A Dead Man's Favor

I0716861

ALSO BY CHRIS TULLBANE

THE MURDER OF CROWS
See These Bones
Red Right Hand
One Tin Soldier

STORIES FROM A POST-BREAK WORLD
The Stars That Sing
The Storm in Her Smile
A Sure Thing

THE STORM WHO RIDES
The Queen of Smiles
The Queen of the Road *

THE MANY TRAVAILS OF JOHN SMITH
Investigation, Mediation, Vindication
Blood is Thicker Than Lots of Stuff
Ghost of a Chance
The Italian Screwjob
A Dead Man's Favor
Godswar *
John Smith Doesn't Work Here Anymore *

*Forthcoming

A Dead Man's Favor

CHRIS TULLBANE

GHOST FALLS PRESS

NEVADA

First published by Ghost Falls Press 2023
A Dead Man's Favor. Copyright © 2023 by Chris Tullbane.

GHOST FALLS PRESS

All rights reserved. No part of this publication may be reproduced, stored or transmitted in any form or by any means, electronic, mechanical, photocopying, recording, scanning, or otherwise without written permission from the publisher. It is illegal to copy this book, post it to a website, or distribute it by any other means without permission.

Publisher's Cataloging-in-Publication Data
provided by Five Rainbows Cataloging Services

Names: Tullbane, Chris, author.
Title: A dead man's favor / Chris Tullbane.
Description: Henderson, NV : Ghost Falls Press, 2023. | Series: Many travails of John Smith, bk 5.
Identifiers: ISBN 978-1-955081-11-5 (ebook) | ISBN 978-1-955081-12-2 (paperback)
Subjects: LCSH: Vampires--Fiction. | Zombies--Fiction. | San Diego (Calif.)--Fiction. | Phoenix (Ariz.)--Fiction. | Private investigators--Fiction. | Paranormal fiction. | Fantasy fiction. | BISAC: FICTION / Fantasy / Urban. | FICTION / Occult & Supernatural. | GSAFD: Fantasy fiction.
Classification: LCC PS3620.U45 D43 2023 (print) | LCC PS3620.U45 (ebook) | DDC 813/.6--dc23.

Book cover design by Jake @ jcalebdesign.com

This novel is entirely a work of fiction. The names, characters, places, and incidents portrayed in it are either the product of the author's imagination or are used fictitiously, and any resemblance to actual persons, living or dead, events or locales is entirely coincidental.

FIRST EDITION

For Nami,
the reason for everything

ACKNOWLEDGMENTS

Nine books in and the number of people to thank just keeps growing. That's a clear sign that I am blessed to know great people:

My angel-wife, Nami, who keeps our life—and my heart—going.

Johanna, dearest friend, who has been a part of this journey from the very beginning. I also told her I would say hi, so… "Hi!"

Jamie, who, as my favorite, oldest, and only brother, has been a part of *everything* from the very beginning.

Claudia, Denise, Kerri D., Mark E., Sam, and Scotty B, who are all fabulous authors and even better friends.

Cory, Mitch, Montie, Tom, and Ziggy, who beat every manuscript into shape while offering qualitative feedback most authors would (fictitiously) kill for.

Charity, Deanna, Kerri K., Kevin, Lara, Lynn, Mike, and Reid, for their continued and ever-appreciated support.

Susan, who knows more about motorcycles than I ever will.

Keith and Shawn, who have yet to solve the riddle required for me to remove them from this list.

And always last but never least, my parents.

Stick around: we're just getting started!

What Came Before

IN WHICH JOHN SMITH GIVES A RECAP
[FOOTNOTES ADDED BY JULIETTE MIDDLETON]

A few years ago, I was just a perfectly ordinary, if thoroughly likeable[1], private investigator. Then crab people tried to kill me, a vampire saved my life, and things started to get weird.

The vampire, Anastasia Dumenyova, a woman every bit as lovely as her name[2], told me I was San Diego's last remaining mediator. That fact that I *wasn't* a mediator but had merely bought a Yellow Pages ad that included mediation in its flashy headline apparently didn't matter… not to the people trying to kill me *or* the people who needed my help.

And so, my career as a supernatural mediator officially began.

That first case showed me just how strange this new job could be. I was called to mediate between the local vampire House, of which Anastasia was a high-ranking member[3], and Lord Beel-Kasan, a demigod of nightmares, terror, and vindication, who appeared to

---

[1] *Thoroughly likeable?* Nobody's buying it, little bird.
[2] Oh, for gods' sakes.
[3] *A* high-ranking member. As in one of many. Including me.

everyone else as their greatest fear, and to me as a seven-foot-tall spear of asparagus.

Yeah… we're all still trying to figure that one out.[4]

Anyway, I bumbled my way through the mediation, but managed to find Lord Beel-Kasan's Nintendo, whose theft had started the whole dispute, and even uncovered a conspiracy within the vampire House to overthrow their admittedly awful leader, the exiled queen, Lucia Borghesi.[5]

With the traitors unmasked, the coup was launched too early, and after more than a few tense moments, the *good guys* managed to triumph.

And yeah… I put *good guys* in italics for a reason. Because after saving the day, Lucia *rewarded* me by trying to make me her human thrall, forced to serve her for the rest of my life.

No wonder people had tried to depose her!

Thankfully, and owing to the same genetic quirk that seemed to make me immune to most forms of compulsion[6], the bond didn't end up functioning quite the way Lucia expected it to. We were connected, yeah, emotionally and mentally, but I kept my free will.

And you'd better believe I used it to get the hell away from Lucia.

Any rational person would have seen that whole experience as a flashing neon sign telling them to get the hell out of the supernatural mediation business, and that was *exactly* what I planned to do… until a pixie came along with her own problems that needed solving. Kristin was too cute to say no to[7], proving once again that most men are idiots.

---

[4] I've stopped even trying.

[5] What the hell? I haven't even been mentioned yet? Agreed on Lucia's awfulness, at least. She's… uh… not going to read this, is she?

[6] Without this, you'd have been a snack on day one. Guaranteed!

[7] Never say yes to a pixie. Even babies know better.

Anyway, a few months after that, I ran into the vampires again, with Lucia[8] having tracked me down to force me to behave as a proper thrall before she lost face with the rest of the supernatural population. And while I initially told her to go to hell, I soon got into a spot of trouble that had me reaching out to the vampires for assistance. A simple adultery case had somehow grown into a divorce mediation for a werewolf pack, and now big, furry monsters were doing their best to kill me.

With the help of Anastasia, who I was busy falling head over heels for[9], and Juliette, a younger vampire who had earned the nickname the Duchess of Snark[10], I survived long enough to learn that the attacking werewolves were members of another pack. They were there to make sure the divorce I was settling ended up anything but amicable, opening a path for their pack to move into San Diego and take power. Things were said, plans were hatched, Juliette and I were *both* kidnapped[11], and for the second time in a year, Anastasia saved us all.

She does that a lot. It's not the only reason I love her, mind you, but it's a damn good one.[12]

When the dust settled, the rival pack's infiltration squad was dead, and the divorcing husband and wife—Jason and Carolyn—decided to become co-leaders of the world's first werewolf democracy.

Also? I convinced Anastasia to go on a date with me.

It was awesome… until she disappeared for six months.

---

[8] And me! Again, feeling like chopped liver here.

[9] Groan. If you start spouting poetry, I'm leaving.

[10] How about that? I do exist! Also, with all the descriptions available, from *cool* to *amazing* to *greatest partner ever*, did you have to go with *younger?*

[11] Your fault, not mine.

[12] Admittedly, she can be pretty helpful for a mass murderer.

By the time she returned, I'd been hired by the White Ladies of San Diego, female ghosts who had all died to some kind of foul play, to track down their missing leader, Graciela. Meanwhile, Lucia was growing increasingly frustrated with the status quo of our broken vampire-thrall relationship, Juliette had quit the House because there was too much paperwork involved and had invited herself on at my agency as a junior partner[13], and unbeknownst to me, my dad's company was looking at moving to Austin.

In the middle of all of that, I made friends with a witch named Nepenthe, who led a coven in Temecula and seemed convinced she could help finally break the bond between Lucia and me. All she needed was a drop of my blood, and I, every bit as blind as the protagonist of your favorite cautionary tale, didn't see the harm in providing it.

Turns out, that was a mistake.

Using my freely given blood, the witches were able to siphon Lucia's power and use it to cast ever-larger spells that allowed them to continue trapping more and more of the White Ladies, whose souls in turn served as batteries for larger incantations.

Yeah, the witches were bad. I probably should have seen that one coming.[14]

In the process, they completely upended the bond between Lucia and me in ways that we're both still coming to grips with. As Anastasia, Juliette and I faced down the coven in their converted warehouse[15], I found myself calling on Lucia's own vampiric Talent to create an icicle the size of a car and skewer a demon who was even larger.

---

[13] Not how *I* remember it. 'Please, Juliette,' you cried. 'Save my agency!'

[14] I don't even have the words.

[15] Let's never do that again. Demons suck.

I also killed Nepenthe. It's something that still haunts me to this day[16], even though it was her blood that ultimately freed the captured White Ladies and saved the day.

Well, that and Lord Beel-Kasan making an appearance to save his ageless ward, Jee Sun. That didn't hurt.

The good news was that the ghosts were saved and the witches vanquished. The bad news—for Lucia—was that there was yet another coup at the vampire House and, thanks to the witches, she wasn't even conscious to try to stop it. She blames me; I'm pretty sure it was just karma doing its thing.

Further stoking the exiled queen's rage, Anastasia, Lucia's oldest friend and servant, finally decided to move forward and continue our relationship.[17]

Which made it all the more shocking when Lucia showed up in my apartment, almost a year later, to tell me that Anastasia had been captured and was being tried for the murder of Lucia's own brother, Tomasso, the vampire king of Europe.

After six years of private investigation, and two of being a mediator, I was suddenly handed a murder case. My only goal: to prove Anastasia's innocence by finding the real killer.

It wasn't easy. It wasn't even fun. There were giant roaches known as the *Illutu*—mercenaries, apparently. There were demons and devils. There was a goddess who called herself Minerva, which I later realized was the Roman name for Athena.[18] And there was way too much death. With a lot of help, and even more luck, I stumbled my way into finding the true killers... Lucia's stepmother, who had faked her own death, and Tomasso's bodyguard, Gaius, who had turned

---

[16] She had it coming. Seriously. Stop beating yourself up over it. It's boring.
[17] The plot twist we *all* saw a mile away.
[18] And who you somehow immediately pissed off. Well done.

traitor for love[19]. In the process, Anastasia asked the queen for her blessing to both court and be courted by me, something I'd assumed we were already doing[20]. Oh, and the bond between Lucia and me was twisted even further, to the extent that we started hearing each other's thoughts in our head, not to mention sharing dreams and memories.[21]

So, a mixed bag, really.

In the end, Lucia's exile was lifted, and while she wasn't restored to the Throne, she *was* made queen-regent until her niece and Tomasso's daughter, Sabina, was old enough to rule. Either that unexpected victory softened her ice-cold heart or the fear of losing Anastasia forever forced her hand… because she gave her blessing to our relationship, and even freed Ana from service for a period of time not to exceed one hundred years.

And that brings us to the here and the now, with Anastasia and me back in San Diego, living the good life, as I run my investigative agency with Juliette[22] and continue to mediate on the side.

Things aren't always perfect, but I can't remember a time when they were better. Which means something bad is probably on its way…[23]

[I've seen more concise recaps from third graders, John. Next time, stick to the important *details, like the amazing business partner and friend who's literally renting you apartment space even as you write this! – Sincerely, Juliette]*

---

[19] Reason #12,346 that love is overrated.
[20] You know what they say about *assume*…
[21] I don't even know which of you got the worse end of that deal.
[22] I'm pretty sure I do all the running.
[23] Well, *now* it definitely is.

CHAPTER 1
IN WHICH VOWS ARE JUST THE BEGINNING

It was a pretty great wedding until the zombie showed up. September in San Diego meant different things than in the rest of the country. It was warm, but not *too* warm, the skies were the sort of blue you usually only saw with painted movie sets, and the breeze coming in off the ocean was content with merely rustling the decorations instead of tossing them about like confetti. Even my rented tux fit almost perfectly, rescued by a second round of last-minute alterations.

The post-ceremony photos were finally done, with the bride and, well, bride now off getting their solo pictures taken. The rest of us were milling about under the giant, open-sided tent that had been erected over the reception tables; seventy-four-degree weather in San Diego didn't mean the sun couldn't still boil you like a lobster if you weren't paying attention.

In a few minutes, those of us in the wedding party would have to form back up again to escort and announce the newly married couple to their own reception, but for now, we were scattered about and mixed in with the guests. I had an icy cold beer in one hand and a plateful of cookies in the other, because I'd very nearly overslept for our

8 a.m. rendezvous at the wedding site, and I'd had to skip my usual breakfast on the way.

The cookies were amazing. Not *breakfast burrito with extra chorizo* amazing, obviously, but I wasn't complaining. And the beer was, as always, the perfect post-wedding treat.

It had been a season of weddings. Mike and Susan had been the first to start things off back in May, and if Susan had spent the entire rehearsal dinner staring me down over what she'd been told about my best friend's bachelor's party, she'd been nothing but smiles during the wedding itself. June, July, and August had then had two weddings apiece, all for old high school classmates who had caught the marriage bug and rightly assumed I still lived in San Diego and would show up with gifts if invited.

And now this, the final wedding of the season, and the third of those eight where I'd found myself going stag. Thankfully, this time, I knew *almost* everyone else at the reception. Even better, none of them had tried to kill me in more than a year.

"How's it hanging, son?"

"Hey Jason." I tapped his beer bottle with mine and tried not to shake my head. "New look?"

"Yeah, what do you think?"

For all that he was still only twenty-two, the werewolf was looking almost professorial in a blazer with honest-to-God leather patches on the elbows. He had tried to complete the ensemble with wire-framed glasses, but the lack of lenses kind of stood out, as did the sheer amount of product he'd worked into his hair.

Not to mention that he'd used that product to give himself a fauxhawk.

"It's different."

"Yeah," he said. "Got to be all respectable and stuff at events like these, you know? Plus, the chicks dig distinguished these days."

"I hadn't noticed."

"It's true. I may be off the market now, but I'm not gonna deny the honeys their eye candy."

"Where is Carolyn anyway?"

"She's at home," he said. "Was feeling under the weather, so I came to represent the pack instead." He gave the phrase *under the weather* special significance, and then looked at me expectantly.

"Uhm… I'm sorry to hear that?"

For a second, he just looked at me. Finally, he shook his head and took another swig of beer.

"Son, speaking as one grown-ass adult to another, you can sometimes be really dense. Even for a human."

"Let's pretend I have no idea what you're talking about," I said. "Because I don't. Also, why are you calling me son now? What happened to bro?"

He rolled his eyes, looking very much like the teenager he'd so recently been. "It's obvious. I'm going to be a dad soon. So, I'm trying it out to see how it feels."

"You're what?"

"Gonna be a dad? Cara's got a couple pups on the way."

"Damn, that's—" I ran through a handful of adjectives, some of them less appropriate than others, before finally settling on something safe. "Amazing! Congratulations, dude!"

"Yeah." He adjusted his lensless glasses and preened. "It's pretty sweet, no lie. We're both young enough still that we've got a good chance of seeing them grow up and have kids of their own."

I managed to hide my wince behind my third-best mediator's smile, recently dubbed The Encourager™. Weres personified the phrase *live fast and die young*, with life expectancies that rarely reached the fifties. It was weird—and sobering—to think that both Jason and his ex-wife, current girlfriend, and soon-to-be baby mama would likely pass around the same time as my vastly older parents.

"Don't expect me to hand out cigars or any of that shit though," Jason was saying. "I'm a soon-to-be dad now. I've got to watch my finances."

"No more Wednesday night bar crawls?"

"I'm a dad, not dead."

"Right."

"Anyway, what's new?" He snagged another beer from the nearby table and popped the cap off with his thumb.

"Not a ton. Juliette's holding down the fort on the P.I. side of things while I deal with the goblins." I couldn't see my business partner, but I knew she was swanning around the reception somewhere with her plus-one. At some point, she'd probably swing by to make fun of my tux again.

"Think the current ceasefire has a better chance of lasting than the last two?"

The Encourager™ cracked under the weight of a question it wasn't qualified to answer, and I shrugged. "We'll see, I guess. The only thing worse than a land war in Asia is a land war with goblins. The Mer are sponsoring the newest round of negotiations, and they want me on hand to work some mediator magic. I guess I should just be grateful they didn't invite Caleb Van Stahl instead." My rival—sort of—mediator usually covered the coastal territories while I handled the rest, but that arrangement hadn't kept him from bogarting mediation cases in the past.

Jason whistled. "I don't care what everyone else says about you, bro; you've got balls of solid steel. I mean, mad respect and all, but that was seriously cold."

Now I was back to being bro. "What are you talking about?"

"Come on; it's not like you left them much choice. They needed a mediator and you're the only one around not pushing up daisies."

"Caleb Van Stahl is *dead?*"

Jason just looked at me for a while, and for the first time in our strange relationship, I saw something like respect in his gaze. "Bro, you're gonna have to teach me how to do that. If I didn't know better, I'd think you were surprised to hear it."

"Because I *am* surprised."

"This is me you're talking to. J-Money, dawg of dawgs, and your bro before all hoes. There's no need to front like you didn't do it!"

I was still grappling with the loss of my long-assumed-if-slow-to-develop bromance with the other mediator, so Jason's words didn't sink in until well after the fact. When they did, I nearly choked on my latest sip of beer.

"You think *I* killed him?" We were in the middle of a wedding, and not *all* of the attendees were supernatural, so I kept my voice quiet. There were only so many times you could laugh off awkward conversations as jokes or movie quotes.

"Of course not." Jason dropped his voice to match mine. "Everyone knows you had your girlfriend do it."

My *girlfriend*—and it still made me giddy to even think the word—was none other than Lady Anastasia Dumenyova, a four-hundred-some-old-year vampire who, through the grace of the Demigod of Unexpected Romantic Pairings, had for some reason taken a liking to me. And yeah, for most of her centuries-old existence, she'd been her queen's *Secundus*, both fixer and assassin, but that wasn't who she was anymore. She didn't kill on anyone's command, and if she'd decided to off Caleb on her own, I was sure she'd have told me.

Mostly sure.

"Jason—" I began.

"Say no more, son." He straightened his glasses and took a long glance around us. "This is neither the time nor the place, ya feel me? Emilio's throwing a barbecue two Wednesdays from now after the pack meeting. You can drop on by and give us the word then."

Before I could reply, or even ask if Emilio was still the owner of the world's greatest mustache, Jason was gone, making a beeline for the last plate of cookies and what I suspected would be his fourth or even fifth beer of the wedding. I went to follow him, but was intercepted by a red-headed, blue-eyed, mediator-seeking missile in a tux of her own.

"John!"

"Darlene." I hugged her back and saluted her with my mostly empty beer bottle. "Mazeltov. How did you like your surprise?"

She turned to regard the two people standing on the far side of the tent, talking to a woman who looked even taller and more beautiful than usual in her white silk wedding dress. While Kayla was a vampire, the people she was entertaining were human: a middle-aged woman with Darlene's eyes and a radiant smile, and a gawky red-headed teenage boy whose resemblance to his newly married sister was almost uncanny.

"I still can't believe it," Darlene told me. "How did you get Mom and Josh to come?"

"Hey, I'm the best man. Or... maid of honor—?"

"Best Man of Honor."

"Right. That. Miracles are kind of what we do." I turned back from the sight of Darlene's mom and brother to regard the woman herself. "Honestly, it didn't take much convincing. I'm just sorry I couldn't talk your dad into joining them."

"I'm not. He had his chance and made his choice, twice over." Darlene shook her head, and her smile made a reappearance, so wide on her small, freckled face that it almost looked crazed. "I'm just so grateful that my old family gets to meet my new one. I swear they're both halfway in love with K already. Thank you."

"Consider it my apology for not being able to attend the festivities in Australia. And for Ana's absence today."

Kayla's former House—and her entire extended family—was in Australia; rather than force either the San Diegans or the Australians to travel, the pair had elected to have weddings in both locations. And if it hadn't been for my role in hopefully helping to end a goblin war—not to mention my thoroughly mixed feelings on airplanes—I'd have been going Down Under to celebrate the second one too.

"You know you're already forgiven for both."

I did, but it was nice to hear anyway. "So, how does it feel? To be Mrs. and Mrs. finally?"

This time, her whole face glowed. "I think it's still sinking in. Have you *seen* K in her wedding dress? How the hell did I get so lucky?"

"By being awesome enough to deserve it."

That earned me a second hug, but before I could say anything more, the DJ was waving at us from across the room. On the far side of the tent, the rest of the wedding party was gathering in pairs, Kayla among them.

"Looks like it's processional time again," I told D, turning her about. "Shall we?"

○○○

I sat with the rest of the wedding party at the main table, which put me in a strange mix of company: a couple of Darlene's fellow recent graduates from UCSD, a handful of vampires from the San Diego House, and one bark-skinned woman with dark, luxurious vines for hair who I was pretty sure was a dryad. Like many of the less human-looking attendants, that woman, Brooke, was no doubt wearing a glamour to let her pass as human amongst those ignorant to the existence of supernaturals. Thanks to me being me, I couldn't actually see that glamour, but her bark skin went well with the off-the-shoulder, deep green wedding dresses that Kayla had picked out for her bridesmaids. And if flowers tended to bloom wherever she stood for any length of time, well, they just added to the décor.

Only two of us at the table were men, and I couldn't help but sense that the second one had been trying to make eye contact with me throughout the meal, long after we'd all stumbled our way through our respective speeches. My relationship with Steve was… complicated… and not just because he was a manpire ninja who had probably never even heard of acne.

Part of me was simply bummed that he'd shaved the mohawk that had always been a close second to Emilio's glorious mustache in the citywide hair and facial hair rankings, but our *real* issues were entirely political. Steve hadn't directly taken part in the coup that overthrew their former House's leader, Lucia Borghesi, femmepire queen and my supposed mistress, but he hadn't joined in the small exodus that followed either.

Instead, he'd opted to support the new leader, Duke Barros… only to have Barros flee both House and country a year later, when Lucia's vigilante accountant, Marcus, had gotten his revenge. It was all a mess, and the upshot was that Steve and I hadn't shared more than a few words over the course of the last year, despite both being in K and D's wedding party.

But, I decided, belly comfortably full with my second slice of wedding cake, *enough is enough. Lucia's back in Rome with the den of snakes—sometimes* literal *snakes—that she prefers, and I'm frankly sick of vampire politics getting in the way of friendship.*

I washed down that last bite of cake with champagne that was far too expensive for me to properly appreciate, and looked across the table at Steve, raising my glass to him in a silent toast. He returned it with a smile, teeth gleaming against the darkness of his skin, and just like that, all was well.

Or so I thought.

A half-hour later, with the reception lunch over, and the party now in full swing, Steve sought me out where I was wallflowering to one side of the freshly assembled dance floor.

"John."

"Steve!" To his evident shock, I took his outstretched hand and pulled him into a bro hug. "How are things? How's Barry?"

He smiled, shoulders subtly relaxing. "He's good. Lord Kala opened up the Bitter End again in July, and we've been meeting almost every night."

"Sorry I was never able to do anything about his situation." Barry was both the wereboar bouncer for San Diego's preeminent supernatural bar and one of its sole permanent residents. At two hundred years old, he was only still alive because Kala, as a demigod of time and death, was able to control the passage of time for individuals within his domain. Barry leaving the bar, however, would remove him from Kala's domain… with likely fatal consequences.

"It's okay. After not being able to see each other at all for a month, being stuck in the bar doesn't seem quite so bad anymore."

I was pretty sure the Bitter End's unexpected summer closure had been my fault, although I still wasn't sure why or how. Even with the bar open again, Lord Kala had yet to make an appearance.

"Anyway," continued Steve, once again looking uncomfortably nervous, "I was hoping we could talk."

"Yeah, of course. But before you start," I told him, "I just want to say this past year has been stupid, and I'm sorry for my part in it. Whatever happened, happened. Lucia's gone, and I'd like to just get back to the way things were. A human and a manpire having a good time and not worrying about vampire politics." I looked for the beer

cooler, but someone had moved it aside to make room for the dancing.
"So, what was it you wanted to talk about?"

Steve coughed. "The House and… uh… vampire politics."

Well, shit.

CHAPTER 2

IN WHICH WEDDING FEVER MIGHT BE
AN EPIDEMIC

"What's up?" I finally asked. I wasn't sure I wanted to know the answer, really, but it was a little too late for that.

"With Barros gone, we've done our best to elect new leadership," said Steve, clearing his throat, "but things are kind of a mess. If Kayla had stuck around, she'd have been one of the oldest of us left. Without her, there's only one person over a hundred, even. And that's a problem because that one person is—"

"Zorana." More than a year later, I liked to pretend just saying the name didn't give me the shivers. It wasn't true, but I liked to pretend it. The pre-teen Blood Witch and I had a long history and very little of it was good.

"Right. Which is a problem at the best of times. But now, she's disappeared, and we aren't sure where she went or why."

"You *lost* the Blood Witch? How?"

"I think she just walked out." He read the look on my face and shrugged. "Do you think any of us would have dared stop her from leaving? We're pretty sure she's in San Diego still, but—"

But that put a millennium-old, possibly insane vampire on the streets, one whose behavior had only barely even been constrained by the femmepire she acknowledged as queen.

A tiny, forever scared part of me was amazed the streets weren't already running red.

"What do you want from me then?"

"I was—*we* were—hoping you could help find her. And then maybe Lady Dumenyova or Queen-Regent Lucia could... I don't know... take care of her?"

"You've got to be kidding, dude. Ana barely survived their last meeting, and I highly doubt Lucia will set foot in this country ever again now that her exile has been lifted."

"It's a lot to ask, I know, but we don't know what else to do. We have people out looking, but even if we find Zorana, there's not a damn thing we can do to control her." He took a step back and held up his hands. "Just ask Lady Dumenyova. Please. The House will help however we can, but the Blood Witch is a bigger problem than we're equipped to deal with."

I sighed. "Ana's in Rome until tomorrow, but I'll at least tell her when she comes back. I'm not making any promises though, and frankly, the less either of us has to do with Zorana, the happier I'll be."

"I get it. And thanks. Seriously."

The DJ was clearing the dance floor and calling for the unmarried men and women in the audience to make their way forward for the bouquet and garter toss. I took advantage of that distraction to make my escape, and joined the small crowd that was starting to form. Marriage wasn't really a vampire thing—this one being an obvious exception—but there were more than a few bloodsuckers in the group around me, and a vastly larger crowd had readied for the bouquet toss. Honestly, both groups were a mix of genders, but almost the entire wedding party was out there waiting for the bouquet.

Kayla, smiling every bit as broadly as her human bride, held the wedding bouquet like a sword, dipping it down as if to knight the men and women hoping to catch it. She spun to put her back to the crowd, her wedding dress skirts flaring like she was some kind of princess, and without further ado, tossed the bouquet over one shoulder.

If she'd used her vampiric strength, she'd have sent the flowers right through the tent's heavy canvas and probably a few hundred yards further, over the cliff and into the ocean. Then again, if the hopeful recipients had used *their* supernatural abilities, we'd have had a tentful of Olympian high jumpers skying for the prize. Instead, it all went off in relatively mundane fashion; the bouquet arced up and then came back down in the middle of the crowd, where a beaming femmepire snatched it and held it aloft like a trophy.

"Tasha," said the manpire to my right, disgustingly fit and handsome as all his kind were.

"You know her?" I didn't recognize either of them from the San Diego House, but it had admittedly been a while.

"We're dating," he admitted.

"Oh. Congratulations on her catching the bouquet. Or… condolences?"

"Definitely the first." He grinned. "I'm Kale."

"As in the vegetable?" I couldn't help but shudder. "No offense, but I'm pretty sure we're mortal enemies. I'm—"

"John Smith, yeah. I know. *Everybody* knows."

He was still smiling, so hopefully that was a good thing.

Meanwhile, after congratulating Tasha, Kayla had joined her new mother-in-law and brother-in-law on the side of the dance floor. It was Darlene's turn to take center stage. More than half of the people who'd been trying for the bouquet joined those of us waiting to catch the garter.

Except, of course, that Darlene wasn't removing the garter from Kayla's leg like in old fashioned weddings. In fact, the item she pulled out from within her vest wasn't a garter at all. Instead, it was a thick loop of buttery soft leather, with a clasp on one side and a metal O-ring on the other.

Because *of course* D would be throwing a *collar* instead.

I didn't have time to see how her family reacted to that little change of custom, as Darlene didn't stand on ceremony any more than her bride had. She just waved at us, spun about with a click of her heels, and chucked the collar over her head in our direction.

Darlene was a human, without any supernatural powers to call upon, but either she'd been preparing for the event or collars flew a hell of a lot better than bouquets. Either way, the leather loop went farther than anyone would have expected, hit the ceiling of the tent, and then dropped like a grenade into my half-heartedly upraised hand.

I almost immediately found myself the center of attention. Kale slapped me on the back, while a femmepire who had just missed the catch glared daggers in my direction. Somewhere outside the throng, I could *hear* Juliette laughing, even if I couldn't quite see her.

Which was great and all, but—I caught Kale as the manpire turned to go and tucked the collar into his hand.

"Might as well make it a matched set," I told him.

"A matched set?"

"You and Tasha, I mean. I'm not saying flowers and collars go together. Although I guess in this case, they—Look, just take it, okay?"

His smile broadened, exposing teeth that passed as human since he wasn't vamping out, and headed for his girlfriend, collar in hand.

"Does Anastasia know you have marital designs on her, little bird?" Juliette, the so-called Duchess of Snark, emerged from the swiftly dissipating crowd, Angel practically welded to her hip. My business partner had poured herself into a little black dress better suited for a club than a wedding, but so had a lot of the other attendees. This had been anything but a traditional ceremony, even before you considered all the different species running around.

"Duchess. And Angel," I added, nodding to the other woman. With their throuple having recently turned back into a couple, the barista-turned-receptionist looked pleased as punch to be on Juliette's arm. "Ana's not interested in that sort of thing. I gave the collar to someone who actually wanted it."

"If you didn't want it, why were you out here at all?" asked Angel.

That was a really good question that I didn't have an answer for. "Solidarity?" I ventured.

"Right." Juliette smirked "Well, better you—or whoever you gave it to—than us, I guess."

Angel's features froze, her smile going flat.

"I'm sure it'll happen when it's meant to," I said, my words intended more for the other woman than Juliette. Angel and I weren't friends—for some reason, she seemed to see me as a threat, just because I lived in their apartment, worked long hours with her girlfriend, and had once been that girlfriend's first choice as blood donor—but that didn't make her reaction any easier to see.

"I don't think so." Juliette swirled the last dregs of champagne about in her glass and tossed it back. "Sweetums, do you mind getting me a refill?"

I waited for Angel to leave and then gave Juliette a look. "Dude. What was that about?"

"What was what about?" The femmepire met my eyes for a moment before her resistance crumbled. "Okay, I know. But ever since I got my wedding invite, she's been all over the place. Anastasia and I don't see eye to eye on a lot of things, but marriage is one of them. It's never, ever happening. Angel knows that and she's okay with it, but…"

"But?"

"It's like wedding fever is a real virus and not something you humans made up just to excuse your terrible life choices."

My long and illustrious career as the city's mediator told me this was probably not the time to pursue the subject, so I shrugged instead. "At least K and D look happy."

Juliette softened, insofar as someone with cheekbones like razor blades *could* soften. "Yeah, I guess I don't have to understand it to wish them the best." She returned my shrug. "Anyway, any news from the Mer?"

"They're still working to set up the first meeting. With Chief Tikky-Wokka Tomlinson… well… dead, and the coup squashed, there's been a bit of a power struggle within the Superchargers tribe." It was probably the only reason they hadn't rolled over the much smaller Clippers tribe, who had declared war as soon as the Superchargers executed Rihanna Mariah Kardashian, the murdered chief's wife, the coup's mastermind, and one of the Clippers' favorite former daughters. "Figuring out who should be attending from each tribe has been difficult."

"Everything with goblins is difficult." She coughed, looking unsure in a very non-Juliette way. "Has anyone said anything about me? Or us, rather?"

"I don't think the chief told anyone we were investigating one of his wives for infidelity. There's nothing to link you or our agency to the coup you uncovered."

"Other than the meeting I set up with him."

"Which was scheduled for some time after his death and therefore never happened." I shook my head. "And it's not like you did anything wrong. You investigated Rihanna Mariah Kardashian, found out she wasn't cheating, uncovered evidence that she was instead planning a coup, but were unable to warn the chief in time. Is it the ideal outcome? No. Was it great advertising for our agency? Of course not. Is the city a less safe place as a result? Obviously." I trailed off. "Where was I going with this?"

"*It's not like you did anything wrong,*" quoted Juliette, her eyes glittering dangerously.

"Right. *We* weren't responsible for what happened. Sometimes, the world is what it is."

"Of all the phrases you've picked up from Anastasia, that might be my very least favorite," muttered Juliette. "But you're right; I'll stop looking over my shoulder for goblin hit squads. Just… try not to piss them off too badly during the mediations. Pound for pound, the little bastards aren't that tough, but they're as numerous as the rats back in New York City, and at least as hard to stomp out."

"I've been hired to stop a war, not start a second one."

"And?"

"And no promises on either front." The Encourager™ made a reappearance, but Juliette remained unimpressed. "You know I'll do what I can, but things have a habit of going squirrely. Still, I'm hoping I can appeal to the tribes' civic pride. They both named themselves after San Diego teams, after all, even if the basketball franchise moved up to Los Angeles. I'm hoping there's common ground there. Maybe they can focus on keeping the town clear of Raiders fans or something instead."

"That's not the dumbest—"

"Excuse me… John?"

"Hey Brenna. What's up?" Like Steve, Brenna had stayed with the San Diego House even after Lucia was driven out. For some reason, I found it harder to blame her for doing so. Maybe it was because she'd never held any kind of leadership role in the House, or maybe I was— as *both* Lucia and Juliette had accused me of in the past—thinking with my eyes and my impossibly stupid *second* brain. Brenna wasn't *Anastasia*, but she was still smoking hot.

"You've got a visitor."

"Here?" I glanced around the reception. The music had started back up again and the dance floor was packed, but even with Juliette and Brenna next to me, nobody seemed to be paying me any attention.

"No. Outside." Brenna rolled her eyes. "It'd be best if he *didn't* crash the party."

Ah. Crap. "Bill is here?" I was pretty sure neither he nor his ward, Jee Sun, had been sent an invite, but that wasn't the sort of thing to stop San Diego's resident demigod of nightmares, terror, and vindication. Especially if there were sweets available. Or pizza. Or sinners.

"Lord Beel-Kasan? No, thank the gods. I'm talking about Simon."

It had been a whole year, so it took me longer than it should have to place the name. But once I had, I thanked Brenna and made a beeline for the place she said Simon was waiting.

I didn't know how the city's zombie prince had found me, or what had brought him all the way out to a wedding on the coast, but I was guessing it wasn't anything good.

○○○

Simon looked much the same as the last time I'd seen him, swaddled in multiple layers of clothes that did very little to limit the stench. His face was the only bit of exposed skin, barely visible between the shapeless hat on top and the ratty scarf below, but it looked like he'd lost more pieces of himself since our last encounter.

As undead, zombies didn't heal. Any damage Simon suffered put him one step closer to a final death, and until someone confirmed that heaven had Netflix, that was something the zombie prince was keen on avoiding.

"What's up, kid?" His lower lip continued to hang on by a thread, waggling out of sync with the rest of his face as he spoke.

"You tell me. You're looking… uh…"

"Yeah, yeah. Pardon me if I didn't get dressed up all fancy like to come see you. Turns out my tailor's been dead since the Great Depression."

"Right. So, not that it's not great to see you again, but—"

"What the hell do I want?"

"Actually, how did you find me?"

He gave me a look. "Same way I find anything in this town."

"Zombie rats."

"Yeah, though I used their eyes rather than checking energy signatures this time."

It was the same thing he'd done to help me find the missing ghost, Graciela, but it was significantly less cool when *I* was the one being tracked. And not just because it meant there were rats at Kayla and Darlene's wedding venue.

"As for what I want?" continued Simon. "I'm calling in my favor."

"Your favor?"

"Jesus Christ on a squeaky unicycle, how quickly they forget." He thumped the Mercedes hood ornament hanging around his neck. "Me help you find missing ghost. You kill shitload of witches. Everybody go home happy. Any of this ringing a bell, asshole?"

"Right. Of course. Sorry… it's been a long year." I cleared my throat. "So, what can I do for you? Need a new iPad? A more permanent place to stay? A friendly ear?" I fought not to gag as the wind off the ocean shifted, bringing the zombie's stench even closer.

"None of that. I… uh… have family, you know?"

"Seriously?"

"Yes, seriously. What, you thought I was some kind of loser in my first life? My wife and I died from influenza after the war, but at least some of our kids survived. And they went on to have kids of their own, and so on."

I didn't ask which war it was. Multiple generations meant we were talking one of the world wars. Or maybe even the Civil War.

"So, you have descendants still walking the earth and possibly adding to the family tree?"

"Right. I don't keep track of most of 'em, because who the hell has time for that? But there's a branch I helped a generation or two ago, and I guess that story's been passed down, because someone reached out to me." He hawked noisily and spat something brown and thick to the side, where I could swear it practically sizzled against the rocks. "Long and short of it is that my however many greats granddaughter and her guy have gone missing. It's been a week already and I want you to find them."

Of all the things I'd expected the zombie prince to call in his favor for, a missing persons case wasn't one of them. Thankfully, it was very much in my wheelhouse.

"Yeah, I can do that. I'll need as much data as—" I stopped as a manila envelope landed in front of me, its exterior only lightly stained.

"That's everything I have on Dulcinea's disappearance."

I picked up the envelope and thumbed through its contents, doing my best to keep it away from my rented tux. There were a dozen or so pages, including black-and-white printouts of the missing couple. At a glance, there was plenty to go off of.

"How did you get this all printed?"

"The FedEx print center down on Sixth." He read my look and shrugged, one of his unseen shoulders twitching higher than the others. "I broke in last night. Anyway, I included contact information for her father. Jeremiah's a bit of a weirdo—thinks technology is rotting our brains and stuff—but he'll have more info for you when you arrive."

"Arrive where?"

"Ghost Falls," said Simon. "Podunk little town in the ass end of New Mexico. You're going there to find Dulcinea."

"To *New Mexico?* I mean… normally, I handle out-of-state cases remotely. The internet's a pretty amazing—"

"Boots on the ground, asshole. You owe me."

He wasn't wrong. And a road trip to New Mexico didn't sound awful… provided I could somehow fit it in between my mediations with the goblins.

"Okay, that's fair."

"Good. I've got *Fargo* to watch." He paused. "I included my newest phone number in there too. Call me once you've got something. And kid?"

"Yeah?"

"This matters to me. *Dulcinea* matters. Don't screw it up. None of your usual stuff where you get everyone around you dead, you hear me?"

"When you come to Middleton & Smith Investigations, satisfaction is guaranteed." It wasn't our actual motto—for both legal *and* financial reasons—but I was betting Simon didn't know that.

"Yeah, that's not how I hear it. Anyway, you do this, and we'll be square."

"I'll find her," I promised, breaking one of the first and most fundamentals rules of private investigation:

Promise to try. Promise to make every conceivable effort. But never, ever promise someone a result that you haven't already achieved.

Still, I'd survived witches, vampires, werewolves, two demigods, and a murder trial in Italy of all places. I was in a personal relationship with the deadliest woman I knew, and a professional relationship with the snarkiest. What kind of difficulties could a simple missing persons case pose in comparison?

CHAPTER 3

IN WHICH PIMPIN' AIN'T EASY

The next day found me working out of our office in Logan Heights. For the first time in weeks, all three members of the agency were present, but thanks to our recently finished expansion into the neighboring 'suite', the combined space still felt roomy. As our receptionist, Angel's desk occupied the room that had originally been the agency's entire footprint, where a fancy glass door led out to the public hallway and bore the name of our agency. Meanwhile, Juliette and I had desks in the new space, connected to Angel's room by an interior door that spent most of its time wide open.

I still wasn't thrilled with Juliette's decisions to hire Angel and expand our business, but with the amount of money she'd been bringing in on solo investigations, it was almost a wash. And the extra space *was* nice. If I squinted and pretended hard enough, I could even almost make out downtown San Diego through the gaps between buildings outside our new room's only window.

Not bad for a twenty-seven-year-old community college dropout.

For some reason, Juliette's new desk was bigger than mine, but it lacked the dents, divots, and damage that gave a piece of furniture character, and her chair was the kind only a *junior* executive would find themselves saddled with. It was squeaking forlornly as she slowly rotated in a circle, playing catch with the paperweight she'd stolen from my side of the office.

"Are you really done with the Peterman case already?" I asked her, somewhere around the seventeenth tortuous squeak. "You don't want to go out and run down some more leads or anything?"

"He confessed. On tape," she reminded me. "And then gave me his home videos. His soon-to-be ex-wife has absolutely everything she needs to take that man to the cleaners. I never even had to pull my camera out of its case."

"I think you mean *my* camera. And that's only because you used your vampire powers to compel him."

"We use what we have, little bird. I've got strength, beauty, mental compulsion, and legs for days, while you've got… well, *experience*, I guess?"

"Nice. Between that and the last two cases, we've got salaries and rent covered through next month. Assuming the goblin mediation goes okay, we should be on easy street for a while." I yawned, and hit Ctrl-S on the excel spreadsheet I tracked our budget in. Nobody had told me that being a small business owner would involve so much work.

Actually, *everyone* had told me that. Even Mike. But still, I couldn't imagine Marlowe or Spade ever doing spreadsheets. I'd become a private investigator to *avoid* being an accountant.

The printouts Simon had given me were spread out across my desk. I'd already reviewed them twice since the wedding. Dulcinea, age nineteen, had left her family's home with her boyfriend, Pedro, age twenty-three, sometime after lunch on Tuesday, the 8th of September. A neighbor had seen them riding out of Ghost Falls on Pedro's motorcycle, but after that, they'd both disappeared off the face of the earth. Dulcinea's youth, and the fact that she'd left *with* her boyfriend, had me wondering if she was missing at all or had just run away from home. After all, my summer to the contrary, eloping *was* still a thing. The town sheriff had come to a similar conclusion, but Dulcinea's father, Jeremiah, was convinced that something had happened.

I'd already asked Juliette's contacts at the SDPD to run traces on the couple's credit cards, but we wouldn't get that information back for another day or so. In the meantime, I'd spent my morning researching Ghost Falls itself. Neither Juliette nor I had ever heard of the place, and it only took one Google search to find out why; the town had less than three hundred people living in it—two hundred ninety-seven, according to the last census. In fact, their main export seemed to be *people*, with the town's population plummeting in recent years as kids grew up and moved down to Santa Fe.

For a town seemingly on its last legs, it was at least picturesque, surrounded by forests with mountains to the north and east. Quaint, as my mom would insist on calling it while reading the description of the town's single post office that had been built all the way back in 1947. I wasn't much of an outdoorsy guy, and I doubted the town had any breweries, but even so… I didn't hate the idea of spending a few days there chasing down leads.

In the other room, the phone rang, and both Juliette and I stilled as Angel went through her usual greeting. I hated to admit it, but Juliette's girlfriend had come a long way since her early days of not taking notes. She even had a tidy stack of post-its on her desk now, just waiting to be used.

A moment later, she hung back up. "Wrong number, unless one of you told someone your name was Ziggy?"

Juliette gave me a look, but I shook my head.

"Not me." Not recently anyway.

Angel went back to whatever she had been doing—browsing on her phone, most likely, not that I could blame her—but Juliette was clearly tired of playing catch. She slid out of her chair with another squeak and crossed over to my desk. "Are you looking through the packet Simon gave you again?"

"Yeah. Unless your pet cops can help us out, there's not much to work with. I guess going to Ghost Falls really does make sense." Simon hadn't given me any choice on that front, but I felt better knowing the trip was warranted. "I'm thinking I might make a little vacation out of it with Anastasia."

"When does she get back?"

"Four hours and twenty-eight minutes."

"Not that you're counting." She smirked, leaning one hip against the desk like a runway model giving the press time for photographs. "This was what… her second trip to Rome since you guys came back together?"

"Third."

"I thought she was done with Lucia?"

"Yeah." So had I, honestly. "She's been released from *Secundus* service for the next century, but they're still… friends? I guess? She's been helping Lucia and her niece, Sabina, with the whole regency thing."

Ana had also been doing a little bit of investigation on the side, but it wasn't the sort of thing our agency handled, and for now, it was on a strictly need-to-know basis. I loved Juliette like the smoking hot, frequently disturbing sister I'd never had, but this was a vampire-politics thing, to my everlasting dismay, and the Duchess of Snark had done a much better job of extricating herself from that arena than me.

"You think she'll want to turn around and fly right back out?"

"Who said anything about flying? I was thinking we'd drive."

"You do realize this town you're going to is at least ten hours away from San Diego by car?"

"It's still better than flying." My flight *to* Rome had left deep emotional scars that the vastly more enjoyable flight *from* it had failed to erase. "When's the last time *you* flew anywhere?"

"People were drinking and smoking on flights. Human people, I mean, not *the* People. So, maybe… the 80s?"

"Well, it's not as glamorous as it was then. Trust me."

"Few things are." She flipped through the pages and tossed them back on the desk. "Anyway, want to go get some lunch?"

"It's ten thirty."

"Yeah, but I'm bored, and all you're doing is shuffling papers around."

I started to argue, then caught myself. One of the reasons I'd started my own business instead of interning at my dad's accounting firm—besides an ineptitude with math that bordered on the supernatural—was that I'd wanted the ability to set my own rules. No suits or ties, no conference calls, and absolutely no slavish adherence to the typical 8-to-5 grind.

"Lunch sounds good."

"I'm thinking sushi."

"It's *ten thirty*," I reminded her.

"I didn't say we'd do *saké bombs* with the sushi." She shifted from foot to foot, acting the part of the teenager she appeared to be, rather than the century-old creature of the night she was. "It's just lunch."

"Fine. Sushi it is."

"Sweet." She was in the next office before I could reply, leaning over the desk in a way that gave Angel a look right down the deep V of her cropped T-shirt. "Can we bring you back anything, sweetums?"

"Maybe an avocado roll and a shiitake roll? And some dessert please?"

"Thanks for holding down the fort, Angel," I said.

"It's what you all pay me for."

"*I* pay you to sit there and look adorable," said Juliette. "But forts need to be held down or whatever too, I guess."

The two traded smiles, Angel actually blushing, and then Juliette followed me into the hall. She scowled at whatever she saw on my face.

"What?"

"Nothing."

"Damn straight."

"I'm just saying… sometimes, you two are awfully domestic. What would your punk rock gods think of you now?"

"I will kill you where you stand, little bird."

"Maybe I'll take that chance?"

"And this is why *you're* paying for saké at lunch."

We both grinned and headed for the stairs.

ooo

Three hours and twenty minutes later, we returned to the office, Juliette swaying slightly on skyscraper-high stilettos that shouldn't have gone with her painted-on jeans, but somehow worked anyway. I nodded to Dale, still camped outside the building with his too-many backpacks and a small hoard of questionable treasures, and the homeless man responded with his usual greeting: a raised middle finger and a complaint about communism.

Nice guy, Dale. He'd pretty much come with the building though, so I passed him the take-home container of sushi.

"What's this?" he grumbled.

"Lunch?"

"A likely story."

I left the sushi with him, knowing eventually he'd eat it anyway, and followed Juliette into the building lobby. Her Ducati was there, chained to the stairwell, and we passed it on our way up to the second floor. It wasn't until we neared the office's front door that I heard the voices inside. We hadn't had any appointments scheduled, but *someone* was in there.

Two years ago, that'd have been enough to have me panicking, but I was made of sterner stuff now. Also, Angel was one of those two voices, and she didn't seem worried. Still, it didn't suck to have Juliette as backup. With Lucia more than six thousand miles away, the femmepire queen and I no longer had to worry about passing emotions and sensations across our bond, but my ability to pull on her powers— or even her strength—was similarly hampered.

Most days, it was a tradeoff I was okay with.

I took a deep breath, just to steady myself, and sent Juliette a nod that she returned with a confused expression. I pushed open the door and found a small, well-dressed blonde sitting on our client couch and talking with Angel.

"Susan?"

"John!" She hopped to her feet, started to say something, and then trailed off as Juliette filed in behind me. "Ugh. Unbelievable."

"I'm sorry?"

Susan shook her head with a scowl. "It's bad enough that you brought an escort to my *wedding*, but you've got one at work, too? Of course *you* would. John in name *and* role. What was I even thinking, coming here?"

"Wait, what?"

"At least the last one was *almost* age appropriate," she continued. "Did you even wait for this girl to graduate from high school?"

"Did she just call me a teenage prostitute?" asked Juliette, her words dangerously barbed.

"I don't blame you for your profession, honey," Susan told her. "Whatever it takes to survive in this economy, right? But you're pretty enough to model, and you can do a lot better than a deadbeat pseudo-daddy half again your age. I swear, every time I think my opinion of John couldn't get any lower, he's out there with a shovel, digging."

I reminded myself, and not for the first time, that Susan was the wife of my best friend, and that he'd *probably* miss her if I had Bill banish her to his private hell dimension, Gehenna.

"Susan, this is Juliette Middleton, my business partner and the other name on the door you came through. And Angel, who you've already been talking to, is her girlfriend." I paused. "Wait, did you just call *Anastasia* a prostitute too?"

"Oh, so *now* you care," muttered Juliette.

"What should I believe? That you're somehow dating a 10 *and* in business with another one? No offense intended," she said to Angel, who wasn't much prettier than I was and was *also* dating a ten. "I'm sure your actual girlfriend is very pretty too, hon, and I wish you both nothing but the best. I even marched in the Pride parade last year!"

"Believe what you want, Susan." Unlike Juliette, *I* hadn't had any *saké*, but this conversation was giving me a headache anyway. "And then let yourself out. Unless there's anything else?"

The usually perky woman's face—always perfectly made up, whether she was headed out for work or dinner or just watching television at home with her husband—fell, and her eyes dropped to the reasonably clean area rug she was standing on.

"I'm not trying to be..."

"You?" I finished.

"Yes. I suppose. If you insist that the woman at my wedding was your girlfriend, I guess I should believe you?"

I tried not to be annoyed that she'd made it a question rather than a statement. This was as close to an apology as I was going to get, and for my best friend's sake, I was going to be okay with that.

"We're an odd pair; I can't argue with that. But as impossible as it is to believe, Ana *is* my girlfriend. And Juliette is my junior partner."

"Who brings in most of the money," muttered the femmepire in question, "and all of the cool."

"Then I guess I'm sorry." Susan directed the words to Juliette, not me, not that I'd have expected anything else. "Making partner at your age is impressive, even in a small business like this one."

Juliette, who hadn't been a teenager for a good eighty years, looked unreasonably mollified.

"What brings you to Logan Heights?" I asked Susan. "And where did you park?" The neighborhood was in better shape than when I'd first set up shop, but the local gang still had an unfortunate taste for smash and grabs on any vehicles they didn't recognize as local.

"I took a taxi, and… could we talk? In private? Please?"

I traded glances with Juliette and nodded. "Sure thing. Why don't you step into my office."

As I escorted her through the interior door, I heard the rustle of plastic as Angel finally tore into her long-awaited lunch.

I closed the door to complete the illusion of privacy, even though Juliette would still hear every word we spoke, and waved Susan to one of the two chairs in front of my desk. I walked around to sink into the plush faux leather of my *senior* executive chair.

"What's going on, Susan? If you wanted to plan a surprise for Mike's birthday, you could have just called."

"Oh, it's a surprise alright," she muttered. "Happy fricking Birthday."

"What?"

"Did you know?"

"Susan, I'm tired, I'm full, I have no idea what you're talking about, and I have roughly thirty minutes before I need to go to the airport to pick up the girlfriend you don't believe I have. Tell me what's going on."

Her carefully composed mask crumbled, and Susan's blue eyes overflowed with tears that coursed down her cheeks, creating messy streaks in both her mascara and foundation.

"It's Michael," she said. "I think he's cheating on me!"

ooo

It took twenty of those thirty minutes to get the full story out of Susan between sobs and far too many tissues. When she was done, I was left with what we in the business would call *an ethical dilemma*. The wife of my best friend wanted me to investigate that friend? I didn't see any way it could end well.

According to Susan, Mike had been leaving their house at odd times during the nights over the past month, disappearing for hours at a time, and offering flimsy excuses when questioned about it. There'd even been instances when he'd come home from his construction job with the faint scent of perfume clinging to him. She'd tried following him a few times, to no avail, and now wanted me to tail him instead so that I could dig up evidence on what—or who—he was doing.

It was a simple cheating spouse case, made considerably less simple because it involved my best friend.

My old boss and mentor, the man who'd shown me the ropes of the private investigation business, would have taken the case anyway as long as he knew for certain the check would clear. I ended up taking it for another reason entirely: there was no way in hell Mike was cheating. It simply wasn't in the man's nature.

"Look, I've known Mike since we were three, and in that time, there've been two things he loved: you and his '66 Mustang. Unless you made him sell it...?" I waited for her to shake her head, because you never knew with Susan. "Then yeah, I don't see either one changing. And even if it did, he'd leave you before cheating. That's who he is."

"But you'll look into it anyway? And you *won't* tell him?"

And *that's* where things got thorny. Spying on my best friend wasn't the sort of thing that would go over well with Mike. Nor would finding out his new wife thought so little of him. But I was pretty sure Susan would just find another private eye if I said no, and I figured Mike would rather have me up in his business than a stranger.

"That's the job."

She dug through her oversized designer handbag and pulled out a checkbook. "How much do I owe you to start?"

"Nothing." I shrugged, feeling way more tired than even four sushi rolls could explain. "You're Mike's wife. That means you're practically part of my family too. I *know* he's not cheating on you, and I'm not taking your money to prove it."

She sniffled and tucked the checkbook away. "That's... that's actually really decent of you."

"I'm a decent sort of guy. I know you've always had a bit of a problem with me, though I never knew why, but—"

"You bring him home drunk at least once a month. And you hired five strippers for his bachelor's party. Five of them!"

If you're going to go, go big. Wasn't that the rule for bachelor parties? Hell, Darlene's had involved an entire bathtub of body glitter. I was *still* finding it in the oddest of places.

"Also, you called me *Suzanne* for the first six months of Michael and me dating!"

From the other side of the door, I heard something that sounded suspiciously like a cackle. Thankfully, Susan was too busy blowing her nose again to pay attention.

"In fairness, I thought it *was* your name! Mike was drunk the first time he told me about you, and… well… maybe he kind of slurred your name? With him calling you Susie after that, I never realized it was short for Susan instead of Suzanne." I waited a second to see if that excuse landed, and then launched my counterattack. "Also, Mike invites you to come to the bar with us, every single time!"

"I know, I know. I just feel sometimes like you're the fun wife and I'm the boring one. But maybe," she allowed, "that's not fair to you."

Gee, you think? I very carefully did not ask. And why was *I* the wife in Mike and my life-long heterosexual bromance anyway?

"Maybe the four of us—you, me, Mike, and Ana—could go out together for dinner or something," I found myself suggesting, to my own internalized screams of despair. "We can all get to know each other better in a more adult and sophisticated setting. You and I are both going to be part of Mike's life for a long time to come. We should figure out how to get along, don't you think?"

"Maybe… yeah," she said, voice firming. "But if he *is* cheating on me, it's over. One hundred percent done, and I don't even care what excuse he comes up with."

"I get it. But this is Mike we're talking about. I'm sure there's another explanation."

There had to be.

CHAPTER 4
IN WHICH HOME IS NOT A PLACE AT ALL

There wasn't time to discuss the case with Juliette; I hurried out of the office a minute or two after Susan's departure. Ana hadn't *asked* me to pick her up at the airport, but her live-in housekeepers and blood donors, Gustavo and Teresa, were getting older by the day, and the less they had to drive, the better.

I checked my wonderphone as I waited in the cellphone lot outside of the airport officially known as San Diego International, but still called Lindbergh Field by everyone I knew. No news from the Mer just yet. Nothing from Mike either, even though I'd texted him on the way out to my Corolla. I wasn't going to tell him that Susan had hired me, of course, but I *could* at least see if anything seemed off before I started tailing him like a wanted fugitive. It had been a while since our last bar crawl, but I'd assumed that was just another consequence of married life. Now, I'd find out for sure.

Whenever he texted me back, that is.

I did have messages from Kayla and Darlene, as well as a cat video from Juliette, so there was plenty to do as I waited for Ana's plane to land. Eventually, my phone buzzed.

I am retrieving my luggage from baggage claim and will meet you out front. – Ana.

Anastasia wasn't keen on contractions, let alone text-speak or emojis, and despite being one of the most tech savvy four-hundred-year-olds I'd ever met, she still insisted on signing her texts with her own name.

On my way, I texted back, *Missed you.*

I added a long chain of heart emojis, just to balance the scales and appease the local Demigod of Overly Emotive Messaging, then tossed my phone aside and pulled out of the lot.

There were a lot of people standing outside the terminal, waiting for rides, but Anastasia stood out as always: stunningly beautiful, elegantly put together, and just… *better*. Some of it was a vampire thing, some of it was her fashion sense, but most of it was just her being her. I didn't even try to fight my grin as I got out of the Corolla, and that grin widened to traditional shit-eating proportions when she greeted me with a kiss.

The agency is doing well, Lucia's still thousands of miles away in Rome, and I'm here, standing on a sunny curb, kissing my dream woman in my dream city. What's not to love?

The obvious answer was the goblin war in that same city and the fact that I'd just been hired to investigate my best friend, but obvious answers were for quitters, and I was no quitter.

I snuck in another kiss and loaded Ana's bags into the trunk before coming around to meet her in the Corolla.

"How was the flight?"

"Quiet and peaceful, truly. I napped for most of the journey and read for the rest of it."

"No inflight movies?" I'd become secretly convinced that Ana was a huge movie buff but had yet to catch her in the act.

"Me? Perish the thought." She pulled on her seatbelt and then laid a hand across mine. "It is good to see you, John. I missed you too. How was the wedding?"

"It would have been better with you, but it was pretty great even so. I caught the collar."

"I beg your pardon?"

"No worries; I gave it to someone else."

"I… see. Thank you for picking me up. Gustavo is a dear, but his eyesight is not what it used to be, and the traffic in Southern California gives Teresa conniptions."

"If it means I get to see you sooner," I pointed out, "I'll drive you anywhere and everywhere."

"And so, we shall ride eternal, shiny and chrome," murmured Anastasia.

I threaded my way between shuttles, taxis, and pedestrians, waiting to give her a knowing look until we were in the clear. "You know, that sounded *a lot* like something they said in Fury Road."

"Did it?" She gave me the slow half-smile I'd fallen in love with years earlier. "How strange."

I filled her in on recent events as we drove, filling the comfortable silence with my usual blend of babble and banter, but as we reached the onramp to the 5, I decided it was time to change things up.

"How was Rome?"

"Largely uneventful. Maria Elena sends her best wishes and wanted me to ask you why you remain inactive on the social media accounts she created for you."

"I'm not sure I'm a Twitter guy."

"Admittedly, the decision to share your inner life on a public forum where anyone can access it does seem imprudent."

"Right?" I shivered. Social media was one of my best tools as a private investigator; I'd found far too much actionable information on there to ever even think of sharing my own. The sort of things my parents posted on Facebook were bad enough. "And how is the royal family?"

"The Kingmaker remains uniquely himself. Princess Sabina is adjusting rapidly to the new status quo. In a few decades, I have no doubt she will be as capable a ruler as any in her line."

"And Lucia?"

"*Queen-Regent* Lucia," corrected Ana, not bothering to hide her smile, "is well, for the first time in decades. Italy agrees with her in a way that this country never did. And I suspect she is grateful that the literal distance between you dulls certain aspects of your bond."

"Me and her both. And speaking of *certain aspects…*" I gave her my very best smolder. "Do you have any plans for tonight?"

"The same ones that you have, I believe. Feed, shower, and then… perhaps retire to the primary suite? It has been a *very* long week."

We shared another smile, this one the kind that puts hair on a man's chest. It wasn't until we'd passed the 8 that something horrible occurred to me.

"Did I just… waggle my eyebrows at you?"

"I believe you may have."

Holy crap. I was turning into my dad.

"Sorry about that. Uhm…" I flailed about for a change in subject. What had we been talking about? Oh, right. Rome. "Any luck with your research?"

"Not as much as we hoped for, although Denarius has promised to continue pursuing any available leads. Gaius' personal effects contained no mention of when or how he gained his Talent or how exactly Jehane faked her death in the Tower."

"And the stone fragments from the Bitter End that they used to frame you with?"

"I was hoping you had made progress on that front."

"No. We went back to the Bitter End, but even with it open again, Kala remains a no-show." I frowned for the first time since I'd seen Ana standing on the curb. The fact that Gaius had refused to reveal his secrets even when he thought he'd already won was still bothering me, all these months later. "There's something we're missing. Too many things just don't add up."

"I think you are correct that there is another party involved somehow," agreed Anastasia. "Yet their identity and ultimate goals both remain unknown. The one piece of information I did come away with was that Gaius was *not* away on King Tomasso's business when the king was murdered."

"Wait, he was still in Rome?"

"No, eyewitness accounts place him in India and then eastern Asia during that time. However, Denarius found mention that it was Gaius himself who suggested that trip, and not King Tomasso as we had originally believed."

"It got him out of Rome and gave him an alibi when Tomasso was murdered," I reasoned. "But why Asia? Especially given how long travel took back then? You think he was doing something for this unknown third party?"

"Indeed. Denarius has agents attempting to reconstruct Gaius' journey. Though the world has dramatically changed in the ensuing century, perhaps one or more clues will be found."

"I'll see if I can step things up with Kala here. I have a feeling that whatever allowed someone to remove pieces of the demigod's home dimension without him knowing will go a long way to answering our questions." I coughed. "Which leaves only Xavier."

Two years after Ana had killed her former lover, I still wasn't sure exactly what to say about the traitorous captain of Lucia's ex-House's Watch.

Hell, even that phrase—*traitorous captain of Lucia's ex-House's Watch*—made my brain hurt. The supernatural races of the world had really cornered the market on coups, power struggles, and betrayal.

"It is still possible that he developed a second Talent on his own," said Anastasia, her words calm and composed, giving no clue to whatever emotions Xavier's mention had provoked. "It has happened before."

"Yeah, but in someone so young, and just in time to suborn some of Lucia's less easily bought House members and stage the coup?"

"Talents are born of blood and age. It seems impossible that someone would be able to create one entirely from scratch."

"As impossible as sneaking into a demigod's own domain and chiseling out pieces of their bar's largely indestructible wall?"

"A fair point. Still, they may not be related. Xavier's second talent at least has an explanation, no matter how unlikely. As for Gaius... some mysteries may never be solved."

"Maybe they should have waited before executing Jehane."

"Perhaps. Yet it was a decision that the council and royal family made together. Better to ensure that justice was finally done than to risk her escaping yet again."

It was a heavy subject and one that followed us all the way up the 5 and past the 52 and the 56. We'd almost reached Birmingham when I remembered Simon's case.

"So, I know you haven't even gotten home yet," I said, breaking the silence that had fallen over our drive, "but how do you feel about taking a road trip?"

"A road trip? To where?"

"Ghost Falls, New Mexico. Fall foliage, Hatch chiles, gorgeous scenery, and, uh… one small missing persons case."

"You've been hired to go to New Mexico?"

"Yeah. Our local zombie prince called in that favor I owed him. It turns out he still has living descendants, and one of them is missing. Honestly, I think she probably just ran away with her boyfriend, but I told him I'd check it out. And I wouldn't hate having you along for company."

"Well, as long as you would not *hate* it."

"I'll even let you pick the music we listen to, as long as I get to choose where we eat."

Her jade eyes danced. "I would say this proposed deal feels a little bit one-sided, had I not once spent several hours with you on an otherwise lovely Sunday listening to grown men grunt and call out obscenities."

I coughed again. "Admittedly, gangster rap's not for everyone. So, we have a deal?"

"This is not a mediation, John." She touched my hand again, her fingers feather-soft for all that they could bend steel. "I wish to spend time with you, and New Mexico *is* lovely this time of year. And if I must eat In-N-Out once or twice on this road trip of ours, I will find my way to accepting that fate," she added, lips curling into a smile.

Best. Girlfriend. Ever.

Gustavo met us at the door from the garage, the elderly man looking like a San Diego native in khaki shorts and a polo, a broad smile deepening the maze of wrinkles in his bronzed face. I handed him one of Anastasia's bags, grabbed the second, and slipped past him and Teresa as Ana hugged her long-time housekeepers and blood donors. The primary suite was up on the second floor, two bedrooms down from where Ana had once nursed me back to health and Lucia had tried to snack on me in her sleep.

By the time I had tucked Ana's suitcase away and gone back into the hall, Gustavo was making his way toward me with the second bag. A frown came to me unbidden. I'd intentionally given the old man the lighter of the two bags, but he was struggling with it, his steps more a shuffle than the careful stride I was used to.

Part of me wanted to offer my help, but Gustavo had his pride, and I didn't think he'd take it well. So instead, I ducked back into the bedroom and then the ensuite bathroom where I made a lengthy show of washing my hands.

Four happy birthdays later, I emerged, trading smiles and then handshakes with the older man. I split my time between Ana's house in Cardiff and Juliette's apartment in Hillcrest... and only stayed in the former when Anastasia was also present. I liked Gustavo and Teresa both and they seemed to return the sentiment, but the elderly couple deserved time to themselves when their employer and friend was away.

Gustavo clapped me on my shoulder, murmured something incomprehensible in Italian, and turned to shuffle back downstairs. I dropped into one of the two easy chairs in Ana's bedroom, fishing out my phone to see if I'd gotten any new messages. The answer to that was no, so I sent a text to Maria Elena saying hi, but making absolutely no mention of Twitter or any of the other social media services she'd created accounts for on my behalf. Then, I messaged Darlene, wishing her and Kayla a safe trip to Australia.

Maria Elena was likely asleep in Italy, but D responded almost immediately with a gif of three men from *The Office*—the American version, of course—all dancing awkwardly and the caption *Party Time!* I sent back two thumbs up, a fire emoji, and a pumpkin, although I wasn't sure what the last was supposed to represent.

The newlyweds were clearly doing just fine.

Ten minutes and innumerable rounds of Candy Crush Saga later, Anastasia made her appearance. Her usually pale cheeks were flushed from feeding, and her eyes locked onto me like laser-guided missile defense systems, even as she toed the door shut behind her.

"Ready for that shower?" I asked.

"I believe it can wait until *after* we've gotten dirty."

ooo

Much later, I snuggled with a delightfully—one might even say exquisitely—clean Anastasia. The sheets were Egyptian cotton, the pillow was a soft cloud, and Ana's nightgown was smooth silk, but the vampire herself put them all to shame.

"That was lovely, Mr. Smith."

"I think I died twice, Lady Dumenyova."

We just held each other for a long while. Between the shower, her feeding, and our own activities, Ana was warmer than usual, her cheek nestled against my bare shoulder, her long hair splayed out on our shared pillow.

This was home. I couldn't bring myself to say it out loud—I felt sort of lame for even thinking it—but it was true.

Eventually, Ana shifted to look up at me. "Thank you for permitting Gustavo to carry one of the bags. No matter what Teresa and I say to him about resting, the dear man does need to feel useful."

"He's a great guy, even if I can't understand a word he says; I don't want him to feel like he's being put out to pasture or anything." Even though it felt like I was betraying the old man, I swallowed and continued. "That said… he was really struggling with your suitcase."

"Yes." Ana's voice was quiet. "I worry about them both. In the long tradition of their family, they have served me well, but I do not know how many years either of them has left."

I gave her another hug, uncertain what to say. Gustavo was the last in a family line that had served Anastasia since shortly after her parents had sold her to Lucia's father, and the old man and his wife had been her primary housekeepers and blood donors for far longer than I'd been alive. I couldn't even imagine what it would be like, saying goodbye to Mike when he was eighty and dying, and yet Anastasia had done something similar again and again over the centuries.

"There is still time yet," said Ana, reading my thoughts and for some reason seeking to reassure *me*. "And they will spend that time cared for and cherished to the best of my abilities."

"What happens when they do pass?" It wasn't a subject I wanted to delve into, but I couldn't help myself.

Once again, Ana knew exactly where I was going. Her voice was soft, and she reached up to stroke my cheek. "I will have to find new donors."

I tried to hide my reaction. A vampire's feeding didn't *have* to be sexual for the vampire themselves, but it inevitably triggered sexual reactions in their donor. It was one thing to see it with Gustavo and Teresa, who had known her all their life and were desperately in love with each other, but someone new?

"We could try—"

"No, John." Her words were steel wrapped in silk. "I have fed from you twice now, once in the Tower and once here at home. There will not be a third such occurrence."

"It doesn't hurt that much," I lied. The same gift that made me immune to glamour was a curse when it came to a vampire's bite. Lucia, who had brute forced her way into my brain to form our bond, was the only exception. With everyone else, Juliette and Anastasia both, there was nothing but pain for me at the end of a vampire's fangs.

Ana's sigh was cool against my chest, and she dropped her hand from my face to snuggle more tightly against me. "We have time yet. We will figure something out."

It was still early, for those of us on California time instead of Western Europe, but I lay there anyway, holding the woman I loved as she drifted off to sleep.

And if my stomach gurgled from time to time, having finally woken up sufficiently to start protesting the *four* sushi rolls I'd fed it, well, nobody but me was awake to hear it.

CHAPTER 5
IN WHICH DOUBT IS A FOUR-LETTER WORD

The next morning found us having a late breakfast in Anastasia's eat-in kitchen. Gustavo had disappeared—age hadn't impacted his ninja-like stealth, apparently—to tackle some sort of maintenance project, but his wife, Teresa, bustled about the kitchen, passing out cups of tea, thermos-sized glasses of orange juice, and platefuls of her own uniquely made avocado toast.

I had thanked her for both with a smile, and she'd returned it, signifying both that this was a good day for her joints and that my long campaign to win her approval was finally bearing fruit. She had started out far more standoffish than her husband, but like mold, I was slowly growing on her.

Anastasia's unmistakable happiness probably helped a lot too.

I was polishing off my second piece of toast when I finally remembered Steve's request at the wedding. I washed down that last bite with some OJ and cleared my throat.

As Lucia's Secundus, Ana had regularly spent her meals on a slim tablet, researching people or events for the queen, but I hadn't seen that tablet since her return. Instead, she was talking in Italian with

Teresa, the warmth of both of their voices a balm even though I couldn't understand the words.

"I forgot to mention; I ran into Steve at the wedding."

"Stephen Grant?" Just like that, I had Ana's attention. She watched me over the brim of her cup of tea.

"Yeah. He was part of Kayla's wedding party."

"And how is Mr. Grant doing?"

"Pretty well, I think. He's happy that the Bitter End is open again so he and Barry could reconnect. But uh… he wanted to pass on a message and a request from the House."

I watched her as I recapped my brief encounter with Steve, but her poker face was in fine form, as usual, and I probably spent at least half of that time just watching her instead. We had gotten up at the same time, but somehow, she looked like a thousand bucks—hair up in a twist, one of her favorite ocean-colored tunics draping over wide-legged pants—while I just looked like death warmed over.

"What do they believe I can or should do?"

"I think the House was hoping you would help them track down Zorana."

"And then?"

"I don't know. Sweet talk her into coming back?"

The look Anastasia sent me spoke volumes.

"Yeah, tell me about it. It wasn't my idea. In fact, I think it's pretty ballsy of them to even reach out at all, given everything that happened last year. Most likely, they're just running out of options."

"So it would seem." Her voice gave away nothing, but I could almost feel her brain churning away, already focusing on the problem and likely devising possible solutions.

"I told Steve I'd give you the message, but that I wasn't making any promises. As much as I like him and a few of the other residents,

I'd rather you *not* get involved." I repressed a shiver. "Zorana is dangerous."

"As am I."

"Sure, but *you* I care about. Zorana? Not so much."

That was a lie. If something happened to Zorana, I'd likely breathe a sigh of relief, and maybe have a few less nightmares. But that wasn't necessarily the same as *wanting* her dead, especially if it put Ana at risk.

Anastasia was as competent and badass as anyone I'd ever met, but the Blood Witch was a thousand years old, and it wasn't Zorana who had come away badly wounded from their last encounter.

"Legally speaking, this is the fledgling House's problem to deal with," she said slowly, as if tasting her words. "However, a Blood Witch running amok in our city poses risks and challenges for everyone, especially given Zorana's altogether questionable state of mind. I should at least meet with Mr. Grant to discuss the situation."

"Maybe suggest he hire the karkino," I said, referencing San Diego's clan of crab assassins. "Not that I think they can take Zorana, but they could at least help find her. They tracked me down without any problem at all."

"If I recall correctly, they simply waited outside your place of business."

"Still… that takes at least *some* savvy."

"I will pass the suggestion on during my visit. When were you planning for us to leave for New Mexico?"

"Sometime in the next couple of days," I said, "although I need to check with the Mer first. They're scheduling my initial mediation between the Superchargers and Clippers, and I need to make sure it's not set for while we're gone."

I eyed the half-slice of avocado toast left on Anastasia's plate, but after a brief but bloody war between my id and my self-control, decided I'd had enough. As good as the toast was, the last thing I needed was another food coma.

"Very well. Would you like to accompany me to the House, or do you need to make an appearance at your office?"

"Juliette should be able to handle the office, and I'd much rather spend the afternoon with you." I tapped out a quick message on my wonderphone and sent it off into the electronic ether. "There. Now, she won't worry or assume that the agency's senior partner is some kind of slacker."

I *was*, of course—and not just because it was already noon and I was barely having breakfast—but Juliette knew better than to expect me at work the day after Ana's return. Given that my junior business partner had gone through her own honeymoon phase with Angel, I think she even kind of understood. Not that she'd ever admit it to my face.

Ana returned her teacup to its saucer and met my eyes across the table. There was nothing supernatural whatsoever about her gaze, but hell if it didn't threaten to swallow me up every single time. "Are you certain that you feel comfortable returning to the House?"

I swallowed. "It wouldn't be the first time."

"To your eternal credit, yes. Even so, I could arrange to meet Mr. Grant elsewhere instead."

After far too long of a pause, I shook my head. "It's been more than a year, and pretty much everyone that tried to kill me—to kill us—is gone now. And I do have *some* good memories of the place. Besides, it's been way too long since I got to ride in an elevator with you."

That won me a smile, small but wry. "If you remain so easily satisfied, Mr. Smith, I might find myself starting to get lazy."

"It's hard to imagine *you* being lazy, Lady Dumenyova, but I'd like to see it at least once." I wiped my mouth with the provided napkin and was just about to take our plates to the sink when my wonderphone buzzed. Twice. "Huh. Speak of the devil."

"Lady Middleton requires your presence after all?"

"No, sorry… different devil. It looks like the Mer have finally scheduled our first meeting. Tonight, in the San Diego Bay. Not *on* the bay. *In* it."

"The Mer *are* aquatic in nature."

"So they are." For some reason, I still hadn't expected them to go with a water venue for the mediation. Their decision raised two immediate concerns. First, I got seasick from even walking *near* the ocean. And second, I didn't have a way to reach the designated location, which was simply a map pin dropped out in the bay. The first issue could be partially mitigated through copious quantities of Dramamine, but the second…

It was late notice, but I could *probably* find a boat to rent, and then bring Juliette along to keep that boat's owner compelled so they didn't wonder what we were doing out in the bay at night and why the creatures we were meeting were recognizably inhuman. Or…

Or I could talk to someone I knew who had a boat of his own.

Yeah, I liked that idea a lot better. For a lot of reasons.

"I'm going to have to pass on the House visit after all," I told Ana. "There's still a lot of prep I need to do before tonight. Sorry about that."

"It is your job. Never apologize for fulfilling your duties, least of all to one such as me."

There was a strange note in her last few words, something slightly discordant that I didn't quite parse, but before I could follow up on it, Ana was up and clearing our plates, dumping the dishes into the sink.

"I will let you know any additional details as I uncover them," she told me, her voice back to its usual chocolatey velvet.

Still…

"If I can do anything at all—"

"You can stop worrying. I love you, John Smith, and all will be fine." She dropped a kiss on my lips, and just like that, life was good again. "Tomorrow, we will toast the successful beginning of your mediation over breakfast."

"Harry's?" I suggested, citing the name of a breakfast spot in La Jolla that made insanely good breakfast burritos.

"It has been a few weeks since I had their pancakes," she agreed.

That was all I needed to hear. I kissed her back and went upstairs to shower, dreams of burritos dancing in my head. There were worse ways to start the day.

ooo

It was only as I was toweling off from what had somehow turned into a forty-minute shower that I realized I'd never asked Anastasia about my deceased fellow mediator, Caleb Van Stahl. Not that I thought she'd killed him or anything, of course, but even in her pseudo-retirement, she tended to pay better attention to the events of the supernatural world than I did.

I'd only met Caleb twice, but both times, he'd been pretty damn likeable; handsome, well-dressed, and funny, in an *I've seen every episode of obscure television ever recorded and thus will charmingly* always *recognize your off-the-cuff pop culture references* sort of way. And yeah, maybe he'd invited himself down to San Diego, and taken over some of the city's ever-active and ever-profitable mediation business, but we *were* a capitalist country, right? Competition kept me sharp, and there were only so many times a year I wanted to engage in potentially fatal conflict resolutions anyway.

Really, he'd been doing me a favor.

Still, he was dead now, and Jason's assumption that I'd had something to do with it kind of poked at me. Anastasia was the least bloodthirsty vampire that I knew—pun *not* intended—but she was *also* a centuries-old assassin with a pragmatic streak as wide as the Grand Canyon. She'd looked into Caleb when he first set up shop and had never been quite as keen on the older man as I was. If she had recently found some piece of evidence that made him a threat to more than just my bottom line…?

Well, yeah. I had very little doubt that Anastasia would do what she thought necessary to protect me. But would she take that step without talking to me first?

I just didn't buy it. Not because she needed my approval or anything… she was just a hell of a lot more considerate than that. She would have understood the optics of my mediator competition being suddenly offed, and that she—and by proxy, me—would automatically become the most likely suspects. At the very least, she'd have given me some sort of heads-up so I didn't look like a complete fool when the subject came up.

None of which stopped me from popping in a Bluetooth earpiece and calling Juliette as I headed toward the 5.

"Little bird, I didn't think I'd hear from you until tomorrow. Is the bloom already off the rose?"

"What rose are we talking about?"

"If you have to ask…" She sighed. "Whatever. Are you planning to grace us with your presence?"

"Not today. The Mer have set the introductory mediation meeting for tonight, so I need to get things set up. I'm just calling to check in on how things are going."

"Things are dead, as usual. Figuratively speaking, that is. The soon-to-be former Mrs. Peterman is coming at one to pick up our evidence and drop off her payment, but otherwise, the day is wide open. No hits on Dulcinea's credit cards, so I'm going to have one of my contacts at the SDPD reach out to the sheriff in Ghost Falls to see if there's anything that didn't make it into Dulcinea's file. Beyond that? I think it's another Netflix and chill sort of day at the office."

I was pretty sure the *and chill* part meant she and Angel would be relaxing, rather than performing sexual acrobatics all over our sole place of business, but it was hard to know with Juliette. Given that I wouldn't be there until tomorrow, and that we now had *multiple* windows to create a cross-breeze with, I didn't really care either.

As the Duchess had told me on multiple occasions over the past few months, semi-regular sex really *had* dislodged the stick up my ass.

"What do you want to do about the *other* case?" continued Juliette. "Your friend Mike and little Susie Homemaker?"

I paused to safely navigate the merge before answering. "Assuming tonight's mediation goes well, I need to head to Ghost Falls with Ana tomorrow. I can check in with Mike before then to see what's going on. I'm sure Suzanne—I mean Susan—is just being paranoid. Again. Dude's probably pulling extra shifts so he can buy her shiny things or something."

"Extra shifts? After midnight?" Juliette's voice was its usual blend of sharp and sweet. "Doesn't he work construction?"

"I'm just saying… I've known the guy since elementary school, when we ate peanut butter, jelly, and banana burritos on the bus together. Mike's not a cheater."

It was a rare thing in our line of business to have any kind of faith in the target of an investigation, but then again, most PIs didn't get hired to investigate their best friend.

"I'll leave that one up to you then, *senior* partner. If there's nothing else, Angel and I are going to order something for lunch on the corporate card."

"Yeah, right. The corporate card." I snickered as I overtook a landscaping truck that was depositing freshly cut greenery all over the highway. "Wait; we don't really have one of those, do we?"

"Of course we do. How else do you think we deduct business expenses?"

"I guess I hadn't really thought about it."

"Seriously, it's a miracle this agency stayed afloat before me."

"I'm a small business owner, Juliette, not some kind of entrepreneurial badass."

"Isn't your dad an *accountant?*"

"Yeah… which meant *he* dealt with all that tax stuff for me. Until they moved to Austin anyway."

"If we get audited—"

"You'll use your magical vampire powers and make it all better, like you do everything else." I shook my head even though she couldn't see the gesture. "Seriously, Duchess, when did *you* start worrying about things like the IRS?"

"I…" She coughed. "Shit, you're right."

"That's what—"

"When the *hell* did I turn into an even lamer version of you? Is this Bizarro Land or something? *I'm* the cool one!"

"I mean, I wouldn't say—"

"This is *your* fault," she decided. "If you hadn't sweet talked me into rescuing your floundering agency—"

It had only been a year, but we had very, very different recollections of how Juliette had become my business partner. Still, I could recognize an impending meltdown when I heard it. Rather than debate trivialities, I decided to head off said meltdown at the pass.

"Hey now," I told her, injecting a carefully prescribed mix of reassurance and confidence into my tone, "you've got a hipster girlfriend named after celestial beings, you're on a buy-you-drinks basis with half the roadies in America, and you can sprint flat-out for miles wearing four-inch stilettos. You're *still* the cool one."

"Damn right I am!" I could somehow *hear* her scowl over the phone. "I swear… you finally lose your virginity and the whole world turns upside down."

"I *wasn't* a virg—" I sighed and let it go. There was no point in arguing with Juliette when she got like this, especially not over the phone. "Anyway, I had another reason for calling."

"Oh yeah?" She at least sounded mollified. Maybe Angel had fed her something. Either that or my secretly amazing mediator powers had struck again.

"Yeah. Did you know that Caleb Van Stahl is dead?"

"Oh, so *now* you want to talk about it?"

"Wait, what?"

"Three weeks! I've been waiting three weeks for you to bring it up! I've dropped hints, I've made casual asides, I even left the obituaries out on your desk to make sure you knew that I knew, and yet nothing! I was starting to wonder just how long you were going to pretend it hadn't happened."

"Uhm…" Hints? Asides? Obituaries? Granted, I would never have thought to expect subtlety from Juliette, but shouldn't I have noticed *something?*

There were times I questioned my vocation as a private investigator.

"I have to admit," purred Juliette, "you defending your territory like that is kind of hot. You lose some points for having Anastasia do it for you, but still… I wasn't sure you had that sort of ruthlessness in you."

"Because I don't!"

"What?"

"Come on, Duchess. I'm a community college dropout. What have I *ever* done to make you think I could have someone killed?"

"Well, you did shoot Ricardo during the first House coup."

"Yeah, but—"

"And vaporized that big boy werewolf out past Santee."

"I mean—"

"And made an ice sculpture of the king's Secundus in Rome."

"That was Lucia as much as me," I muttered.

"And we can't forget the witches."

"Okay! I get it!" Lord Kala, the demigod owner of the Bitter End, had called me a nexus of death, and maybe, just maybe, I was starting to think he was right.

Juliette's voice softened. "You know you saved us all when you killed her right? Not just me, but Anastasia and the White Ladies too?"

I blinked away images of Nepenthe, a forty-something yoga instructor and the leader of the coven that had tried to take power in San Diego, blinked away images of her clutching at the knife I'd driven into her chest. Maybe it was racist—or species-ist—of me, but her death still haunted me in a way that the vampires, weres, and mercenary roaches never had.

A loud honk—more suitable for a barge than anything even remotely automotive—brought me back to myself and I made way for the F250 careening down the highway.

"Anyway," I said, clearing my throat. "I didn't have anything to do with Caleb's death. I didn't even know about it until the wedding this past weekend."

"Seriously?"

"Seriously."

"Shit." She gave me a moment or two in an uncommon show of courtesy, but then couldn't resist asking. "You think Anastasia…?"

"No."

"Are you sure? Because I think she'd kill *me* in a heartbeat if she thought I was a threat to you. And I'm unreasonably pretty."

"And *cool.*"

'Exactly. Also, Van Stahl was murdered during one of the few weeks your girlfriend was in town."

Well, shit.

"It really is a good thing he's dead," she insisted. "I never understood your attachment to the guy when he was taking money right out of your pocket."

"We had a bit of a bromance going."

"A bromance? Since when are *you* into silver foxes?"

I frowned. "Wait, he was an Infected? I didn't even know werefoxes were a thing!"

"*Silver fox* is code for an older human who is distinguished, handsome, and rich, you moron."

"Oh." That made more sense. "You know I'm not into guys. Not even old ones." That qualifier hadn't quite come out the way I'd intended, but I shrugged it away again. "There's just a special bond between mediator dudes."

"A special bond."

"Yeah. Two good guys doing their best to deal with difficult clients and dangerous situations."

"Caleb invaded your territory."

"Only because he didn't know me at the time. Once we met, we agreed to divvy up the greater San Diego area."

"An agreement he promptly broke by mediating for the chupacabras in Ramona."

"Apparently, his best friend growing up *was* a chupacabra."

"Naturally." She sighed. "I should have known you would never do anything I might perceive as hot. Anyway, I'm just saying… him being dead isn't the worst thing ever. And if Anastasia did it—"

"She didn't."

"But if she did, maybe she had a good reason."

"Maybe," I admitted.

"Have you asked her?"

"I will. I just forgot last night. But *when* she says she had nothing to do with it, we should probably investigate who or what *did* kill him."

"Why?"

"Because it's the right thing to do?"

Nothing but silence over the line. I tried again.

"And I might be next?"

"Okay, that makes more sense."

"Maybe you can get started on that while Ana and I tackle Simon's case in New Mexico?"

"If I must."

"And here you were complaining that we didn't have any cases. Between Dulcinea, Mike, and Caleb, I've gotten us three!"

"And how many of those are we getting paid for, little bird?"

I coughed.

"That's what I thought. Hey, be careful with the Mer and the goblins tonight. Both have had human on the menu at various points in their species' history."

"As opposed to vampires, who still do?"

"That's totally different."

"How so?"

"We're hot. Humans will forgive anything if the packaging is attractive enough."

I could hear Angel say something in the background, but the words themselves were too indistinct to make out.

"And speaking of humans," added Juliette, "I need to feed mine so she can return the favor. Thanks for the credit card, partner."

That settled it; I needed my own corporate card.

CHAPTER 6
IN WHICH PREPARATION IS EVERYTHING

I parked my still-shiny, if no-longer-new, Corolla in one of the overpriced and barely attended lots downtown. Before getting out and messing with the QR code I needed to scan, I gave Mike a call. No answer, but that wasn't too unusual when he was on the job; I left a voicemail suggesting we hit Pacific Beach for drinks ASAP. A beer or two with my big Mexican friend would help smooth the way for questions about his late-night excursions, and then I'd have the case crossed off my list almost as fast as Juliette had taken care of the Petermans. And *without* vampiric powers to compel my key witness.

Of course, *best friend* status was its own kind of mojo.

It was another beautiful day in San Diego, and even though it was a weekday, the tourists were out in force. I wove my way through the crowds at Petco and the convention center and then cut across to the marina on the other side of one of our town's plethora of Marriotts.

As I'd told Ana, the Mer had set our meeting for midnight in the bay, and that meant I needed a boat. Boat rentals were, of course, very much a thing in San Diego, but I was pretty sure renting one overnight would cost extra, and Mrs. Peterman's check hadn't arrived yet, let alone cleared.

Thankfully, I had friends with boats. Or one boat anyway.

Roughly two-thirds of the way down the rightmost pier, I stepped up the gangway and onto a reasonably sized, conspicuously clean boat, all in white except for the chalk graffiti that its youngest resident had scribbled across the upper decking. That budding artist was standing nearby her latest masterpiece, small hands over both eyes, her increasingly tattered Superman cape blowing in the breeze off the water.

"Jee Sun?" As ever, the small Korean girl was wearing a school uniform under her cape, despite never having been to school in all the time I'd known her. That wasn't the only thing that remained unchanged: two years later, she still seemed to be the exact same age as ever… something I very nebulously called five-to-ten-ish. Jee Sun was human, as far as anyone knew, but for some reason, time seemed to skip her by.

"Shh," she told me, not removing her hands from her eyes. "We're playing hide-and-seek!"

"Are you hiding or seeking?"

That won me a look of near outrage, delivered through spread fingers. The effect was only slightly weakened by the coke bottle glasses she wore beneath thick black bangs.

"Right. I'm supposed to be quiet." I zipped my mouth shut, locked it, and tucked the key away in my pocket.

"Where oh WHERE has Tiny Flower gone?" The voice was deep and incongruously Southern, and it came from below deck, where I could hear someone stomping around.

Moments later, the speaker emerged into the sunlight, all seven feet of him, with green skin, coal eyes, and a mouth that moved freely despite having been drawn on with magic marker. Lord Beel-Kasan, Demigod of Nightmares, Terror, and Vindication had grown one arm from the recognizably oversized asparagus spear he called a body and was using that arm to cover his own eyes, even as the mouth beneath wiggled back and forth. "I know she MUST be around HERE somewhere!"

Jee Sun giggled as Bill tromped off along the deck in the exact wrong direction, narrowly avoiding marching right over the edge. I was never entirely sure how Bill walked, given that he didn't have feet or even legs, but it was probably the least strange thing about my demigod friend. He marched up to the bow—or the stern… I could never remember which was which—and leaned out into open space, defying gravity as he peered down at the water despite the arm over his eyes.

That was when Jee Sun decided to strike. She pulled her hands away from her own eyes, spun until she had located the demigod, and then charged across the deck as fast as her Mary Janes could carry her, rocketing into the base of Bill's stalk like a child-sized projectile.

"I got you!" she crowed.

"Oh no, were YOU the SEEKER and I the HIDER in THIS GAME OF BOTH HIDING AND SEEKING?" Bill's eyes rotated all the way around his body until he was looking down at the little girl, and then two extra arms grew to toss her into the air, catching her again moments later to the little girl's clear delight. "I COULD not REMEMBER!"

Even outside, with the noise of the marina around us, Jee Sun's squeals had a certain penetrating quality. I spared a glance at the boats moored to either side of us, but either the owners were absent or they'd learned to avoid their neighbors. Given that Bill manifested to everyone but me and apparently Jee Sun as that person's deepest fear, I couldn't blame them. Even Juliette still needed a few drinks before she truly relaxed around the goofy, unpredictable, and ultimately terrifying immortal.

I gave the pair a few moments, knowing from personal experience that Jee Sun would be anxious to do something else in moments, and that that something would probably involve food.

"Ice cream?" she asked, when the giggling finally stopped.

"YES! ICE CREAM FOR EVERYONE! AND WE WILL EAT IT WITH THE SPOONS AND THEN WE WILL ALSO EAT THE BOWLS MADE OF WAFFLES AND THEN—" Bill stopped as Jee Sun gave him a poke. "What is it, TINY FLOWER? Do you no longer like the BOWLS MADE OF WAFFLES?"

"Mr. John is here," she informed him, squirting out of his grip to run downstairs, in search of the elusive ice cream and what I assumed were waffle cones.

Both coal eyes rotated around the stalk even further until they pointed in my direction. The magic marker was slower to make its journey, but when it arrived, it widened into a cartoon-like O of surprise.

"Johnny Law! Is Mickey's small hand pointed at the eight already?"

"No?"

"So, it is not time for DRINKS AND CHEESE PUFFS with you and Lady PAC-MAN?"

"That's next month," I reminded him.

"Are you here for ICE CREAM then? Do you too NO LONGER like the BOWLS MADE OF WAFFLES?"

"No… I mean… yeah, I wouldn't turn down some ice cream. And waffle bowls or cones sound pretty good, honestly. But that's not why I'm here."

"Then wiggle your face at me, AMIGO, and we will unspool what must be unspooled until all that remains is miles and miles of yarn."

Two-plus years of getting to know Bill had not made him any less strange, but I had, at least, gotten better at translating his words into something that made sense.

Occasionally.

"I was hoping I could borrow your boat for the night," I told him. "I need to do a mediation out in the bay."

"Our boat?" That magic marker mouth reshaped itself into a straight line. "But this is the HOME of Tiny Flower, Johnny-On-the-Spot."

"I only need it for one night. I have to—"

"It is where she RESTS HER SMALL BUT APPROPRIATELY SIZED HEAD."

I winced and pulled out my number-one smile, the Dealmaker™. Bill was a friend, but he was also insane, and quite possibly capable of destroying all of downtown San Diego. I didn't think it would come to that, but a little bit of mediator magic probably wouldn't hurt.

"Why don't you guys come with me?" my mouth said, before I could think to stop it. And then, as I desperately tried to undo the damage I'd potentially already done: "To the meeting site, I mean, *not* the actual mediation."

He paused, and his mouth wiggled back and forth like a sine wave.

"Will there be ice cream?"

"I mean… yeah, as long as we bring it."

"And CARAMEL FRAPPUCINOS WITH EXTRA CHOCOLATE SYRUP SAUCE?"

"I can make that happen."

"ICE CREAM AND FRAPPUCINOS!" He hooted, dancing around the deck. "It will BE A FIELD TRIP except WITHOUT A

FIELD and NOBODY WILL BE DOING ANY TRIPPING unless they get PERMISSION FIRST!"

He fixed me with one coal eye at that, and I just nodded. I didn't think it was possible to trip Bill at all, and anyone dumb enough to do so with Jee Sun deserved the endless torment in Gehenna it would win them.

"I'll be back tonight then?" I asked as much as told him. "With Frappucinos in hand."

"Roger that, good buddy." He made what was either a call-me sign or a shaka. "You know how to reach us if anything changes."

So, it had been a call-me sign. Good to know.

"Did you guys get a new phone?"

"Why would we do that when the previous phone was perfectly fine and covered in stickers of Pooh and Piglet and Eeyore and—"

"Because Jee Sun dropped it in the bay. Back in June."

Bill's mouth formed another O, this one somehow larger than the first. "That's right! And I WENT DOWN TO LOOK FOR IT, but it was dark and the seaweed felt like SNAKES." He leaned in, looming over me without even trying. "I do not suggest you call the snakes, Johnny-Be-Good. They have NOTHING sunny to say."

○○○

I didn't stick around long after getting Bill's cautious—if mildly confusing—approval. The truth was, I still had a lot to do before I came back that night to the marina. I needed to get something more to eat, because mediation on even a partially empty stomach was a huge no-no. I needed to pull out one of my suits from wherever I'd stashed them upon returning from Rome. And most importantly, I needed to actually prep for the Clippers and Superchargers tribes.

Contrary to popular belief *and* local folklore, I was, in fact, a thinking animal. And that meant, with enough time, effort, and positive (or negative) reinforcement, I could learn from past mistakes.

Going into the situation in Rome effectively blind had been one such mistake, and even if everything had worked out okay in the end, it wasn't something I wanted to repeat.

When I got back to the apartment I still shared with Juliette and Angel, the first thing I did was, obviously, make myself a sandwich, with lettuce, tomato, two thick slabs of honey wheat, and at least a half-dozen layers of thinly sliced roast beef… but the *second* thing I did was dig up the folder that contained my notes on the case.

This was not a normal mediation, for a lot of reasons. As an intra-species conflict instead of an inter-species one, it wasn't subject to the Toulon Concordat, aka the set of rules and regulations older, more powerful, and presumably wiser beings had created to keep the supernatural world from attracting too much attention with their bloodshed. That meant mediation wasn't a requirement; in fact, the only reason I'd been hired at all was because the Mer, as one of San Diego's two remaining ruling powers, had demanded it. Apparently, the fish folk had grown tired of goblin corpses being dumped into the ocean and fouling the nearby waters.

The good news was that, even without the Concordat's rules to protect me, I could still rely on the Mer, as the hiring body, to keep me safe. The bad news was… well, everything else about the mediation itself.

Goblins weren't precisely dumb, per se, but they often operated more on instinct and animal cunning. That made the prospect of mediation a challenging one, even before getting into the whole blood feud thing. As far as I knew, the Clippers tribe hadn't been involved in Rihanna Mariah Kardashian's attempted coup, but the execution of one of their former princesses had certainly galvanized them. Meanwhile, the Superchargers were just a mess. Tonight's meeting suggested one of the tribe's internal factions had finally seized control, but I had no idea which faction it was, or how long they'd remain in power.

It's not a murder trial, I reminded myself. *You're just going to meet the clients, get them talking, and slowly try to work your way to common ground. Or, failing that, find some sort of compromise that both tribes hate but will accept in lieu of continued bloodshed.*

I'd been joking about trying to get them to focus on Raiders fans, but I couldn't deny that the idea had some appeal. With the Oakland Raiders being in many ways the Chargers' archrivals, the goblin tribe who'd taken the latter team's name would be easily moved to violence. And the Clippers, as a tribe whose team totem had abandoned the city before I was even born, could *probably* be persuaded to turn their ire on competing franchises from a different sport entirely.

Of course, having a bunch of human NFL fans go missing in the city would create its own kind of mess. I doubted the Mer would care, as long as the goblin corpse pollution stopped, but the last thing any of us wanted or needed was human law enforcement getting involved. With Lucia's former House in shambles, I wasn't sure there was anyone truly focused on keeping my species unaware of the very many things in San Diego who liked to go bump in the night. And humans, as individually weak and universally derided as we were, were, as a species, the bogeyman of… well… the actual bogeymen. If knowledge of the supernatural ever went mainstream, I was pretty sure there'd be a bloodbath that put our little goblin war to shame.

Also? Not even Raiders fans deserved to be killed and eaten.

Now, *Dodgers* fans, on the other hand…

I browsed through the bios of the Clippers leaders, and then turned to the larger stack that represented the various Superchargers factions. Anastasia had put the profiles together, and each was short but succinct, listing known associates, personality traits, and even general likes and dislikes. I was pretty sure she had files like that on most of San Diego's supernaturals from her time as Lucia's *Secundus*, but it had only recently occurred to me to take advantage of that fact.

Knowledge is power. I didn't know who had said it originally—Sun Tzu? Churchill? Cookie Monster?—but it was as true now as it had been then, and that meant reading pages of surprisingly dry data about the stomach-high, green-skinned individuals I might be speaking with tonight.

It wasn't the best couple of hours I'd spent in my life, but it wasn't the worst either. When you'd been kidnapped and imprisoned as regularly as I had, you tended to adjust your parameters for unpleasantness.

When I was done, I raided the pantry for some of Angel's prized Pepperidge Farm Sausalito cookies. I left one in the bag, just to keep her from flipping out on me for no reason, and tossed back the Dramamine I'd bought on my way home. The box had said it was non-drowsy, and I could only hope it would live up to its advertising. Slurring my words *would* be better than projectile vomiting on my clients… but probably not by a whole lot.

It was hard to know for sure with goblins.

I took a quick shower before pulling on one of the suits Lucia had made for me in Rome. The jacket was actually a little bit loose, which was quite possibly the first time I'd ever had that happen to me. I hadn't changed my diet at all, so either I was suffering from some sort of secret illness or the exercise I'd been doing with Ana was starting to pay dividends.

It didn't totally suck, although I was a very, very long way from being able to see my abs. Or having abs, for that matter.

The skinny pants, on the other hand, remained as distractingly tight as ever. I'd thought about tossing them out entirely upon our return to San Diego, but… well, Ana liked the way they looked, and I wasn't a total idiot.

A comb through my hair changed absolutely nothing, and I then spent a solid ten minutes practicing my various smiles and expressions in the mirror. Lucia being over six thousand miles away meant neither of us felt each other's thoughts or emotions—and thank every conceivable god for that—but it also meant I couldn't draw on her abilities across our bond. And *that* meant I was back to relying only on my God-given gifts as a mediator and generally affable human being.

My track record as a mediator made that a cause for concern, but I stiffened my spine with a dose of the Encourager™, followed by my best attempt at Derek Zoolander's Blue Steel. The latter was still very much a work in progress, despite the movie being a decade and a half old.

Even my reflection looked kind of embarrassed.

ooo

Downtown San Diego is a whole different beast at night, and the marina was too. Lights reflected off dark waters and I could just barely hear the distant roar of intrepid tourists who had decided *Monday night* was the perfect time for partying. Bill was on deck waiting for me, Jee Sun at his side in footed pajamas with cows on them. She also had on a domino mask like you'd see in low-rent superhero movies.

"Are we going… incognito?" I asked her, handing over a Frappuccino almost as big as she was.

"I don't know what that word means, Mr. John!"

"Johnny Banana wants to KNOW if you are NOT who you are, Tiny Flower," said Bill, clarifying very little.

"I'm a cow burglar!"

I blinked.

"That's a 10-4, LITTLE BUDDY, but even the best cow burglars NEED THEIR COATS in CASE the night is VERY COLD."

Jee Sun's pout left little doubt about her feelings on wearing a coat, but she hugged the demigod and went below anyway.

Bill turned his eyes and mouth to me. "Are YOU the CAPTAIN now?"

"I didn't know you'd seen that movie."

"HAHAHA." Bill's mouth wiggled uncertainly, almost impossible to see in the marina's dim lights. "What movie, AMIGO?"

"Never mind. I don't think Jee Sun's old enough to watch it anyway. I'm just going to be a passenger if that's alright with you."

I gave him the coordinates for the meeting spot. Boats and I didn't mix, and I sure as hell didn't know how to drive one. Or sail one. Or... boat... one? Whatever it was you did with the things. The last time I'd been out on open water had been during high school, with a would-be girlfriend and her father, and I'd spent the whole trip sharing my breakfast with the denizens of the deep.

By the time Jee Sun was back on deck, wearing a pink puffer coat that was at least three sizes too big for her, Bill had unmoored the boat, raised the anchor, and we were easing our way out of our berth. I took a death grip on the railing and tried to keep my eyes fixed straight ahead and not on the water sloshing against the hull below.

A mediation between warring goblins, hosted by fish people in the middle of the bay, with Bill and Jee Sun too nearby and me at least partially high on medication...

What could possibly go wrong?

CHAPTER 7
IN WHICH MANY THINGS GO PREDICTABLY WRONG

Apparently, Dramamine took longer than I'd thought to kick in, because I had lost my sandwich *and* all three cookies by the time we reached the designated meeting spot. I was starting to feel better though. It still wasn't *fun* being out on the water, but I was mobile and in possession of what Lucia would call my *limited faculties*, so I wasn't going to complain. The medicine seemed to be living up to its billing.

Unfortunately, when we reached the coordinates I'd been given, there was nobody else there. The Coronado bridge sketched a bright line across the night sky to our south, but we were alone.

"Now what?" I muttered.

"Pooh!" suggested Jee Sun.

"Maybe later, sweetie." I scanned the horizon for any boats coming our way, and then fished out my wonderphone.

I'm here, I texted. I still didn't know the name of the Mer I'd been communicating with, but they had taken point on the preparations for this mediation.

When their reply finally came, it wasn't via cellphone. Instead, I heard splashing from off the side of the boat. After verifying that Jee

Sun hadn't jumped into the water to burgle some cows, I leaned out over what the little girl had informed me was the bow.

A figure was scaling the side of Bill's boat despite the lack of a ladder, webbed fingers somehow finding purchase on the hull's sheer surface. The boat's running lights shimmered off wet scales and they were naked except for some kind of loincloth that barely hid their dude parts. As they climbed over the railing and onto the deck, I saw a face that only a mother could love: wide bulging black eyes, a lipless mouth full of multiple rows of sharks' teeth, and flaps of skin pulsing below the absence of a jawline.

Clearly, ancient tales of the unearthly beauty of mermen and mermaids had been drastically exaggerated. I drew on all my mediator experience to keep my face composed as I went to meet the Mer.

He took one look at me and made a sort of coughing gurgle. "Believe me," he said, the words careful and precise, "you look every bit as horrific to us as we do to you."

Apparently, my poker face needed some work. I shrugged and extended my hand.

"I get that a lot, believe it or not. I'm John Smith."

The Mer's hand was larger than mine, webbed fingers long and tipped in hooked claws that even a werewolf might find impressive. "Glubrialusos."

"Glubrialu—"

"Just call me Glub," he sighed. "The others are below already, We need to get—" His voice trailed off, black eyes fixed on something beyond me.

"Howdy-doo," said Bill, words flat and so empty that even his accent was missing. "Are you the snake in my grass?"

I still didn't know what Bill's beef was with snakes, but I knew that was *not* a road we wanted to head down. I turned, keeping myself between the demigod and the Mer that was dripping seawater all over the deck.

"This is my contact, Bill," I said, keeping my voice calm and soothing. "From the Mer? Remember?"

"I remember many things, John." Out of the marina, it was too dark to see his magic marker mouth, but something told me it was a straight line. And that wasn't good for anyone, least of all Glub.

I looked to the Mer for help, but he was frozen, staring at Bill with what, even on his species' alien features, was identifiable as terror. Whatever it was Glub saw when he looked at Bill had temporarily robbed him of speech.

"Glub came to get me for the mediation." I stepped in front of the Mer, doing my best to break his sightline. "If you and Jee Sun don't mind camping out here, we'll be—"

An oof came from behind me. I spun to find Jee Sun had wrapped her body around one of Glub's scaled legs.

"A cow, Mr. Bill! I got one!"

That, as much as anything I'd done, was enough to break the Mer's horror-stricken trance. He looked down at the small girl clinging to his leg and then at me. "What is going on?"

"I think she's trying to burgle you." I crouched down next to her. "This isn't a cow, I promise."

"But he's white!"

He wasn't white. Not at all, but Jee Sun saw supernatural species as colors. Vampires were yellow, werewolves were red, and apparently, we now knew the Mer were white.

"Even so, he's not a cow. And he's not a snake either, Bill. He's more fish than anything, I think."

"That's not—" Whatever Glub had been about to say, he mercifully stopped as I gave him a look.

"Are you SURE?" asked Bill, all the menace gone from his voice. "He HAS SCALES and a tongue that twists."

"So do fish."

"And cows," agreed Jee Sun, ignoring the images all over her pajamas that suggested otherwise.

"Right." I peeled the little girl off the creature of the seas and handed her back to Bill, who grew two arms to accept the literal and figurative burden. "This is Glub. Like I said, he is one of the Mer."

Glub kept his eyes averted but gave a sort of cross between a bow and a curtsey. "It is an honor to make your acquaintance, Lord Beel-Kasan. Truly a story I will tell my children."

"I'm a children!" volunteered Jee Sun.

"Yes, you ARE, Tiny Flower. The BEST OF ALL." Bill patted the head of the child in his arms, taking care not to dislodge her domino mask. "Do the FISH CHILDREN like CANDY?"

Glub stayed low, although I wasn't sure if it was a sign of respect or simply to avoid looking at whatever Bill had manifested as. "They do indeed, although with teeth like ours, there are limits—"

"Tiny Flower, would you LIKE TO SHARE your candy with the fish children?"

"Baby fishes?" She twisted her mouth back and forth like she was swirling around mouthwash, then gave a bright smile. "Okay!"

She headed belowdecks again, somehow shrugging out of her pink puffer as she ran. One of Bill's arms extended a good ten feet to pluck the garment off the deck. "Good candies make good eating and good eating makes good friendships, AMIGO," he told Glub, me, and the world at large.

Glub stayed in his bow/curtsey, but I could see him twitch.

A moment later, Jee Sun rushed back onto deck, carrying an orange plastic pumpkin overflowing with candy, from tootsie rolls to Red Vines to at least one chocolate bunny that had had its left ear conspicuously bitten off. She wove her way around Bill's stalk, and then pranced over to Glub and me.

"Here you go, Mr. Fish Cow!"

"I and my children thank you, little one," said Glub, taking the pumpkin in his webbed hands. He risked a look in Bill's direction, and then turned back away with a shudder. "And you as well, Lord Beel-Kasan. Word of your kindness shall spread beneath the waves."

"OK!" Bill turned to me and visibly double taked. "Johnny-Come-Lately, when did you get here?"

"He was always here, Mr. Bill!" giggled Jee Sun.

"Well, of COURSE he was." I didn't need daylight to read the confusion in his expression.

"Glub is going to take me to the mediation…" I looked to the Mer and got a nod in response. "If you two don't mind hanging out for a few hours to bring me back when it's done—"

"Actually, we can see you directly back to shore," said Glub, his words thickening as he spoke. "But my time out of water is nearing its limits. If you are ready…?"

I wasn't sure how I felt about relying on the Mer more than I already was, but recent events had made me reconsider the wisdom of Bill being anywhere near the mediation. "You and Jee Sun can go back home, Bill. I'll talk to you later."

"Will there BE ICE CREAM, Kemosabe?"

"I'll make sure of it."

"YAY! Ice cream!" screamed Jee Sun, in a voice that probably carried all the way to the marina.

"Let's get going while we can," I told Glub quietly. "Although I'm not sure where we're going or how."

Glub gathered the tattered remnants of his dignity around himself like they were a cloak. "We go down, Mr. Smith. Into the depths. I will dive in, and you will come after me."

"Underwater?"

"We are the Mer."

"And this is Italian silk," I said, motioning at my suit. At least, I *assumed* it was silk… it was hard to imagine Lucia dressing me in anything less. "Also, I don't breathe any better underwater than you do out of it."

Glub flashed me his shark's smile. "The water is our domain, mediator. You will be fine, as are the goblins already awaiting your presence."

With that, he stepped over the rail, pumpkin in hand, and dropped into the water below.

I looked down into the darkness of the bay, shrugged, and before I could talk myself out of it, jumped in after him.

ooo

The anticipated splash never came.

Instead, I found myself slowly descending through the water, surrounded by a bubble of air, thick enough to keep me aloft in its center but still breathable, if somewhat… dank. Glub was just a shadow in the deeper black of the bay's depths, darting in and out of the space around me.

I couldn't see anything else, but when several minutes had passed, and I *still* hadn't hit the floor of the bay, I realized that my pocket of air had to be moving on its own, horizontally as well as vertically. Apparently, the Mer had their own kind of taxis.

On the one hand, my suit was still perfectly dry. On the other, I couldn't see where we were going, and being underwater somehow made my motion sickness even worse, Dramamine notwithstanding.

Whoever had killed Caleb Van Stahl—assuming, once again, that it *wasn't* Ana—was rapidly climbing up the ranks of my theoretical shit list. If Caleb had still been around, *he* would have been the most likely mediator hired for this job, and *I* could have spent the night with Ana instead of being dragged around the bay.

But wishes and fishes and beggars or however the saying went.

Eventually, the unrelieved darkness gave way to light; not above us, but below. That single point of reference finally told me just how fast we were traveling, as it quickly swelled from a single distant spark to a string of submersible LEDs, ringing a cave where no cave should have been. A half-dozen Mer were waiting there for us. Based on the variety of clothing, there were both men and women, but the so-called mermaids were every bit as alien and odd as the men.

Glub gestured to the closest Mer, another loincloth-wearing individual holding a spear fashioned from something that clearly wasn't wood. In my bubble, I could only faintly hear their ensuing conversation—whistles and high-pitched clicks that bore no relation to the English language—but the other man nodded, and we headed for the cave.

Glub stopped at the entrance, giving me a solemn nod as my bubble went by. Moments later, my feet touched down on the cave's floor. My air pocket didn't so much dissipate as expand, losing its tight sphere to mix freely with the atmosphere already present in the cave.

Apparently, we were doing this mediation at the bottom of the bay, in an oxygen-filled cave that was otherwise surrounded by the Mer and whatever other terrifying things secretly lived in the ocean. On the bright side, I wouldn't have to worry about anyone storming outside before I'd said my piece.

The interior of the cave was bone dry and almost homey, with more LEDs hanging in strings above us like bodega lights, an area rug spread across the rocky floor, and a table with five chairs in the middle of the room. All it needed was a couch, a 75" TV, some questionable art choices, a certain level of funk, and a mini-fridge full of beer and it would have been a literal mancave.

Four of the five chairs were taken, two on each long side, with the one empty chair at the end left for me. I nodded to the four goblins and took my seat at the head—or foot—of the table. By the looks of the crumb-covered plates in front of them, both tribes' representatives had been there for a while, but I didn't let that bother me. Much like wizards, a mediator always arrived precisely on time.

"You're late, human!" snarled one of the goblins. The jersey she'd altered into a terrible dress was powder blue and gold, making her part of the Superchargers tribe, and I recognized her from my files as one of Chief Tikky-Wokka Tomlinson's wives. *Not* the one who started the coup, killed the chief, and was then executed for it, obviously. The beehive hairstyle was new, but I was almost one hundred percent sure this was Madonna Adele Beyoncé Swift.

Even better, I'd *met* the goblin next to her. Wubby-Lubby Rivers Tomlinson was Tikky-Wokka's only son, and the reason I'd first been hired by the goblins, two years prior. He looked a hell of a lot better now than he had then, a sure sign that the shaman-sent nightmares Bill had put a stop to had never returned.

"I'm sorry for the delay," I told the goblins, giving them a professionally respectful smile. "Traffic was a mess, you know?"

By the scowls on at least two green faces, they did *not* know. I turned to the two members of the Clippers tribe. The first was their current chief and wartime leader, Charlemagne B. Free, but the second was a bit of a surprise. He was half again as large as his chief, and his skin was an unpleasant mottled mix of green and brown.

"My son," said Charlemagne, bestowing a shit-eating grin on me and the Superchargers. "Charlemagne Alexander Genghis B. Free the Second, Esquire."

I blinked.

"Hi, Mr. Smith," said Charlemagne Alexander Gengh—

Junior, I decided. I was calling him Junior. At least in my head.

Junior's voice was surprisingly high-pitched for his gargantuan, near-human-sized form.

I said something agreeable back as I wracked my brain for details on the chief's son and came up empty. He hadn't been in my files, which… given that those files had originally come from Anastasia herself, said a lot. Where had Charlemagne the Elder been hiding him? And… why was he so big?

"I'm part troll," volunteered Junior.

Apparently, I'd asked that last part out loud.

"That's right he is." Charlemagne the Elder turned to the Superchargers, still grinning. "Been living with his mom up in Seattle, but he'll be here for the fall. Staying with me and my tribe. Tell Wubby-Lubby how much you bench, son."

"Uhm, six-fifty?" came the squeak of an answer.

"Maybe we can all share weight training tips later," I interjected before things could go further off the rails.

"*You* work out? Are you sure?" Charlemagne the Elder looked me up and down with a frown.

"Respectable paunch," mused Madonna Adele Beyoncé Swift, in an accent that was every bit as Russian as it was fake, "but your arms are tiny like noodles. Angel hair, not linguine."

Apparently, she liked Italian food. I was adding new information to my files all the time.

"And just like that, you two have found something to agree on," I said, giving them an admittedly underpowered version of my best smile, the Dealmaker™. "I think that means we're ready to start."

ooo

Almost two hours later, my personal bubble transportation device deposited me just south of the marina, to the surprise and confusion of a handful of Japanese tourists who had been looking for Seaport Village, wandered in the exact opposite direction, and ended up taking pictures of the bay and star-filled sky instead. I gave them a nod, tipped my imaginary hat to the family's matriarch, and walked away, as dry as a bone despite everything. In a testament to modern pharmaceuticals, I wasn't even *that* queasy.

I was roughly eight blocks from where I'd parked the Corolla in one of those open public lots that charged an arm and a leg per hour despite a complete lack of security. Even so, I found myself whistling as I walked. Absolutely nothing had been resolved during our first mediation, but that hadn't been the point. We—meaning the Mer and me—had gotten the goblins—and one half-troll—to the table, and that was a start. I'd sent both tribes home to draft lists of complaints, demands, and concerns, and I'd told them to rank each in their order of importance. Knowing goblins, that ranking would take days and probably involve at least a few outright brawls. And *that* meant I'd have time to head to New Mexico.

In fact, we'd scheduled our next mediation meeting for a week from Saturday. That would give me space for individual client sessions before we got the whole gang together once again.

I turned up Fifth Avenue and wove my way around a section of sidewalk that had been cordoned off for no visible reason. Normally, I'd have taken the opportunity to stop in at the Bitter End, but it was late, and I had breakfast with Ana in a few hours. It was time to go home. To Juliette's home, anyway.

As the Corolla came into sight, I spared a thought for the goblins' younger generation. For all their differences in size, both Junior and Wubby-Lubby seemed kind of sweet, a far cry from their parents.

To paraphrase Whitney Houston's cover of some '70s song… maybe the children *were* our future.

CHAPTER 8
IN WHICH A FAST IS BROKEN TWICE

I woke the next morning from dreams of fluffy singing unicorns racing around an Olympic-sized pool of chili, the shrill beeping of my alarm loud in my ears. Between the mediation, the drive after the mediation, and the post-mediation shower and sandwich, I'd managed a little over four hours of sleep, but that was okay. If there was one thing I'd gotten lately it was sleep.

I could hear the shower going, so I pulled on a T-shirt and a pair of shorts and wandered out of my tiny bedroom and down the hall into the kitchen.

"Duchess."

Despite leaning back in her chair with both feet up on the table, she somehow made a theatrical double take. "Is this possible? A wild John Smith sighting before the hour of nine in the morning? It can't be!"

"Funny."

"Angel started a pot of coffee when she got up. Feel free to get yourself a cup."

Technically, I was going to be getting coffee with my breakfast with Ana, but I snagged a mug anyway. After all, Harry's was a good thirty-minute drive away, and my chances of arriving there alive would only be improved with a jolt of caffeine.

"We've got pastries too," added Juliette, nose practically buried in her phone.

"I'll pass," I said bravely. "Ana and I are meeting at Harry's in a bit."

"I'm surprised you even slept here last night then."

"I finished with the goblins sometime around two-ish. I didn't want to wake up Teresa or Gustavo."

"Ah." Juliette didn't seem as impressed by my courtesy as I would have hoped, but then she *did* claim to be punk to the core. "I see you didn't get eaten; how were the green skins?"

"Somewhat less green than expected." I told her about Junior, and for the first time, she looked up from her phone.

"Huh. Half-troll, half-goblin?"

"I guess so." I carried my mug of coffee over to the breakfast table and grabbed a seat. One scalding hot sip had me setting the mug back down. I was very, very happy that Lucia, holder of my bond, was back in Italy, but I was going to miss the convenience of being able to access her Talent. Now, I had to wait for my coffee to cool on its own. "Honestly, I didn't even know that was possible."

"Your girlfriend would know better than me, but maybe the two species have a common ancestor or something." She frowned. "Trolls are nasty, little bird."

"Well, Junior seems like a sweetheart."

"I'm sure that'll be a comfort when he rips your limbs off."

I hid a wince. Given my gym-related allergies, I didn't really have a frame of reference for what *I can bench six-fifty* really meant, but it *did* seem like that limb-ripping might be on the table. Still, as a mediator, I had to trust my instincts.

And it wasn't like those instincts had ever led me wrong before, right?

"Anyway, I gave them a week and a half to think about things, and some homework to do in the interim. When I get back from New Mexico, I'll line up one-on-one interviews with the principals. From the outside, this whole thing looks pretty simple—partially successful coup, favorite daughter killed in retaliation, war erupts—but if I can get them to broaden their perspectives, maybe a compromise will be possible."

"Make sure you bring Anastasia with you to those individual meetings."

"Yeah. I'm not dumb, despite what the stories and your own questionably sourced evidence might have you believe." I grinned. "No more getting kidnapped or imprisoned, I promise. Did your police contact hear back from the Ghost Falls sheriff yet?"

She shook her head. "Not yet, but you know how small towns are. I'm hoping we'll hear something today. What about you?"

"I don't have any police contacts."

"I know that, doofus. Did you hear back from Mike?"

"Oh. No." I shook my head. A year ago, this many cases at the same time had driven me to distraction, but now, it felt like we were staying on top of things just fine.

"What are you smiling about?"

"Just thinking it's good to have a partner."

She rolled her eyes. "Gods, she really does have you whipped, doesn't she?"

"I meant *business* partner. With so much going on, it's good to be able to divide and conquer."

"Oh." She coughed, and then shot me a glare for no reason whatsoever. "Well, that's why my name is on the door, obviously."

"And here I thought it was because you paid someone to add it while I was in Rome."

"I was expanding the office anyway. It seemed fitting, *partner*."

We traded grins.

"I'm going to call Mike again," I decided, fishing out my wonderphone and putting words to action. "With his birthday coming up, it won't be *too* weird if I get a little clingy."

"Caleb, Jason, Mike… you really are the bromance king, aren't you?"

"There's nothing wrong with strong male friendships built on a foundation of mutual respect and trust—" I stopped. "Wait? *Jason?* At best he's—"

"Hello?" Mike's voice, deep, slightly accented, and clearly annoyed, came over the line.

"Hey dude, it's John."

"Bullshit. John doesn't wake up before ten. Ever."

"I was up at nine for your wedding."

"Shit, I guess that's true. What do you need, wey? I'm beat."

"Late night?"

"You better believe it. Long day at work, and then Susie and I went out and—"

I waited, but he didn't finish the sentence.

"Mike?"

"Sorry. Just tired. We had dinner or something. Only the best for my querida."

"Well, I'll let you get back to bed. Just wanted to see if you were free tonight. Figured I'd take you out for an early birthday dinner."

"I can't believe we're both nearing thirty, but yeah that'd be cool. We could maybe—" His voice trailed off again, but this time he resumed speaking all on his own. "Sorry, I just remembered I already have a thing tonight. It's been crazy. Can we postpone it to next week maybe?"

"It's your birthday dinner. We can do it whenever you want."

"Wanna bring Ana and make it a double date?"

"I was thinking it could just be the two of us instead."

"Sure thing. It's been a while since we cut loose. Did I ever tell you that Susie was convinced your girlfriend is an escort?"

"You don't say."

"Yeah. I tried to tell her that you've got moves most people haven't even dreamed of, but you know Susie. Once she gets her mind set on something, it's hard to change it. And brother from another mother or not, there's no way I'm risking my domestic bliss on behalf of your dating life."

"So, everything's good? Married life, I mean?"

"Other than some maniac calling me at all hours trying to invite me out to birthday dinners? Yeah, it's great. I think we might even start trying for a niño in the next year or so."

"Damn, dude. You really *have* gone domestic on me."

"Better believe it. Now, get off the line so I can go back to my beauty sleep."

"I don't think it'll help," I told him, but I was laughing and so was he.

I ended the call and shot Juliette a victorious look. Seated three feet away from me, even a mundane human could've heard most of that call. As a vampire, I knew she'd listened in on every word.

"Does that sound like a guy cheating on his wife?"

"No," she admitted, "but Susie didn't say anything about going out to dinner with him last night, did she?"

"Maybe she didn't think it was necessary. I mean, they *are* married."

"And what about his mysterious plans for tonight?"

In SoCal parlance, Juliette was swiftly harshing my buzz.

"If he's busy, he's busy."

She just fixed me with her yellow eyes and waited. Eventually, I caved.

"So, you think we should still check him out?"

"It's what we're being paid for. Or *not* paid for, in this case." She read the look on my face and softened her voice. "Why don't I handle it? One talk with him and we'll know for sure."

"I don't want you messing with his head."

"But I barely *ever* break people anymore!" She cocked her head as the silence grew. "You know that was a joke, right?"

"Yeah. But still." I knew for a fact that Juliette had used her vampiric mojo to erase any memories of vampire-like activities from Brian aka Bobo, the long-gone third member of her short-lived throuple, and that she'd used that same mojo on many of our investigative targets, all with no visible lasting impact. But Mike was family. It wasn't the sort of thing I was willing to risk or even permit.

"Fine. We'll do things the long, slow, and boring way instead. I'll follow him around town and see where he ends up. But that means you'll have to leave the camera behind when you go off to honeymoon in New Mexico."

"Deal. I'll just take pictures with my wonderphone."

"Great."

My coffee still wasn't the right level of tepid, but I had places to be. I tossed back the full mug and went to rinse it in the sink.

"Sorry to be a pain in the ass, Duchess. It's just—"

"I get it. Heterosexual soulmates or something. It's fine. It's not like I don't know how to do a stakeout. But I'm putting my expenses on the company card."

"That's what corporate cards are *actually* for." The sounds of the shower finally stopped. "I'll see you both at the office after breakfast. Give Angel my best."

"Believe me; she's used to far better than your best." The familiar smirk crept out across Juliette's angular features, and then vanished in an instant as she looked me up and down. "But where do you think you're going?"

"Breakfast? With Ana? At Harry's?" Hadn't we already been over this? Or had that part of the conversation only happened in my head? With the caffeine still slowly working its way through my body, it was hard to be sure.

"You don't think you should maybe wash your face? Comb your hair? Put on something nicer than a Homestar Runner tee?"

"I showered last night when I got in… and this is an *awesome* shirt. Don't be jealous, Duchess. Besides, it's just breakfast."

For the first time since I'd come into the kitchen, the femmepire swung her feet down off the table and stood up. Two long strides brought her to my side of the kitchen, and she grabbed hold of my jaw with one supernaturally strong hand.

"Little bird, your relationship is none of my business—and thank every god in existence for that—but I want you to do me a favor anyway, okay?" She forcibly nodded my head up and down. "Good. I want you to close your eyes and picture your lover. Lady Anastasia Dumen-yadda yadda. Can you do that for me?"

I could, and happily.

"Good. Now, imagine her at breakfast in public. Think about what she looks like. How she carries herself. What she's wearing."

I cracked open one eye to find Juliette practically in my face. I was more than happy to think of Ana, but it felt kind of weird and creepy when Juliette made me do it. While the Duchess of Snark swung both ways, I had it on the best of authority—meaning hers—that Ana was not at all her type.

"Don't look at me, you idiot," she hissed. "Do what I'm telling you to do."

"Fine." The word came out mangled with her vise-like grip still wrapped around my jaw, but I was pretty sure she got the picture. I closed my eyes and tried again. It was anyone's guess whether my femmepire love would have her auburn hair up or down, but she'd be beautiful either way. She'd most likely have something ocean colored on, paired with a long black skirt or pants. It wasn't a uniform, per se, but like many of the longer-lived individuals I knew, she'd found what worked for her and tended to stick with it. "Done."

"Now imagine standing next to her, in your current attire and state."

It… wasn't a pretty thought, and not just because Ana was a solid eleven and I was a borderline five. A T-shirt and long shorts made for perfectly acceptable breakfast burrito attire by myself, but when I was out with Ana…

"Exactly," said Juliette, reading my thoughts without any need for vampiric abilities at all. "Now, go pretty yourself up or whatever it is you do."

I passed a towel-clad Angel in the hall, the two of us studiously ignoring each other's presence, and took her spot in the steam-filled bathroom. I was *really* starting to question Juliette's devotion to punk, but when she was right, she was right.

ooo

I arrived at Harry's with almost two minutes to spare, but Anastasia's burgundy Jag was already there, tucked into the small lot behind the coffee shop. I parked the Corolla a few spots away—to lessen any hurt feelings it might otherwise incur from being compared to the Jag by passing strangers—and walked around to the front.

Ana stood alone in a bubble of empty space, the warm sunlight picking out the red highlights in her hair. Two and a half years later, she was as tall and elegant as when we'd first met and would remain so long centuries after I was dead and gone. I'd correctly predicted the color of her top—sapphire silk this time instead of emerald—but instead of the usual blouse, this one was high-necked and sleeveless, showcasing the long lines of her strong arms. Her skirt was black, fitted, and calf-length, with leather boots peeking out from underneath. She looked like a hundred million bucks, something the men seated out on the patio behind her seemed far too aware of, and her lips quirked up in the half-smile that I loved as she took in my own appearance.

"Mr. Smith," she said, voice a low purr. "You look good."

Apparently, I owed Juliette a drink or three.

"It's worth it just to see you smile." I went in for a kiss and let my hand settle on her hip as we finally separated, ignoring the almost obnoxiously surprised reactions from her unacknowledged admirers. "Shall we?"

"Indeed."

Moments later, we were seated at a table inside the always busy coffee shop. Before I could ask how things had gone with Lucia's former House or give her the blow-by-blow recap of my mediation, our waiter was there to take our orders. Instead of pancakes, Ana had a cold brew along with granola and yogurt, as if to make it clear that she wasn't *entirely* perfect, while I ordered an extra-large mug of hot chocolate. And as for food...

"A carne asada California breakfast burrito," I told our waiter, who had introduced himself as Caden, "with extra guac."

"You got it—"

I held up one hand and waited for him to stop, maintaining eye contact the entire time, like a predator staring down my prey. *"Extra* guacamole, Caden."

At first, he seemed confused, but I could see when he finally got it. His face changed and a light went on behind his eyes as he fully internalized the sheer importance of properly proportioned guacamole in my forthcoming breakfast burrito. It was only then that I let him slip away.

Ana grinned. "Should I ask what that was about?"

"People in this town have developed an unfortunate habit of skimping on the guac, even when the exact opposite is requested. But that's all going to change, starting today. I'm a man on a mission."

"A man wearing slacks and a polo shirt, no less." Her eyes danced. "What exactly occurred while I was away?"

"Nothing of importance or value." I shrugged, offering a grin of my own. "Maybe I just wanted to give you a small teaser of what our road trip will be like."

"John…" Her poker mask slid briefly into place and then faded just as quickly. "I cannot accompany you to New Mexico."

"Because of the guacamole?"

"Steven requested my assistance with locating and capturing Zorana," she explained. "I felt honor bound to agree."

"Why?"

"Outside of San Diego's immortals, the Blood Witch is quite possibly the most powerful individual left in the city."

"All the more reason to leave her be." I still remembered Ana bleeding all over me after their last encounter.

"Yet she has grown increasingly less stable over the past few years. You know that better than anyone." Her eyes darted down to my covered chest and the unseen scars I bore from my brief time in Zorana's care. "I would not have others subjected to torment or slaughter because I chose to stand back and do nothing. The House is ill-equipped to deal with Zorana, even should they find her."

"And you think you can take her?"

"With assistance? Yes." She shook her head. "But it will require a significant amount of time and effort, and you—"

"Need to get this New Mexico trip over with ASAP, both because I have a small window of time in the middle of the goblin mediation, and because the longer Dulcinea is missing, the less likely we find her at all."

"Precisely."

I sighed, watching my dreams of a romantic getaway with a minor side course of missing persons go up in smoke. I couldn't blame Ana. In fact, I should have probably anticipated her decision. And considering I'd gotten into mediation in the first place to help save the unsuspecting humans of my hometown, it was pretty hard to hold it against her that she was now forgoing a vacation to do the same.

But still… a couple's trip would have been *amazing*.

"That's fine," I said, desperately rallying. "It'll be a quiet car ride without you, but I can't argue with your priorities. I'll bring back some chiles for you."

"You still intend to drive instead of fly? I would be more than happy to purchase your round-trip fare."

"Nope, I'm good. A road trip is easier, and I can bring whatever I need." And I wouldn't potentially get stuck next to a hyperactive demon in child's form for multiple hours again without recourse or hope of escape, but that part kind of went without saying.

"Will Valentina be accompanying you?"

By reflex, I put my hand to my chest where a plain wedding band normally hung. That ring was safely stashed in my nightstand at Anastasia's house.

"No," I admitted. "Whatever Minerva did to her, she's still recovering. Graciela and the other White Ladies think they've found something that might help, so I'm going to leave her node behind so she can focus on getting better."

"Then may I suggest you bring Lady Middleton?"

We both paused as Caden dropped off two steaming hot mugs. I admired the mountain of whipped cream slowly sinking into hot chocolate, and then turned back to Ana.

"Juliette? Why?"

"Company and protection. I would ask Steven to accompany you instead, were he and the entire House not needed for the forthcoming witch hunt."

"I'll be fine," I said, ignoring all past evidence to the contrary. "This isn't Rome."

"True, yet the American Southwest has long been carved up into domains and territories, and you are no longer just another member of the faceless mass of humanity. Your passage *will* be noted. Juliette is young, but her presence alone may ease your travels. And she is not without her strengths."

Including, unsurprisingly, *literal* strength. My partner might not be able to match Junior on the bench press, but she could toss *me* around like a dishrag.

"The choice is yours, of course, but I would feel better if I knew you had accompaniment." Her eyes, enormous in the delicate beauty of her face, ensnared me as effortlessly as I had our waiter. "Will you do that for me, John?"

Well, shit.

CHAPTER 9

IN WHICH PEOPLE SPEAK IN CODE

"I'll ask her," I said, "but there's a lot going on with the agency, and there's Angel to consider too. I can see Juliette wanting to stay behind in San Diego."

"Then perhaps *I* will have a word with Lady Middleton about partnerships and the obligations that come with them."

The words were mild, the voice soft, but I could almost feel the danger lurking just out of sight, like a conversational iceberg upon which the S.S. Duchess of Snark would run aground and be torn into a thousand pieces.

It was ridiculously hot.

Either my poker face remained as lousy as ever or I must have made a noise, because she dropped her eyes to her cold brew.

"I know," she admitted. "For all my words of partnerships, here I am abandoning you to pursue other obligations."

"You're literally risking your life to help save my city. I don't consider that abandonment. And I'm not annoyed or irritated."

"Then what is that expression on your face?"

"Can you really not tell? You?"

She blinked, at a loss for words for one of the few times that I could remember. The smile that slowly slipped onto her face was at least one-half disbelief. "What about *this* conversation has you thinking of carnal matters?"

I could feel the blush coming on. God, I *loved* how she worded things sometimes. *Carnal matters* sounded so much classier.

"It's not the conversation. It's just… I never thought I'd have someone like you so invested in my safety."

"You are mine, Mr. Smith, body and soul, until you choose otherwise. There is little in this world that I love; I will spare no effort to protect those things and people."

Which… unfortunately touched on a subject I *didn't* want to talk about, but probably needed to. Just as unfortunately, it was going to absolutely kill the mood.

"Did you know that Caleb Van Stahl is dead?"

If the change in subject threw Ana, she didn't show it. She took a long sip of her coffee and nodded. "I did."

I swallowed. "Did he fall under the heading of you sparing no effort to protect me?"

Before she could reply, the rest of our breakfast arrived. I checked the burrito—extra guacamole successfully achieved—and gave Caden a silent nod of respect and appreciation, but all the while I could feel the femmepire's eyes on me.

When he was gone, she spoke. "Are you asking if I killed Mr. Van Stahl?"

"Yes?" I couldn't meet her eyes. "I know you had some concerns about him. I thought if you had maybe uncovered something new—"

"Then I would have brought that information to you so that we could collectively decide on a course of action."

"Of course you would have." I sighed and rolled my eyes. "Which is what I *keep telling* everyone."

"Everyone?"

"The pack. Juliette. Anyone else who asks. Apparently, Caleb's murder is an open secret, and everyone thinks they've already identified the culprit."

"Your pet monster." There were poker faces and then there were *poker faces*, and right now, Ana's was the latter, as close to her moniker as the Stone Lady as she could get without transforming into stone.

"The woman I love," I corrected her, "who happens to be as hot as a chile pepper and a legitimate badass with a reputation almost as impressive as she is."

"As hot as a… chile pepper?"

"I have peppers on the mind with New Mexico looming." I threw out another grin. This one didn't have a fancy name or pedigree, but it felt good on my face. "And if the spice shoe fits…"

Anastasia shook her head, but the cold mask had slipped from her face and a smile was threatening to break through.

"Anyway," I added, keeping my tone light, "since neither of us had anything to do with Caleb's murder, I kind of feel like I owe it to him as a brother of the profession to figure out who did."

She raised an all-too-expressive eyebrow.

"I mean, I solved the Rook's murder too, and I'd never even met the guy before *his* death." Frankly, I wasn't sure I'd have liked my predecessor, given his… proclivities. Although his taste in outerwear *had* allowed me to stay fashionable during San Diego's cooler winters.

"With Queen-Regent Lucia returned to Rome, my network of local contacts has dwindled accordingly, but I will reach out to them, if you wish it."

"Please. It'll have to stay on the back burner until I've found Simon's granddaughter, finished the goblin mediation, and put a pin in this whole Mike thing, but if someone *is* killing mediators, it's probably a good idea to find out who."

"By *this whole Mike thing*, are you referring to your friend, Mike, whose wedding we attended?"

"Yeah. Did I not tell you about that case?"

"You did not."

"Right." I frowned. "So, I should probably start with when Juliette and I walked in to find his wife Susan waiting in our office. Or maybe I should start with that same wedding and her misconception about our relationship." I winced and shook my head. "Actually, let's start back when I thought her name was Suzanne for literal years. But first…"

I manhandled my overstuffed burrito into my mouth and took an enormous, guacamole-filled bite. It was only then that I realized our waiter, Caden, was directly in my line of sight. I gave him a nod of appreciation and threw in a shaka sign for good measure.

After I'd put the burrito down, of course. I'd learned my lesson with one-handing gargantuan burritos as a teenager, and that lesson was *don't* unless you want to be stuck with the clean up afterwards.

Caden nodded back and we had ourselves a bit of a moment, one burrito bro to another. But it was time to bring Anastasia up to date.

ooo

"So, Mike's new bride suspects him of infidelity?"

"Yeah."

"And you agreed to take the case."

"Better me than some creep of a stranger." I shivered. "Have you met other private eyes? Mike deserves better."

"And this is one of the things that Juliette would have been doing had she not chosen of her entirely free will to accompany you to New Mexico?"

"Right." I gave the vampire across from me a suspicious look. "Of course, she *hasn't* chosen to accompany me."

"Yet."

'Right." I shrugged and let it go. Anastasia being protective of me wasn't new, but it *felt* different since we'd declared our feelings for each other. And honestly, I didn't hate it. Besides, Ana knew how I felt about Juliette, so I highly doubted any secretive discussions she had with the Duchess about when and why she would be joining me on this trip would end in bloodshed. And that was about as much as I could ask for, really. "Yeah, she was going to investigate Mike while I was gone."

"If you wish, I could—" She trailed off. "Actually, no. I do not believe I will have time to assist on that front. San Diego is not a large city, but the hunt for Zorana will be intensive."

"That's fine. Susan can wait a few days; we'll deal with it when we get back."

"If he is innocent—"

"He is."

"—will you then inform him that his own wife lacks faith in his fidelity?"

I sat back, mid-chew. That hadn't even occurred to me. Generally, the adultery cases I worked only came to the attention of the other spouse *after* I had found evidence. The few times I'd come up empty, the targets of those cases had been left to go about their lives without ever knowing they'd even been investigated. But I already *knew* Mike, and honestly, the fact that Susan was already acting suspicious of him only magnified my own doubts about her.

"I don't know," I finally decided. "He loves her, which is why I agreed to be best man at the wedding, despite, well… *Susan.* It's also why I *know* he'd never cheat on her. But does he deserve to know she doesn't trust him, or would it be better to let him live in blissful ignorance?"

Professionally, the answer was clear, but I'd abandoned professionalism the moment I decided not to refer Susan to some other private dick.

"Perhaps, the answers you uncover will make those next steps clear."

"You mean like if I find out he's secretly learning tap dance to impress her or something? Maybe she'll tell him on her own once I've resolved her suspicions?"

"Indeed, although I struggle to imagine him dancing tap."

"You'd be shocked. Dude's got moves most people haven't even dreamed of yet," I said, unconsciously repeating what Mike had said about me.

"Perhaps the greatest surprise will be when one of your friends *fails* to shock me."

I lowered what was left of my burrito to the plate and gave her a look. "I'm going to take that as a compliment, I think."

"I think you should, Mr. Smith."

We stayed at Harry's for almost an hour, long after her granola and my burrito were both gone, but eventually all good things had to end. I made eye contact again with Caden, who'd been waiting and watching us, no doubt eager to provide further guacamole at a moment's notice, and he swiftly brought the check over.

There was no competing with vampiric reflexes, so I knew Anastasia *chose* to allow me to grab the check before her. I flashed her a smile of thanks. We'd gone through a phase where she wanted to pay for literally everything, and while it made sense from a purely practical and financial perspective, my parents had raised me better than that. Breakfast was the least I could do.

I dropped my distressingly non-corporate card on the check, and Caden swooped in to retrieve it. This was the first time we'd had him as a waiter, but I hoped it wouldn't be the last. Service was always good at Harry's, but this was above and beyond.

When the receipt came back, I was fully intent on expressing my appreciation through the sheer magnitude of my tip. Unfortunately…

"He left you his number," I told Ana, tapping the offending digits with the clicky part of my borrowed pen. "And here I was just starting to like him."

"Are you certain that was intended for me? It is *your* credit card, after all."

"I…" I looked up to find Caden watching us from across the room. No, watching *me*, eyes smoldering blue before he closed one of them in a slow and very unsubtle wink. "Huh. I think you're right. Maybe *extra guacamole* is code for something else around these parts?"

I returned Caden's smile and turned back to the bill. There was no way I was going to call him—not unless Steve and Barry broke up and I decided to set one of them up with a rebound—but I was honestly kind of flattered. Generally, gay dudes only hit on me when they were too drunk to see straight.

I added another dollar to my tip as a silent apology for my impeccable straightness.

Ana's crowd of admirers were long gone by the time we emerged back into the sun. It was a shame; the kiss she gave me before we parted might have put hair back on their freshly waxed chests.

"You do know," she told me, looking up at me in a way that always surprised me, given that in my mind's eye she was seven feet tall, "you could have come over to my house last night after the mediation."

"I thought about it, but it was late, and I didn't want to wake up Teresa."

"I suspected as much. Which is why I wanted to give you this."

I blinked down at the small metal object she'd slipped into our clasped hands. "Is this…?"

"A key to the house, that you may come and go and stay as you please."

Truthfully, I already spent most nights up in Cardiff with Ana, but this was still a big step, especially for someone as private as the femmepire. I coughed, and swallowed, and did my very best not to tear up like a middle-aged woman watching the Notebook for the 27th time.

"Thank you. I'll try not to lose it."

CHAPTER 10
IN WHICH EVERY JOURNEY BEGINS
WITH TOO MANY BAGS

"You're an idiot, little bird." Juliette's look could best be described as a cross between *disappointed* and *irritated*. It was a combo that went surprisingly well with her hair and fashion choices.

"I'm not saying *only* middle-aged women cry over the Notebook, Duchess. My dad wept buckets."

"I'm not talking about that. I'm talking about Anastasia."

"What do you mean?"

I'd gone straight back to the apartment in Hillcrest and had been surprised to find Juliette still there instead of at the office. Somehow, the femmepire had sniffed out Anastasia's parting gift before I even walked through the door and now, a scant few minutes later, was engaged in her favorite non-sexual pastime: pointing out my shortcomings.

Instead of answering my question directly, she asked one of her own. "What do you think it says when a woman gives you the key to her house?"

"That she trusts me and wants me to be able to come and go without waking up her septuagenarian blood donors."

"But that's not what she *actually* said, is it?"

I frowned. I was pretty sure it was.

"You told me her exact words were 'that you may come and go and stay as you please.'"

"That's literally what I just said."

"No; you said come and go."

"And?"

"And *stay* is the important part of all of that." She read my textbook look of confusion, and it was her turn to sigh. "Why are you still paying me rent, John?"

"Because you'd kick me out without it?"

"Well, obviously. But aside from that."

"I don't…"

"You spend virtually every night with Anastasia anyway, presumably playing cribbage or parcheesi or something. Why pay for space you don't use or really even need?"

"Because it's *her* house. Hers, Teresa's, and Gustavo's. I'm not going to just invite myself to move in there…" I trailed off, looking down at the key still in my hand. "Oh."

"It's like watching a baby deer take its first steps."

"But she didn't actually say *John, I think you should move in.*"

"No, but she opened the door. Literally and figuratively. Do you already have a drawer in her bedroom?"

"A whole dresser, actually." I didn't really have enough clothes to fill it, but I'd done my best.

"Exactly. So, this is step two."

"And step three is me suggesting we make it permanent?"

Juliette's sigh filled the entire kitchen.

"What? I've never done this before."

"I doubt she has either. As a *Secundus*, she lived apart."

"Even with Xavier?"

"That was before my time, but yeah."

For some reason, hearing that made me feel better. Not just that I was emerging from under the shadow of the uber-handsome and very dead manpire, but that there were some things that were as new for Anastasia as they were for me. Her age and experience sometimes made me feel like she'd done and seen everything, but apparently there were still some things that were new to both of us.

"Look," said Juliette. "You two have kissed. You've probably even seen each other naked in between long, dreadfully dull conversations about economics and world politics."

She had a very strange view of my relationship with Ana.

"What I'm saying is that maybe you shouldn't let your own fear keep you from taking that next step."

It ranked among the best pieces of advice Juliette had ever given me on my love life, and that naturally made me suspicious.

"You need my room, don't you?"

"There may have been discussions of tearing down the wall, and expanding the kitchen and living room, but that's neither here nor there."

Of course it wasn't. Still, she'd made a good point… and the apartment *would* feel much more spacious after the proposed renovation. What I didn't bother telling Juliette was that Ana had already raised the possibility of me moving in once before. Subtly, yeah, but not *so* subtly that I hadn't caught on. And yet, I'd chosen to play dumb.

It wasn't that I didn't *want* to live with Anastasia. I did. I *really* did. Waking up next to her had quickly become top three on my list of activities, period, and the other two *also* involved Ana. There was just some part of me that couldn't help but point out that it was *her* house.

Her house, her food, her servants. I'd paid for breakfast today, yeah, and I even paid for the occasional dinner date—especially In-N-Out—but when it came to the financial side of things, our relationship was totally imbalanced.

"You're an idiot," Juliette said again, interrupting my thoughts. "Of course it's imbalanced! One of you used to work with royalty, the other thought Burger King was a real person."

I let the insult go, focused on more important things. "How much of that did I say out loud?"

"Everything from 'It's *her* house.'"

And just like that, it was time to change the subject.

"What are you doing home anyway?" I asked her. "I thought you'd be at the office."

"Apparently, it's Partners-Play-Hooky Day." She shrugged. "We have nothing on the calendar and Angel's there to answer the phone. I decided to stay home and get some peace and quiet."

"Aren't you the woman who headbangs to *Anarchy in the UK* while running around the apartment like you've been set on fire?"

"That was last week, and I was ruthlessly drunk. Sometimes, a woman needs her space."

"So, I guess you *don't* want to spend the next fourteen hours in a car with me?"

She cocked one eyebrow, somehow making the gesture a thousand percent less elegant than when Ana did it. "Are you asking me to go to Ghost Falls with you?"

"Yes?"

"Fine. Let's go."

"You don't want to talk to Angel first?"

"She'll be okay; she has a key. I do need to pack though." She paused, halfway out of her chair. "This means Anastasia's *not* coming, right?"

"She's going to take the lead on the whole Zorana hunt instead."

"Now, there's an encounter I'd sell tickets and popcorn for," mused Juliette. Her smirk disappeared when she saw my face. "It'll be fine, little bird. Really. Assuming they even *find* Zorana. Your girlfriend wasn't Lucia's assassin for nothing."

"I know," I lied. "And maybe if we finish with Ghost Falls fast enough, I'll be able to help with the hunt somehow." I wasn't sure how, and I couldn't stop the tremor that ran through me at the thought of it, but I knew people; maybe some of them would be willing to help.

"Better you than me. I'm not getting near that dumpster fire." Juliette clearly wasn't one of the willing.

ooo

It only took me a few minutes to throw a notebook and pen, most of my remaining clean clothes, and a collection of toiletries into my bag. To my surprise, Juliette was ready almost as fast. When she emerged from her bedroom a minute after me, carrying three fully packed suitcases, I knew something was up.

"When did Anastasia call you?"

She cocked her head, holding the three bulging suitcases like they weighed nothing. "What?"

"Asking if she was coming with us was a nice touch," I said, ignoring her question. "Added some real verisimilitude."

"Are you sure you're using that word correctly?"

"Not really?"

"I knew that word of the day calendar was a mistake."

It had, in fact, been an *awesome* purchase, but I refused to be distracted. "Duchess…"

"Oh, fine. The great and noble *Lady* Dumenyova called about thirty minutes before you made it back."

Or basically right after we'd said goodbye at Harry's.

"You know, regardless of whatever Ana said, you don't have to come with me. It's your choice."

"Well, obviously. You think she *made* me agree?" Juliette raised herself to her full height, helped liberally by the platform heels I was pretty sure she'd stolen from Angel. "You think *anyone* could make me do *anything*, least of all her?"

The obvious answer was *yes*, but recent history had taught me that people don't always appreciate the obvious answer. So, I sidestepped that minefield of a question and asked one of my own. "What did she say then?"

"The usual ridiculousness. That she felt it was her duty to assist the House that overthrew her liege lady in their hunt for the world's most dangerous thousand-year-old pre-teen witch."

"And?" I was reasonably sure Ana hadn't phrased it quite like that, but Juliette had her own unique perspective on these things.

"And that you're utterly hopeless by yourself, and if left to your own devices, will no doubt end up kidnapped and naked somewhere in New Mexico while simultaneously triggering the apocalypse."

I coughed. "She didn't actually say that... did she?"

"Maybe I inferred *some* of it. Still, she's right."

"Why didn't you just tell me that when I came in? Why pretend?"

Juliette shrugged. I was starting to think she'd forgotten she even had the bags in her hands. I missed having my own conduit to vampiric strength. "I wasn't sure if you knew she'd be asking me."

More like *telling*, but again, I wasn't going there. "And if I hadn't known?"

"I'd have painstakingly fed you clues over the course of the drive. By the time we reached New Mexico, you'd have hopefully pieced everything together and your irritation would be at an all-time simmer. And then I would get to listen in as you gave your meddling girlfriend a piece of your mind. It would have been glorious."

I just stared at her.

"What? Other than a minor goblin war, things have been *so* dull lately. I almost wish I hadn't kicked Brian to the curb; at least he kept things exciting!" She scanned my face and looked disgusted. "You're not even the tiniest bit annoyed with her, are you?"

"With who?" Or was it *whom?* Hell if I knew.

"Anastasia! That woman moves the people in your life around like chess pieces, and you're totally cool with it?"

I managed to avoid pointing out that Juliette had just cast herself in the role of a pawn, but it was really, really hard.

"She's protective. That's not a bad thing. Besides, it's not like she's wrong. I *could* use the backup. And the company, I guess."

"Ugh. You really are the worst." But she grinned as she said it. "So, you won't move in with her because of weird, outdated notions of masculinity, but you're totally fine with her swaddling you in bubble wrap to keep you safe?"

"I've almost died like ten times since you people came into my life."

"I really think you're undercounting."

"Maybe. Still, life is good right now and I'd like to make it to thirty. Besides, Ana has literal centuries of experience when it comes to security. Questioning her judgment on something like this would be like questioning your taste in music."

"Which you would never *dare* do, given that your tastes aren't much deeper than whatever the radios have decided is Top 40 schlock."

"Exactly."

"Huh." She finally looked down at her armful of suitcases and scowled. "This is going to be a really long ride, isn't it?"

"Unless a comet falls out of the sky and drops an army of aliens on our heads."

"Aliens aren't a thing, little bird." She paused, then shrugged. "But given that you're the kind of bad luck magnet that prophecies should be written about, we can always hope."

By the time I'd carried all four bags downstairs and tucked them into the Corolla's trunk, it was early afternoon and our chances of reaching Ghost Falls that day had completely vanished. Thankfully, splitting the fourteen-hour trip into two smaller chunks had always been my plan. We'd look for a hotel outside of Phoenix. Preferably something upscale enough to offer a complimentary breakfast.

I fished my wonderphone back out of my pocket and called Ana, who picked up after a single ring.

"John. Did we not just see each other?" she asked, her voice full of a humor that her peers would have never believed her capable of.

"It already feels like forever," I said, only halfway joking. "I just wanted to let you know I'm headed out."

"Alone? Or did Lady Middleton elect to accompany you?"

"I think you already know the answer to that."

"Good." She didn't raise her voice, but the shift in tone made it immediately clear her words were meant for the femmepire slouching against my car's passenger door. "I entrust him to you, Juliette. See to it that no harm befalls him."

Juliette opened her mouth to reply, but I stepped in before my business partner said or did something we would both live to regret.

"I'll be fine," I said. "I'm more worried about you. Zorana—"

"Is exceedingly dangerous," finished Anastasia. "Both myself and the members of Queen-Regent Lucia's former House are aware of this fact. Assuming we locate her at all, be assured that we will consider every angle before engaging."

I'd seen Zorana beat another vampire to death with her bare hands and use that vampire's blood to annihilate a roomful of mercenaries… to say nothing of the alpha werewolf she'd literally decapitated. I wasn't sure geometry was going to be the great help Ana seemed to think it was, but then, I'd never been a fan of math in any of its forms.

"Just… stay safe," I urged her. "As safe as you can, anyway. Gustavo and Teresa would be crushed if something happened to you, and you know I don't like it when old people are sad."

"As you say. When do you anticipate on returning?"

"We should reach Ghost Falls by Thursday sometime. I figure two or three days there, and then another two back. So…"

"Sunday," supplied Juliette helpfully. "Monday at the latest."

"Yeah, that. I'm going to run my one-on-one interviews later next week, so we'd have to be back by then anyway."

"Very well," said Anastasia. "I will see you upon your return. Good luck to you, Mr. Smith, and please stay safe."

"You too, Lady Dumenyova." I ended the call and found Juliette giving me one of her own patent-pending looks. "What?

"*Good luck to you, Mr. Smith. You too, Lady Dumenyova.* Can't either of you say goodbye like normal people?"

"That *was* pretty normal."

"Right. Do you even kiss or do you just trade curtseys instead?"

"Are you sure you want to know?"

"Ugh. No. Forget I asked and please let me scour the image from my mind." She gave a theatrical shudder, then grinned. "To be honest, I'm surprised she's okay with you heading out on your own."

"On my own?" I gave the femmepire a once-over and raised an eyebrow in a far less elegant rendition of Anastasia's expression.

"You know what I mean. Out of town without her."

"I guess she trusts you to protect me." And then, because my mother had raised an honest son, I couldn't help but add, "And I'm pretty sure she just wants me out of San Diego."

"What? Why?" Juliette was inexperienced and frequently distracted, but she was also a long way from dumb. After a moment of silence, she put two and two together. "Zorana."

I swallowed. My reaction to the name didn't seem to improve no matter how many times I heard it. "Yeah. I have to imagine if she had decided to target me, it would have happened when Ana was still out of the country and none of us even knew the Blood Witch was loose, but…"

"But you never know. Especially with her."

"Exactly." And Steve was smart enough that he'd have likely pointed out my vulnerability if Ana hadn't thought of it. After all, I made for a pretty damn convenient reason for the femmepire to get involved.

"Huh," said Juliette.

"Huh?"

"I'm starting to think Anastasia is better at playing people-chess than I realized."

"At the end of the day, we have to go to Ghost Falls anyway. If it makes things easier for Ana, so much the better." I'd never even met Dulcinea or her family, but I could imagine how much panic her disappearance had caused. We didn't get a lot of missing persons cases at the agency—and too many of *those* were of the skeevy stalker variety that I immediately rejected—so it would be nice to turn my investigative powers to a truly good cause for once.

"On that note, I heard back from the town's sheriff while you were out. Not much new to report there; he's still convinced she ran away with her boyfriend. Said it's the sort of thing that happens a lot in a town that small; kids start to feel trapped and then end up just taking off. There's every possibility that she'll have called home by the time we arrive."

"That would be ideal. Then we could just turn around and come back—" I cut off as my wonderphone chimed with a notification. Ana had sent me an email, and while that email lacked both a subject and a body, it *did* have an attachment.

In a direct refutation of every information security tutorial ever, I opened the pdf. After all, it seemed unlikely anyone would even know who Ana was, let alone dare to spoof her address.

Sure enough, the pdf opened without anything nefarious manifesting in my wonderphone's digital innards. Instead, I found pages and pages of text. There were pictures too: some of them photographs, others little more than sketches.

"What's all that?" asked Juliette.

"Information from Ana's files on Arizona and New Mexico. Who and what we might encounter on our trip and why it's best not to piss them off."

"Does she know you can't control that last part?"

"I think hope springs eternal."

I scrolled through a few more pages of documentation and then pocketed my phone. I'd review the data when we stopped for lunch or dinner, and then again before I went to sleep in Phoenix. My trip to Rome had taught me that information *mattered*. Whether it was the vampire capital of Europe or some tiny town in New Mexico, I wasn't going to make the mistake of going into any situation blind anymore.

At least this time, the notes hadn't started off with a comprehensive review of the genealogies of every prominent bloodsucker in Western Europe.

CHAPTER 11

IN WHICH NOTHING SAYS FUN
LIKE FUNGUS AND CHEESE FRIES

Rush hour in most cities starts around four and ends around six or seven. In San Diego, it starts at two in the afternoon… or even earlier during the heights of summer. And the whole downtown/North Park/Hillcrest sprawl had, for as long as I could remember, been a mess to get in and out of even on the best of days. So, I knew starting our road trip mid-afternoon wasn't the brightest of ideas even before we hit the glut of cars trying to reach the 8.

That's why I had Juliette drive.

The Corolla was a year old at that point and had already sustained a few inexplicable dings over its short lifespan, damage that was even *more* visible because of Lucia's preferred white color scheme. I was still plenty protective of the car, as the nicest thing I'd ever been allowed to drive—one nearly disastrous test ride of Juliette's Ducati notwithstanding—but I wasn't quite as possessive of it anymore. And since we were going to be stuck in traffic, I didn't have to worry about the femmepire's usual insane driving habits; it's hard to properly terrify your passenger when nobody's going faster than twenty.

In return, Juliette got to choose the music, something I'd previously promised Anastasia. I sagged low in my chair and did my best to ignore the relentless bass of some garage band that she swore would've been the second coming of Warsaw Pakt had their lead singer not found Jesus and cocaine, in that order, on one late spring weekend.

"Did you know there's something living under Phoenix?" I asked, raising my voice above the tortured strains of someone who wanted the world to know how desperately it needed to be burned down.

"There's something living under most cities, little bird."

"Ana's notes say this is some sort of intelligent fungus."

"Oh, right. Kevin."

I watched as Juliette forced her way into the right lane, onto the shoulder, and then back around another car, all to end up behind the car she'd been initially trying to pass. The femmepire had both eyes scanning the road, like a creature on the hunt.

"Kevin?" I pressed.

"Yeah. Its real name is like all consonants, right?"

"Yep." Twenty-one characters long, and only one vowel. Assuming *y* counted as a vowel… I vaguely remembered from grade school that *y* was to vowels what tomatoes were to vegetables.

"That's why we call it Kevin. Anyway, it's nothing to worry about. Other than bugs and vermin, it mostly eats thoughts."

"Thoughts?" I checked the info on my phone and sure enough, the fungus was supposed to be psychic.

"Yeah. When it first arrived on the scene, it was a problem, but after it spread to Tempe, the subsequent decades of munching on the stray thoughts of ASU students really mellowed it out. I mean, I'm not saying Kevin puts the fun in fungus or anything, but you could certainly learn a thing or two from its attitude to life."

"You've met it?" I didn't wait for her nod. "If you want, we could stop by on the way back, and let you say hi."

"I'm not sure your delicate constitution is up for it, or that Anastasia would be too happy with me if we did." She looked over at me even as she blindly forced her way into the left lane, a lane which was moving exactly as slowly as the lane we'd just left. "Its spores can have psychotropic effects."

"Wait, so there's a smart fungus living under Phoenix that eats thoughts and…"

"Farts hallucinations. Yeah. Also, Kevin's gotten really into philosophy. Like really, *really* into it." She shrugged. "It's all Nietzsche this, Foucault that, Categorical Imperative yadda yadda. It gets old, you know? Even so, I might have still settled down in Phoenix back when I first passed through if the summers weren't so brain meltingly awful. And if San Diego hadn't existed."

That was honestly more than I had ever wanted to know… about Phoenix and this Kevin besides. On the bright side, if my city was going to have a giant, intelligent fungus as one of its neighbors, at least that fungus seemed to be of the peaceful variety. I hadn't seen Ana's notes on Los Angeles, and I didn't want to either. Just driving to L.A. was often enough to ruin my mood. As long as whatever was up there *stayed* up there, I'd be happy.

By the time we reached El Cajon, I was twenty pages deep into the menagerie of the American Southwest, and traffic was finally starting to clear. Juliette spotted a half-inch of daylight and took it, careening around two cars and going from thirty to seventy in a span of time that had me reconsidering everything I knew about the Corolla.

"You won't get any points for keeping me safe from Kevin if we die before even getting out of California," I reminded her.

"Keep your pants on, little bird. Nobody's dying today."

I didn't know what pants had to do with anything, but I grabbed onto the 'Oh Shit' handle and turned all my focus to keeping mine clean.

ooo

Thanks to San Diego traffic, the expected two hours and change trip to the Arizona border took well over three. We stopped in Yuma for gas and caffeine, at which point Juliette insisted I take over the driving.

"We can swap back when we get to Phoenix," she said, munching on a Twix bar she'd bought at the gas station, "but driving's boring when there's no real risk involved."

Since I preferred it when we were the only car on the road, that arrangement suited me just fine. I moved the driver-side seat back a handful of inches, tilted the steering wheel down, and adjusted literally every mirror in the car so that I could actually see again, and then we got back on the road.

I'd spent most of the trip so far reviewing Ana's notes, but Juliette was far more interested in toggling between different playlists on her phone and making the occasional pointed observation about the other drivers we encountered on the road. When that grew old, she pulled a family-sized bag of Skittles out of her purse and spent a solid thirty minutes chewing her way through it.

Vampire metabolism remained high on my private list of completely unfair superpowers. The fact that I'd never been able to borrow *that* from Lucia through our busted-up bond was some sort of cosmic punishment.

We were about an hour from Phoenix, and my stomach was making various gurgles of discontent, when Juliette got back on her phone.

"Ghost Falls is the north end of New Mexico, right?"

"Yeah. Why?"

"I was thinking… instead of coming back through Phoenix, we could head west and hit Sedona, then Vegas."

"You're *that* focused on avoiding Kevin?"

"It's not about Kevin. Have you ever been to Sedona?"

"This is my first time in Arizona in general."

"Well, you'd like it. It's all nature and Zen and stuff. You could sit around and navel gaze with the trees while I got a three-hour massage."

"What part of *navel gaze with the trees* sounds like me?"

"Mostly the navel part," she admitted. "Still, it's a cool town. And a *great* way to decompress before we hit Vegas."

"I *have* been to Vegas before."

"But never with me. Trust me, one night in Vegas with Mama Juliette will blow your mind, change your religion, and turn your hair white, above and below."

There was so much in that sentence that for a moment I couldn't even figure out where to start unpacking it.

"*Mama Juliette?*"

"It sounded better in my head. Auntie Juliette?"

"More like annoying much, much, much older sister."

"I can live with that." As ever, Juliette seemed genuinely pleased to have me comment on her age.

"Anyway, I'm sure Vegas would be cool, but we don't have the time, irrespective of its potential effect on my brain, beliefs, or… uh… hair color. This trip is cutting things close as it is."

"Then maybe we should have flown. I can't believe you're letting one hyperactive little girl scare you off planes forever."

"She wasn't just a girl. She was a demon in child form."

"Sure she was."

I didn't have much to say to that because Juliette was right. Even with airports and plane travel sucking these days, a flight to

Albuquerque and a three-hour car ride to Ghost Falls would have made a hell of a lot more sense than a full-on road trip. But admitting so would mean she had *won,* and after four-plus hours of punk music infiltrating my eardrums to slowly make itself at home in my brain, *surrender* was no longer in my vocabulary. So, I decided to change the field of battle.

"When this is all done, maybe the four of us could hit Vegas together?"

"You, me, Kevin, and…?"

"I'm sorry?"

"Who's our fourth?"

I frowned as I turned off the 8. As a proud son of Southern California, I'd never even heard of this so-called *85,* but the GPS swore it would get us to the 10 which would in turn take us to Phoenix, and the one thing I'd learned as a young driver—other than that parallel parking was a test designed to break even the strongest of us—was to always trust the GPS.

"I meant you, me, Ana, and Angel. We could make it a couples vacation. A double couples vacation."

"Oh." Even out of the corner of my eye, Juliette's shrug was expressive. "Maybe."

I wasn't the world's expert on relationships, despite multiple months dating a four-hundred-year-old, temporarily retired vampire assassin, but even I could pick up on the fact that *something* was going on. As Juliette's friend, it was my duty to help if I could. However, experience had taught me that matters of the heart were often problematic and deeply difficult to talk about, and that meant I'd have to carefully consider my approach.

"What is going on with you and Angel?"

Or… I could just ask her, which apparently my mouth had decided to do all on its own.

"What?"

"You were irritated at the wedding. You jumped at the chance to come on this road trip. And now—"

"Your girlfriend basically ordered me to come along."

"I'm pretty sure no one can make you do anything you don't want to do," I said, paraphrasing her own words. "And I can get and even appreciate that one or both of you might be worried about my safety… but you didn't even call Angel to let her know you'd be gone."

"I sent a text."

"That's what I'm talking about. Six months ago, you were practically living in each other's air space. You even gave her a job at our agency. Now, you're taking off on trips with little more than a text? And you'd rather go to Vegas with me than her?"

"So?"

"Doesn't that seem weird to you?"

"Are you saying *you* don't want to go with me?" There was an edge to her words, but some other emotion lurked beneath, intense but indecipherable.

"No, I'm not saying that at all. I'm sure it'd be amazing and that we'd probably spend at least some of it in jail until you sobered up enough to work your mojo. But why not bring Ana and Angel with us when this is all over and done?"

"You don't get it."

"I guess not. Because it kind of feels like you're just looking for reasons to spend time away from Angel. And while I'm Team Juliette all the way, I still don't want to see her hurt."

"That's not—" She shifted about in her seat, finally bringing her bare feet down off the custom white dashboard. "Whatever. I don't want to talk about it."

"Okay."

"And don't even think of using one of your stupid mediator smiles on me. They just make you look ridiculous. And slightly crazed."

"Fine." I carefully tucked the Encourager™ back away, knowing that its time would come, and that it would be that much more effective in the right moment.

"Fine," she echoed, focusing back on her phone.

One thing that both mediations and my first long-term relationship in half a decade had taught me was the power of silence. So, I didn't press for more information as I slowly followed my GPS directions onto the 10 and then into Phoenix. I'd originally planned a stop at a nice hotel in the city with Ana—something with a view, a soaking tub, and a king-sized bed—in the sort of lavish romantic gesture that would have hoovered up my disposable cash for the month. The change in companions, and my new knowledge of 'Puts the Fun in Fungus' Kevin had convinced me to instead push on to a town called Payson. It added an hour and a half to the route but would make the next day's trip that much more manageable.

Juliette kept quiet as we moved through the city. She even let her playlist finally end… although she'd no doubt tell me it had burned out rather than faded away. The only sounds in the Corolla's still pristine interior became those emanating from my increasingly displeased stomach. It had been almost seven hours since brunch, and not even the extra guacamole Caden had provided could keep the hunger pangs at bay.

"Are you going to feed that thing or do I need to put it out of my misery?" Juliette finally asked.

"I figured we would wait to eat when we stopped for the night in Payson. My stomach's not happy about that plan."

"What the hell is Payson?"

"It's the heart of Arizona." I had both eyes fixed on the road, but I could *feel* her glare. "That's what Wikipedia said. Anyway, it's a town about ninety minutes northeast of Phoenix. No worries about Kevin eating our thoughts while we sleep. Plus, it'll give us an easier drive tomorrow."

Juliette sighed. "Fine."

The Duchess of Snark had her moments of irritability, like anyone else, but it had been a long while since I'd seen her this out of sorts. That, more than anything, told me I'd struck a nerve asking about Angel. Still, I wasn't going to push it. I'd opened the door, to badly mix metaphors. If she wanted to talk, she would have to walk through it.

"There's a Comfort Inn just off the 87 in Payson," Juliette volunteered a few minutes after we'd left Phoenix behind. "With Mexican next door or a diner down the street. Which do you think will prevent your stomach from attaining full sentience and murdering us both while we sleep?"

"Let's do the diner. I'm starting to think there might be such a thing as too much guac."

"And you say *I'm* acting strange," she muttered.

I let the opportunity to renew that line of questioning skate by, reminding myself of the difference between mediations and friendships. Besides, if Juliette did end up wanting to discuss whatever was going on with her, it made sense to do so when neither of us was hangry anymore.

An hour later, we checked into the Comfort Inn, and twenty minutes after that, we were seated at the bar and grill Juliette had found online. A friendly waitress with tired eyes took our orders and came back a minute or two later with our drinks... a beer for Juliette and another soda for me. I scrunched down into my booth and rolled my head about, hearing the cartilage in my neck crack and pop in a way it had never done in my early twenties.

"It'll be about eight hours to Ghost Falls tomorrow," I said, breaking the silence that had followed us all the way from the car. "I figure we can wake up early, get some food, and then head on out."

"That's fine."

I studied her over my glass of Diet Coke, playing with the straw in my mouth, and finally gave in. Maybe it was incumbent on *me* to walk through the door that I'd opened.

"I'm sorry if I overstepped, Duchess."

"What?" That got her attention; yellow eyes narrowed as she finally looked up from the beer she had yet to touch.

"Your love life is your business." Technically, that wasn't true, given that she'd hired her girlfriend to be our employee, but bringing that up would probably sour the olive branch I was attempting to offer. And besides, it was impossible to have an HR nightmare when we didn't have an HR department at all, right? "I'm not trying to stick my nose where it doesn't belong." I waited for her nod and continued. "But I'm also your friend, and a decent enough listener that only half my mediation clients have tried to kill me. If you want to talk, I'm here."

"What I *want* are my cheese fries, and a nice glass of O-negative."

One part of me—my stomach—couldn't help but rumble its agreement regarding the cheese fries that had yet to arrive. Another part of me was just glad that she'd gone with O-negative instead of my blood type, AB-negative. The rest of me recognized a brush off when I heard one.

"Fair enough. But beer's not a bad consolation prize, right?"

She stirred, as if seeing the beer in front of her for the first time, then tossed back a good third of the glass in one long sip. For the first time in well over an hour, she grinned.

"It doesn't suck, admittedly. And it won't keep me up all night either, unlike what you're drinking."

"I'm a caffeine veteran," I told her with no small amount of pride. "The stuff barely even affects me anymore."

"Except when you don't drink it."

"Well, that goes without saying." I matched her grin. "Besides, I drove for multiple hours and now I'm having cheese fries and a half-pound burger; I'll be lucky if I stay awake long enough to walk back to the hotel."

Before Juliette could respond, the much-anticipated cheese fries arrived. A few minutes passed as we collectively tore into the small mountain of potatoes and cheese.

When there was nothing left on the plate but crumbs, I sighed happily. I wasn't sure if I even had room left for the burger I'd ordered, but I was going to give it my best effort. To say nothing of dessert…

"I don't see a future for us," said Juliette out of nowhere.

I carefully swallowed the Diet Coke I'd almost spit out and scooted my half-full glass to the side.

"Why? What did I do?"

"Not *us*. Me and Angel."

Oh. I'd never practiced, let alone named, my non-smiling mediation expressions, but I did my best to adopt an agreeably interested demeanor anyway… and then secretly named it the Listener™.

"How come?"

"She wants something different. Something more like you have with Anastasia." Juliette looked away, swallowing more than just another sip of beer.

"Meaning…?"

"Something serious. Something more permanent." Her eyes glittered. "As if humans even know what permanence is."

"If my relationship with Ana is causing you problems—"

"It's not. Angel is twenty-nine and suddenly thinking about the rest of her life. Family, kids, a white picket fence, and 2.5 dogs."

I was pretty sure dogs didn't come in fractions, but not *so* sure that I was going to force the issue.

"And you?"

"I'm not even a hundred yet. I want to have fun."

We both leaned back as the waitress dropped off our burgers and whisked away the cheese fries plate I'd practically licked clean.

"I can feel you judging me from all the way across the table," muttered Juliette.

"Only because you decided to ruin a perfectly good hamburger with relish." I shivered theatrically, but my grin faded as I looked at the femmepire. "Seriously, Juliette. I'm not in a position to judge anyone."

"No? You got the storybook ending. You flew across the oceans to save your one true love and managed to win her freedom—and yours—from Lucia at the same time."

"Yeah, and almost died like a dozen times in the process. Hell, I almost got her killed along the way. Not to mention Lucia and her niece Sabina."

"But—"

"I know. I lived, the bad guys got caught or killed, and my life is perfect now, right?"

Juliette set down her burger and gave me a hard-eyed stare. "Are you saying it's not?"

"No. It's amazing. Ana's amazing. I go to sleep every night struggling to believe I got so lucky."

"Well, then—"

"And I wake up every morning convinced that *this* is going to be the day I screw it all up. That she sees me for who I am and realizes she deserves so much better. Someone even half as good-looking as she is. Someone more talented and better read. Someone she can fricking drink from without feeling guilty as hell over the pain she's causing."

"Little bird—"

"I'm not trying to make this about me," I told her. "I'm just saying… I'm not in any kind of position to judge. Relationships are brutally hard, even when it all goes right. You've been a PI long enough to see that for yourself."

"John—"

"So, yeah. I'm here to listen and to help if I can. Just—"

"Would you shut up already?" hissed Juliette, yellow eyes blazing gold. "We have bigger problems than Angel or Anastasia."

"What?"

She dropped her voice so that it was barely a whisper, even as she looked past me toward the restaurant's front door. "We have visitors. Three of them. Just came in from outside."

I went to look over my shoulder, but her grip on my hand tightened to fruit-pulping levels. I settled back in the booth and looked to her instead.

"Three of who?"

"Infected." And then, because that didn't narrow it down much at all, given the very many types of weres in the continental United States… "Wolves."

Well, shit.

CHAPTER 12

IN WHICH A WOLF CRIES BOY

I had nothing at all against werewolves. In fact, some of my closest… well, *acquaintances*, no matter what Juliette said to the contrary, were werewolves. But those acquaintances were all part of the San Diego Pack, a living, breathing, lycanthrope democracy led by Jason and his hippie ex-wife-and-now-girlfriend, Carolyn. It took them ages to come to a decision on damn near anything, but the members of that pack were all generally good people.

The New Mexico Pack was very, very different, in size, reputation, and demeanor. They had tried to conquer the San Diego pack, first by marriage and then by force. During the chaos that followed, I'd personally shot and killed one of them, while at least a dozen others had been executed by vampire hit squads. And then, when the dust had seemingly settled, Anastasia had taken a trip out to their home state to give a message of her own, one where the presumptive heir to the pack, his two lieutenants, four of their enforcers, and the she-wolf that was his fiancée all took a one-way trip to the afterlife.

They'd had it coming, by the laws of the Concordat, but something told me that wouldn't hold water with the rest of their pack. Still, it shouldn't have ever been a problem.

"They're not supposed to be here," I murmured back to Juliette, the hairs on the back of my neck standing straight up as if I could feel the wolves closing in. "The pack is based out of Albuquerque."

"Maybe they're unaffiliated. Keep quiet and follow my lead."

All expression fell away from her face as three leather-clad individuals, two men and a woman in their early to mid-twenties, tromped over and took the table next to our booth. They looked like they'd just come in off the road, dust and dirt making even the one Caucasian almost as dark as his companions. The woman remained standing, cocking her shaved head to the side, and tilting the chair back and forth on one leg. She finally spun that chair about so that it was facing our booth, and dropped into it, giving her back to the other two wolves.

"We don't know you," she told Juliette in a soft drawl, the bone white of her eyes suggesting her wolf was riding somewhere just below the surface. "An unknown fanger in our town? It makes the boys kind of nervous."

Juliette let her gaze flick past the lady werewolf to her companions and then shrugged. "Boys are trouble that way. Good thing you're in charge, pet."

"That I am."

Something passed between them… maybe the metaphysical equivalent of a pissing contest. Finally, Juliette shrugged a second time.

"We're just passing through," she said, the words light. "We'll be out of your… hair… in the morning."

I wasn't sure if that was a shot at the other woman's lack of hair in human form or the fact that it became fur in wolf form. Either way, I fought to keep my tension hidden.

"Your donor here seems a bit nervous."

"Like I said, boys are trouble."

The other woman looked me over, dismissed me in a nanosecond, and turned back to Juliette. "You could do better, girlie."

"Are you offering?"

One of the male wolves growled, the low rumble hitting me like it had physical weight.

"Not in this lifetime," said the female were. "I'm Hyacinth."

"The flower?"

'What? Don't I smell sweet to you?" Hyacinth's skin rippled, as if the wolf was trying to break free. "Maybe you should give me your name now."

"Juliette. And this here is Ziggy."

"You don't look like a Ziggy," Hyacinth told me.

"What's a Ziggy supposed to look like?"

"I don't know. Cool maybe?"

"I guess my parents were optimists."

"Seems like." She turned back to my companion. "And where are you and your overfed blood bag from, Juliette?"

"City of Angels." Juliette spread her hands wide, as if presenting herself. "Didn't you see the halo?"

"I must have missed it somehow."

"Long hours on a bike will do that to you. What do you ride, flower girl?"

"American steel."

"Good for the open road," said Juliette. "I've got a Ducati."

"That's a lot of ride."

"You know it."

I wasn't entirely sure, being notoriously bad at the sport, but it kind of seemed like these two were flirting. I could feel my anus unclench, if only a little bit.

"Do you have it with you?"

"Left it back in L.A. so this one could chauffeur me around in a manner I'd like to become accustomed to."

"Well, that's a real pity."

"I'm starting to think so. Tell me, flower girl, do you always give passers-by the third degree?"

"Only those too rude to announce themselves."

"Last I heard, the pack was located in Albuquerque."

"We've been expanding."

"Celebrations are in order then, I guess. Buy you a drink? The beer here's not complete rat piss."

"Sadly, we've got things to do tonight. We'll be out of your… hair… in just a few moments," she added, with a pointed glance at Juliette's own do. "Ezra?"

The wolf who had growled rose to his feet. He didn't look much like an Ezra. With the extra heel provided by his riding boots, he had to be pushing six-four and I was guessing he topped the scales somewhere around two-forty. Which was intimidating until you realized even Hyacinth's hybrid form was probably significantly bigger.

Juliette didn't move a muscle, but I could feel her tension as the other were approached our table, one figurative paw reaching into the interior pocket of his riding jacket.

Instead of a weapon, he pulled out a phone. Three taps later, I heard the audible click of a simulated camera shutter.

"Something to remember you by," drawled Hyacinth, "on those cold, lonely nights."

Ezra turned to me and took a second picture.

"I'm flattered," I said.

"That one's just for our files," said Hyacinth, stomping on my already bruised ego with one heeled boot. "If y'all change your minds and decide to stay more than the night, we're gonna need to have a longer chat."

"We'll be gone after breakfast," said Juliette.

"I guess we'll see." The two male wolves headed for the door, slipping past Hyacinth and the waitress only now coming to take their order. With one last, searching look, the female werewolf gave Juliette a mocking salute and turned to follow her men.

"Hey," called Juliette, stopping her in her tracks. "If you ever make it to Long Beach, look me and my flock up. Not all our donors look like this guy."

I reminded myself that I was dating a centuries-old badass with more sophistication in her pinky finger than these two women possessed combined. It helped… just not as much as I'd hoped.

"Maybe I'll take you up on that someday, fanger."

"I'll be waiting with bells on, flower girl."

I stayed twisted about in my seat so I could watch the last of the three weres departing the building. Moments later, loud engines rattled the windows as multiple motorcycles peeled off into the night. I turned back to Juliette, shaking my head. "I have to admit, that was *not* how I expected things to go."

"We need to get out of here," said Juliette. I'd expected a lazy, self-satisfied smirk on her face at the semi-successful flirtation, but the femmepire's eyes were glowing gold, and her features could have been carved from granite. "Now."

"What? Why?"

"What do you think they're going to do with the pictures they took, little bird?"

I coughed, fighting back a blush. "Well, from the sounds of it, she's going to use your picture as fantasy material…"

"Only after sending it and yours back to the pack for recording." She flagged down our waitress before she could return to the kitchen and tossed her a handful of wrinkled bills.

"And?"

"And don't you think at least *someone* in the pack will recognize the mediator who thwarted their invasion of San Diego? Who's now *dating* the woman who killed off half their leadership? It's only been two years. That's not nearly enough time for the rest to die out of old age."

"Shit." I was out of the booth moments after Juliette, not vampire quick, but as close as I could manage with my bondholder all the way back in Italy. "So much for our nice stay at the Comfort Inn."

"It's like Warren Zevon said," she told me, hustling us both out the door. "You can sleep when you're dead."

ᴏᴏᴏ

I tensed as we left the restaurant, expecting wolves to leap out of the darkness, but the parking lot was quiet and still, and the handful of cars making their way up and down the cross street didn't pay us any attention. I shivered in the surprisingly cool night air and followed Juliette. My companion wasn't running, but she wasn't moseying along either, and despite my longer stride, I found myself almost jogging to keep up with her.

"You start the car when we get there," she told me. "I'll fetch the bags."

I passed her the keycard to our hotel room. "You really think they'll be on to us that fast? The pack must have groups like this all over. I can't imagine a flirty vampire and her overfed blood bag are going to jump to the top of the identification queue."

"You thought I was flirting? Seriously?"

"I'm pretty sure you both were." We hustled across the 87, not waiting for the crosswalk.

"She was interrogating me, little bird, and I was giving it right back while trying to keep their focus from shifting to you. Trust me: bald and furry isn't my type."

"What are our chances if they come back?" Juliette was almost a hundred years old, but I wouldn't have bet on her in a fight against anybody in her former House's Watch, let alone three werewolves. And while the Infected were vulnerable to compulsion unless actively calling on their bestial side, anyone who came for us would be doing so forewarned.

"I guess that depends on whether you have another of those flamethrowing hell guns you used in Santee."

"I wish. Every time I bring it up to Bill, he just starts talking about snakes."

"Then it's a good thing we're already running away."

Thankfully, the Comfort Inn was only a block away. Its lot was every bit as quiet as the one we'd just left, and the Corolla was where we'd parked it, slightly less pretty after a day driving through the desert, but still almost new and unmistakably mine.

"You sure you don't want help with the bags?"

"Just get the trunk open and the engine running," she told me over one shoulder as she headed for the lobby. "The sooner we're out of here, the happier I'll be."

Both tasks were well within my capabilities, even after a half-plate of cheese fries and a hurriedly consumed bacon cheeseburger. I started the car and made sure the passenger door was unlocked, my eyes trained on the second-floor hotel room whose light had just flickered on. I couldn't see Juliette inside, but the fact that she'd already made it there was one more sign that she wasn't messing around.

I backed the Corolla out of its space and pulled around to idle in front of the lobby. I was pretty sure we had time before the unfortunately named Ezra sent our pictures back to the pack, and even more time before whoever was on duty got to identifying us, but I'd also been *pretty sure* that the pack operated exclusively in southern New Mexico. Their presence just an hour outside of Phoenix blew that to hell, and the fact that they'd located us—or at least Juliette—within an hour of our arrival in Payson told me they had some level of basic surveillance in town.

Sad to say, Juliette was just too pretty to go unnoticed unless she spent her energy continually compelling everyone around her. In San Diego, it didn't matter so much. Here in Payson, she'd clearly stuck out like a sore thumb.

And that meant getting the hell out of Dodge as soon as possible was the right decision.

Juliette reappeared in the lobby, two bags in each hand, and hurried towards me. I popped the trunk, and a succession of thumps preceded her slamming that trunk shut again with a little more force than the owner's manual recommended. A moment later, she was sliding into the passenger seat.

"Let's go."

We didn't even make it out of the lot before the Corolla's own pleasant purr was drowned out by the rumble of overjuiced motorcycles. Four of them melted out of the darkness to block the route to the 87, and another half-dozen rolled in to flank us, cutting off any retreat.

"What was that you were saying about queues?" spat Juliette. "Give me your gun. I'll clear some space and you drive right through. Maybe we can lose them in the night."

"I already told you I didn't have a gun."

"I'm not talking about the hell gun. I'm talking about the nine that Anastasia's been training you on."

"Why would I have brought that with me?"

"Why *wouldn't* you have?"

"I'm not licensed to carry it in Arizona or New Mexico!"

"They're both open carry states. You don't need a license if you're over eighteen."

"Seriously? That seems… questionable."

"You're the worst, little bird. I want that on my tombstone."

Someone tapped on my window, and I looked to find a shotgun barrel, as wide and dark as the devil's road, pointed in my direction. Against my better judgment, I rolled down the window.

"Kill the engine," growled an unfamiliar voice, "or I spread your insides all over this pretty white car."

In the movies, I'd have knocked the shotgun barrel away, cleverly angling it so that the resulting buckshot would tear through Juliette's passenger window and shred the wolves on her side, even as I stomped on the gas and blew through the Harley Davidson-sponsored roadblock in front of us. Sadly, I'd been through enough in the past few years to understand the difference between Hollywood and reality.

I turned the key in the ignition and held up my hands.

Hyacinth dismounted from her motorcycle and stared us down, illuminated in the Corolla's headlights. "John Smith," she said, voice carrying easily as the motorcycles around us quieted. "I knew you didn't look like a Ziggy."

"It's the name I used to dance under in college," I told her.

"You'll have plenty of time to tell us all about it." She turned to Juliette. "Lady Dumenyova. If reputations are to be believed, even the ten of us might not give you pause. Thankfully, your boyfriend here is a lot less durable than you are. Come with us voluntarily or he dies here and now. The choice is yours."

I traded glances with Juliette. Apparently, the pack knew what *I* looked like, but their files weren't quite as comprehensive when it came to the vampires of San Diego. It felt like there should be some way to use this to our advantage, but I was drawing a blank on how. In fact, it meant that Hyacinth had brought more than enough wolves to subdue us physically, even without the threats to my very fragile, very mortal body.

"You have three seconds," said Hyacinth. "Starting now."

"Don't get your tail in a knot, flower girl," said Juliette, but her hands swiftly joined mine in the air.

"What do you want?" I was proud of just how steady my voice was, despite the shotgun practically caressing my cheek. "Like we said in the restaurant, we're just passing through."

"You *were* just passing through. Now, you've got a meeting with the big cheese." She glanced at the wolves on either side of my car. "Take them."

My door ripped open, and I was pulled out into the cool Arizona air. A moment later, Juliette stepped out of her own volition. There were four wolves on her side, but they all hesitated, bone white eyes wide as some sort of internal debate passed between them. Finally, the smallest man stepped forward to force Juliette down to the asphalt.

A second wolf moved in, dropping a knee into Juliette's back and dragging a grunt from the downed woman. I could hear the telltale sign of multiple sets of handcuffs being clicked shut around her wrists and ankles, and then a third wolf joined the other two over Juliette's now-bound form. This one stripped off her leather vest and shifted right there in the parking lot, gaining a foot in height and doubling her mass as she assumed the wolves' monstrous hybrid form.

"My name is Shae," she said through a maw never meant for human speech. "Laika, Georgie's fiancée, was my sister. This is for her."

The nightmarish creature pulled back her leg and soccer kicked Juliette's supine form. With the Corolla between us, I couldn't see the blow land, but I heard the crack of bone, and the whoosh of air departing Juliette's lungs. A second kick arrived almost as swiftly as the first, chased by Shae's snarling laughter.

What happened next was pure reflex, sourced from that free, empty space between rational thought. I dropped my weight, slipping out from under the lax grip of the wolf who'd paused to watch Juliette's beating. There was no chance in hell of me wrestling the shotgun from the wolf's other hand and I didn't even try. Instead, I ducked behind him, tugging backwards on the biker's thick belt as I kicked down at the back of his knee.

Gun training wasn't the only thing Ana had been *strongly* encouraging me to do with her on the weeks she was in San Diego, and if every single one of our matches on the mat had inevitably ended with me pinned and then thoroughly smooched by my vampire girlfriend, there'd still been quite a few less enjoyable lessons along the way. Things like wrist escapes and judo throws that used your opponents' greater strength against them.

Unfortunately, there was strength and then there was *strength*, and werewolves tended towards the latter. The wolf dropped down as I kicked his knee out from under him, but when I tried to rotate my hips and drive his upper body to the pavement, I encountered the limits of my technique: with a halfway stable base under him, the dude didn't even budge. Instead, he twisted about and took hold of me. I drove a thumb towards his eye, but apparently, he'd seen that move before; he swayed aside from my attempted strike and then physically hurled me into the side of the Corolla.

The initial impact of body on car was followed almost immediately by a second one, momentum sending my head snapping back to bounce off fiberglass and chrome. Just like that, the world went fuzzy around me. I watched as doubles of the wolf I'd just tried to throw stepped forward. Two fists tore through the night air in my direction, and as I attempted to dodge, all I could do was guess which was real and which was the phantom brought on by my sudden head trauma.

I guessed wrong.

Chapter 13

IN WHICH NUDITY MAKES A COMEBACK

Two things quickly became clear as I woke up. First, I'd been moved while unconscious… the stone beneath my cheek was smooth and cool and not the parking lot's rough asphalt, still slightly warm from the day's long-gone sun.

And second, judging by the fact that I could feel that same smooth stone with my *other* cheeks, I was, against all rhyme, reason, and basic laws of morality, once again naked. Naked, kidnapped, and judging by the cold metal around my wrists, handcuffed.

This was starting to get ridiculous.

There *was* good news, at least. It wasn't dark, and once I finally convinced my eyes to open, I found myself in some sort of cellar, dusty shelves covering three of the four walls around me. The fourth wall contained the door leading out, not that I had any chance of opening it with my hands cuffed behind me.

The second piece of good news was that I didn't immediately vomit upon waking. In fact, my vision seemed fine, and even the expected headache was muted, a dull throb instead of the marching band I'd been anticipating. Apparently, I'd avoided a concussion despite my unfortunate encounters with both my own car and an asshole wolf's oversized fist.

Those two minor victories aside, however, things looked bleak, and not just because I was on full display to whoever wanted a peek. There was no sign of Juliette and zero chance of me escaping my handcuffs, let alone breaking out of the locked room and what was almost surely an entire den of werewolves on my own. Meanwhile, Anastasia was hundreds of miles away and had no idea we were in trouble, and Lucia was *thousands* of miles away and equally ignorant. But my biggest and most immediate concern was that all the soda I'd had during our drive from San Diego and then dinner was doing a number on my insides.

I really, really, *really* had to pee.

I lay there for a good ten minutes or so, working whatever muscles controlled the bladder like I was an Olympian power lifter, when I finally heard footsteps approaching my impromptu cell. A moment later, the insertion of a key confirmed that the door had been locked, and a moment after that, the door opened out onto a well-lit hallway.

"Rise and shine," drawled Hyacinth. She reached down and yanked me to my feet, then steadied me as my legs took their time remembering how to function. "Your presence has been requested."

"By who?"

"Isn't it supposed to be *by whom*?"

I gave her a hard look that she didn't even pretend to be bothered by. "Seriously, who are we going to see?"

"I told you back at the hotel. The big cheese himself."

"Your pack's alpha?" I tried not to make a face as I said it. According to science, the alpha/beta hierarchy wasn't actually a thing with real life wolves, but weres still insisted on adopting the outdated methodology.

"Georgie's Dad, yeah." Something almost like sympathy flashed across her face, there and gone in a moment. "Can't say I'd want to be in your shoes right now."

"I'm not wearing shoes."

"You're not wearing *anything*," she said, finally deigning to acknowledge the elephant—and I was *definitely* only being metaphorical—in the room. "I'm guessing Nero didn't much like you taking a swing at him."

"My heart bleeds for him."

"Not yet it doesn't."

I coughed, deciding that that particular topic of conversation was played out. "Is there any chance I could get some pants before this meet and greet?"

She met my gaze again. Without the wolf shining through, her eyes were a pleasant celery green. "I'm not sure pants will help all that much, mediator."

I disagreed rather vehemently, but nobody seemed to care.

The hallway was unremarkable except for its length. Cement floors, unfinished drywall, and a lack of windows told me we were probably underground in some sort of basement or, worse yet, a *lair*. We passed two other rooms like the one I'd been stashed in, reached an intersection where we took a right, and then walked for another few minutes before we reached a cased opening and what could only be described as some sort of vestibule or foyer. If my guesses were correct, the closed set of double doors on the far wall led to whatever passed for a werewolf's throne room.

Honestly, the building was kind of a dump. I'd expected better from the largest pack in North America, even if that pack appeared to be a supernatural biker gang. But then, I'd also expected them to be based over in Albuquerque, not hanging around a stone's throw from Phoenix.

A stranger waited at the door, wearing a suit instead of the ubiquitous black leather. Slim and small, he gave Hyacinth a look as she pushed me into the vestibule.

"How is he today?" she asked him.

The other wolf didn't speak, but he held out one hand and waggled it back and forth.

"Lovely," muttered Hyacinth. "Is the other one already inside?"

"They are in the process of fetching her." The man's voice was smooth as jazz, each consonant rolling around in his mouth like something to savor. "Boss wanted her collared."

For the first time since I'd woken up, my mind focused on something other than my aching bladder.

"Did you say *collared?*"

"Your girlfriend has earned herself a bit of a reputation," muttered Hyacinth, although something in her tone suggested she wasn't any happier about it than I was. "Can't blame us for taking no chances."

"You're all making a really, really big mistake," I said, directing my words at both wolves. "I'm a pretty easygoing guy, but there are limits."

"You might want to gag him," suggested the doorman. "For his own safety."

"To be honest, I didn't think he'd even be able to walk," she said. "Let alone talk. I guess Nero needs to be taught how to throw a punch again."

"I heal fast," I said. "Latent werewolf virus."

"Latent *what?*"

"Werewolf virus. The last *alpha* who kidnapped me tried to turn me. It didn't take and now he's dead."

The two wolves exchanged glances. The doorman looked unruffled, but Hyacinth was frowning.

"That's not how it works," she said.

"And yet here I am, shrugging off a concussion like it was nothing. You do the math."

I wasn't entirely sure what math I was talking about, but I was naked, I had to go to the bathroom, and these assholes had apparently just *collared* Juliette. The time for rationality was clearly over.

A few minutes later, my partner finally made her appearance, dragged in by two wolves who made Ezra look small. They were followed by another four wolves, including the woman named Shae. In human form, she was tall, muscular, overly tattooed, and wearing entirely too much leather.

Juliette still had her clothes on, but that was the only good news. A thick metal collar—almost a medieval gorget—had been locked into place about her neck and not even her vampire constitution had been able to erase the bruises and swelling across the pale skin of her face. Her yellow eyes rolled about in her head before finally landing on me. "Like my new jewelry?" she asked, voice slurred. "Angel always wanted me to accessorize."

"I think she meant suspenders or one of those fancy berets. Are you okay?"

"Couldn't be better. Thanks for asking."

"In retrospect," I admitted, "we probably should have flown."

"Don't be ridiculous." She grinned, her fangs exposed. "Don't you know how dangerous airplanes are?"

"Enough," said Shae, holding up what looked like a garage door opener. "You ain't impressing anyone."

"What's that?" I asked, eyes trained on the device.

"I thought you'd never ask." The wolf clicked the plastic box's only button, and Juliette fell back to the ground, flopping like a fish out of water. "Shock collar. Pure cruelty when used on animals, of course, but fangers? They have it coming."

Before I could even take a step toward her, Hyacinth was standing between us. "Enough. Boss wants to see them both." She looked Juliette up and down and scowled at Shae. "See *and* speak to them. If your lack of control means she's not able to talk back, there's gonna be problems."

"Boss can tell me himself, if so. I don't answer to mouthy upstart nobodies. Only reason you're even invited is because your little patrol found them."

The werewolf at my side stiffened, then shrugged. "It's your poorly tattooed ass on the line." She turned to the doorman. "I guess that means we're ready."

The man in a suit nodded and turned to the interior chamber, one hand on each heavy door. He threw those doors open, then stepped in and off to the side.

"The prisoners you requested are here, Ezekiel."

The voice that came in answer was so deep it made my bones vibrate. It was also thick with an emotion even I could recognize as rage.

"Send them in. I have words to say to my son's killers."

ooo

The throne room was not what I expected. For starters, there wasn't a throne. Nor was there anything I would describe as creature comforts, from carpeting or area rugs to tapestries or paintings on the wall. Instead, there was a thin mattress to one side that looked like it had been purchased on clearance at TerribleBeds.com, and a card table to the other side with a handful of folding chairs arranged around it. What light there was came from overhead cans and a halogen torch that had been almost desultorily parked in the far corner. The whole room smelled musty and, though I wasn't going to be dumb enough to say it, just a bit like wet dog.

Maybe my time in Rome had spoiled me, but this was disappointingly primitive by comparison.

Shirtless and shoeless, Ezekiel was just as primitive looking, but when it came to the New Mexico Alpha, disappointing was not the adjective I would use. Scary, maybe? Borderline psychotic, even? He looked like a mountain man serial killer, all hair and overwhelming size. I could easily picture him with an axe in his enormous hands and ice threaded through his unkempt bushy beard and equally unkempt chest rug. His hair must have once been black, but it was now salt and pepper, with the salt clearly winning the field. Brown eyes blazed within a sun-weathered face, drilling first into me and then into Juliette as she was dragged in to join us.

He turned to the doorman, who had entered the room along with the other wolves.

"What is this, Chase?"

Before the other man could answer, Shae stepped forward. "That's the San Diego mediator, John Smith, and *this*," she added, knocking Juliette back to the floor, "is the so-called Stone Lady, Anastasia Dumenyova."

I winced as she butchered the pronunciation of Dumenyova.

Ezekiel glanced at me again and then back at the now supine vampire. His entire body rippled, as if moments away from a shift. "Is this some kind of joke?"

Shae went pale beneath her face tattoos. "I don't—"

I didn't see Ezekiel take a step, but he was suddenly across the room, and Shae's body hit the wall behind her so hard the drywall crumbled. She fell to the floor in a shower of off-white plaster. The alpha spun on the other wolves and roared, the noise too loud for the basement room, wordless but full of rage and pain.

My own experience with the San Diego Pack told me Shae was fine, or would be, soon enough, but the werewolf stayed down, careful not to make herself a target. The wolves around me had dropped their heads, careful to avoid eye contact with their leader, and I followed suit. For a long moment, all we could hear was Ezekiel's heavy breathing, massive lungs working as if he had just sprinted a marathon. When he finally spoke again, his voice was barbed, each successive sentence gaining in volume until he was screaming the final words.

"Did you believe I wouldn't know the face of my son's killer? Do you all believe me so far gone? Is this what passes for respect now in my pack?!"

The rustle of fabric told me Chase had moved, and I peeked over to find him rising from a deep bow. "None would dare disrespect you, Alpha. Not now or ever. If there has been some mistake, only tell us what it is—"

"That's not Anastasia." A half-dozen set of bone white eyes turned on me, and I fought the urge to take a step back. "We told you so at the diner. Her name is Juliette. She's not even associated with the House in San Diego."

Anymore, I carefully didn't add.

"Surprise, assholes," muttered Juliette, speaking for the first time since making her reappearance.

"But…" Shae climbed to her feet and spun on Hyacinth. "You said—"

"John Smith was correctly identified," said Hyacinth, only slightly defensive. "We lack visual identification for Dumenyova, but a single female vampire traveling with the mediator through our territory. I thought—"

"You thought wrong." Ezekiel's voice cut through the other two wolves' chatter. The rage was gone from his voice, leaving something cold and empty in its wake. "You thought you had caught a grizzly unaware, and instead came away with little more than a rabbit. And yet, even rabbits have their uses."

He turned and walked back to turn one of the folding chairs around. The metal frame shuddered, just a bit, as the big man took a seat. From the motion of his beard, his lips were moving beneath all that facial hair, but no words appeared to be forming.

"Alpha?" Chase finally asked, after a long, uncomfortable minute had passed.

"Eliminate the vampire however you wish," Ezekiel finally said. "What is left of her can be fed to the dogs."

"And the human?"

Ezekiel's cackle came out of nowhere, unprompted, and more than a little bit maniacal. I felt Hyacinth flinch behind me.

"Bait for my trap," said the old wolf. "It appears we will have to bring the grizzly out of her cave. How better than with her mate as hostage?"

Apparently, Ana was the grizzly in the scenario, and I was a rabbit. I hated how quickly I'd figured that out, and how much sense it made.

"With respect, boss," said Hyacinth, choosing her words more carefully than at any time since I'd met her, "shouldn't we focus our energies on recovering Audrey? A conflict on multiple fronts will—"

"By the time the vampires arrive, Audrey will be back with the pack," said Ezekiel, teeth gleaming white in the darkness of his beard as he adopted an almost congenial tone. "Tomorrow, we ride to Phoenix to reclaim my niece from her captors."

"Alpha, are you—"

"The time for talking is done, Chase. The time for waiting and weakness is done. This is a time for war. The streets will run red and what is mine will be reclaimed."

"War!" Shae pumped a fist, entirely healed from whatever damage Ezekiel had done. The wolves around her were smiling, exposed teeth a match for the bone white of their eyes.

"Summon your fellow lieutenants, Shae. We have work to do."

Shae was still smiling as she left, several of her wolves in tow. That left Chase, Hyacinth, Ezekiel, and two other wolves behind. If Juliette really *had* been Anastasia, I would have liked our odds, even with the shock collar. As it was, there might as well have been fifty guards surrounding us.

"We'll need food and drink for the war council," continued Ezekiel. "Preferably beer."

I couldn't tell if he had forgotten I was there or not, but then, I honestly had no idea what was going on. Ezekiel's niece was in Phoenix and being held prisoner? By who? Or *whom*, for that matter? And how was an entire werewolf pack riding to battle in Phoenix going to do anything but make things worse? For the most part, humans remained ignorant of the supernatural species living among them, but it was hard to hide a rampaging horde of the Infected. Especially in the day of social media and camera phones.

"Of course, Alpha." Chase paused. "And the prisoners?"

"Throw the human back in his cell."

"And the vampire?"

"Are you mocking me, boy?" Just like that, Ezekiel was back on his feet.

"Never, Alpha."

"Everywhere I turn," muttered Ezekiel, pacing back and forth in front of us. "Cowardice and stupidity. At what point does it cross the line from incompetence and into outright insurrection?"

"Alpha?"

"I told you what to do with the vampire. If you are loyal… if any of you are loyal…"

"Why not let her go?" I suggested, finding my voice again. "I'm the bait you need. Send Juliette back to San Diego as a peace offering, and you'll only have to worry about Anastasia instead of the whole House."

"Why would the House care about someone who is unaffiliated?" asked one of the wolves next to Juliette.

"San Diego's a small town. Everyone knows everyone." I swallowed. "Let her go and I'll make sure they don't make any trouble for you."

"This is not a mediation, and we are not your clients, human." Ezekiel waved a massive hand, dismissing me like yesterday's news, and turned to the man in the suit. "Why are you still here, Chase?"

"It will be as you said, Alpha." Chase bowed again, but his features were carved from granite. "I will see to it myself."

I went to speak again, but Hyacinth's hand clamped down on my shoulder, the pressure almost enough to send me to my knees.

"And the beer?"

"Domestic only, Alpha."

"I can always count on you," purred Ezekiel. "Make it so."

CHAPTER 14
IN WHICH THE WORM THAT TURNS
IS A WOLF

The double doors boomed shut behind us as Chase and the other two wolves dragged Juliette down the hall, Hyacinth pushing me along behind them. We stopped at what appeared to be the basement level's main intersection.

"Chase," said Hyacinth, her voice low.

"Yeah, I know." He turned to the two male wolves accompanying us. "Guillermo, the alpha's beer is in the main kitchen on the primary floor. Go retrieve a few cases for the war council. Nothing light and nothing foreign. Morgan and I have this vampire handled."

"You got it." Guillermo left, moving lightly for someone his size.

"And now there's just three of you," slurred Juliette. "Which of you thinks they're man enough to finish the job?"

"Be silent, vampire."

"You, in your pretty little suit?" She shook her head as best as she could in the tight metal collar. "Nah, I'm pretty sure Ezekiel has your balls in his pocket. Better leave the *real* work to someone who's still got the stones."

Chase ignored the comment, turning to Hyacinth. "The council will likely continue into the early hours of the morning, but Ezekiel will summon the squads a few hours after sunrise. See that you are present."

"Not a problem," said the wolf at my side.

"Nine o'clock. Don't be late."

"When am I ever?" The two traded serious, if incomprehensible, glances, and then Morgan and Chase started to drag Juliette away.

Naked, weaponless, and lacking my access to Lucia's power, I had no chance whatsoever against three werewolves—assuming Chase was a wolf like the others—but if they planned to use me as bait, it meant they didn't dare kill me. As the others turned to go, I threw my head back at Hyacinth to clear some space and then charged the suit-clad man in front of me.

That was the plan anyway. The problem was Hyacinth didn't even stumble… she just took my headbutt and stood firm. As I tried to push forward, she wrapped me up in both arms and lifted me into the air like a struggling kitten.

"Be calm," she hissed into my ears.

Shockingly, I chose *not* to listen. My arms were pinned to my side, but my legs were free; I kicked back with a heel, aiming for a knee or something vulnerable, but finding only air as she swung me about.

"Juliette!"

The femmepire was struggling between the two wolves dragging her, but between her injuries and a clearly overwhelming size and strength disparity, she was faring even worse than I was. She tried turning to look back at me, but the collar didn't allow it.

"Stay alive, little bird," she croaked. "And tell Angel…"

I finally gave up my futile attempts to escape from Hyacinth's grip, going limp in the werewolf's arms. "I will."

There were a dozen more things to say but it was too late for any of them. The wolves hadn't even slowed their stride, and just like that, Juliette was out of sight.

Hyacinth didn't even give me a minute to grieve. "Are you going to behave, or am I going to have to carry you?"

"Go to hell."

"I'm pretty sure I'm already there." She didn't ask a second time, carrying me through the corridor like I was a baby. We soon found ourselves back at my cell, but instead of opening that door, Hyacinth kept on going, winding her way to a small flight of stairs leading up. The werewolf dropped me to the hard ground and knelt over me.

"I take it I'm not going to live long enough to be bait?" All the fear had left me. All I could see in my mind was Juliette being dragged away to her horrible fate.

"There's no time for fishing." I was trying to puzzle my way through her words when the handcuffs around my wrists came free. "Is it true what they say about you, mediator?"

I rubbed my wrists, confused. "I don't know what you mean."

"That you can talk a robin out of her eggs? Because so far, I just don't see it."

"I'm good at my job," I said, mildly overstating things.

"You have to be better than just good." She tugged me back to my feet and up the stairs. There, Ezra was waiting with a bundle of clothes I recognized as mine. Hyacinth passed them over. "Get dressed. We don't have a lot of time."

"What's going on?" asked Ezra.

"Boss just decided to invade Phoenix."

"Shit. We're moving on to Plan B, I take it?"

"More like Plan F. Three guesses what the F stands for."

"What's Plan F?" I wanted to know.

"You are. We're taking you to Phoenix tonight and you're going to negotiate for Audrey's release."

"And why would I do that?"

"You just met Ezekiel." The pair flanked me as they escorted me through the largely deserted wing of the building. As far as I could tell, the pack was squatting in an abandoned office building of some kind. "What was your impression of him?"

"He's a few years past his expiration date."

"Exactly. Georgie was supposed to have succeeded him by now, and Ezekiel would have been free to give his life for the pack, as tradition demands. Unfortunately, your *girlfriend* screwed all of that up. And now, he gets worse by the day."

"Why keep following him then?"

"Because his heir isn't ready yet. A few of us are doing what we can to keep things from going completely off the rails, but we need her here to help."

"Audrey?"

"Yeah. She's only fifteen, but Ezekiel listens to her. With Georgie dead and Jason banished, she's the only family he has left."

For the first time since waking up, I felt a small glimmer of hope. "I'm not lifting a finger if Juliette dies."

"She'll be fine, provided we get Audrey back in time. Chase is part of our coalition."

"And Shae?"

"Not so much. Some wolves enjoy the freedom Ezekiel gives them in his dotage. Blood has its allure. Still, Chase will take care of Morgan and get your fanger somewhere safe."

"Are you sure about this play, Hy?" asked Ezra.

"The first thing Audrey's captors will do when the squads roll into town tomorrow is kill her. I'm not going to watch the pack tear itself to pieces. This is our only option."

I frowned. "So, I sweet talk some people into letting a werewolf princess go, she helps calm down her crazy uncle, and then…?"

"You two will be free to go. And we'll return to our hunting grounds where we belong."

"You're only out here at all because of Audrey," I realized.

"Yeah. She was doing a school tour of ASU with friends two days ago. One of them saw her get taken and spread the word to our ears and eyes in the state."

That clarified some things, including why the whole operation seemed so hastily thrown together, but there were a *lot* of questions that still needed answering. Unfortunately, we'd already reached an exterior door. Ezra cracked that door open and looked out.

"We're golden," he said.

I wasn't sure how long I'd been unconscious for, but it was pitch-black out as I followed the werewolves across the empty back lot. A line of bikes stood a few hundred feet away.

"You could have just asked me for help back in the diner. And skipped a kidnapping and—" I trailed off. If I knew Juliette, these wolves had just made an enemy for life, but saying so didn't seem wise.

"Maybe we would have if you'd told us who you were then and there. But as soon as your picture got flagged, Ezekiel was notified. I had to take you in."

"And now you're letting me go."

"No, now I'm using you to solve a problem." She shook her head. "Audrey's the future of this pack. Ezekiel putting her at risk to satisfy his need for blood left me no other choice."

For once, it wasn't a coup. Or at least, it wasn't one *yet*. As long as an increasingly insane wolf remained in charge, a violent rebellion seemed almost inevitable. Still, that wasn't my problem. If I could recover this Audrey, I'd happily leave the pack to their own politics. A surprise mediation wasn't *ideal*, but it beat the hell out of Juliette dying and me being used as bait to lure Ana into a trap.

And speaking of Juliette…

"I don't work alone."

"That's good to hear, because Ezra and I are coming with you." Hyacinth's bike was the kind of motorcycle that gave other motorcycles self-esteem issues… a chrome and leather behemoth that probably cost as much as most cars. She ran one hand almost lovingly down its quilted seat.

"I was talking about Juliette. She's my partner."

Ezra frowned. "I thought you were dating the other bloodsucker?"

"I mean *business* partner." I really needed to start clarifying that up front.

"Oh."

"You're going to have to do this one without her," said Hyacinth, tossing me the helmet that had been dangling from her bike's handlebars. "I'm sure you're trustworthy and all that, *Ziggy*, but the fewer potential complications we have in the field, the better, and that girl is a walking complication."

She wasn't wrong, but hell if I was going to just accept that.

"I'm not helping you until I know Juliette is safe."

For the first time since she'd freed me, Hyacinth let the wolf shine through her eyes. "Y'all are starting to annoy me, Mr. Smith."

"It's a gift." I met her eyes and didn't look away. She could kill me as easily as breathing, but I'd stood toe to toe with a lot worse over the past few years. "Put yourself in my shoes. You don't trust me, but I don't trust you either. *Prove* that she's still alive."

"We gotta go, Hy," said Ezra. "Longer we wait…"

"Fine." The other werewolf glared at me as she pulled out her phone and tapped in a quick number. "Chase, put her on. The mediator wants to know she's alive."

"John?"

"Duchess?" I felt a huge weight lift just from hearing her voice. "Are you okay?"

"I'm hungry, I'm hurting, I'm a prisoner, and this walking insurance salesman won't tell me what's going on. So, just another day as your partner." Chase said something in the background and Juliette answered. "*Business* partner, asshole. How about you, little bird?"

"I'm not naked anymore, so things are looking up. I'll give you two guesses as to what we landed ourselves in."

She only needed one.

"Pack power struggle?"

"Kind of. I'm going to help get Audrey out before Ezekiel and the others turn Phoenix into a war zone. After that, we'll be free to go."

"So that we can get kidnapped and held prisoner by whoever or whatever's next, no doubt."

"Every day's an adventure." I couldn't help but grin. She sounded better than she had even ten minutes earlier, which suggested Chase was treating her okay. We were both alive, and we had a path forward. And with Phoenix a reasonably short ride away, we might even be done and back on the road again by the morning.

After all, I had a timetable to keep.

"Try to get some sleep," I suggested to Juliette. "And keep an eye out for any other wolves. The last thing we need is Shae or her flunkies paying you another visit."

"You know that sleeping and keeping an eye out are mutually exclusive, right?" There was another conversation on their end of the line. "Insurance Boy says we're out of the way and should be safe for now."

"Until someone notices he and Morgan are missing," muttered Ezra.

"By then we'll be back with Audrey," said Hyacinth. And if it sounded like she was trying to convince herself, well, I couldn't blame her. "But we need to go. Now."

"Stay frosty, Juliette."

"Don't do anything dumber than usual."

Hyacinth ended the call and shot me a look. "Well?"

"Congratulations; you just bought yourself a mediator."

Both werewolves just looked blankly at me for a second, and I sighed. Honestly, it had sounded cooler in my head.

ooo

We made it almost three blocks before my bladder reminded me of its existence, and the sense of impending doom returned in an entirely new fashion. It took another half-block before I was finally able to both get Hyacinth's attention and explain through gestures what the problem was.

I couldn't hear whatever she was muttering as we pulled back off to the side of the road, but I didn't think it was complimentary. Ezra, riding solo on the bike behind us, just shook his head, and kept his thoughts to himself.

One incredibly satisfying minute later, I returned to find Hyacinth waiting with Handi Wipes, and twenty somewhat less satisfying but far more sanitary seconds after that, we were back on the road.

I spent most of the ride to Phoenix trying to plan for a situation I knew almost nothing about. Neither wolf had told me exactly who had captured their princess, and I didn't have my phone with Ana's notes to at least review what threats the city held outside of Kevin the Fungus. Still, if I was understanding Chase's coded messages from earlier, we needed to be back with Audrey before nine in the morning. There was time for me to be briefed in Phoenix. The bigger problem was the negotiation itself. I hadn't ever had a mediation take less than a couple of weeks; a couple of hours might be pushing even my fabled skills past their limit.

Finally, I shrugged and tried to relax into the ride. I'd never tell Juliette, but Hyacinth's Harley was a hell of a lot more comfortable than the Ducati. I wasn't quite so wedged in, either, to our no doubt mutual relief.

The 87 wasn't much less busy than when we'd come north on it, but the two wolves wove from one lane to another and then back again, carving up what traffic there was like a Thanksgiving turkey. As much as I loved my Corolla, for reasons that needed absolutely no enumeration, there was something exhilarating about being on a motorcycle. It would have probably been even better if I'd been in the driver's seat, but riding bitch meant all I had to do was hold on, and I didn't hate the lack of effort that required.

Hell, I didn't even have to navigate.

I didn't have my watch *or* my wonderphone to tell time with, but I thought it was an hour or two later—and at least twenty minutes after we hit Phoenix itself—when Hyacinth finally pulled off onto a local side street. The buildings around us seemed to be mostly residential… a mixture of apartments and single-story ranch homes.

I looked for a sign that said "Werewolf prisoner here" but found nothing, so I pulled off my helmet and turned to Hyacinth instead.

"*This* is where she's being kept?"

"Of course not. We're parking here and walking the rest of the way. No point in spooking them before you can do your thing."

Do my thing was a new mediation euphemism, but I let it go. If I was holding a werewolf hostage, I'd probably be listening for the sound of her biker gang family's motorcycles too.

"I think it's time you finally told me what we're up against. Skinwalkers? Elven eco-terrorists? Chupacabras?"

Admittedly, I threw the last one in more out of hope than expectation. I'd always wanted to meet a chupacabra. Caleb Van Stahl taking that mediation had been the closest thing to a wrinkle in our burgeoning bromance until someone killed him.

Ezra stayed impassive, but Hyacinth shook her head.

"Crap," I said. "It's not Kevin, is it?"

"Who is Kevin?"

"The Phoenix Fungus among us. Twenty-two consonants and one y, so everyone just calls it Kevin," I told her, acting like I hadn't just found all that out less than twelve hours earlier.

"How would a fungus ambush and kidnap anyone?" asked Ezra.

"Spores, I think."

"It's not… *Kevin*," growled Hyacinth. "Audrey's captors aren't supernatural at all."

I blinked. "Wait, what? She was taken by humans? How? Why?"

"Maybe you can ask them that when you negotiate her release. Scouts on the scene tracked the scent back to a safehouse, but the humans had it locked down tighter than a drum. Guns, reinforced steel doors, the works. All we got was a few snippets of conversation and a name."

"One Life," added Ezra. "Ever hear of them?"

They sounded like a health and wellness company; I started to shake my head and then paused. Actually, I *had* heard it before… just not in English.

"Vita Unica?"

"Gesundheit," said Hyacinth.

"What? No… that's their name in Italian."

"So, you *do* know them?"

"Yeah."

Just enough to know that we were screwed.

CHAPTER 15

"**I**'d have preferred eco-terrorists," I admitted.

"Sounds like the sort of thing someone who never met an elf would say."

There was a story there, but I didn't have time to hear it, no matter how badly I wanted to.

"Vita Unica held me prisoner in Rome. Apparently, it's their thing. Well, that and gathering intel on things that go bump in the night."

"You were their prisoner too? And you talked your way free?" Hyacinth looked almost impressed.

"Actually, no. A bus-sized roach crashed the party and killed everyone. I made my escape in the chaos."

"They all died?"

"Yeah."

"That's not ideal."

"From what I know, they work in cells, so hopefully my part in all of that never came to light. Regardless, these guys are fanatics… conspiracy theorists who looked out their window one night and discovered that all their nightmares were true. I don't think they're going to want to negotiate. From what I've read, they don't think of supernaturals as anything but vermin."

"That's the sort of perspective to get someone dead." Hyacinth chewed on a finger. "What do they want then?"

It was a weird feeling being *more* informed than someone else, but I had Ana to thank for that. "From what I've been told, some cells focus on gathering evidence to eventually expose your world, while the rest…"

"Yeah?"

"They're more about figuring out how to take you all out in the war that would follow. Whichever type this cell is, they probably won't have killed Audrey yet, but…"

"But they will eventually. And in the meantime, they might be doing anything to her."

"Yeah. Turns out you guys don't have a monopoly on treating prisoners like shit."

Ezra, at least, had the grace to look vaguely ashamed. Either that or he'd swallowed a bug on the ride into Phoenix.

Hyacinth, on the other hand, stayed laser focused on the problem. "So, how are you going to convince them to release Audrey?"

"I don't think negotiation works with fanatics."

"Think of something! We didn't bust you out of prison and put our own asses on the line for nothing, human."

Someday, when I was old and gray—assuming I ever lived to be old and gray—I would write my memoirs, and those memoirs would include a chapter on just how quickly other species turned to calling me *human* once things went poorly.

Then again, I was thinking of my forced companions as *wolves* practically every step of the way. Maybe this was one glass house that didn't need rocks being thrown at or from it.

"Let's scope out the place they're keeping her," I suggested. "Maybe we can figure something out."

Hyacinth pushed back the sleeve of her motorcycle jacket and checked her watch. "It's a little after one in the morning. Assume it'll take two hours to get back to Payson if nobody needs to stop and take a piss along the way. That means—"

"Six hours, yeah. I can do the math." Basic math, anyway. Anything else would require my wonderphone which, much like my Corolla, was a long way away right now. "So, maybe we should get moving? Besides, standing around in the alley behind an apartment building like this is like holding up a neon sign saying we're up to no good."

"It's one in the morning on a Thursday," said Hyacinth. "Nobody on the streets right now is up to any good."

Ezra just grunted.

Ten minutes later, we were tucked behind a dilapidated building and looking down a long street at our target, another apartment complex that looked like it had been abandoned sometime before most of its units' windows had been broken. The neighborhood had worsened the further we walked, and either the area had a problem with cars backfiring repeatedly or there'd been at least two shootings along the way. Even as someone who rented office space in Logan Heights, I found myself unexpectedly relieved to have two werewolves at my side.

"I'm not sure the authorities would care if your pack *did* roll right into town and tear this place apart."

"The police aren't the problem. One Life killing Audrey the moment the battle starts is the problem."

"And you're sure she's still in there?"

Hyacinth tapped her nose. "Like I said, one of our scouts followed the scent trail."

"Yeah, but how many hours ago was that?"

She and Ezra exchanged a look and the big man sighed. He passed her his vest and then his body shifted and condensed, the rest of his clothing dropping to the dirty concrete as if passing through mist. Moments later, an oversized wolf sat before us, black-furred, with a patch of gray along one flank. Other than its size, only the eyes suggested it was anything other than a normal wolf; they were bone white and cold as the Pacific.

I shivered under that inhuman gaze, and then Ezra was gone, blending easily into the shadows, moving silently through the urban wasteland.

"Have you all thought of just… sneaking up on them and taking them out, one by one?"

"Spoken like someone dating an executioner. We're warriors, not assassins." Hyacinth shrugged away the look I sent her. "Okay, yeah, we thought about it. Problem is, there's at least three layers of security." She pointed first to the ground floor, where a few shapes could be seen loitering around the building's exterior, then the second floor, and finally across the street to the rooftop of a boarded-up building. "Add in the cameras there, there, and there, and not even the Stone Lady could crack this particular nut without an alarm being raised."

I resisted the urge to defend Anastasia's efficiency. This wasn't the time, and a pack she'd already practically decapitated wouldn't want to hear it anyway.

"How many exits are there?" I asked instead.

"Four aboveground, if you include the fire escapes."

I raised an eyebrow. "There's something below?"

"A basement, we think."

That was weird enough. San Diego didn't have a lot of basements, and not just because of all the fault lines and flooding. "You think there's an escape route down there?"

"Maybe? For a city built on caliche, Phoenix has a surprising number of tunnels under it, holdovers from some colony of burrowers that lived here up until last century, I think. A lot of those entrances have been buried or forgotten, but…"

"But it would explain why One Life chose this building to be their base of operations."

"It sure as hell wasn't the view."

"Or the ambiance."

"I won't tell your fanger girl you're talking French to me if you don't, mediator. It can be our little secret."

I didn't have anything to say to *that*. Thankfully, a wolf big enough to ride manifested out of the shadowed alleyway directly in front of me and I could instead put my focus into being thankful I'd already voided my bladder. Something that big should *not* be so stealthy.

Wolves didn't care quite as much about nudity as I did, but I still turned around, giving Ezra his privacy to shift back and get dressed. When he was done, I turned about and leaned in to hear the word.

"Scent is still strong," he said. "Trail leads in, but not out. I'm guessing they have her down below."

"Makes sense," I said. "With the aboveground windows mostly broken, there's not much to muffle sound. If you're going to experiment on someone, you don't want their screams to carry."

Both wolves stared at me.

"That sounds like personal experience," said Hyacinth, about ten seconds after the silence had gotten truly awkward.

"Like I told you back in Payson, you guys weren't the first to kidnap and imprison me. It's been a rough few years."

"That explains the scars."

I swallowed. I'd somehow forgotten she'd seen me naked. "You should have seen the other guy."

Thankfully, she didn't follow that up with a question. I wasn't in the mood to talk about Zorana, especially with Anastasia no doubt out hunting her even now.

"So, we know she's in there," I said, clearing my throat for no reason whatsoever. "And our chances of sneaking in undetected are…?" I glanced to Ezra for confirmation.

"Nil. I caught the scent of several dozen people and plenty of guns."

"That many people means they need a lot of food and drink." I frowned. "We could ambush whoever they send for supplies? Maybe get them to smuggle us inside?"

"I don't think that works outside of video games," said Hyacinth, "and we don't have time to wait for a supply run that may never happen anyway."

"What about a fire?" suggested Ezra. "Whole block goes up in flames, it'd force them to evacuate."

Hyacinth shook her head again. "We don't know if they'd bring Audrey with them or just cut their losses and kill her on their way out."

"We can find the tunnel and come in that way," I suggested.

"It'll be guarded too. And we won't have any room to maneuver down there."

"Do *you* have any suggestions?" I asked.

"Yeah: we stick with the original plan. You go in and negotiate. That's what you're here for."

"With all due respect—"

"I don't want to hear it. Y'all got five and half hours. Figure this shit out."

"Maybe we could gas the place?" mused Ezra.

"Ezra, I love you like a brother from another mother, but if you don't have anything useful to say, kindly shut the f—"

"That's brilliant!" I said.

"What?" Hyacinth scowled as she turned on me. "No, it's not. We don't have anything to gas them with, and this place hasn't been hooked up to any external lines in years, maybe decades. Besides, most of the windows don't have any glass left. Any sort of gas leak is going to dissipate before it can have an impact."

"The windows above ground are all busted," I agreed, "but the basement's a whole different story."

"So, you want to find an access point to the tunnels, a route through those tunnels, *and* a handy supply of knockout gas? In five hours?"

"Five and a half," I reminded her, grinning for the first time in far too long. "And I've got something better in mind than knockout gas."

"Like what?" asked Ezra to my delight.

"Spores, my dude. Spores."

It had occurred to me, when Hyacinth mentioned tunnels and Ezra suggested gassing the enemy, that there was an entity who both lived belowground and, per Juliette, *farted hallucinations*. Kevin was potentially the solution to both of our biggest problems… finding our way to One Life's presumed escape tunnel and incapacitating those inside for long enough that we could free Audrey and get away.

Of course, that introduced a third problem: finding Kevin.

"Two hours," said Hyacinth, who'd been rubbing her bald head angrily ever since I dropped my latest brilliant plan on her. "If we don't find him or it or whatever in two hours, we're coming back here and going with Plan M."

Unlike Ezra, I didn't have to ask what the M stood for.

"Deal."

"So, where do we start?"

I frowned. The truth was, I had no idea. Kevin lived underground—insofar as a network of fungus lived at all—but beyond that, all I knew for sure was that it had spread under Tempe and ASU at some point in the past few decades.

"Tempe's not that far to the east," said Ezra. "Should we ride over and just… uh… look for accessible drains or something?"

"You took the words right out of my mouth," I lied. "We need to get underground and we need to find a place where fungus would accumulate. Does Phoenix even have water?"

"We literally crossed the Salt River on our way here."

"Oh." I shrugged at Hyacinth. "I must have missed it in the dark. Still waiting for the latent werewolf virus to reach my eyes, I guess."

"Latent what?" asked Ezra.

"Don't get him started. Anyway, it's more a riverbed than anything. Barely a trickle of water in it, especially this time of year."

"More homeless encampments than there is water," agreed the other wolf. "Except near the lake."

"There's a lake?"

"Tempe Town Lake. It's man-made, but if you want water, that's the place to go."

"Huh. Did you live here once or something?"

He shook his head. "Nah, but I was bitten instead of born. Had a few friends from summer camp who lived down here before we lost contact after uh… well, my change."

It was weird thinking about the bruiser werewolf who'd helped capture Juliette and me having a childhood at all, let alone a childhood where he'd been human. Clearly, I'd been spending too much time with vampires who, despite the legends, had never been human to begin with.

"Sounds like we're headed to the lake," I decided. "Then we can park, follow the riverbed, and look for a way underground."

"One hour, fifty-seven minutes," said Hyacinth.

I really didn't need the reminder.

ooo

Finding the lake was easy. In fact, it was basically part of the Salt River that had been dammed off to form a reservoir. There was a bike path and walking trail ringing the whole thing, but what I didn't see were storm drains or tunnels large enough for us to enter. So, instead we started working our way west along the riverbed. It was bizarre, even in the dead hours of the morning, to go from a vibrant, almost lush reservoir to the dry riverbed I associated with desert living. It was even stranger to see the homeless tent cities flanking the barely-there river, just a few hundred yards from a lake that seemed intended to be a tourist attraction.

Those tents did, however, give me an idea. I made my way to the closest campfire and the handful of still-awake people huddled about it, motioning to Ezra and Hyacinth to stay back. If my experiences with Dale, the man who squatted outside my office, had taught me anything, it was that intimidation tactics, even unintentional ones, had a tendency to backfire.

"Hey dudes," I said, hands open and spread as I stopped a good ten feet from their fire. "I was wondering if you—"

"Screw off!" barked a gaunt shadow, not even looking up from the fire that barely illuminated his features. "Don't need no Jesus, don't want none neither."

"I'm not part of a church."

"Don't want no handouts neither."

"I hear you. I'm not offering help, I'm asking for it."

"Pshaw! We look like a bunch of suckers to you?"

I gave it a moment, but none of the others at the fire said a word, content to let Mr. Unfriendly be their spokesperson. This was one of those times where Juliette would have *really* come in handy. "Fair enough. I'll ask at the next camp."

I was halfway back to the two wolves and doing my best not to stumble over the unfamiliar terrain, when someone small melted out of the shadows in front of me, preceded by a smell that was half body odor and half cigarette smoke.

"You trying to buy drugs, hoss?" asked a voice that was somehow simultaneously deep and reedy.

"No."

"You selling then?"

"Sorry, dude. No drugs here."

"Good. Because we don't need that shit."

That was… unexpected, but I was cool with it. "Maybe you can help me out?"

"You or the two wolves hanging out over there, trying to look inconspicuous?"

Now *that* got my attention. "They're with me. Can I ask who you are? And maybe what?"

"Just a guy who took a dance on the other side of death, y'know?"

I really, really didn't.

"Well, I'm glad you made it back."

"You and me both." He stepped closer, but we were far enough from the fire that I didn't get much more than an impression of long, dark hair and a hooked nose. "As for a name? Names have power. You should know that better than anyone. But I guess you can call me Coyote."

"As in the god? The trickster?" I tensed. I'd had exactly one experience with a god of the non-demi variety and it hadn't gone very well.

"Nah man, it's just a name. He's more like a patron whatchamacallit. What's the word?"

"Saint?"

His bark of a laugh turned into a cough, and I could hear spittle hitting the dried soil around us. "Shit, way I hear it, Coyote's not a saint and neither am I."

"Fair enough." Hyacinth didn't move, twenty feet away in the darkness, but I could practically *feel* her growing impatience. Time was running short. "Well, it's nice to meet you, Coyote."

"Gotta lift my tail if you want to blow smoke up my ass, wey."

"Right." There was no way to build up to it, and talking around the issue wasn't doing me any good, so I decided to just go with the basics. "We're looking for Kevin."

"Tall bastard with great hair, a smile nobody should trust, and a truckload of used Magic the Gathering cards? Because I've never heard of him."

"Not that Kevin. The intelligent fungus living under this city."

"Ohhhh. You mean—" He rattled off the chain of consonants effortlessly, like he'd been doing it all his life. "Yeah, we've met. What do you need to see it for?"

"We need his—its—help rescuing a girl."

Coyote grunted and then said nothing else for way too long. "Kevin's pretty far out, you know?"

"Physically?"

"Spiritually. I don't know if it's the sort of creature that does the real prosaic shit like rescues."

"I'm hoping to change that, if you can help me find him. It."

"What's in it for me if I do?"

I didn't have a great answer for that, considering the only thing I had on me were the clothes I'd been kidnapped in. "What do you want?"

"Not drugs."

"Yeah, I got that part."

"I'm not gonna ask for a favor neither. That shit always goes wrong somehow."

Coyote was smarter than he seemed.

"I don't have any money on me, but…"

"Who needs money when you've got the mysteries of the universe camping out behind your eyelids, am I right?"

"Uh, right."

"I *am* hungry though. Think one of your furry friendsters over there wants to spring for some poke?"

I knew both Hyacinth and Ezra could hear Coyote just fine, but they left it to me to respond.

"We buy you a poke bowl, you take us to Kevin?"

"Is Venus making itself felt in your pants today?"

"I mean… it *is* a Thursday."

"Then you got yourself a deal."

CHAPTER 16
IN WHICH THERE ARE MILES TO GO
BEFORE ANYONE SLEEPS

Tempe had a surprising number of eateries still open at two in the morning on a Thursday. The place Coyote directed us to was called Shade Park and nice enough that I worried about whether they'd have a *no shirt, no shoes, no service* policy. Thankfully, we didn't have to find out... they offered takeout, so Ezra went in to order while the rest of us waited outside.

Once Coyote got his poke bowl, he sat down there on the curb and went to town on it, paying the rest of us no attention at all. Ezra kept an eye on the man, while I joined a visibly impatient Hyacinth at the corner.

"Are you gonna make it?" she wanted to know. "You look dead on your feet."

"I had to mediate for goblins under the Pacific before we left San Diego, so I didn't get a ton of sleep the night before last. And then today..."

"Yeah."

We watched Coyote eat for a few minutes.

"We're running out of time," she reminded me.

"If he can get us to Kevin, it'll save us hours of wandering around on our own."

"If we can't find the fungus and convince it to help us, we're going with Ezra's fire plan."

"Okay." I turned from the skinny, shirtless man chowing down on his bowl of raw fish to people-watch the college students passing us by in search of late-night munchies. When even that had gotten old, I turned back to the wolf. "We'll be fine. I may not be able to negotiate with humancentric fanatics, but Kevin won't even be my first vegetable."

"I'm not sure fungus is a vegetable."

"I'm not sure Bill is either." I shrugged. "Either way, this is going to work."

"It had better."

Maybe it was the encroaching sleepiness, but I couldn't resist asking: "Once Audrey is free, are you *really* going to let Juliette and me go?"

She shot me a look. "If I was planning to betray you, why would I admit it before Audrey's safe?"

"Good morals?"

"You're an odd man, mediator."

"I get that a lot. And it's okay to just call me John."

"Okay then. The fact is, Georgie broke the Concordat. I won't deny it chaps my ass that we have to live by rules set down in a foreign country by beings I'll never even meet, but the law's the law. Your fanger girlfriend was in her rights to do what she did, legally speaking, and the fact that we never saw her coming or even found actionable evidence of her involvement is one part scary and two parts impressive."

"Impressive is a great adjective for her."

"What I'm saying is that I, personally, don't care about getting revenge on your girlfriend, let alone you or Spunky Brewster."

"Spunky who—?"

"Your business partner."

I eyed the wolf. If I had to guess, I'd have put her around twenty-two or twenty-three. "You're way too young to be making Punky Brewster references. Hell, *I'm* almost too young for it."

"When this is over, I might introduce you to something magical called basic cable reruns, John."

I nodded to acknowledge the point.

"Anyway, if you help Audrey get out of this alive, Ezra and I will do everything in our power to make sure that you do too. Does that settle your nerves?"

"It helps, yeah."

"Good. We have enough on our plate without all of us worrying about getting stabbed in the back." She raised her voice. "Hey, song dog! Hurry up with your bowl."

Coyote ducked his head deeper into his poke.

"Song dog?"

"Never heard that one before? Maybe it's a New Mexico thing."

Five minutes later, Coyote was done with his food, and a minute or two after that, he'd polished off the extra-large Coke he'd talked us into buying with it. We returned to the bikes and followed his directions west.

Instead of going back to the river like I'd planned, he led us to an industrial park and then to the back of one of that park's gray concrete buildings. At two in the morning, we were the only people in sight. The rear door was locked, but he pushed a few numbers into the analogue keypad, and moments later, we were inside.

"How'd you get the combo?" I asked.

"I've seen some things, you know?"

Fair enough.

We followed him down a mundane hallway and into the stairwell near the rear door, but there were no stairs leading down like I'd expected. In fact, the posted evacuation map only showed three floors, all of them above ground.

"Isn't Kevin below ground?"

"Above… below… you really gotta broaden your mind, brother." Instead of climbing the stairs, Coyote went to the shadowed corner under them and leaned his weight on the wall. There was an audible click and that wall swung open.

"Original builder was part of the local freedom militia," he told us as we joined him. "Decided to include a bolt hole for weapons and ammo storage."

"I thought Arizona was an open-carry state?"

"For firearms, yeah. Less so for RPGs, anti-tank weapons, and the kind of explosives that can bring down a building." He laughed at whatever he saw in my face, crooked teeth yellow in the dim interior lighting. "Don't worry; all that shit got cleared out when the militia went on the run. Turns out the Feds aren't as dumb as they look on TV. Now, it's just a cubby hole nobody even remembers, but it has a backdoor exit onto the tunnels you're looking for."

The storage room was entirely empty. Empty and small, its air quickly filled with the dual fragrances of Coyote's smell and the wolves' leather. None of the walls were finished, but the one the other man led us to was crude stone.

"In you go," said Coyote, motioning to an almost invisible passage in that far wall. "This'll get you to the tunnel systems."

Alarm bells went off in my head.

"You're not coming with us?"

"Nah man. *Kevin* and I ain't seeing eye to eye as of late. Different cosmic views, if you get what I'm saying. Won't be hard to find it once you're in there though. Good luck." Without another word, he darted past us for the exit.

"Ezra!" Hyacinth's unvoiced command sent the other wolf after our squirter. Even though he'd only been a handful of steps behind Coyote, it was several minutes before he returned; he came back empty-handed and shaking his head.

"Gone. I couldn't even find a scent trail."

"Goddamn mystics," growled Hyacinth.

Huh. I'd read about mystics. Like witches, they were humans who had found their way to some small connection with a mystical power. However, in lieu of grimoires, rituals, and spells, that power seemed to alter a mystic's perceptions. Second sight, fortune telling… if it was something you could imagine being offered from a tent in a run-down carnival, it was probably a mystic instead of a witch.

How any of that allowed Coyote to somehow outrun a freaking werewolf was a question for later. Or for never, depending on how the next few hours went.

In the meantime, we had a fungus to find and chat with.

I stopped Hyacinth before she could squeeze through into the tunnels. "Do either of you have a phone?"

"It's 2015. Of course we do."

I tried not to let the absence of my wonderphone make me bitter. With the various gods and demigods of the universe as my witness, I swore a solemn vow that it, the Corolla, and I would soon be reunited. "Can you turn on the flashlight then? Some of us don't see that well in the dark."

"Seems like you're doing just fine," said Ezra.

"Better than most," agreed the other wolf.

"Latent werewolf virus," I explained again, ignoring that I had only just told them it hadn't reached my eyes yet. There were times I genuinely had no idea what the hell was going on with my body. Thankfully, there was almost always something more interesting to focus on, like food, or Ana, or underground passages to tunnel networks that weren't supposed to exist under Phoenix.

Hyacinth and Ezra traded glances I could barely see, and then the bigger wolf pulled out his phone and clicked on the flashlight. My earlier impressions of the now-empty explosives room had been more or less accurate. The path down was little more than a crack, narrow enough that we'd have to turn sideways to slide through. Ezra's light showed the pathway traveled for at least a dozen feet before it took a hard right turn. If Coyote was to be believed, it would eventually open into the tunnel system we'd been searching for.

And if he was lying, whoever went in first might just find themselves wedged in between rough stone, effectively entombed beneath the building's foundation.

"I smell earth and vegetation," said Hyacinth after a long moment. "Maybe the mystic didn't screw us after all."

"We did get him his poke." It hadn't been my finest negotiation, especially given the dude had ghosted us already, but it was still a long way from my worst.

"I'll go first," she decided, "and call back up when I've made it. You'll be second, John, then Ezra. Try not to tear yourselves up on the way through. No idea what else might be living in these tunnels that could be attracted by the smell of blood."

And just like that, I had something new to worry about.

Hyacinth wasn't a small woman, especially in her leather, but she navigated the interior of the passageway far more easily than the hulking Ezra or my slightly fluffy self were likely to do. A minute or so later, her voice echoed back up to us.

"Did that sound more like *Hey guys, I made it, you should come down* or *Oh no, there's an army of flesh-eating toxic slimes here; run away and save yourselves?*" I asked Ezra.

He just gave me a look. A hand in my back propelled me towards the moderately hidden passage.

I was about four inches taller than Hyacinth, and at least fifty pounds heavier. I also still had a bit of a gut, even if the training efforts of Kayla and Anastasia had shrunk that down to a size I barely remembered from my early twenties. In short, I was not at all confident about my ability to squeeze through the narrow space.

Sadly, nobody was giving me a choice. I held my breath as I started my approach, then blew it out again as I realized doing so would only expand my body.

The passageway was dark, the light from Ezra's phone mostly blocked by my own bulk as I descended into the depths. The ceiling, at least, was high enough that I didn't have to crouch, and that went a long way to calming my fears of ending up wedged in like the cork in a bottle of wine.

The width of the passageway, however, was another thing entirely. There were no less than three spots where I had to suck in my belly or twist my hips and torso about to squeeze through, and if I didn't leave any blood or tissue on the rocks behind me, I was pretty sure my T-shirt and jeans had gone from pleasantly worn-in, to the kind of distressed that rich kids would pay top dollar for from vintage shops.

When I finally reached the turn, I expected to be plunged into darkness, but there was a strange, soft glow coming from further down the tunnel, pale and ethereal. The path continued to angle downwards, but I could just see part of Hyacinth's silhouette against that light. It was a relief to realize she was only another fifteen or so feet away.

I crossed *spelunker* off my list of potential post-mediation professions.

I made it down to Hyacinth and then turned back to the tunnel I'd just squeezed through. Ezra was a fair bit bigger than I was, at least in the shoulders, and I had no idea how he'd make it through.

The answer was one I'd failed to anticipate:

He cheated.

Moments after I emerged, an enormous wolf did too, dragging a carefully tied bundle of clothes behind it. I turned to give the dude privacy again as he shifted back and got dressed, finally getting my first real look at the tunnel we'd found ourselves in.

Whatever species of underground burrowers had dug it, they'd done a hell of a job. While the walls and floor were mostly covered in lichen, the tunnel was as perfectly round as anything mankind had dug with our machines, and tall enough that Ezra wouldn't be able to touch the ceiling, even wearing Hyacinth's boots. Not that I'd have suggested he try… the source of that soft light was located along the tunnel's ceiling, hundreds, maybe thousands, of whitish filaments dangling down and giving off their own white glow. I couldn't tell if they were fungi, or plant roots, or some bizarre mix of the two, but having them hanging over our heads was making me nervous.

"Are those Kevin?" asked Hyacinth, waving at the tendrils, "Or is it the lichen?"

"I'm not sure." Technically, it could be both. Or neither. "Juliette's the only one of us who's met the uh… guy… before."

"That seems problematic."

"Hey, *I* wanted to bring her with us." I looked at the fungi around and above us, and then turned to the left and the right. The tunnel we'd emerged into extended in both directions, and despite my best hopes, nobody had left any signs or even a mall directory indicating which way we should go. Or where the damn Cinnabon was, for that matter. Still, Juliette had said Kevin had spread *to* Tempe, and that meant it had encompassed more area than just that.

"Kevin?" I asked, raising my voice. "Can you hear us?"

Nothing, other than the echoes of my voice making it back to me, somehow losing all its steely resolve and deep gravitas in the process.

"Juliette Middleton says hi," I added. "She couldn't come with us, but she thought you might be able to help."

"Coyote showed us the way."

Hyacinth and I gave Ezra matching stares.

"What?"

"Dude, can we maybe *not* announce our association with someone the city's underground fungus is on the outs with at the moment?"

"Too late for that," muttered Hyacinth.

"Sorry," said Ezra, shrugging. "It's not like it seems to be listening any—" He stopped as a loud whisper of sound filled the tunnel. It took me a moment to place the noise, but when I did, I looked up.

All those tendrils above us were swaying in a breeze that wasn't there, rubbing against each other to create that susurration.

"Kevin?" I asked again. "Can we talk?"

The whispering didn't stop, but it did lower in volume. Along the center of the tunnel's ceiling, a three-foot wide pathway of tendrils stopped swaying about and instead curled up and inward toward the ceiling. I was struggling to interpret what that meant, when I realized something… they had all curled in the same direction.

"I think it wants us to go that way." I motioned down the left-hand tunnel.

"We should have gone with Ezra's plan," said Hyacinth, so softly I clearly hadn't been meant to hear it.

I decided not to let the creepy tunnel, the creepier vegetation, or the blatant lack of enthusiasm from my captors-turned-possible-allies get me down. This would all just make my inevitable success that much more satisfying, right?

As we walked, the tendrils continued to lead the way like some sort of ceiling-mounted red carpet. Eventually, our tunnel intersected another, and sure enough, the 'carpet' turned into that new tunnel. It would be fair to say I was lost by the third or fourth such turn, but it would also be fair to say I'd been lost shortly after we entered the city. No wonderphone meant no GPS which meant I was mostly just going where the wolves, then Coyote, and now Kevin itself had guided me.

A less confident mediator might have seen that as a metaphor for his entire fratman life to that point, but then, a less confident mediator wouldn't have somehow convinced the woman of his dreams to fall in love with him.

We traveled the tunnels under Phoenix for at least half an hour, Hyacinth's deadline looming more prominently with every step, when our latest tunnel finally ended, opening into a cave system that must have been the nest of the original burrowing species.

Now, it was occupied by Kevin.

CHAPTER 17

IN WHICH COMMUNITY COLLEGE IS WORTH
EVERY PENNY

The enormous cavern's ceiling was a forest of roots and glowing tendrils. The walls and floor were covered with lichen as well as several species of moss that should never have been able to survive desert climates. All that growth glowed: whites, blues, and even reds combining to create an unnatural sunlight a hundred feet below the surface. A narrow path wound its way through the vegetation to a monolith at the cavern's center. A circle of mushrooms ringed the base of the monolith, and more lichen covered the stone. It glowed like a neon sign in Vegas, flickering through a spectrum of colors as we approached.

"Alright, mediator," murmured Hyacinth. "Time for you to talk vegetable."

Apparently, she'd come down on the side of fungus being a vegetable after all.

"Hi," I said to the monolith, "I'm John Smith, the mediator for San Diego."

The mushrooms at the monolith's base swelled suddenly, like balloons that had been filled with water, and then shuddered, an almost invisible wave of *something* spreading out from them and washing over us.

Next to me, Hyacinth and Ezra went still. I turned to find them paralyzed, only shallow breathing and the occasional eye blink to prove that they were alive and not dead.

Well, shit. Maybe my reputation preceded me.

"Whatever you've heard, I promise I'm not here to cause any trouble. For you, I mean."

The lichen on the monolith writhed in a thoroughly disquieting way. It took me a moment to realize it was actually moving, rearranging itself on the rough stone beneath it. First, a three-by-three space on the stone appeared, and then lichen invaded that space in an orderly fashion, coming together to form a speech bubble and words within that bubble.

This was different.

I waited for the words to form, and then read them aloud.

"Why. Can't. You. Hear. Me?" it asked.

I wasn't sure why every word but the last ended in a period, but I wasn't here to debate grammar with a city-sized fungus. "Because you're not saying anything? Or weren't, anyway?"

Again, the lichen reshaped itself into words, and again I read the ensuing message.

"In. Your. Head. You. Do. Not. Hear. Me. And. I. Cannot. Taste. You."

"Oh." I hadn't been exactly sure how Kevin communicated, but as a thought-eater, it did make sense it might be telepathic. "I think it's a combination of latent werewolf virus, broken vampire bond, and something genetic. I can't turn it off, unfortunately."

"This. Interests. Me."

He could join the club. It had also *deeply* interested the Endless Empire's ambassador, Ti An, to the point that she'd tried to buy me from Lucia in Rome. It said something about my deep terror for Ti An that

Kevin's statement of interest was significantly *less* disturbing. "I wish I had more to tell you about it. Outside of the werewolf and vampire bits, I've always been this way, I think. The San Diego House never figured out exactly what it meant, but if I ever learn more, I'm happy to let you know."

"What. Do. You. Want?"

"We need your help. There's a werewolf who has been kidnapped in the city and—"

I stopped. The lichen was already responding, and this message took significantly less time to form.

"No."

"No?"

The lichen just kind of shivered, but the message stayed the same.

"Do you mind, uh, elaborating on why not?"

"I. Am. Present. I. Do. Not. Interfere."

"Like the Watcher from Marvel comics."

"You. Understand."

"Hey, I can respect that. And at least you're not bald." I winced, shooting Hyacinth a look of apology before I remembered she was… well, whatever Kevin had done to her. "But a young woman's life is at stake, and there are a lot of other lives, human and otherwise, that hang in the balance."

"I. Do. Not. Inter—"

"Yeah, yeah, I get it," I said, not waiting for the lichen to finish spelling out *interfere* again. As a successful, if untrained, mediator, I understood that there was a give and take to these discussions. Everything was always a compromise. "Maybe there's something we can do for you in trade?"

"I. Watch." The vegetation around us came to life, tendrils and lichen and moss and mushrooms and every other strange classification of organic matter waving in unison. "I. Listen. Experience. Is. Understanding. Understanding. Is. Bliss. Life. Is."

I puzzled through that, the process made harder by me having to figure out where the sentences truly started and stopped. "So, you don't need anything?"

"No."

"And chaos and bloodshed in your city don't concern you?"

"Life. Is. Death. Is. Life."

I just nodded. In retrospect, it was exactly what I should have expected a fungus to say. I was starting to understand the nature of Kevin and Coyote's disagreements.

Unfortunately, a creature without any charitable instincts who also neither needed nor wanted anything made for a tough negotiation, even by my somewhat lofty standards. I couldn't threaten it, given both my own physical fragility and the shocking reality that my werewolf companions had been paralyzed beyond even their healing abilities to counteract. I couldn't bargain with it because it didn't want anything. I couldn't play on its sensibilities because it didn't seem to have any.

In short, I only had one potential route left to me, and given how long it had been since my single semester in college, it was just as likely to blow up in my face as succeed.

"That's fine," I told Kevin. "As Plato said, the formation of causes and belief systems are left to our individual volitions. If your belief system doesn't include the concept of community, then…"

The speed at which the lichen formed new words suggested I might be on to something.

"You. Know. Plato?"

"I studied his work, yeah," I said, simultaneously shading the truth considerably while being deeply grateful that Kevin didn't have eyes and therefore couldn't see through my notoriously awful poker face. The fact that it could hear my voice and interpret that into actual words was already spooky enough. "But I think what I liked most was his concept of abstract ideals."

That's what I vaguely remembered at least. Something about a cave and how reality was comprised of poor physical representations of the singularly perfect Platonic ideal.

"What. About. Ideals?"

"That they're something to strive for. Human love, for example. It's messy. It's flawed. It sometimes ends with you crying by yourself in an alley because three beers just weren't enough to get over her walking away. But…" I paused. Where had I been going with this? Love. Plato. Ideals. Oh, right. "But it's still something worth pursuing. We strive for the impossible and make this reality a little better in the process."

"I. Do. Not. Know. Love."

"And that's okay! I'm sure asexual reproduction has its own perks too. But you do know community, right?"

There was a long pause.

"Students. And. Faculty. Late. Night. Coffee. Social. Contract."

"Exactly. I believe in the Platonic ideal of community. And that means people help each other. Life is hard enough on its own… it shouldn't have to be experienced alone."

"Nietzsche. Decries. The. Idea. Of. The. Common. Good."

Well, shit. My single semester of Intro to Philosophy hadn't covered more than the basics, like Plato and Aristotle, although the teacher had assigned us Hegel as reading homework. I did vaguely recall a few other names at least.

"And what would Kant say about that?"

It was a genuine question: I had no idea. But given how transgressive people seemed to think at least some of Nietzsche's philosophy had been, I was hoping that, whoever Kant was, he'd disagree.

"The. Categorical. Imperative. Is. Distinctly. Judeo-Christian. In. Its. Formulaics."

"True," I admitted, as if I knew what it was talking about. "And I bet we could stay here all night and bring up different philosophers that agreed and disagreed on all of these points."

"Yes."

"I'm not questioning your belief system, let alone your knowledge. But you *are* part of a community. Part of an ecosystem. And maybe if you were a more involved part of both, you could do more than just be present. You could do more than just listen."

The cavern plunged into darkness, only the lichen on the monolith and the mushrooms around its base still glowing.

"What."

"You could be part of the conversation. Debate philosophy with other students. Speak to more than just the occasional person like me or Coyote who finds their way down here. There's more to life than just being, right?"

"This. What. What."

It was starting to feel like I'd just changed Kevin's religion. And *without* us going to Vegas.

"Is that something you would want?"

"YES."

Thank you, Jesus, I very carefully did not say. The sweat trickling down my back had become a flood, but hell if I wasn't mediating the shit out of this conversation.

"That's good to hear. Really, really good. But community means giving as well as taking, regardless of what Nietzsche had to say on the subject. Help us and we will help you. You have my word as a mediator."

Given what I knew about my predecessor, the Rook, that word wasn't always worth the air used to give it, but I was channeling people like me and my departed brother, Caleb Van Stahl. True, blue, honest mediators who just wanted the best for the world around us. I had no idea how I would be able to even partially integrate Kevin into ASU's student body, but I'd give it my best try.

"How. Can. I. Help?"

"That werewolf I mentioned. Her name is Audrey. She's alone and scared and being held by humans. We think the building housing her has an escape route into your tunnels."

"I. Am. Neither. A. Lover. Nor. A. Fighter."

It sounded like something I would have said before meeting Ana.

"You don't have to be either one."

"Then. What."

I nodded to the frozen wolves flanking me. "I'm told that your spores can cause a variety of effects for those who breathe them in."

"Yes."

I felt a smile slowly spread across my face.

"Then if you don't mind waking my companions back up, I think we've got the beginnings of a plan."

○○○

I wasn't sure if the cavern we'd found the monolith in was Kevin's primary residence or just one of many such spaces sprinkled through the impossible underground network beneath Phoenix, but after an hour traipsing through the tunnels at the fungus philosopher's direction, I was leaning towards the latter. Everywhere we went, we saw more of the creature's body: lichen on the walls, tendrils on the ceiling, even the occasional carpets of moss on the floor, somehow slippery despite the lack of moisture.

New York had its hordes of rats, living in pseudo-symbiosis with the city. Phoenix just had Kevin.

"It's already almost 4," Hyacinth announced grimly, as we trekked through yet another tunnel. She'd been less than amused to realize she and Ezra had both been paralyzed by the fungus' spores, and she'd taken to marching right across the patches of moss we'd found rather than going around it, her heeled motorcycle boots leaving a trail of organic destruction behind her.

As far as I could tell, Kevin hadn't even noticed.

"That still gives us two hours." I looked up at the tendrils above us that were serving as directional signposts. "That should be plenty, right, Kevin?"

The tendrils waved in what I took for general agreement, even if no words were formed anywhere that I could see.

"See?" I gave Hyacinth a look. "We're doing fine."

"And if we reach the building in question and they *don't* actually have an access point to the underground tunnels?"

"Then we'll have wasted a lot of time," I admitted. "But we knew that from the start. And we'll just go to the nearest exit. If it's close enough, maybe the whole spore plan will still work. If not, we always have Plan F."

"The F is for fire," said Ezra.

"We can go with that." I shrugged tiredly under Hyacinth's still-sharp gaze. "If this works, we're golden and Audrey will be as safe as can be. If it doesn't work, we'll still have time to improvise instead. That's the best I can do. If you're not satisfied with the service—"

"Then your partner dies and you serve as bait." She nodded.

"I was going to say you can leave a 1-star review on Yelp, but yeah. Sure. Whatever."

In the past day, I'd nearly died a dozen times before we even made it out of San Diego, thanks to Juliette's *avant-garde* approach to driving. I'd suffered through six-plus hours of obscure punk bands that never even made it out of their parents' garages. I'd been forced to eat my bacon cheeseburger far faster than I would have preferred… only to then still be victimized by a werewolf attack that had added new dents to my Corolla. And I'd just debated philosophy with a city-sized fungus.

Fist-induced naptime notwithstanding, I'd been up for eighteen hours straight, after only getting a few hours of sleep the night before. Worst of all, it felt like I'd been walking for *at least* half that time. I was rapidly hitting the point where threats on my life lost all meaning and even started to gain just a little bit of appeal.

Thankfully, our root tendril nav system soon took us to a small offshoot of a tunnel, maybe twenty feet deep and only four or five wide. Unlike the other tunnels we'd been introduced to over the past few hours, this one was clear of detritus. It also ended in a door, thick and solid.

So far, Kevin had held up its end of the bargain, but that door was a problem. First of all, it was locked. Second, it opened *into* Vita Unica's lair, which put the hinges on the wrong side for us to remove the pins and then the doors entirely. I was pretty sure Hyacinth or Ezra could eventually smash the thing down, but that would alert whoever was inside and put Audrey at risk. And my plans to gas the interior would be severely hampered by that same door blocking the air flow.

In short, it was time for me to save the day once again through the magic of lockpicks and my YouTube-sourced skills.

"I need a tension wrench and a rake," I told Hyacinth, my eyes never leaving the lock in front of me. It was important to set the tone for this sort of encounter; never, ever show fear, even to an inanimate hunk of metal.

"You need what? Why?"

"To pick the locks."

"Why would I have either of those on me?"

"You're a biker. Don't you all use wrenches?"

"Not the sort that are small enough to fit in a lock… and I sure as hell don't carry them around with me. And aren't rakes for leaves anyway?"

It was always difficult dealing with amateurs.

"Do you have any paper clips then?" Before she could say something about office workers and their supplies, I explained: "My tools are back with the car that I'm guessing you all abandoned in the Comfort Inn parking lot."

"Why does a mediator know how to pick locks?" Despite her grumbling, both she and Ezra started going through the pockets of their jackets and pants.

"I'm not always a mediator."

"So, you're a blood bag *and* an international man of mystery."

I didn't hate the second half of that, to be honest.

As it turned out, neither wolf had paper clips, but Ezra passed over a few strands of metal wire—the intended purpose of which might never be fully known, given Hyacinth's own confused expression. It took me a bit of time, and some carefully directed werewolf muscle, to twist those metal bits into the necessary shapes, but eventually, I had a set of jury-rigged tools that were only moderately inferior to my usual bargain-bin set.

And then, like all the great detectives, craftsmen, and action stars of history, I got to work.

Unfortunately, whoever said *doing what you love means you'll never work a day in your life* hadn't known what the hell they were talking about. Picking the lock took *way* longer than it should have. Mostly because of the quality of my tools, I was sure.

It took almost twenty-five minutes to hear the click I'd been waiting for. I nodded to Ezra, and the big man carefully turned the handle. The door swung inwards, enough to let the light from within spill out, both brighter and more artificial than that in the tunnel and accompanied by a rush of hot, stagnant air. It was September, not August, but I still struggled with the idea that Vita Unica had voluntarily opted to squat in a building without electricity or, more importantly, air conditioning.

There was pro-human, anti-supernatural fanaticism and then there was just outright stupidity.

We waited for the air between our tunnel and their hideout to reach some sort of equilibrium and then Ezra and I retreated to join Hyacinth. I'd sent the female wolf back to the main tunnel eight minutes into my recent lockpicking marathon… or roughly two seconds after she'd broken my concentration for the seventh freaking time with a reminder that we needed to hurry. "It's all you, Kevin."

There were no words of acknowledgement slowly written across the wall, but a wave of organic material rolled past us and into the side tunnel. It reached the now open door and thickened until there was something like a mold carpet or doormat growing up and into the entryway. From that foundation, mushrooms sprouted as if in a time lapse video, growing larger and thicker than even the ones that had ringed Kevin's monolith. I watched, oddly fascinated, as those new mushrooms repeated the previous ones' actions, the stems swelling for a solid minute before the caps above shook, expelling the spores that we couldn't even see.

Kevin had said something about using a different type of spore this time, for improved aerodynamics and coverage, but all I saw was a bunch of alien-looking mushrooms doing their weird, alien-looking dance. Everything else had to be taken on faith.

"How long do we wait?" asked Hyacinth.

"Let's give it ten, just to make sure the spores have taken effect but are no longer… uh… active?"

The werewolf spent those ten minutes frowning. I was starting to worry she was developing a morbid obsession with time. Even with the lock having proven *somewhat* harder than expected to crack, we still had a solid ninety minutes to retrieve Audrey and return through the tunnels to an exit near our parked bikes. And sure, a bigger buffer would have been preferable, but even so, we were kind of kicking ass with this whole *Mission: Impossible* setup they'd forced me into.

John Smith, secret agent and international man of mystery, was once again saving the day.

When the ten minutes had passed, each second carefully—and again obsessively—tracked on Hyacinth's phone, we re-entered the side tunnel and soon reached the open door.

I nodded at Ezra to enter first. I didn't know if I'd avoided Kevin's paralytic spores earlier because there was some sort of mental component to them or if the fungus had simply controlled the spores so they only hit my companions, but it made sense for the burly werewolf to serve as our nigh-indestructible guinea pig.

He took a cautious step inside, breathed in and out, and then froze. Both Hyacinth and I stiffened too, thinking he'd been paralyzed yet again, but a moment later, he was moving. He turned back to wave us in.

"Bodies on the floor," he said, voice a low rumble. "All of them armed, but with their weapons holstered. They seem to still be breathing, so I'm guessing the mushrooms put them to sleep."

"We'll need to stay quiet then." Hyacinth stepped past me. "And hurry too. We don't know if the spores traveled upstairs or whether they would even have any effectiveness in rooms that are open to the outside."

Before I joined the two wolves, I turned back to the tunnel. "Thank you, Kevin. We'll be back shortly with the girl you've helped us rescue."

The mushrooms by the doorway had already crumbled, the '70s shag carpet thinning even as I watched, but the glowing tendrils along the tunnel's ceiling waved cheerily in response. I was really going to have to figure out how to hold up my end of our deal. Telepathic thought-eating fungus though he was, Kevin had totally come through for us.

CHAPTER 18

IN WHICH THINGS GET GRIM
BEFORE THE DAWN

There wasn't a lot to see in the first room. Shelves with supplies lined one wall—enough canned food and bottled water that we'd have been waiting forever to ambush someone making a supply run—and a second door opened onto a hallway. One of the bodies that Ezra had spotted was in the storeroom, the other splayed out in the hall. I took a peek at both people as we stepped over them and deeper into the building.

Other than the handguns holstered on their hips, they looked… normal. Both were men, both in jeans and T-shirts, both with medium-length hair. One had a full tattoo sleeve on his arm, and the other was a little bit stubbly, but I could easily imagine drinking beer next to either of them without giving it a second thought.

It was disquieting. As far as I knew, I had just been a curiosity when Vita Unica captured me in Rome, but part of me wondered if I now had my own file in the organization's archives. Were there people in Europe with my photo and orders to capture me on sight? Or, given their clear presence in the United States… was there a cell in San Diego watching everything I did?

I felt a moment of unexpected gratitude that my dad's accounting company had decided to move to Austin and that both he and my mom had chosen to move with it. I hated my parents being so far away from me, but at least it meant they were safe.

The hallway was lit with a couple of portable LED lamps, solar panels allowing them to recharge when taken upstairs into sunlight. The door directly across from ours looked in on the stairwell leading up, while several other doors, also open, led off the hallway to our left. We followed Ezra down that hall and found several more bodies, all of them as unconscious as the first two.

We passed a storeroom. Another storeroom. A bathroom so foul it was all any of us could do to even peek inside. Some sort of meeting room, overstuffed with a table and way too many folding chairs. By the time we rounded the corner, the hallway was starting to feel like just another tunnel to me after our long night underground.

There, we found one final door. This one, however, was closed. Worse, we could hear voices inside.

"Just gas them," muttered Hyacinth angrily, her voice so quiet that she was clearly talking to herself and not the rest of us. "Better yet, use spores. What could possibly go wrong?"

"They won't be expecting intruders," I reasoned. "We'll just open the door, real quiet like, and then rush them before they can raise any sort of alarm. And by *we*, I mean the two of you."

She rubbed her shaved head nervously and nodded, trading glances with Ezra as she pushed past me to join the other wolf at the door.

"On three," I told them. "One…"

Ezra gently twisted the handle and eased the door open, the movement as quiet as could be. He and Hyacinth flowed inside, moving at a speed no mere human could match. A second or two later, soft thumps inside told of bodies hitting the floor.

"Or you can go on one," I decided. "One works too."

I pushed the door the rest of the way and joined them, blinking at the unexpected glare. Where the hall and other rooms had been shrouded in shadow, this room was almost over-bright, LED lamps standing in a steady circuit along the exterior wall, each one pointed inward. A desk to one side held notebooks filled with a doctor's unintelligible scrawl, and two bodies in lab coats lay on the floor in spreading pools of blood, but my eyes were pulled to the table in the center of the room. Stainless steel and rectangular, it could have come straight out of the ER in any low-budget hospital show if it weren't for the attached wrist and ankle manacles. A camera had been mounted next to it on a large black tripod, and a stool sat next to the table, to insure whoever was *operating* could do so in comfort.

The only thing that kept the scene from immediately taking up residence in my nightmares was that the table was clean and unstained, the manacles as shiny as if they'd just been bought from Kidnappers-R-Us. As far as I could tell, drawing upon my unfortunate experience as a multi-time kidnappee, whatever was scheduled to occur on that table had not yet happened. And judging by what Ezra and Hyacinth had done to the people they found inside, it never would.

Which raised one question.

"Where's Audrey?"

Hyacinth didn't answer me with words. Instead, she was in motion, vaulting the table entirely in her hurry to reach the other side of the room. There, masked behind the other pieces of furniture in the small space was something that made my blood run even colder than the sterile, gleaming, inimitably sinister operating table:

The far wall held a row of four cages, heavy-duty and large enough to hold any dog. Or wolf.

Hyacinth ignored the first three, making a beeline for the fourth and bending down out of sight. I couldn't make out what she said to whoever was contained within, but I could hear the anger in her voice, poorly hidden even beneath heartfelt concern and compassion.

She raised her voice, calling out to us despite the half-dozen unconscious or sleeping bodies we'd stepped over on the way in. "Find the keys. Please."

I looked to Ezra, but the big man had slipped back out the door, no doubt going to watch our six now that the action was over. I hurried over to the dead people whose lab coats had no doubt begun the day as pristine as the operating table. The first was face down and male. I did my best not to look at what had been done to him from the shoulders up, patting down his lab coat and then pants pockets while listening for the jingle of keys. When that turned up nothing, I moved on to the second body. This one was lying face up, eyes fixed on a ceiling she couldn't see anymore. Other than the savage gash in her throat that had ended her life even as it removed her ability to scream, her corpse was whole and unharmed.

Honestly, I wasn't sure which was worse.

I swallowed, trying to keep from looking at anything too closely, and repeated my inspection. This time, I was rewarded with a jingle of metal. I pulled out a ring of keys, all of them as bright and shiny as the table, as the manacles, and as the cages, and slid them across the floor toward Hyacinth. Then, I turned to the side and threw up what little remained of my bacon cheeseburger.

By the time I was done, Hyacinth had the cage door open, and a mid-sized, rust-colored wolf padded out onto the bloodstained tile. It led the way across the room to a series of cubbies near the desk and whined, nosing the lid of the first. Inside was a pile of clothing. I retreated into the hallway to give the new wolf—Audrey, I assumed—privacy to shift and get dressed.

Ezra was nowhere in sight.

With a frown, I ventured back down the hallway we'd come through. It wasn't until I reached the end that I found the dude, crouched over one of the Vita Unica members, enormous hand cutting off the unconscious enemy's air flow.

"What are you doing?"

"What needs to be done." He didn't even look over at me. "We can't risk them sounding the alarm. And every enemy that never wakes up is one fewer we'll have to face down the road."

Unconsciously, I turned and scanned the hallway behind us. I hadn't noticed it in my search for Ezra, but none of the bodies in sight were still breathing.

I didn't know how to feel about that either. Killing someone in battle was one thing. Doing so when they were helpless was something else entirely. And yet…

Cages. An operating table. We'd arrived in time to save Audrey from that fate, but how many other people or species had been captured and experimented on or even vivisected by Vita Unica across the world? Did it make any sense to leave people like this alive to try again? Would we be complicit in the survivors' actions?

I didn't like where those thoughts led me. I was a mediator, not a soldier. I was supposed to prevent war and killing, not rationalize it.

Focus on the good, I told myself. *Audrey is safe, which means Juliette will be too. There's a lot of horrible stuff in the world, and too much of it is human, but your part in this specific conflict will be over soon.*

It didn't help. I was tired, I was nauseous, and now that the euphoria of negotiating with Kevin and picking the lock on the door had faded, I was sick in a way that had nothing to do with my stomach.

It was a relief when Hyacinth joined us in the hall. Behind her, almost hidden in the taller woman's shadow, was a slim teenager with dark hair, dressed all in black and wearing a pair of chunky framed glasses. Her eyes, red-rimmed even behind thick lenses, widened as she took in the scene.

"Ezra? What are you doing?" Audrey's voice was a whisper.

"What I had to." Ezra rose from the corpse at his feet, towering over the teenager. "They needed to die."

"And the ones upstairs? Will you kill them too?"

"What's done is done," said Hyacinth, before Ezra could respond. "But we need to get out of here now. Back into the tunnels before anyone knows that you're free."

Audrey blanched at the word *tunnels*, but she followed the rest of us willingly enough, averting her eyes from the bodies—now *actual* bodies—she had to step around. Moments later, we were back in the soft half-light of Kevin's phosphorescence.

"Hey Kevin," I said to the lichen on the wall. "Any chance you could lead us back to where we first met you? Our transportation is nearby."

There was no reply. Even the tendrils dangling from the ceiling stayed still.

Right. Our bargain. "I have an idea on how you can attend classes, but it's going to take a bit of work to set up, and I can't do it all from here."

Still nothing. I got the sense that Kevin was waiting for more, but I wasn't sure exactly what it was. So, I went big.

"I am John Smith," I said, desperately trying to remember how I'd been announced in Rome, "bonded to Queen-Regent Lucia Borghesi of the Italian courts and loved by the Stone Lady, Anastasia Dumenyova. I have been called Pack-Friend and Ghost-Blessed, a breaker of covens, a defender of Houses, and a slayer of demons."

Audrey and Hyacinth were both staring at me now. I did my best to ignore them.

"I give you my word, as a Padres fan and a mediator for the *great* city of San Diego that I will uphold my end of the bargain, no matter how long it takes. May the powers above and below us smite me now if I am lying."

I winced and held my breath a bit after that last part slipped out. I didn't know most of the powers above and below us, but if they were anything like Minerva, they might just smite me for even mentioning them. Thankfully, the moment passed without any lightning strikes or hellfire or… well, whatever else smiting might conceivably involve.

"Who is he talking to?" whispered Audrey.

I didn't pay attention to Hyacinth's response because the glow coming from the hanging tendrils had strengthened. Finally, they bent to one side, directing us down the right branch of the tunnel.

It wasn't the way we'd come, but I didn't question it. My wonderphone might have Waze, but I had something even better: I had Kevin, fungus and future ASU undergraduate philosophy student.

ooo

It only took us fifteen minutes to reach the narrow trail that led up and into the building where Coyote had ghosted us, but Audrey was struggling by the end of it. According to what she'd told Hyacinth, her captors hadn't done much more than force her to shift and shove her in the cage, but the combination of lights, sound, and fear had made sleep impossible. The ordeal had left her even more tired than I was.

She was tough though, in a way that I was pretty sure had nothing to do with being a werewolf, princess or otherwise. She hadn't complained once during the entire trip, intent on Hyacinth's explanations.

"I'm not going to move against Uncle Zeke," she told the other wolf. "I know it's his time, and as his only relative, it's my responsibility, but…"

"Nobody's asking that. We just need y'all there to help keep him balanced." Hyacinth sighed. "I'm sorry, Audrey. It's a hell of a burden for anyone to bear, least of all a teenager."

"It's still better than killing him, whatever tradition thinks."

I kept my opinions to myself.

"I'll squeeze through first," said Ezra, "and make sure the coast is clear again."

By this point, all the shifting was almost becoming passé. I turned to Hyacinth and ignored the big wolf dragging his pile of clothes into the yawning crack.

"So, how are we going to do this?"

"What do you mean?"

"I've held up my end of the bargain. To you, at least, if not Kevin."

"Chase will release the fanger and we'll drop both of you off at your car."

"What fanger?" Audrey looked between the older woman and me. "What's going on?"

Apparently, Hyacinth hadn't covered the whole kidnapping and blackmail part of the story.

"You've heard of John Smith, right?" she responded, answering a question with another question in a conversational gambit as old as time.

"The Padres fan. I heard his weird speech, yeah."

"He is… connected to the individual who killed your cousin."

"Oh." She frowned at me. "Georgie wasn't a nice person, like, at all, but that doesn't give you or anyone else the right to kill him."

'Technically, the Toulon Concordat said otherwise,' was what I *should* have said. Instead, I went with another old standby.

"In fairness, he tried to kill me first."

"Oh. So, Uncle Zeke made you help free me to pay for your crimes?" She read the answer in my face and turned on Hyacinth. "You did this on your own?"

"It was the only way. Ezekiel was going to lead the pack here in a direct assault on the building holding you prisoner. It would have gotten you killed."

"And this fanger he was talking about?"

"My business partner," I said. "Insurance to make sure I did my job. Which I'd say I have."

"Yeah, you have." Hyacinth was the freshest of the three of us still underground, but she didn't sound it as she sighed. "I'll call Chase as soon as we have a signal. You and your—Juliette—will be free to leave and Ezra and I will take Audrey home where she is safe."

"And Ezekiel?"

"Uncle Zeke will be fine. He just gets worked up when I'm not there to talk him down," insisted Audrey.

"Fair enough." I eyed the narrow crack and sighed. Maybe all that walking we'd done, coupled with the loss of my remaining bacon cheeseburger, would make the squeeze a little bit less challenging.

○○○

Spoiler alert: it didn't.

○○○

Much, much too long later, I emerged from the crack to find Ezra waiting, fully dressed. He gave me a once-over, pulled me up and out of the way, and then leaned in to help Audrey, who'd been right on my heels after the first overly tight bend.

Maybe the rumors of my fatness *hadn't* been greatly exaggerated?

Hyacinth was last to emerge, but there was a skip in her step that hadn't been there while we were underground. "I'm going to call this in to Chase," she said. "There should be enough time for him to get the fanger out before he informs the boss of our success. With luck, he'll even call off the attack."

"Now that Audrey's out, we have the luxury of time," said Ezra. "It will be our turn to hunt."

"And nobody does it better." They shared wolfish grins. "Keep watch over them please. I'll be back shortly."

After she left, Ezra took up a guard position by the secret door, close enough to stop me if I ran or did anything stupid, but far enough away to give his princess the illusion of privacy.

Audrey flopped down onto the floor, hugging her arms to her chest, as she squeezed her eyes shut. "Is this real?" she asked, voice wavering.

"I ask myself that a lot." I took a seat too, making sure to give her space. "But I keep reminding myself only reality can hurt this much."

"So, you really did promise some sort of plant that you'd help enroll it at ASU?"

"I'm not sure fungi are considered plants."

"Then what are they?"

"Vegetables?"

"No. Definitely not."

I shrugged. "No idea then. But the answer is yes. Kevin helped us, and I'm going to help in return."

"Just like that? Even though he's a whatever he is?"

"I'm not sure Kevin has a gender, but yeah. I said I would."

"It's not like that in our pack. We keep our words, sure, but it's family first, you know? Blood, then pack, then friendships, then everyone else."

"It doesn't have to be that way."

"Says who?"

The obvious answer was *me*, but in twenty-seven years, that answer had never impressed anyone. "I can think of at least two people. Did you ever meet your cousin Jason?"

"A few times, yeah." She grinned, in spite of herself. "He was a lot older than me, but kind of funny."

"He still is, I guess. In his own way."

She glanced over and then away. "Oh. You're *that* mediator."

"Yeah. He and his ex-wife, now-girlfriend and baby mama, Carolyn—"

"Jason is having kids? No way!"

"Right?!" I shivered. "He'll either be the best dad ever or the worst. I'm not sure there's any room for in between. Anyway, they run *their* pack as a democracy. They've even worked with the other species in San Diego from time to time."

"Huh."

"I'm not saying it's the right way to go for you or your pack; I'm just saying there are options. When you're older, you'll be the one making those decisions."

"I don't know if I want to. Make decisions, I mean." I could feel her dart another look at my face before returning to staring at her knees.

"When I was your age, I didn't either." I wasn't even thirty yet, but I felt ancient, giving advice to a teenager who hadn't necessarily asked for it but seemed badly in need of a friend.

"What changed?"

"Somedays, I'm still like that." My grin came and went. "The rest of the time, I guess I'm just trying to keep the people I love safe. Not deciding anything is kind of a decision too, right?"

"You sound like Auntie Kyla used to."

I didn't ask what happened to Auntie Kyla. With werewolves' short lifespans, the answer was almost always the same.

"She sounds like she was a smart woman."

"Did you… just compliment yourself?"

I played back the words in my mind. "I guess I did."

"Laaaaaaaame." She coughed. "But uhm thank you for the advice. And for helping rescue me."

"It's what I do. More the rescue part than the advice, admittedly"

"Really?"

"Kind of. Mediation's a weird business. Hey, did you find your phone with your clothes?"

"No. I guess I have an excuse to upgrade now, right?"

Jesus. Kids really did bounce back fast these days.

"I guess so. In the meantime, can you memorize a phone number if I give it to you?"

"Obviously," she said with the sort of confidence held only by the young or criminally insane. She frowned as I rattled off the numbers. "Wait. 619 is San Diego, right? You're not… I mean, this isn't…"

"I'm taken." I scowled. "And also not some sort of predator, whatever you've heard."

"I mean—"

"Send me a text when you have a phone again, and I'll put you in touch with your cousin and his… well… Carolyn." The two werewolves really needed to figure out what they were to each other. Divorced, dating co-parents? Any label I could think of just invited questions I wasn't interested in answering. "I'm sure Jason would love to hear from someone in his family. More importantly, I bet Carolyn has some helpful thoughts about running a pack as a woman."

"What can you tell me about her ? Is she nice?"

"Very," I said, shading the truth with remarkable aplomb. "She's pretty passionate about the environment, but she likes just hanging out too. They have movie nights and game nights every week, but otherwise, I think she likes to just, you know, read, watch anime, and listen to music."

"Which animes?"

"I… don't know?"

"That's okay; there are so many good ones."

"So I hear."

"I hope she's a K-Pop stan."

"There's only one way to find out, really." Maybe I'd put her in touch with Sabina too. It couldn't hurt to foster inter-species cooperation between princesses, right?

Diplomat John Smith didn't have much of a ring to it, if I was being honest, but I was starting to think it might be my true calling.

CHAPTER 19
IN WHICH *PARANOID* HAS AN I
BUT *I'M TIRED* HAS TWO OF THEM

The entire way out to the bikes, I expected something to go horribly awry. Maybe Vita Unica had tagged Audrey with some sort of tracker and was closing in our position even now. Or maybe Shae had gotten wise to Hyacinth and Chase's joint plot to rob them of their bloody fun and would ride out of the darkness to stop us. Or hell, maybe Coyote had decided to take our bikes with him when he pulled a fade.

Nope on all counts. Hyacinth finished her call, came in to collect us, and the four of us exited through the same back door we'd entered, where the two motorcycles were waiting, dirty but otherwise untouched and unguarded. I think Audrey wanted to ride with Hyacinth, but simple physics made that a terrible idea: it would put me on a bike with Ezra and I wasn't sure even a Harley could support our shared… awesomeness.

So, I rode with Hyacinth again, and Audrey rode with Ezra. It would have been the perfect opportunity for the swarthy werewolf to shock us all with a surprise betrayal, riding off with the werewolf princess as his unwitting captive. Instead, he fell into formation about four feet off my ass, content to draft behind us.

I was tense the whole way out of Phoenix, waiting for an attack that never came, then somehow even *more* tense once we hit the open highway where, my brain stubbornly insisted, *absolutely anything could now happen.*

What happened was roughly ninety-seven more minutes of peaceful riding that neither my anxiety nor my tired legs particularly appreciated. By the time we pulled into the Comfort Inn's lot where my Corolla waited, dirty from a day on the road and a night at a motel, I was almost irritated that nothing had happened.

I climbed down off Hyacinth's bike, holding onto the quilted leather seat for support as I waited to see if my legs felt like holding me or not, and scanned the lot for Juliette.

She wasn't there.

Finally, that little voice in my head crowed. *Finally, the other shoe drops.* I didn't know when the first shoe had dropped, and I didn't really care either. The betrayal I'd been fearing and anticipating had finally arrived, and now it was—

"Hey little bird." Juliette exited the Comfort Inn, a water bottle in hand. At some point, the femmepire had showered, changed clothes, and lost her shock collar. She even looked like she'd gotten some sleep, yellow eyes bright and familiar smirk forming as she crossed the asphalt. She ignored Ezra, traded considering glares with Hyacinth, and cocked her head at the bespectacled Audrey. "Is this who all the fuss was about?"

"Juliette, meet Audrey. Audrey, this is my friend and business partner, Juliette."

"Hi Sparkles," said Juliette. "I'm glad you're safe… and not just because my life literally depended on it."

"Uhm, thank you?"

"She's adorable. More kitten than wolf if you ask me." Juliette drained the water bottle and yawned, stretching in a way that would have stopped traffic if there'd been any to speak of. "Shall we?"

"Just like that?"

"I'm sure they want to get the kid home before the big bad wolf loses his shit again, and *I* don't want to spend one second longer in this parking lot or city." Juliette tossed me the keys. "I call shotgun."

"I haven't slept in like twenty-two hours."

"And?"

"And it'll be a long walk to New Mexico if I wrap the Corolla around a tree. Or God forbid, another Corolla." I threw the keys back at her, ignoring that her catch was a thousand times more effortless than mine had been.

"She's right though," said Hyacinth, who hadn't dismounted from her motorcycle. "This *is* goodbye. For now, at least. The sooner we get back…"

"I get it." I gave a general nod in the trio's direction. "I can't say it was fun, but at least it all worked out. And if we do ever see each other again, I hope it'll be over burgers and beers and not whatever the hell this was."

"Only if it's five years from now," said Hyacinth. "Otherwise, Audrey's drinking lemonade."

"Text me when you get the chance," I told the werewolf princess in question.

"I will," she said, eyes still big behind her lenses. "I owe you one."

"I might need your help with that whole enrollment thing," I admitted. "But until then, stay frosty."

We didn't wait for the two motorcycles to leave but instead headed for the Corolla.

"Is that your thing now?" asked Juliette.

"What?"

"Telling people to stay frosty. It's dumb."

"It's from a tv show."

"Based on a non-fiction book about the military. I know; we all streamed it together like a month ago."

"So?"

"So, it sounds dumb when you say it. Stop ruining things."

I grinned through my tiredness. "It's good to see you, Duchess."

"Likewise. And thanks for saving my ass, John. Seriously."

"Angel would have mine if I didn't."

"I guess she would. Are you really too tired to drive?"

"Honestly? I'm too tired to even have this conversation."

"But you'll at least tell me what happened as we go?"

"I'd rather sleep. *Seriously.*"

"That sounds like a man who doesn't want his phone back."

I paused in the act of opening the passenger door to my beloved Corolla. "Maybe I could spin a story or two."

"And maybe I could see my way to buying you a dozen Egg McMuffins. And an extra-large coffee."

"At first, you had my curiosity," I quoted, "but now, you have my attention."

ooo

I woke up much later, somewhere in New Mexico, a bag of used McMuffin wrappers at my feet. I must have told Juliette the whole tale of my time in Phoenix, because she had let me fall asleep, but damned if I could remember the telling. I barely even remembered the mountain of processed breakfast food I'd shoved down my throat, which was a crime against the better parts of humanity.

I looked over at the femmepire. She was wearing one of the hats Angel had given her and a pair of coke bottle sunglasses and was drumming her fingers against the steering wheel as if playing along to music I couldn't hear.

Because there *was* no music. No punk gods who left us too early but also precisely at the right time. No *this band could have been famous if it wasn't for the Doberman incident.* No *this is how you tell the difference between punk, post-punk, goth, and shoewave.* Just simple, blessed, slightly worrying silence.

"Is everything okay, Juliette?"

"Why wouldn't it be?"

"It's quiet."

"You somehow won a philosophy debate with a vegetable," she said. "I figured you deserved some peace while you slept."

I'd have called it the nicest thing she had ever done for me if the evidence of something even nicer wasn't still crinkling under my feet.

"I've been told fungus isn't a vegetable."

"By who?"

"Audrey."

"That's ridiculous. What is it then?"

"Hell if I know." The answer, as with most answers, was available via the device sitting in my front pocket, but I couldn't be bothered to look it up.

"Any idea how you're going to hold up your end of the bargain with Kevin?"

"Kind of. I have to check if ASU allows remote study. I figure I can get it a laptop and some sort of solar hookup, if so. Kevin might not be able to hang out and do bong hits with the other students, but at least it would have access to classes. And I figure if it can spell, it should be able to learn to type."

"Is there a Plan B?"

"I skip the laptop entirely and ask my business partner to go and compel everyone on campus to ignore the intelligent fungus walking among them."

"I'm a rockstar, not a miracle worker, little bird."

"Too many people?"

"And too much ground to cover with way too much variance."

"Variance?"

"It's a university. People are coming and going every day, not to mention the influx of new students every quarter or two. You'd need someone in admissions, and even then, I doubt even one of the old monsters in Europe or Asia could maintain that many compulsions. There's a difference between slightly editing someone's memory of something and actively making them continue to ignore something they shouldn't ignore."

"Laptop it is then. With some sort of accessibility accessories so that it's usable by... well... Kevin."

"Sounds expensive."

"I'd say our lives were worth it." I coughed. "Speaking of admissions though, I might still need you to go to sweet talk someone into accepting his enrollment. I'm not sure *century-old fungus with interest in philosophy and no test scores or school records to speak of* will exactly qualify otherwise, even with affirmative action."

"Maybe you should reach out to the other species in Phoenix? Some of them have to be sending their kids to ASU or U of A, right? Study groups in this cavern you found might be a little more feasible, not to mention exciting for Kevin."

"Look at you with the good ideas. I really wanted it to get a diploma though. And one of those little graduation hats."

"As one of the two people in this car without a college degree, it sounds to me like you're projecting, just a bit."

"Nah, that's not it." I frowned. "I don't think so anyway."

"You know you can go back to school anytime you want, right? SDSU isn't all that expensive, and if your amazing, elegant, and empathic business partner could get a fungus into real college, I'm sure she could do the same for someone who actually went to school once."

"I think I'm a little bit old for college."

"If you tell anyone I said this, I'll smother you in your sleep with a lavender scented pillow, but you're twenty-seven, not dead. You've got most of what you humans call a life left ahead of you. Our agency is doing well, and your mediation side-hustle only causes issues a few times a year; this is the time."

That was a *lot* more thought than I'd have expected Juliette to put into anything, least of all my academic career.

"Are you sure you're okay?" I asked her. "The pack didn't like infect you with some sort of ancient tapeworm of unanticipated kindness or anything, did it?"

"I will punch you so hard you fly right through your window."

The physics of that seemed kind of questionable, but after a moment's thought, I decided not to take the risk.

"Okay, *now* you sound like you." We shared grins. "As far as college goes… I don't know. I kind of felt like that ship had sailed, but maybe you're right."

"Sooner or later, you'll learn I'm always right." Somehow, she even managed to say that with a straight face. "I rescued your agency, I single-handedly kickstarted your love life, and now I'm turning my powers toward—"

"Wait… you what?!"

She shot me an arch look while simultaneously weaving through the small cluster of cars on the road. "Which part of that was unclear?"

"I can sort of grant you the agency part, although I'd say the credit goes more to your biological cheat codes than anything, but how did *you* help my love life?"

"The facts are undeniable."

"The facts don't exist."

"And this is why I really should be the senior partner." She sighed and started ticking off points on her fingers, ignoring the fact that she was also driving well over ninety. "Fact one: you hadn't had sex in *five years* before we met."

It had only been *four* years when we first met, but now that my dry spell was over, I found I didn't care quite so much what people had to say about it. After all, that was ancient history. Or… *several months ago* history, anyway.

"Fact two: you couldn't even get a date with Anastasia until I gave you her cellphone number."

"You mean until I cleverly tricked you into calling it even though I already knew we didn't have a signal."

"Fact three: somehow, you dropped the ball so badly on your one date that she left the country for six months."

"Okay, that's not technically—"

"Fact four: when she came back, she ended things with you."

"Yeah, but—"

"Fact five: I then kissed you, and despite the utter disaster *that* was for both of us, it was still sufficient to trigger her possessiveness, at which point she reversed her breakup decision. And that, kids, is how Auntie Juliette helped your father meet your mother."

"I think you're leaving out some important bits, like my kidnap and torture and, oh yeah, me flying to Rome to put my life on the line to defend her." Not to mention that vampires and humans couldn't even have kids, making this *How I Met Your Mother* impression flawed from the start.

"Those are just details. Scut work for the engineers out in the field. As the genius CEO of this whole endeavor, I had the vision. It only makes sense to leave some minor aspects of the implementation up to you."

I… didn't really have any comebacks to that. She was wrong, I knew, but had somehow still laid out a halfway persuasive argument. Clearly, it was time to change the subject.

"Is me going back to college a part of your vision?"

"Hell no. As someone who never even attended high school, I don't get what the fuss is all about."

"But—"

"But you mention that you're a college dropout every other week, often in the middle of some sob story about how the woman who asked for a century off from her job just to date you is going to suddenly change her mind."

"I literally said that *once*, and I was trying to make you feel better about the whole Angel thing."

"Do you really wake up every day worrying you'll screw up your relationship?"

"Are *you* really going to dump our receptionist and roommate just because she wants more than just a casual, carefree romance?"

"About that… I may have given her a promotion before we left."

"To what? Senior receptionist?"

"Junior detective." For once, Juliette was keeping her eyes on the road, but she somehow *still* read my expression. "On a trial basis! She'll still answer phones and stuff, but this way, she can get out of the office occasionally to do some work in the field."

"Why are you promoting someone you're likely going to break up with?" In any other company, the whole thing would be a massive lawsuit liability. I was pretty sure we didn't have to worry about that, but even so…

"Job experience. She's been a barista, she's run the register at a tattoo parlor, and now she's a receptionist. This way, she'll get a taste of the investigator lifestyle too. The more options she has…"

"The better you'll feel."

"I mean… I guess so?"

We both sat there in silence for a bit.

"How much longer to Ghost Falls?" I finally asked.

"You can read the GPS as well as I can."

With a sigh, I rubbed my eyes and leaned forward. One hour to go. The nap had done a lot to cure my exhaustion, but the last day of travel still felt more like a week. It was somehow only Thursday and we'd ended up leaving Payson far earlier than I would have on my own. That gave us most of the afternoon, and all Friday and Saturday to investigate and talk to friends, family, and the town's sheriff before we had to head back to San Diego.

I was pretty sure that would be ample time, but the lack of a credit trail for either of the two missing kids was a concern. There weren't a lot of people these days with enough cash on hand to survive for even a few days, let alone more than a week.

"What do you say we drive straight through on the way back?"

"You mean you don't want to stop in Payson again? But it went so well for us the first time."

"I'd like to skip Phoenix too until I have a solid answer for Kevin."

"That's probably for the best. Before switching to a diet of philosophy thoughts, it really knew how to hold a grudge." She shrugged. "I'm fine with a long drive. Flower girl and Sparkles seemed okay, and I guess insurance guy was too, but the rest of the pack can burn, as far as I'm concerned. Shae especially."

"I wasn't sure if I'd have to talk you out of seeking revenge."

"I thought about it. I thought about it a lot. But as I sat there, waiting for you to do whatever it is you were doing, I realized there's nothing I can do to them that will be worse than what karma has in store."

"That's surprisingly evolved—"

"And by karma, I mean your girlfriend."

"Oh." I chewed that over, as we slowly ascended into foothills that would become mountains. "I know Ana has a past, but she's not anywhere near as bloodthirsty as people think. In fact, I think one of her favorite things about this *Secundus* sabbatical is *not* having to kill people on command."

"John, sweetie—"

I tensed up. Nothing good came of Juliette using endearments.

"—we really need to do something about this massive lack of awareness you have. It reflects badly on our shared profession."

Yup, totally called it.

"What are you talking about?"

"Anastasia might not be the foaming-at-the-mouth murderer the stories paint her as, but her trail of bodies could still fill at least two cemeteries."

"That was then. Now, she's—"

"A woman in love, and the man she has chosen to share her next century with was just kidnapped, imprisoned, and forced into a dangerous situation under direct threats on his life. Part of me is worried she'll kill *me* for not protecting you better... do you really think she won't have something to say to the New Mexico Pack?"

"I..."

"Exactly. Which is why I'm not worried about getting revenge. Once you make it painfully obvious to her that I did the right thing in all ways and at all times and was therefore in no way responsible for this debacle, I plan to just sit back and wait for karma to make headlines. *'Entire biker gang found dead from gas leak.'* Or maybe *'Albuquerque natives perish in freak meteor shower.'* I'd even be okay with *'Southwestern militia dies in inter-gang shootout.'* Whatever it is, it'll be glorious, and I won't have to lift a finger to make it happen."

There were times I forgot Juliette was a vampire, and there were times it was impossible to see her as anything but.

CHAPTER 20
IN WHICH A SMALL TOWN
SMALL TOWNS

It was a little after one when we finally reached Ghost Falls, a collection of a hundred or so buildings grouped around one road and a dozen or so cross streets. The central thoroughfare, which I was pretty sure was required by law to be called Main Street, seemed to be what passed for the town's commercial hub, sporting a handful of restaurants, two bars, a scattering of stores, a clinic too small to be a hospital, and a single-garage fire station. There was also a sheriff's office, just past the *Welcome to Ghost Falls* sign that had lost one of its Ls.

Again, my mom would have called the town quaint.

"Hell, I'd run away too," was Juliette's one-line review.

"It's small, but the view's pretty amazing." Ghost Falls was nestled in the mountains, giving it gorgeous vistas on multiple sides. The titular waterfalls were nowhere to be found, but we *were* still in a drought.

Or maybe that's what made them *ghost* falls? I'd have to ask a local.

I made note of the sheriff's office, knowing we'd want to stop by later, but directed Juliette down Main Street to the seventh cross street, creatively called Seventh Street. The roads turned to dirt as soon as you left Main, but the Corolla had already been through worse on a pie-buying trip to Julian that had taken us through the dusty back roads of Ramona.

"According to Simon's directions, it should be this one to the right," I said.

The house we stopped next to had been built in the traditional Pueblo-style adobe, squat and square, with rounded corners and arched openings above and below indicating the balcony and entryway. It all looked very New Mexico, and honestly kind of cool compared to the hodgepodge of different styles we had in San Diego.

"I guess Jeremiah's home." There was no garage, but the house did have a long gravel driveway, and a small work truck in faded red paint had been parked a few feet from the house.

"Either that or they have two cars."

I shrugged. "Might as well go find out. I'm pretty sure Simon told him to expect us. Or at least me."

Exiting the car was its own feat of heroics, as I pretty much had to roll myself out onto legs that had fallen asleep with the rest of me and then opted not to wake back up again afterwards, all while *not* bringing any McMuffin wrappers along. The sheer number of breakfast sandwiches I'd consumed was borderline impressive, but my stomach's rumbling said it was ready for lunch anyway.

Work first, I told it, *then eat Hatch chiles.* It was hard to believe I'd been in New Mexico for like half a day and hadn't had *something* chile-focused yet.

"Try to be compassionate," I reminded my partner as we headed toward the house. "Simon says Jeremiah's a bit of an oddball, but he also just lost his daughter."

"Please." She rolled her eyes. "Both of my parents were diplomats. I know how to fit in."

"So, you *didn't* get kicked out of the New York House?"

"I don't want to talk about it."

My laugh won a yellow-eyed glare from the femmepire. I didn't know her dad, but I *had* met her mother, and while Juliette and Deanna looked like sisters, they couldn't otherwise have been any more different. My business partner was many things, but diplomatic wasn't one of them.

"Just let me do the talking."

The door to Jeremiah's house was wooden, worn, and tall, its top portion curved just like the arch we'd walked through. There didn't appear to be a doorbell, so I grabbed hold of the large, cast-iron knocker, and rapped it against the wooden frame three times.

Three, because all the books swore it was a magic number. And also because it took that many to really figure out the correct ratio of force to noise; my first knock had been too quiet, and the second had sounded like I was trying to force my way in.

It took a while—long enough for Juliette to grow visibly bored and begin contemplating how many kicks it would take to knock the whole thing down—but eventually we could hear footsteps inside. The door didn't have a peephole, so I wasn't surprised when whoever was there just yanked the door open to reveal a mid-forties man with olive skin, a noticeable paunch, and graying hair.

"What?" From the scratchiness of his throat and the redness of his eyes, he had been crying, and from the cloud of pot smoke and bourbon fumes that moved to envelop us, he'd been treating that grief medicinally.

"Jeremiah?"

"Depends who's asking." He squinted up at me then over at Juliette where he did the kind of double take that usually only happened in movies or cartoons. His next words were directed at her. "Well, *you're* not from around here are ya, darling? Whatever you're selling, I'm buying."

"He doesn't look like Simon, but he kind of acts like him," said Juliette.

It took a while for that comment to percolate through the cocktail of controlled and uncontrolled substances Jeremiah was operating under, but when it did, the change was immediate. His bloodshot eyes widened, and he straightened up, losing the indolent slouch.

"You're the people he sent?" he rasped. "Did you find my Dulcinea?"

"That's what we're here to do," I said. "I'm John, and this is my partner, Juliette. We're the investigators that Simon hired to find your daughter. If you have someplace for us to sit and talk, I wanted to fill you in on our progress so far. I'm also hoping that you can elaborate on what information we already have."

"Of course, of course." He stepped aside and waved for us to enter.

I hadn't been sure what to expect from the interior. Simon had described Jeremiah as a weirdo Luddite—a particularly telling comment, coming as it did from someone who had died around the turn of the century and yet spent his undeath streaming what he insisted was the golden age of peak TV. Between that and the *very* traditional exterior, a part of me was anticipating gas lamps, dirt floors, a wood-burning stove, and maybe a butter churn. Instead, the home seemed reasonably modern, with tile floors and high ceilings. While it lacked central a/c and heating, a window unit was visible in the living room, and a tiled fireplace was set into the opposite wall.

All in all, it would have been almost homey, if it didn't look like someone had set off a bomb just before our arrival.

"Sorry," said Jeremiah, running back and forth, gathering up clothes. By the time he was done, he had an armful of laundry. He seemed at a loss as to what to do with it.

"Maybe dump the clothes in the hamper?" I suggested.

"Right. Right." He was roughly Juliette's height, but seemed smaller as he scurried out of the living room. He was back, moments later, and by the look of it, had splashed water on his face and at least made an effort to run a comb through his hair.

I would have told him not to worry about it. His daughter had been missing for a week; as far as I was concerned, he was doing pretty damn well holding things together.

Juliette sat down next to me on a couch older than I was, and we waited as Jeremiah rushed back into the small kitchen just off the living room, returning with water in handmade ceramic mugs. He waited for us to take sips and then leaned forward eagerly.

"What can you tell me? What have you found so far?"

It didn't take long because we didn't have much. Still, I walked him through what we'd done so far and the dead ends we'd encountered.

"If Dulcinea did run away—"

"She didn't. Not my daughter. She loves Ghost Falls."

"And her boyfriend?"

He frowned. "She could do better, but I guess she loves him too."

"No… I mean does *he* love Ghost Falls?"

"Oh." He chewed on that a bit. "Pedro's the kind of boy who's never happy with where he is, the kind who's always looking ahead to the next step or the next score."

"And by *score*, you mean…" I pantomimed taking a drag on a joint. It seemed odd for Jeremiah to be throwing stones at anyone over drug use, but if Pedro was an *actual* addict, it might open new avenues of investigation.

"No, he doesn't do drugs. Neither of them do. They're good kids." And then, as if realizing we could smell the evidence of his own habits, he grumbled. "I have glaucoma. I've got a medical card and everything."

"We're not here to judge." Somehow, pot *still* wasn't legal in California, even fifteen years into the new millennium, but at least half the state had medical marijuana cards, prescribed to help them treat anything from mild anxiety to maladies that only existed in textbooks and fantasy novels. "All we care about is finding Dulcinea. And Pedro."

"Right. Sure. Yeah, I'm good with that."

"Okay. What I was originally going to say was that *if* Dulcinea had run away with Pedro, I would have expected to find some evidence of their passage online. Kids are smart enough to know that phones and credit cards both leave trails, but there's a limit to how far someone can go on cash." I paused and reconsidered. Maybe *Luddite* carried over to banking institutions? "Or… did either Dulcinea or Pedro have a habit of carrying large sums of cash on them?"

"Pedro liked to flash a roll," admitted Jeremiah, "but it was mostly ones, wrapped inside a couple of twenties. All sizzle, no steak, that boy."

"And your daughter?"

His laugh quickly turned into a cough that was eerily reminiscent of his ancestor's. "Our money goes to bills, John, and to keeping that old truck of mine running."

"What do you do?" asked Juliette.

"I'm a handyman, Miss." He puffed up his chest. "If I can't fix it, you probably need to go buy a new one."

"Good slogan," she admitted.

"So, if I'm understanding things correctly," he said, turning back to me, "y'all have been working the interwebs for some sign of my daughter's cybertrail but are coming up empty?"

I nodded. It wasn't *exactly* how I'd have phrased it, but as my dad would say, it was good enough for government work.

"So, what're your plans now? How are you gonna find her?"

"Our first step," I told him, "is to gather as much information as we can. From you, from the sheriff, and from any friends or other family your daughter and Pedro have in town. We need to build as comprehensive a picture as we can of the day in question."

"Like one of them there murder mysteries on TV."

"Right."

He blanched. "You don't think…"

"No. Not yet. There's no bodies or crime scene. From what I understand, they haven't even found Pedro's vehicle?"

"His dirt bike. Always hated that thing, but I'd give everything I have to see it again."

"Has anyone gone looking for them?"

Jeremiah gave Juliette a look. "Did you grow up in a small town, young lady?"

"Manhattan." From the looks of it, Juliette couldn't decide whether to be annoyed or amused by the *young lady* comment. Looking like an eighteen-year-old had its drawbacks.

"That's a no then." He harumphed. "In a small town, everyone knows everyone. Admittedly, that means you end up disliking a big chunk of them, but when push comes to shove, the whole town comes together. We've had search parties out in the hills for days. Problem is, it's a lot of ground to cover, and nobody's seen anything. Not even a trail for the bike. It's like they just rode out of town and disappeared."

"Did they leave town a lot?"

"I mean… they're kids?" He scowled. "Not a lot of privacy in a small town, so people look for places they can be alone, if you get what I'm saying. Sheriff Abbas can tell you we checked all the usual spots though and didn't find a thing."

"Do you mind if we take a look at Dulcinea's room?" So far, we hadn't gotten much of anything that wasn't in the papers Simon had sent over.

"You think she left some sort of clues behind?"

That was exactly what I was hoping, but it sounded kind of unlikely when someone else said it. "I'm not sure," I said instead. "Sometimes, finding someone means getting into their headspace first. Seeing where she grew up might help with that."

"Down the hall," he said, waving us past the kitchen. "Only door on the left. I haven't touched it, but the sheriff and his deputy came through once already."

The hall in question was small and the bedroom to the left was too. I carefully closed the door behind Juliette and me before I looked about.

"Sometimes, finding someone means getting into their headspace first?" quoted Juliette. "Did you get that from a serial killer show?"

"Probably. Still, it seems like good advice, right?"

The bedroom was considerably cleaner than the living room had been, but not in an obsessive sort of way. The bed wasn't made, but clothes were tucked away, and all but a few books were arranged on shelves instead of carpet. An oil painting of the town's mountains took up most of the wall, occupying the space where I'd have expected posters of movies or bands.

"Where do we start?"

"I need you to go back and talk to Jeremiah some more," I said, trying not to wince. "He seems genuine and genuinely upset, but if this really isn't a case of two teenage runaways, if there was some kind of foul play…"

"Then the first place to look is with family."

"Yeah." I was pretty sure I'd gotten *that* from crime documentaries, but it didn't make it any less true. And one thing I'd learned as a private eye was that there was always more going on beneath the surface. "Especially with his wife and Dulcinea's mother having died too."

"I thought that was cancer?"

Apparently, Juliette had done her own research. "That's just what the obituary said. I'm not saying he's responsible, for his wife or for Dulcinea, but we need to be sure."

"I'm pretty sure he's not just going to confess to being a killer."

"I know. I was thinking you could… you know…"

"So *now* you're okay with me compelling someone?"

And *that* was why I'd been wincing inside. Hypocrisy didn't look good on anyone, least of all late-twenties fratmen with a penchant for T-shirts and board shorts.

"There's a life at stake now instead of just a marriage. Two lives, potentially." And then, to ease my conscience. "It won't cause any damage, right?"

"He'll be fine. It'll be like it never even happened."

"Then maybe see if he has access to Dulcinea's social media accounts too? Simon's information packet didn't mention any, and my search didn't turn anything up under her name either, but she's a teenager. It's hard to imagine her not being online."

She nodded and slipped back into the hallway, leaving me alone in Dulcinea's bedroom. I eyed the closet, the dressers, the bed and the shelves, all possible hiding places from a prying father's eyes. This sheriff—Abbas, Jeremiah had called him—had either done a lousy search or a phenomenal job of putting everything back in its proper place.

I'd know which of the two it was soon enough.

ooo

By the time I was done in Dulcinea's room, Juliette and Jeremiah were laughing like old friends. That, by itself, didn't mean much… my business partner was a beautiful woman who could be charming on the rare occasions she bothered, and that was a potent cocktail for anyone, let alone a slightly drunk, slightly high widower who was already emotional. Still, the look the femmepire sent me told me that yes, she'd compelled the poor guy and no, he hadn't had anything to do with his daughter's disappearance.

The look I sent back said I hadn't found anything of note in the bedroom, but at least had a few more names to add to the list of people we needed to talk to.

Our powers of nonverbal communication had come a very long way in the past few years.

"Thank you, Jeremiah," I said, injecting just a little bit more sincerity into the words now that I knew for sure he wasn't a suspect. "We might come back by, but for now, I think we have everything we need."

He nodded slowly, like someone just waking up. "I'll be here unless I'm out on a job. Drop on by anytime. I gotta admit, I wasn't entirely too sure about you when you showed up on my door, but Juliette here says you always get your man."

That was painfully far from the truth, but I wasn't going to tell a client that. Or a client's relative, for that matter.

"We'll do everything we can to find Dulcinea," I said instead, offering up a silent prayer to any local deities of lost children *and* lost causes that she'd be alive when we did. "But now, we need to get set up in town."

"Tell Pearl at the bed and breakfast that you're here to help with my daughter," he said. "She's a sweetheart, that old woman. She'll give you one of the better rooms, no upcharge."

And that was that. Juliette finally deigned to rise from the ancient couch, and the two of us slipped back out into the bright sunlight, leaving Jeremiah to his bourbon, his weed, and his empty home.

As we neared the Corolla, Juliette turned on me. "Did you really find her?"

"What? No!"

"Then what on earth was that goofy nod about?"

"I was letting you know that I hadn't found any real leads but did find a yearbook with notes from what look to be friends in the back. Our interview list is growing."

"That's not what came across at all. You should tilt your head more to one side, and maybe squint a bit next time."

Okay; maybe our nonverbal communication still needed work.

"Jeremiah's not a suspect though, I take it?"

"No. Drunk and a little bit high, but he told us the truth. Originally, a small part of him *was* worried she and Pedro had just run away together, but he believes she would have made contact since, if that was the case."

"See, I *did* get that from *your* nod."

"Exactly. I'm just that good." She slid into the driver's seat without even asking. "Shall we go say hi to the sheriff?"

"Let's get set up at the bed and breakfast first. From the way Jeremiah was talking, it didn't sound like we'd have a hard time finding a room, but I'd rather have our stuff packed away than stuck in the trunk."

"Do we know the name of the place?"

"Of course I do." I gave her a look that reeked of smugness. For once, I'd done my research. "It's called Pearl's Bed & Breakfast."

Juliette wasn't impressed.

ooo

From Jeremiah's description, I'd expected Pearl to be pushing ninety, hard of hearing, and capable of whipping out a plate of freshly baked cookies at a moment's notice.

Turned out only the cookie part was true. I was pretty sure Pearl was the same age as Jeremiah, and almost as sure she was sweet on the widower. She definitely perked up (while somehow also deflating) at the mention of Dulcinea, and the next thing we knew, Juliette and I had the best suite in the whole place. Between the wood on the walls, the wood on the ceiling, and the furniture inside, it looked kind of like a woodworker's shop had exploded.

Juliette froze on entering. "That's a whole lot of wood."

"Tell me about it. What do you think it is? Knotty pine? Red oak? Laminate?"

She stared at me.

"What? I watch a lot of HGTV."

"It's mahogany, you dumbass."

"Seriously?" I frowned at the wood around me. "Huh."

"You didn't know what mahogany looked like?"

"Clearly not." I took a picture, just for my records.

Wood notwithstanding, we couldn't complain about the rest of the room. There was a large picture window off the back of the building that looked toward the mountains, a full sitting room, a standalone tub *and* shower, and a spacious balcony that we were advised to never actually go out on, for *reasons*.

It also, in direct refutation of any and all romance novel tropes, had two queen-sized beds. Even so, Juliette got squirrely as soon as she saw them.

"Let's not tell Anastasia we're staying in the same room, okay?"

"We literally share an apartment in San Diego, Duchess."

"Still. The whole werewolf incident is already going to be problematic enough." She placed her last suitcase in the walk-in closet and came back out into the bedroom. "Speaking of which, have you texted her yet?"

I hadn't, and I really needed to remedy that fact.

"Remember," said Juliette, "None of this was my fault."

"You know, you've gotten a lot more skittish since Ana and I started sleeping together."

"Yeah well, that's when the equation flipped."

"What equation?"

"My net value. When you two were just kind of sort of dating, and I wasn't directly working against Queen Bitch Lucia's designs, I was fairly confident that Anastasia wouldn't care enough to move against me. But now, she's got nothing but you and an awful lot of time on her hands."

"You're my friend. My obnoxious older sister. My Auntie Juliette, even. Ana's not going to do anything to you. Seriously."

"One day, I hope to be as blindly in love as you are, little bird. Except I'd end up stabbing myself in the heart with a letter opener just for being a cliché."

"We're all clichés to someone."

"You say that like it makes it okay."

I sent Ana a quick text—leaving out all mention of werewolves, just in case—while Juliette cleaned up in the bathroom, and then we swapped places. I splashed cold water on my face and armpits, tried to decide if the three-day-old stubble made me manly or just unkempt, and pulled on a clean T-shirt and a pair of jeans that didn't have my own blood on them.

Maybe it was a good thing that Jeremiah hadn't been sober when he met us.

By the time I was done making myself presentable, Juliette had finished texting with Angel. She tucked her phone away and gave me a look. "Sheriff or food first?"

The only possibly correct answer was *food*, especially given that my stomach was audibly trying to insert itself into the conversation. Still, we were here on a job, and there were two people's lives potentially at stake.

"Let's go see Johnny Law," I sighed.

Turned out Sheriff Abbas was way ahead of us on that front.

CHAPTER 21

We left Pearl's B&B to find a patrol car parked outside, and a small, dark man in a pristine white cowboy hat leaning against it. Sharp eyes moved from me to Juliette and back, and then he tugged on the brim of his hat and ambled over to us.

"Afternoon, folks," he said. "My name's Abbas. Sarosh Abbas. I'm the sheriff of Ghost Falls. Heard we had some visitors so thought I'd be neighborly and come say hello."

Sarosh dressed and talked like a cowboy, but he looked and sounded Middle Eastern. He made for an unexpected sight in northern New Mexico. I shook his outstretched hand, grateful that neither of us was doing that thing where we asserted our dominance by trying to crush the other. And not just because Abbas was armed.

"Nice to meet you, Sheriff Abbas. After speaking with Jeremiah and getting settled in at Pearl's, we were just on our way to meet with you."

"Jeremiah?" He cocked his head and turned to Juliette. "Are you the young woman I spoke to on the phone. From Middleton & Smith Investigations?"

"It's Smith & Middleton, actually," I said, interjecting. "I'm John Smith, and this is my business partner, Juliette Middleton. We were hired by a distant family member of Jeremiah's to lend our aid to the search for Dulcinea and Pedro."

"Could I see some identification?"

"Sure thing." I pulled out my license and handed it over. To my surprise, Juliette did too. I honestly hadn't known she'd ever even bothered getting an ID.

"Much appreciated." He scanned them briefly, then passed them back. "Glad to have you both."

"Really?" Television had taught me to expect a cold welcome and a long speech about jurisdiction… although that was mostly municipal or state police dealing with the feds.

"Yup. Normally, I might have something to say about big city private dicks coming into our town to throw their weight around—"

At least we'd watched the same shows. I could feel a sense of kinship forming already.

"—but at this point, I'll take whatever help I can get. It's been a week, there's been no sign of Dulcinea or Pedro in neighboring towns, and we've combed the local trails without any luck."

"Does that mean you don't think they ran away anymore?"

"It's still a possibility, but how many nineteen-year-olds do you know who can cover their tracks so well that they might as well be ghosts? Either they've been planning this for a while, and frankly I can't fathom why they'd need to—Jeremiah dotes on the girl, and Pedro's liked well enough in town—or…"

"You suspect foul play." I wasn't going to use the M word, not out in the streets where, according to tradition and small-town stereotype, there were likely at least a dozen sharp-eared septuagenarians listening in.

"I hope not. It's possible they rode Pedro's bike up into the mountains and something went wrong," the sheriff admitted, "but like I said, we've gone up the trails a good ways in every direction. Even had a helicopter from down south do an overhead flyby to see if they could spot anything. Smoke, a fire, debris... nothing. Either they were taken and nobody saw a damn bit of it happen, or they wound up off trail and deep enough in the mountains that we can't find them." He shook his head, the cowboy hat on his head not even wobbling with the motion. "I don't suppose either of you is trained in Search and Rescue?"

I hesitated. Did rescuing Audrey count?

"We aren't," said Juliette, answering on our behalf. "But we're damn good at putting the pieces together to solve a puzzle."

"If we can find out what happened before they left town, we might be able to figure out where they were going," I added. "Having a direction or a destination to work off of has to be better than trying to search everywhere at once."

"You got that right." He thought about it for a moment, then nodded. "Stop on by my office around three, and I'll show you what we've put together so far. That'll give me time to meet with Jeremiah and make sure your story checks out."

I just nodded. At least he was upfront about things. Also, a 3 p.m. meeting meant we'd have ample time for lunch.

"Sounds good to me. We plan to leave Sunday at the latest."

"That doesn't give you a whole lot of time."

"It's just enough to talk to some of Dulcinea and Pedro's friends," I admitted, "and maybe start working out hypotheses. But you know the area a lot better than we do. We'll run anything we find past you, if that's okay?"

"Better than I expected, to be frank."

I shrugged. "We're doing this to help out a friend; I don't care about anything but results."

"Then I think we'll get along just fine." He tipped his hat to us and ambled back to his patrol car. "If y'all are looking for something to eat, Mama Nita puts out a good spread, and her diner is only two blocks west of here."

He didn't say which street because only one street in the whole town really mattered, and we were already standing on it.

Juliette watched him drive away, and then turned to me, rolling her eyes. "I have no idea what we're doing here."

"We're looking for—"

"I get *why* we're here. I just don't know how we're supposed to accomplish it. You're a San Diego boy, born and bred, and I'm only slightly more comfortable in the wild. And given that I can't compel animals—or communicate with them, for that matter—I don't know what value I'll bring if Dulcinea and her boytoy are stuck in the wilderness somewhere."

"If they were up there, I'd think the search parties would have found some trace." I shrugged as we started the two-block hike to the restaurant. "Honestly, I don't know what to think yet. They could be being held prisoner in someone's house here in town for all we know."

"So, we just take it as it comes? Break some shit and see what happens?"

"Maybe without the breaking part, but yeah. We'll see what Sarosh has put together and then have our own talks with any people of interest, including Dulcinea's friends. With you here to assist in the questioning, we know we'll get the truth."

"You think some of them might be involved?"

"Maybe? I know exactly as much and as little as you do, remember? But even if they had nothing to do with the disappearance, maybe we'll learn something new that cracks open the case. After all, teenagers don't have the best track record of telling the whole, unvarnished truth to authority figures."

"I'll take your word for that. I don't even remember my teens."

"I'm sure Deanna has some stories."

"Which she will not tell you, on penalty of death."

"Come on now, Duchess, you're really going to threaten your own mom like that?"

"I meant *your* death."

"I'm telling Ana you said that."

We traded grins until my stomach spoiled the mood by growling.

"Gods, little bird. You should really get that looked at."

"Honestly, it's easier—and cheaper—to just feed it."

○○○

Mama Nita's was as good as advertised. I didn't recognize half the dishes on her menu, but she used chiles the way Michelin-starred chefs used truffles... abundantly and to spectacular effect. By the time we were on our way to the sheriff's office, conveniently only another couple of blocks further on Main Street, I was pleasantly full and more than ready to crack the case wide open.

An hour later, I was still pleasantly full, but a little bit less optimistic about the investigation. Sheriff Abbas was every bit as meticulous as he had seemed in our first meeting, his case files neatly organized and laid out for us in the single back room used for official police interrogations. He'd already spoken with all of Dulcinea's friends, including the names I'd found in her yearbook, as well as Pedro's older brother, who was the only family Dulcinea's boyfriend had left in town. We read through the transcripts of those conversations and the notes Abbas had made before, during, and after each one.

Nobody seemed to know anything, and what information there was matched the information packet Simon had given me back in San Diego. The couple had been spotted riding through town on Pedro's bike on the day of their disappearance. In fact, the witness had tried to file a complaint about Dulcinea not wearing a helmet. They had been traveling eastbound along Main Street at the time, which would have taken them up into the mountains, but nobody had actually seen them leave. Ghost Falls didn't have traffic light cameras or much in the way of CCTV in general; digitally, it was like the pair had just vanished from existence.

When the town mobilized to search for the missing teenagers, they'd sent search parties in every direction, but the majority had focused on that eastbound road, and the numerous animal and dirt bike trails that branched off from it as it cut across the mountains. They hadn't found anything to build on. While there'd been no shortage of tracks and tire treads, dirt biking was a popular activity for the locals; Pedro's bike trail, assuming he'd even left one, was indistinguishable from that of a dozen other similar bikes that had ridden up and down those same hills. A few townsfolk had even taken their dogs with them, thinking the canines might be able to sniff out a trail, but those pooches hadn't found a thing.

In short, the sheriff's well-planned and well-organized search, utilizing all the resources of Ghost Falls, and a few on loan from neighboring counties, had turned up a big, fat donut.

And not the delicious kind.

By the time we left the sheriff's, it was already late afternoon. Abbas had given us the addresses of the family members and friends he'd already interviewed, but first we decided to speak with the one eyewitness on the day of Dulcinea's disappearance.

Lacey Goodfellow was pushing ninety, but as tiny as she was, she hadn't gone frail the way most people her age did. She was deeply tanned, her white hair bleached even whiter by the sun, and the wrinkles on her face, arms, and legs reminded me of the bark and burls of a tree. She was quick to let us know that she wasn't impressed with our *big-city credentials*, glaring up at us through rheumy eyes. Still, as the oldest person in town, she considered herself the unofficial mother of damn near everyone else in it, including Sheriff Abbas, and Dulcinea had held a special place in her wizened heart.

"She's a peach, that one," said Lacey, her voice precisely as scratchy and thin as you'd expect upon meeting her. She used her chin like Mike's mother used her hands, visual accompaniment and emphasis all-in-one. "Never understood what she saw in the boy, but I was young once too. Good Lord knows, I let a boy or two chase me that I probably shouldn't have!"

"What is it about Pedro you don't like?" I asked.

"Shiftless and lazy, like his dad before him. Wears his hair long like a girl, with a big leather jacket like one of them rockers from California." She leaned in conspiratorially. "Sometimes, he even walks the streets without a shirt on!"

Juliette made appropriate noises of horror.

"The mother, Elloquis, God rest her soul, was the only good one of the bunch, but Dulcinea's a sweetheart with a good head on her shoulders. Either she'll shape him up or she'll ship him out." Lacey frowned up at us. "How come you haven't found her yet? Sheriff Abbas is a good boy, but he can't do all the work, you know?"

"We're doing our best, ma'am," I said. "That's why we're talking with you. We're hoping you might remember something more about what you saw on the day of their disappearance."

"I told the sheriff everything." That chin wagged back and forth like a terrier trying to ward off intruders. "Dulcinea and the boy on that terrible motorcycle of his, riding down Main Street like they didn't have a care in the world. I was on my way back from Otto Green's store with my groceries for the week. He lets me push one of his carts the whole way home on account of my license being suspended a few years back."

"And they were headed east?"

"Sure as the day is long."

"Can you recall how they seemed?"

"How they seemed?"

'Yeah; were they happy? Sad? Arguing? Anything could help."

Even her chin paused to consider the question. "Well, Pedro had a helmet on, so I couldn't see his face, but he was whooping it up like one of those damn fools down in Duke City or something. Dulcinea wasn't wearing a helmet—did I say that already? Eeeeee, I was shocked to see it. Smart girl, but all the brains in the world won't matter much if they end up spread across the road, you know?"

"But otherwise, she seemed… normal?"

"Yeah. She was laughing. Arms wrapped around Pedro and hair flying behind her like a flag."

That was almost poetic.

"That's it," said Lacey. "They went down Main Street and then I pushed my shopping cart home. When I returned the cart to Otto there was no sign of them."

"How much later was that?"

"Oh, I don't know. An hour, maybe? I don't walk so fast anymore."

Given that she was ancient and tiny, I believed it.

ooo

We managed three other interviews that day before the sun went down, and they all went pretty much the same way. Juliette stepped in on two occasions, eyes flashing gold, but while we learned a few things about the local gossip and hidden lives of Ghost Fall's teenage population, we were no closer to finding Dulcinea by the end.

"I thought small towns like this were supposed to be hotbeds of concealed sin and corruption?" she grumbled on our way back to Mama Nita's.

"I guess Ghost Falls is the exception." I shrugged. "I'd been half hoping we'd uncover some sort of secret cult, myself."

"Only half hoping?"

"It's been a week since the pair went missing. I feel like any cult worth their salt would have already done something to the people they kidnapped."

"Oh." Juliette shivered theatrically. "Okay, maybe it's a good thing this town is as dull as it looks."

"Good for Dulcinea and Pedro, anyway. Less so for our investigation."

Mama Nita's had six booths and just as many stand-alone tables, but once again, we were the only people in it. The host/waiter, who I was pretty sure was Nita's husband, son, or brother, escorted us to one of those booths, and we sank down onto worn but comfortable cushions. Twenty minutes later, I was working my way through some sort of stew, and Juliette was on her fourth taco.

"If I ever leave San Diego," I decided, "I'm moving to New Mexico. I could spend my whole life just walking from Pearl's to here and back again every meal."

"You'd be three hundred pounds in a year or less."

"Worth it."

"So, what next? Recon? Stakeout?"

I shook my head. "Where would we go? Who would we watch? So far, everyone's been accommodating and truthful, if not always pleasant. I vote we hang out here a bit and then head back to Pearl's. We've got a lot more interviews ahead of us tomorrow."

"I'm going to have to make a pit stop before that."

"Too much information, Duchess. Besides, the bathroom's right over there." I'd already visited it twice. Something about the combination of chiles—Christmas, as our waiter had called the mix of red and green—and beer was causing everything I ate and drank to go right through me.

"That's not what I'm talking about." She licked her lips and, for the first time all day, I saw a hint of fang. "Some of us need more than just food."

Oh. Well, that complicated things.

"Didn't you feed before we left?"

"Yeah, and I'm old enough now that a feeding can last me a few days in the right conditions. And no," she added, reading my face like a book, "those conditions don't include getting my ass kicked by a bunch of Infected. Healing all that took its toll."

Whereas I'd recovered just fine on my own. Then again, Juliette had gotten it a lot worse than I had, especially from Shea.

"Okay. So, uh… how do you want to do this? Just pick someone out, do your mojo, and get your drink on? Wham, bam, thank you ma'am?"

"No, I figured I'd invite them out for a night of poetry under the stars." She rolled her eyes. "Yes, that's how it usually goes."

"Can I help any?"

"Are you offering?" Just like that, her eyes were golden instead of their usual yellow. "I didn't think you'd be up for it."

"Wait, what are we talking about now?"

"Blood, little bird."

"You mean *mine?* Yeah, not in this life. Not again anyway."

The glow faded from her eyes. "No need to be an ass about it."

"Even if it didn't hurt like hell—and you know it does—how do you think Anastasia would feel about you snacking on me?"

"You're right." She sighed. "I never thought she'd be as territorial as Lucia. Sharing is caring, after all."

"Juliette—"

"It's fine. I get it. I'm just tired, bored, and hungry, and you—"

"I know. I smell amazing."

"Your blood does anyway." She wrinkled her nose. "Everything else? Not so much."

That was… unkind but probably accurate.

"Anyway, if I can help some other way…?"

"I've been feeding almost as long as little Lacey's been alive. I'll be fine on my own."

"Okay. Make sure you don't take too much, okay? We don't need anyone suddenly showing up with anemia a day after our arrival."

"Yes, Mom."

"Also, maybe pick someone who *isn't* on our list of suspects or contacts?"

She shot me a look.

"I'm just saying; this is a small town. Be judicious with your choice."

"I'm about twelve seconds away from just stabbing you with a fork and drinking straight from the tap."

I mentally calculated how far I could get in twelve seconds, and just how quickly Juliette would be able to cover that same ground. The odds were not in my favor.

"Maybe we should drink some more beer instead?"

CHAPTER 22
IN WHICH BAD NEWS TRAVELS FAST

Juliette and I split up on the way back to Pearl's. As she'd pointed out, she didn't need my help to hunt, and that was more than okay with me. I was dating a vampire, in business with another, terrible thrall to a third, and friends with a fourth, but the whole drinking blood thing just wasn't my scene.

Except when Lucia does it to you, whispered a voice in my mind. *Then you can't get enough of it.*

Which just went to show that life would always find a way to make things difficult. If I could somehow transfer my bond from Lucia to Anastasia, I would have done so in an instant, and not *just* because Ana would then be able to get the blood she needed from the man she loved… although that would definitely be a bonus.

With Lucia being the only one who could drink from me without it being torture, I was pretty much permanently off the menu. And I had no interest in being a bystander, regardless of what my relationship with the vampire in question might be. Voyeurism wasn't my thing any more than exhibitionism was. So, I wished Juliette the best and headed back to our suite at Pearl's. At least there, I'd have the one thing I'd been missing since leaving San Diego: privacy.

We probably should've just sprung for separate rooms, especially given the multiple vacancies at the bed and breakfast. But I was a small business owner and despite my best efforts to be a terrible one, minding the budget was something that had become an unconscious habit over the years. Our agency was doing reasonably well now, mostly thanks to Juliette, but running a business that involved more than just me had added a ton of expenses—health care for Angel among them—and this pro bono case for Simon was going to suck up most of our net profits for the month. Sharing a suite saved us almost $300 a night, and that extra thousand dollars could be earmarked for better things.

Like paying off the corporate card, apparently.

I hopped in the shower and washed away the day's stink. My multi-day stubble was now showing signs of possibly evolving into a beard, but I once again let it be. We were up in the mountains, after all, and it seemed to fit the general vibe. All I needed were some hiking boots, an axe, a face transplant, and about thirty pounds of fat magically transforming into muscle, and I'd be the kind of mountain man to make romance heroines swoon.

Juliette had claimed the bed closest to the window, so I hopped into the other one, wonderphone in hand. I'd already noticed that cell signal was a little bit sketchy in Ghost Falls off the main road, but Pearl's had Wi-Fi and I connected to it straightaway. With my partner out snacking on a local, it would've been the perfect time to give Ana a call, but we'd traded texts over the course of the afternoon, and I knew she, Steve, and others were out on the streets of San Diego, searching for Zorana.

In some ways, they were facing the exact same issue we were… too much space to cover and not enough manpower to cover it. Juliette and I were working to narrow *our* search area, but Anastasia and Steve had another option: drastically increasing the manpower available.

Or... the crab and rat power available, technically. My suggestion of employing the karkino had gone over so well with Steve that I'd doubled down and pitched the idea of them using Simon's zombie rats too. No word yet on whether Simon had agreed, but I had high hopes.

I sent Ana a goodnight text, one which Juliette would have gagged over if she'd seen it, and then checked the rest of my messages. No word from Kayla and Darlene, although I hadn't expected any. I was pretty sure they'd be radio silent until they returned to San Diego with a hundred gigabytes worth of pictures and at least three drunken stories. In the meantime, I'd happily let them be so they could enjoy their honeymoon.

Maria Elena *had* messaged me, mostly to tell me about the club she'd gone to with some manpires as well as her friend and Lucia's niece, Sabina, aka Queen-In-Waiting Sabina Borghesi. The pictures of that excursion were already up on literally all of her social media accounts, and even though it was something like four in the morning in Rome, I messaged back to let her know I'd check them out.

Shockingly, I had even received a text from Sabina herself, only the third such message since leaving Rome months earlier. Like the first two, this one was just her complaining about Lucia. While the aunt and niece had learned to work together and maybe even appreciate one another, they were far too similar in far too many ways to ever truly get along. I sent back words of commiseration, trying not to be too smug about having finally gotten away from Lucia myself. Literally nobody in the world knew better than me what a pain in the ass the formerly exiled vampire queen could be.

As always, thoughts of Lucia activated our bond—which had gone from being a small knot of thoughts and emotions in my brain to a five-lane superhighway—but being a thousand miles closer to the femmepire queen meant we were *still* almost six thousand miles apart; I could sense her general direction—east—and nothing more.

It was all kinds of glorious.

Those were the only texts I'd received all day, which probably said something about my social life. Wedding season was dying down, and the chance of former high school classmates popping back into my life unexpectedly had dwindled accordingly. I checked my email—most of it spam, albeit with slightly fewer penis enhancement treatments than normal—then opened the YouTube app on my wonderphone.

Roughly two dozen cat videos later, my phone buzzed, this time with a message from a new and unknown number.

Hi, it read.

I rolled my eyes. What had spammers and con artists even done before the digital age?

I'd like a pepperoni pizza, I replied. *Hold the pepperoni, add extra pineapple, and slather the whole thing in Ranch.*

What?

What what? I replied smartly.

Isn't this John, the mediator?

That stopped me in mid mocking reply. It wasn't unusual for spammers to know my name, but my second career shouldn't be in any searchable databases. Hell, not even the IRS knew I mediated as a side hustle, and they knew practically everything.

Uh, who is this? I finally answered.

Audrey? This is the number I was given.

Oh. Sorry, Audrey, this is John. I thought you were a spammer.

And a pizza place?

Something like that.

You do know ranch dressing is gross, right?

I didn't know that, not at all, but she was still young. I was sure she'd learn better on her own.

How's everything going with the pack?

Good! She added two smiling emojis and a thumbs up. *Uncle Zeke calmed down almost as soon as Hy and Ezra brought me in. He didn't even care too much that Chase let your business partner go, although I wouldn't recommend she show her face around again anytime soon.*

I think we're all in agreement there. Are you headed back to Albuquerque soon?

In a week or so, I think? There's still the matter of the people who kidnapped me. A few of our stronger squads are already in Phoenix on the hunt.

Once again, I wasn't entirely sure how I felt about that. In all likelihood, humans were literally dying to werewolves in Phoenix even as we traded texts. Did those people deserve it? Thinking of that cold, sterile operating table made me say yes, but even so…

Maybe I wasn't cut out for this whole silent species-war thing.

I sent back my own thumbs-up emoji and a sweating smiley-face.

Anyway, she continued, *I wanted to reach out to you.*

What do you need?

You said you'd give me the numbers for my cousin Jason and his… what was it… co-leader?

Oh, right. Carolyn. I sent both numbers over, and then checked the time. It was almost eight here in Ghost Falls, which made it seven in San Diego, according to the murky and slightly unknowable laws of time zones. Seven on a Thursday night… *I think this is the pack's new game night. If you call Carolyn directly, you might be able to chat with more than just her.*

I was just planning to text.

That'll probably work too. Let me send her a quick message letting her know, so you don't get another pizza order.

By the time I'd sent that text to Carolyn and came back to Audrey, she'd sent me three skull emojis and a diagonal laughing face.

I waited for more, but no other texts ever came. Apparently, Audrey and I were done with our chat.

I put down my phone and stretched out on the bed. I was glad she was reaching out to Carolyn, and that she had a friend in the pack like Hyacinth. In the long run, she'd need both when it came time to assume a leadership role… and in the short run, the more people she had to lean on, the better equipped she'd be to cope with her kidnapping in Phoenix.

Not that I was a specialist in that sort of thing.

Juliette still wasn't back, so I turned my mind back to our case. This whole job had started out as a way to repay the favor I owed Simon, but after talking to the townsfolk, it was hard not to be invested personally. Dulcinea and even Pedro seemed like nice kids, and I'd had enough of nice people finishing last. The zombie prince had entrusted me with finding his many-greats granddaughter, but we hadn't made any progress yet. Juliette had questioned what value she added, and now I found myself in the same position. Sheriff Abbas was a more experienced and more capable investigator than I was. That much was undeniable. So, what the hell had Simon expected me to bring to the case?

The answer, when I finally realized it, seemed obvious. I flipped over my wonderphone and swiped back through my email.

A few minutes later, Juliette made her return, cheeks rosy with someone else's blood and the energy that feeding produced in a vampire. Even her features looked a little less sharp than usual.

"What's got you grinning?" she asked me.

I looked up from the dossier of supernatural species that Anastasia had sent me. "Sprites."

Juliette shivered. "Flying disease vectors. What about them?"

"There's a symposium of them in these hills."

"And? You think Dulcinea was killed by *sprites?*"

"What? No!" I frowned. "Is that possible?"

"In the same way as someone can die if they willingly stand still and let a thousand or more mosquitoes feed at their leisure."

"So… yes?"

She rolled her eyes again. "It's not likely."

"That's fine. I wasn't thinking of pinning the kidnapping or attack—if there was one—on the sprites. But they do offer something we're sadly lacking."

"Which is?"

"Manpower." I ticked the relevant points off on my fingers. "They fly, they know the area, and apparently they can get damn near anywhere undetected."

"They also have brains the size of gnats and are notoriously distrustful of strangers. Especially ones that *don't* have wings."

I let the Dealmaker™ spread across my face, bringing peace and joy to all who saw it.

"Don't worry; I've got a plan for that."

ooo

"Hello?"

The woman's voice was high-pitched and chirpy, as cute as the rest of her, even somewhat dulled by sleep. I could practically see her in my mind's eye, ten inches tall in heels, with prismatic butterfly wings that beat the air a thousand times a minute.

"Hey Kristin, this is John Smith."

"I didn't do it!"

"Are you sure? Because I've been told otherwise." I had no idea what *it* was, but one thing I'd learned about pixies in general, and Kristin's congregation specifically, was that if there was something shady going on in San Diego, they were always in it up to their wings.

"Okay," she admitted. "One of my direct reports *may* have been involved, but I promise you, that's as far as it goes, and her next performance review will reflect it!"

"I'm going to trust you on that, just this once." I made a mental note to ask Anastasia what she thought the pixies might be involved in. Forewarned was forearmed, after all. "In the meantime, I need something from you."

"Oh?" I could practically hear the calculation ooze into her Disney-esque voice. "Tell me what you need! I'm sure we can come to a mutually beneficial arrangement."

"Like you did with the witches, you mean?"

There was a moment of silence.

"Now John, you know that wasn't my fault! Nepenthe *seemed* trustworthy, after all. How was I to know you'd choose to give her your blood?"

"When someone I think is an ally vouches for a third party, it goes a long way."

She squeaked. "Aww! My congregation is honored to be considered your ally, John. And because of that, I think we can even give you a special discounted rate—"

"Kristin."

"I mean, nothing *too* significant—we need to make a profit on the deal, after all—but I bet—"

"Kristin!" Something in my tone had Juliette looking up from her own phone even though she was sprawled across her bed on the other side of the room.

"Yes, John?"

"You owe me. Not your congregation. You. I'm calling in that debt."

She shifted tactics on the dime she could have easily fit at least one of her feet on. "You know I'm always happy to help a friend."

"What are your thoughts on sprites?"

"Love them," she replied immediately. "Every single one is a born consumer. Play a catchy jingle, show them something shiny, and they'll be trading their life's savings in tree pollen for the cheapest of manufactured goods."

Small, I reminded myself for the hundredth time, was just another word for sneaky.

"We're trying to make a deal with a local symposium," I told her.

"In San Diego? I don't know any—"

"No, New Mexico. Outside a little town called Ghost Falls. I was hoping you could act as our go-between."

"Hmm."

Even her hum was cute. It was really hard to remember that she had, unwittingly or not, set the stage for everything that had gone down in San Diego the previous year: the kidnapping of Graciela, the House coup, and of course the further warping of my bond with Lucia.

Granted, I had as much, if not more, to do with all of it, but *I'd* already paid the price for that.

"We have a franchise deal with another congregation in Santa Fe," she finally said. "Let me reach out to them and get the contact info for your sprite symposium. Do you want to tell me what it's about or just set up a meeting?"

"We need their help searching the territory."

"For anything specific?"

"We'll tell them that ourselves, pixie," said Juliette, speaking up for the first time.

"Who is that?"

"My partner, Juliette Middleton."

"I thought you were dating the *other* vampire? The skinny and scary one?"

"*Business* partner." Juliette said the words at the same time as I did. I wasn't sure if she was more annoyed by the continued misunderstandings or by the fact that *Anastasia* was the scary one.

"Business partners are the best kind," chirped Kristin. "No hurt feelings when you trade them for a twenty-second spot on NPR. Okay, I'll set up a meeting so you can tell them what you need. Do you have any money on you, John?"

"Why?"

"I might work for free, in honor of our longstanding professional relationship and our mutual hopes for future joint ventures, but the sprites won't."

"I have a few bills," I admitted.

"Exchange them for coins. Sprites like their currency shiny. And maybe bring some sweets too. They'll try to bargain with you, but they're slaves to their eyes and stomachs."

"Sounds like someone I know," mused Juliette.

"When do you think they'll be able to meet us?" I asked, ignoring my *business* partner.

"I'll get my best people on it. It'll probably be sometime tomorrow? Sprites aren't good with maintaining technology, so they have to make do with other people's."

I wasn't sure what that meant, but I didn't really care either. "Tomorrow would be great. I really appreciate this, Kristin."

On her bed, Juliette shook her head despairingly. She recognized a faux pas when I'd committed one.

"Well of course, John! That's what friends and allies do, isn't it? And speaking of friendships, I wouldn't be able to sleep in good conscience if I didn't tell you about an incredible business opportunity one of my junior executives recently discovered."

"Is it a multi-level marketing scheme?"

"Of course not! It's way better. I'm talking a truly boutique, bespoke operation. These products are too good for general consumption. All you need to do is pick the five friends you like the most and introduce them to the opportunity. Every purchase or sale they make trickles back up to you, giving you a cut of the proceeds. If they choose out of their own free will to then share the opportunity with some of *their* friends, well, guess what? You get some of those proceeds too!"

"That's exactly what a multi-level marketing scheme is, Kristin." Between condo timeshares and pyramid schemes, I'd seen more than a few scams in my day.

"No, this is more like a pyramid, really! The closer to the top you are, the better things go."

"I think I'll pass, but thanks."

"I'll give you a few days to think it over," she said. "Talk to you tomorrow when I've got sprite news!"

I tapped to end the call and rolled my eyes. "Go ahead."

"With what?"

"With whatever it is you so badly wanted to say about Kristin. Or sprites. Or both."

"Oh. That. I stopped paying attention after she mentioned bribing the sprites."

"Then why were you shaking your head?"

She looked at me from across the room, yellow eyes oddly serious. "Because I got a message from Angel. You're going to want to see this."

She tossed the phone across the room with a flippancy only the rich or supernaturally athletic could afford. I bobbled it—twice—and managed to redirect it so it fell onto my bed, rather than the floor. When it had stopped moving, I flipped it over and blanched.

"Jesus, Juliette. Why would I want to see that?"

"What?"

"I don't care how freaky you guys get behind closed doors. Seriously, it's all cool, even if it gets really loud sometimes, but I don't need to read the foreplay. And I don't even know what the hell *that thing* is for." Whatever it was, it looked like some sort of alien technology.

"Oh, for the love of—you must have scrolled up when you butterfingered the catch. Just scroll down, you moron."

"Yeah, *I'm* the moron." I did as requested, skipping past a surprising amount of raunchy pillow talk for a relationship possibly on its way out, and finally found another image at the very bottom.

"What's this?"

"Remember how I promoted Angel to junior investigator?"

"Yeah. Why?" I frowned at the image. It was grainy and dark, but I recognized the coastline. There were two figures on the pier, and one of them— "Wait, is this Mike?"

"She decided to take over the stakeout, since we were both out of town."

"That's a huge invasion of privacy, Duchess."

"It's our job, little bird. Anyway, she struck gold on the very first night."

I studied the image more carefully. Apparently, Angel hadn't used my dad's camera and her phone was the next best thing to an early-2012 potato: the low-light photography left *everything* to be desired. Still, it was recognizably Mike, bent down toward a woman who was identifiably *not* Susan, and while I couldn't see anything of the woman other than her dark hair, the two were very clearly kissing in a way that left absolutely no room for debate.

"Well, shit."

"I'm sorry, John. I know he's your friend."

"This just doesn't make sense." Even as I spoke, I couldn't help but compare myself to every spouse I'd had to deliver the bad news to over the past years. Few people hired a private investigator unless they already *knew* deep down what was going on, but the shock and protestations when actual evidence was produced never changed. And yet… "I'm telling you; this isn't like him at all."

"Angel's going to tail him for a couple more nights," said Juliette. "I told her she could take the days off to sleep."

"Yeah, that's fine. Our voice mail can get any callers, and it's not like we're there to take new cases anyway." I swallowed past the inexplicable lump in my throat. "Have her bring my dad's camera with her next time. The less ambiguity there is the better."

"Are you okay?" Juliette's voice was uncharacteristically soft.

"Yeah. No. I don't know." I shook my head. "I was best man at his wedding *four* months ago! I don't particularly like Susan, but she deserves better than this. I just hope there's some sort of explanation that I'm not seeing, because this… Man, this would kill my parents to see. Not to mention Mike's mom."

"I guess I didn't realize it was that big a deal." She held up both hands at whatever look I gave her. "I'm serious! With Kayla an obvious exception, you know my kind don't get married. And as far as I can tell after a year of working with you, humans don't let marriage keep them from doing whatever they want anyway."

"We're private eyes; we see the bad side of humanity. That doesn't make marriage itself a joke or change the fact that there are good people in the world who I'd expect more from." I tossed Juliette's phone aside and picked up my own.

"What are you doing?"

"I'm texting him."

Just like that, the femmepire was standing over my bed, and if she wasn't anywhere near as fast as Anastasia or even Kayla, she was still quick enough to take my phone before I even realized she was moving.

"What the hell, Duchess? Give me my phone."

"Not until you take a breath and stop behaving like an asshole."

I made a grab for the phone and she rolled her eyes, holding it up in the air, while her other hand pinned me to the bed like a butterfly to a page.

"John, I say this as your business partner and your friend: you need to chill the hell out. I know you're disappointed and—apparently?—feeling betrayed, but confronting Mike now will blow up our case. Gather the evidence, put it all together, and only then present it. Isn't that what you taught me?"

I frowned. "I don't think I've ever said that in my life."

"Oh. I must have read it somewhere. Too bad; I thought you'd given me some wisdom somehow." Her smirk came and went. "Seriously… who's our client?"

"Simon?"

"Gods, I'm actually starting to feel bad for Lucia. *Lucia!*" She took a long slow breath, in and out, and tried again. "Our client on the Mike case, little bird."

"Susan, obviously."

"Right. She's the spouse. She's the one being betrayed here, not you. So, maybe you should pump the brakes on your own emotions and think about the person who hired us?"

I took my own long breath, and when that didn't work, took another. Juliette's hand on my chest felt like Mjolnir; I had as much chance of getting out from under it as I did bench pressing an SUV. Worse, despite the jumble of emotions coursing through me, she was depressingly right.

If Mike was having an affair—and it was hard to argue that fact—Susan, as our client, deserved to get all the evidence of that affair. And me flying off the handle at my lying, cheating best friend would only make gathering that evidence more difficult.

I was starting to understand why all the textbooks recommended never taking a case involving friends and family.

"Fine," I said, meeting Juliette's serious gaze. "You're right. But before we meet with Susan, I want to see it with my own eyes. I don't know what other explanation there could be, but—"

"I get it."

"Mike's a good guy."

"Sometimes, good guys do dumb things."

I winced. That one I *had* told her.

CHAPTER 23

IN WHICH ONE FLYING PEST DESERVES ANOTHER

It wasn't a great night of sleep, and not even the breakfast Pearl served us the next morning could change that. I was tired and a bit grumpy by the time we started our interviews and a solid four hours later, I was also frustrated.

"Was your murder case like this in Rome?" asked Juliette.

"Sort of." I paused to finish chewing. We were back at Mama Nita's, this time for lunch, and I was having a sandwich that seemed like New Mexico's—or maybe just Nita's—version of a Po Boy: fried pork, crisp bread, lettuce, tomatoes, and of course, chiles. Like everything else I'd eaten in Ghost Falls, it was good. "I think I spent two solid days interviewing. More, if you included the council members."

"And that's how you cracked the case?" Juliette was having some sort of stew. And a beer. On the table next to us, the jar of honey we'd bought at Ghost Falls' general store remained unopened.

"Didn't I already tell you all of this when I got home?"

"I don't know. Honestly, you said a lot of things and I only listened to about half of them."

"Right. Well, I didn't so much crack the case as have most of the answers fall into my lap," I admitted. "Courtesy of whatever the Rag Lady did to me."

"So, we have no guarantee this approach even works?"

"I mean... no? But what else are we supposed to do?"

She replied with a grunt that told me she was as frustrated with our lack of progress as I was. We'd only been in Ghost Falls for about a day, but I think we had both kind of hoped that things would already be resolved.

"Anyway," I said, "we have... what... three people left on our list?"

"How would I know? You haven't even shown me the list. I'm just here to look pretty and keep everyone honest."

So far, that last part hadn't been a problem, for all the good it did us. Not all of Dulcinea's friends were as enamored with Pedro as she was, but even his most vocal detractor limited her criticisms to his fashion sense and general lack of ambition. Nobody believed for a second that he would have done anything to her. As for Pedro's brother, he'd been an unmitigated asshole—recalcitrant and lazy—at first. Once Juliette worked her mojo, he'd been as forthcoming as the others, with just as little insight to offer.

Dulcinea and Pedro loved each other. Everyone seemed to agree on that. They fought, like most couples, but never for more than a day, and their last blowup had been all the way back in the spring. Unlike many of their peers, neither had seemed interested in leaving Ghost Falls, Pedro looking to help his brother at their small auto shop, and Dulcinea having dreams of creating an online clothing business.

They both *did* have social media accounts, despite what Jeremiah had thought. I'd pored over the Instagram feeds, hoping to find a clue, but every picture had been filtered to within an inch of its life, rending them largely useless. If a stranger was lurking in the background of any of them, they'd been blurred to hell and back with portrait mode, and if either of the teenagers was up to anything even vaguely illegal, they'd concealed it from their friends, their family, *and* their own online presence.

In short, all we'd found since coming to Ghost Falls were dead ends.

"We'll finish our interviews this afternoon," I said, "and then if we haven't heard from Kristin yet…"

"Let me guess: dinner?"

"I was thinking we'd walk the town. See if maybe vamp senses picked up anything the sheriff might have missed."

"That's not a terrible idea." Juliette broke off a piece of bread from my po boy and ran it along the inside of her now-empty bowl. "What happens if I don't see, smell, or hear anything?"

"Then we hope to hell you taste something at least." I met her roll of the eyes with a shrug.

"We should've brought Jason or one of the other San Diego wolves with us. They've got better noses than I do."

It wasn't a terrible idea, but… "Unless there was a clear trail leading out from town, we wouldn't even know where to start. We need the sprites to help us canvas the territory first."

"Then I'm going to get another beer." She eased herself up her feet and wandered over toward the kitchen where the restaurant's one waiter spent most of his time. After only three meals at Mama Nita's, both Nita and her employee had started treating the femmepire like she was family.

Juliette swore she hadn't used her mojo on them, but I was reserving judgment.

When Juliette returned, her second beer was in an enormous glass, closer in size to something you'd see people wandering the Vegas strip with than anything you'd find in a restaurant. She downed a healthy sip and leaned back in the booth, eyes halfway closed like a cat lazing in the afternoon sun.

"Having fun there, Duchess?"

"More than I was this morning, anyway."

"We've only got about twenty minutes before our next interview." I checked my phone just to be sure. "If you need help finishing that monstrosity off…"

"It's fine. Henry already said I could take it with me if need be."

"Who's Henry?"

"Our waiter? Mama Nita's husband? Aren't you supposed to be the people person in this business?"

"He's not wearing a nametag."

"Neither was I when we first met, yet we somehow got along swimmingly anyway."

That wasn't how I remembered things, but I'd long since learned that arguing with Juliette's revisionist history was a lost cause.

"Fine. Bring it—" I stopped, mid speech, as the phone in my hand buzzed with an incoming call.

"Hey, Kristin."

"John, who's your favorite pixie?"

I was pretty sure that was a trick question and that any answer I gave would get me into trouble somehow.

"You got in touch with the symposium?"

"Of course I did! They want to meet with you at two."

"In the afternoon?"

"Obviously! I wouldn't set up a 2 a.m. meeting without contacting you first. I know you humans need your beauty sleep."

"Some more than others," muttered Juliette.

"It's like ten to two right now."

"Don't be silly; it's only 12:50, John." Kristin's voice went sweet. "You know, if you're looking for supplements that promote mental acuity, I have an incredible deal—"

"We're in New Mexico. They're in a different time zone."

"Oh. Right. Actually, that makes a lot more sense, now that I think about it. Well, you better get moving!"

"Where are we meeting them?" I waved for our waiter—Henry—to bring us the bill, and scooped the jar of honey into the backpack I'd bought along with it.

"Most of them won't go near Ghost Falls—something about bug zappers and at least one pet toad—but they're sending a contact to wait near the anthill outside town."

I waited for more details, but they never came.

"I'm not familiar with the location of the town anthill," I admitted. "Did they give you anything more than that?"

"I think they said the east road. Just keep going and they'll flag you down. I gave them your description."

"East it is." I handed Henry my card, which he popped into a card reader then and there. "We'll see them soon."

"Great! I have to say I'm loving this synergy we've got going here. Have you given any more thought to the opportunity I outlined for you last night?"

"The pyramid scheme?"

"I think of it more as a pyramid plan, really."

"Yeah, I'm still not interested."

"Of course. I'll give you a few more days to consider it."

"That's not—"

She had already ended the call.

I sighed and tucked my phone away.

"After this, you might want to just block that number," said Juliette with a smirk. "And I'm warning you now: you're not selling

Tupperware out of my apartment. Sex toys? Maybe. But not Tupperware."

Henry guffawed, the older man patting Juliette's shoulder as he gave the femmepire a fond smile. "There you go again, Juliette."

"I have to keep things light, Henry. Otherwise, you'd have to roll me out of here after every one of Mama's meals."

"Don't I know it." The wrinkles on his worn brown face deepened as he gave her another smile. "Speaking of, she wanted me to give these to you." He handed her a bundle, neatly wrapped in colored paper and tied in a bow.

"Macarons?" Juliette bowed her head. "You shouldn't have."

I blinked and looked back and forth between the two.

"Nonsense! Gotta keep your energy up as this one drags you all over town." The smile slipped from his face as he handed me back my credit card, flipping the card reader around so I could read the screen. "Please choose your tip and then enter your signature, sir."

I went with the twenty-five percent tip option, but the stern expression on his face never changed. He scanned me head to toe, grunted a thank you, and then marched back to the kitchen.

"Did I do something to piss him off?"

"I think he and Mama Nita are concerned you might be taking advantage of a sweet young thing like myself. You do look like you're half again my age, after all."

"Only because you chose to have your first drink of blood at eighteen and will now be stuck as a teenager for the rest of your life."

"You say stuck, I say blessed." She grabbed her macarons in one hand and her beer glass, still half full, in the other, and stood back up. "I hear we're looking for an anthill?"

○○○

We never found the anthill.

In fact, part of me wasn't convinced it existed.

Thankfully, it was a moot point. About five minutes after we had walked out of town, following the east road in what could have been an exact retracing of Dulcinea and Pedro's steps were it not for the fact that they had been on a motorcycle and we were walking, something flashed in front of our faces. *Literally* flashed, like a giant firefly despite the fact that it was still daytime.

Thankfully, neither Juliette nor I tried to swat it away, because a moment later, it resolved into a small glowing orb, maybe the size of a baby's hand. Unlike the Mistborn at Lord Kala's Bitter End, they were more than just light though... at the center of that sphere was the silhouette of a person.

"Sprite?" I asked Juliette.

"Sprite."

The sprite buzzed around us a bit. I couldn't tell if it was trying to communicate, just excited to see us, or maybe trying to communicate *that* it was excited to see us. Eventually, it turned away and, bobbing up and down like beachball in a swimming pool, floated off the road and away from us.

I wasn't an expert in interspecies communication, or anything else really, but I was at least reasonably sure it wanted us to follow it. So, I did. With a sigh, Juliette removed her heels, sharp, pointy, and already showing wear from too much walking, and packed them away in my backpack with the honey.

"Let's go, little bird."

Within twenty seconds, I was hopelessly lost. No doubt, there were all sorts of indicators about where we were going or even where we had come from, but to me, every tree could be categorized as big or small, and was otherwise indistinguishable. I kept my eye on the dancing ball of light, and hoped it wasn't luring us into quicksand.

Assuming New Mexico had quicksand. Ana hadn't included it in her briefing, but quicksand was, as far as I knew, entirely mundane in nature. Maybe she had just figured I was already well versed in quicksand lore? Maybe she thought humans learned about it in elementary school?

If I was going to start my life entirely over again as an infant… well, I'd learn martial arts as soon as I could walk. But the *second* thing I would do as a chubby little baby boy would be to study up on quicksand. After all, ignorance really *could* be deadly.

Luckily, the little sprite didn't lead us to our slow, suffocating doom, but instead on a long and winding route through the woods. My quads started to burn as each step took us further up the barely visible incline, but a sip of Juliette's beer and the macaron she had finally given me after ten minutes of puppy dog eyes helped fortify me for the journey.

The exercising I'd been doing with Kayla, Darlene, and even Ana probably helped too, but I was giving the lion's share of the credit to that macaron.

By the time the floating special effect that was our guide slowed down, it was a quarter to three, my phone had no bars, the backpack slung across my shoulder weighed about a thousand pounds, and even Juliette was looking a little bit hot and sweaty. Of course, on her, it looked good; I was pretty sure *I* looked like a zombie movie extra. I leaned against a tree like I was holding it up instead of the opposite, and pretended not to see the tiny gestures the sprite was making inside its sphere.

Ten breaths. In and out. Then another ten until my heartrate started to slow and my limbs remembered what they were and who they belonged to. I brushed sweaty hair out of my face, lamented my decision not to shave, and nodded to Juliette.

"I'm ready if you are."

"I'll go first, just in case, but you're doing all the talking."

"Deal." She wasn't the most impressive of vampires when it came to combat, but she was still a hell of a lot more durable than I was. And presumably had enough energy left to actually dodge or run away if this was all a trap.

I followed my friend into a clearing. It was still in the afternoon, but the trees formed a canopy above us, casting the open space into a field of dancing shadows. As our guide darted ahead, even those shadows faded, banished by a new light.

"That's… a lot of sprites."

My earlier thoughts of fireflies came back in force as hundreds, if not thousands of glowing spheres poured into the clearing like waves of an unseen ocean. I didn't know a lot about sprites, other than that they were one of the last remnants of nature spirits in the United States and that they had some sort of ancestral connection with the far more cosmopolitan pixies. To hear Juliette talk, they were more annoying than dangerous, but I'd been in enough bad situations to know that numbers mattered. Give each of those sprites a toothpick and I'd be a giant-sized Swedish meatball in literal seconds.

I wasn't sure who to address. Each sprite's body—assuming they had physical bodies at all—was little more than a silhouette, and both those silhouettes and the spheres of light surrounding them seemed largely identical to my inexpert eyes. Thankfully, after the clearing was uncomfortably full of tiny, glowing forest spirits, one sprite floated forward.

"Hi—"

I stopped, mid-greeting, as the sprite made an imperious gesture with their tiny hand, one that I recognized from way too many arguments with Lucia.

"Did it just cut you off?" murmured Juliette.

Before I could reply, a second sprite floated toward us, taking up a space several inches to the right and several more inches down from the first.

"Their Exalted Eminence, Emperor Emeril Ellington, Esquire, has consented to grant this audience despite your species' long history of collective misdeeds. What reparations do you offer?"

"What?"

Juliette's elbow found my doughy midsection. "Give him the honey."

"Weren't we using that as payment for them finding Dulcinea?"

"Little bird…"

"Fine." I pulled the backpack off my shoulder and dug out the jar of honey I'd placed within it. The thick liquid glowed like gold in the sprites' light.

"Exalted Emin—" I began, only to be cut off yet again, this time by the second sprite.

"Their Exalted Eminence, Emperor Emeril Ellington, Esquire, shall not lower themselves to speak with or be spoken to by one of your ilk. Direct your words to me, giant stain, or not at all."

Giant stain was a new one. I was starting to get why Juliette didn't like sprites.

I cleared my throat, and focused on the sprite who was doing all the talking. "My apologies. Please inform his Exalt—please inform the *emperor* that we bring this jar of premium honey and offer it up freely in an apology for our ancestors' actions."

My ancestors hadn't set foot in New Mexico, as far as I knew, but I doubted the sprites were interested in specifics.

The two sprites buzzed, making contrasting noises that sounded like the thrumming of hummingbirds, despite the absence of visible wings. As their unintelligible conversation continued, I started to wonder if the emperor even spoke English at all. Maybe all this theater had been to disguise that fact?

Finally, the buzzing ended. The second sprite turned back to us.

"Your offering is accepted."

Over a dozen sprites darted forward, like fireflies on speed, and the jar of honey was plucked from my grasp. Those sprites immediately retreated into the forest with the honey, as if not wanting to give us a chance to change our minds.

Given their size, bees might actually present a real threat to the sprites, so I could sort of see why honey would have value to them.

"This audience," continued the emperor's appointed spokesprite, "is now open. Their Exalted Eminence, Emperor Emeril Ellington, Esquire, will hear your pleas."

"Don't screw this up," murmured Juliette.

"Don't worry; I was born for this."

Chapter 24

IN WHICH EVERYTHING IS SHINY

I had barely finished my long, possibly *too* detailed summary of the events that had brought us to Ghost Falls and the help we now sought when the spokesprite bobbed forward.

"You wish us to find a giant stain?"

Damn, I was good.

"Yes. Two of them, really, but if you can only find Dulcinea, that works too." I gave their descriptions and then, for good measure, placed the photo of Dulcinea from Simon's files on the grass between us.

"And what will you offer in exchange for this boon?"

I dug back into my backpack and pulled out four rolls of dimes.

"The symposium does not care for paper sticks." I could hear the disdain dripping from the miniature sprite's unseen lips.

"What?"

"Try again, and this time, be certain that your offer does not enrage the paragon of power and puissance that is their Exalted Eminence, Emperor Emeril Ellington, Esquire."

"I don't—" I looked down at the rolls of dimes in my hands. This was $20 worth of so-called shinies. It was supposed to be my trump card in any negotiations, but now they weren't inter—

Oh.

I picked up one of the rolls and tore away the paper wrapping. Dimes spilled out into my waiting palm and the entire symposium of sprites went still.

"The paper sticks create shinies?!"

"They don't create them… the paper is a mask for the shinies within."

"A dull lie to hide the shiny truth."

"…yes?"

"What truths do the other paper sticks hold in secret?"

I awkwardly opened another roll of dimes while trying not to dump the fifty coins I already had in that hand.

"The same truth. Each… uh… paper stick contains fifty shinies."

There was some buzzing between the emperor and spokesprite, and then the latter turned back to us.

"Show us."

"Duchess? Do you mind?"

"Do I have a choice?" She didn't wait for my answer but put down her empty beer glass and the bag of macarons so that she could cup her hands and hold them out to me. I dumped the hundred dimes I'd already unwrapped and then unraveled the remaining rolls.

"Two hundred shinies," I said, into a clearing that had gone as quiet as a cemetery at midnight. "All of them yours if you find this human."

More buzzing, but this time, there was an almost tangible air of excitement to it, so I wasn't surprised at all when the spokesprite turned back to us and said:

"Your offering is considered acceptable."

"Fantastic. When can you start the search?"

The other sprites in the clearing scattered, some darting up into the trees, others zipping around the trunks. Within moments, there were only two sprites left in the clearing.

"We have already begun," said the spokesprite.

Their attitude towards customer service wasn't great, but I couldn't argue with their work ethic. I opened my mouth to thank them when every sprite that had left returned just as quickly. Only this time, they weren't clustered behind their emperor, but around me instead.

"The symposium has found the giant stain."

"That fast? That's… honestly, that's amazing." I couldn't see Juliette through the cloud of sprites around me, but I shot her a look of triumph anyway. There were good ideas and then there were *good* ideas, and this had clearly been one of my best. "Where is she?"

"In this clearing, roughly one deer-length in front of me."

I wasn't familiar with deer-lengths as a form of measurement, but I got the general idea. The bigger problem was that the only human standing in front of the emperor and their voice was…

"You mean *me?*"

"Yes. The giant stain you asked us to find."

I heard a noise from Juliette but couldn't determine if it was laughter, or crying, or some strange combination of the two.

"I don't need you to find *me*," I said. "I need you to find Dulcinea. The human I told you about. Whose picture I showed you."

This time, the buzzing continued for more than a minute. Surrounded by layers upon layers of sprites, I tried not to move. I'd never been much more than mildly claustrophobic, but it was starting to feel like a fear I could really develop.

Finally, the buzzing stopped.

"You wish us to find a giant stain that is not yourself?"

"Do you all not see faces? Do we all look alike to you?"

"There is leaf and tree and blade of grass, brook and creek and mountain pass. There is shiny and not shiny, symposium and congregation, giant stain and blood-drenched. These we know and see."

Well, shit.

"In other words, no."

"No," admitted the spokesprite. "Will you give the shinies now?"

"You haven't done what we asked you to."

"We found the giant stain."

"Not the right one." I blew out a frustrated breath, and a half-dozen sprites directly in front of me went pinwheeling through the air. If they couldn't find Dulcinea or Pedro, what use were they to us?

"Maybe have them look for their ride instead?" suggested Juliette. "There's enough chrome on the thing to keep them invested."

"And I doubt there's too many bikes out in the mountains right now, especially with two of the town missing." It was about as far from a foolproof plan as I could imagine, but I didn't have any better ideas.

"We want you to look for something else," I announced, trying to speak past the layers of sprites still surrounding me.

"Not a giant stain?"

"Not a giant stain. Do you know the vehicles that giant stains sometimes ride through your territory. Some on two wheels and some on four? They make noise and breathe fumes while carrying the giant stains back and forth? Shit, I don't really know how else to describe—"

"Do you mean motorcycles and ATVs?"

"You can distinguish between recreational vehicles, but not people?"

"As their Exalted Eminence has already told you, the symposium *can* distinguish between people. There are sprites and giant stains or blood-drenched, hawks and vultures—"

"Right. Sorry." I didn't dare roll my eyes, with sprite bodies literally inches in front of those eyes, but I really wanted to. "What I mean to ask is… can you visually distinguish one motorcycle from another?"

"Two rubber wheels. Frame partially wrapped in armor and animal hide. Shiny truth masked in dirt, like your paper sticks."

That sounded like a no to me, but as I'd said to Juliette, I doubted there would be any motorcycles just hanging out in the mountains, and recreational activities by the townsfolk were at least temporarily curtailed.

"Fair enough. We're looking for a motorcycle that is outside of town, not on one of the main roads—the black roads—but instead somewhere in the hills and mountains. It could be any direction from town. If you can find it, we will give you these shinies." I gave them the description I'd gotten from Sheriff Abbas.

The buzzing started up again, all the worse because this time I was in the middle of it. I eyeballed the sprites in front of me but couldn't see what was actually making the noise. They didn't appear to have wings, but I couldn't see their mouths moving either.

Sprites, I finally decided, were weird. And *I'd* spent a night talking to a philosophy-obsessed fungus.

The buzzing cut off and the cocoon of light around me vanished, as the horde of sprites once again darted into the woods.

"Their Exalted Eminence, Emperor Emeril Ellington, Esquire, has agreed to your terms with one condition."

"Yeah?"

"The shinies must not leave this place."

"The emperor wants us to wait here until the symposium has found our motorcycle?"

"Yes."

"Why?"

"We have met giant stains before. We do not trust giant stains not to hide shiny truth behind lies a second time."

Part of me wanted to be offended that my trustworthiness was being called into question. The other part of me recognized my species' deservedly horrible reputation had been built one shitty brick at a time.

"Okay."

"Okay?" said Juliette, still holding two hundred dimes in her cupped hands. "Are you serious?"

"Sometimes, even giant stains have to be shiny," I told her.

"You're the worst, little bird." She rolled her eyes and took a seat in the clearing, her bare feet already green with grass stains. "Mama Nita's *definitely* going to hear about this."

Hopefully, Ghost Falls had more than one restaurant.

ooo

I won't say it was the longest two hours I'd ever spent—I'd been a student for like thirteen years of my life, after all—but it was definitely up there. At first, the emperor seemed content to just float there, bobbing up and down like a nightlight buoy, and their spokesprite was, if I interpreted the noises correctly, asleep and snoring within seconds. Now that her beer was done, Juliette was eating her remaining macarons one loud bite at a time, her expression doing a pretty phenomenal job of communicating that I wasn't getting another. Meanwhile, we had no cell service at all, so I couldn't order a pizza, check baseball scores, or text any of my friends.

Was this what life had been like when Anastasia was younger? Or hell, when Juliette was young, even?

It was horrible.

About an hour into the silent vigil, the emperor stirred. A dozen sprites entered the clearing, and I sat up straight, expecting news. Instead, they carried the jar of honey that had been the price of our audience, setting it down onto the grass below their ruler. It took five of them to twist the lid off, but then it was gone, and what was already a strange setting got just a little bit stranger.

Two sprites, a vampire, a human, and an open jar of honey all walk into a bar. I didn't think I'd ever heard a joke that started *quite* like that, but it seemed like there should be one.

The spokesprite was still sleeping, Juliette was still eating, and my phone still didn't have any service, so I watched as the ball of light that was the ruler of this symposium of sprites slowly descended into the open jar. Despite the creature's size, there was something regal about its slow, steady motions… right up until I realized what it was doing.

"Is it taking a bath? In honey?"

Juliette spared a moment from her vengeful macaron consumption. "Yup. A bath of the adult variety."

"That's what I thought. This is weird."

She started in on the last of her macarons, paying no attention to the anguished look I sent in that cookie's direction. "Yup."

"How long do you think this will take?"

"The bath?"

"No, the search."

"Until they find something with two wheels and a bit of chrome." She shrugged. "If the sun starts going down, I'm leaving you here with your so-called shinies."

"To bring us back pizza?"

She snorted with a laugh she had tried but failed to contain. "I suppose I should be grateful that we haven't been eaten by a dragon yet. By your standards, this day must be going pretty well."

"I haven't even met any dragons. Not unless Ti An counted as one back in Rome."

"I think the *Jade Dragon* title is figurative, not literal."

"You think?"

"International studies was never a focus of interest for me."

"Even though your parents are both diplomats?"

"Maybe because of it."

There wasn't much I could say about that; my dad was an accountant, but I'd opted to pursue the prestigious profession of staking out late night motels instead.

"Did you ever figure out what she wanted from you?"

"Your mom?"

"Ti An, moron."

"No. It's one of the mysteries Ana has been trying to solve in her return trips to Rome. With Ti An back in China, and Lady Manassa not knowing anything more than what she already said about my scent, we haven't made much progress on that front."

"You seem pretty human to me. I don't think the sprites would call you a giant stain otherwise."

"And my parents are human too. All I can think is that it has something to do with my broken bond."

"I don't think bonds have a smell."

"Trust me… being bound to Lucia stinks."

That got another laugh out of her, and just like that, things were good again. Or as good as they could be with her smugly licking the last macaron crumbs off her fingers.

"Seriously, I'm not going anywhere," she said, "but the longer we sit here, the more likely I really do complain to Mama Nita about you and your treatment of my delicate young self."

"I'm not sure that threat has any teeth. If they find the motorcycle—and it's the right motorcycle—we might locate the kids and be gone by morning. And then neither Mama Nita nor her husband will be able to glare at me."

"Do you really, even for a moment, think things will work out that easily?"

"I plead the Fifth."

"I'm sure you do."

I risked a glance over at the jar of honey sitting in the middle of the clearing and looked away again. For someone who loved food as much as I did, I'd never really entertained the idea of a food fetish… and now I never would.

"Should we talk about Angel?" I asked.

"Only if *you* want to talk about Anastasia."

"I *love* talking about Ana."

"I mean the truckload of angst you apparently have when it comes to your relationship."

"Oh. That." I frowned, but there was quite literally *nothing* else to do. "I guess I'm game."

"Fine, but you start."

I shrugged. "I'm not sure what there is to say. Have you ever finally gotten something you dreamed of forever only to—"

"Realize it's not what you wanted?"

"What? No! I was going to say only to realize it's even better than what you dreamed of."

"Of course you were. You're an XXL Hallmark card, little bird." It was her turn to frown. "What's the problem then?"

"I don't see how it can last."

"That's fair."

"It is?" This was not the kind of support I'd been hoping for.

"Yeah. Technically, it *can't* last. You'll be dead in a matter of decades, after all."

"That's not what I meant."

"I know, but you're being stupid." She cast the last few beautiful macaron crumbs aside and met my eyes. "Is it the blood thing? Or the fact that you feel inferior to her?"

"I don't feel *inferior*. I just know she could do better."

"That's the same thing, idiot."

"Tomato, potato."

"What?"

"I don't know. Look, the blood thing is a problem. Even you can agree with that, right? Would you date someone you couldn't drain like a juice box?"

"No," she admitted, "but I'm still in my first century. I have to feed regularly. With Anastasia, it's more of a twice-monthly thing unless she exerts herself, right?"

"Yeah, but even so, she has to go elsewhere for it."

"And does that bother her or does it bother you?"

"Does it matter?"

"Yeah. If she doesn't mind the hassle, then it's just a matter of you being jealous."

"And what if it is?"

"Then you need to get your head out of your ass and decide whether you're going to let something that neither of you can change upset the whole apple cart."

I didn't know why we were talking about fruit now, but it was hard to otherwise argue Juliette's point.

"Yeah, I get it. And honestly, it's not a big deal right now. She has her blood donors already, and I like them both. I'm just thinking about ten years from now, when they've both either passed or gotten too old to provide that service."

"You're worried she'll bring in the new hotness?"

"No. Maybe. I don't know." The more I talked, the dumber I sounded, even to myself. "I'm already a five dating an eleven. Is it so weird I'd be having self-esteem issues?"

"Honestly? Yeah! Remember, that so-called eleven chose to date you. That alone upgrades you to at least a six."

I tried and failed to contain my smile. I'd never been a six before.

"Besides, it's not like mass murderers' dating cards are as full as you seem to think."

"I'm not even sure what a dating card is."

"I guess that was before your time since you're a literal baby. Look, do you have any *actual* complaints about Anastasia?"

"About Ana? Of course not. She might not be perfect for everyone, but she's the best woman I've ever known."

"Rude, but whatever." Juliette scowled. "And do you have any complaints about your relationship?"

I shook my head. "I wish we got to spend more time together, but half the reason she keeps going to Rome is to dig into the mysteries we both want resolved."

"So, the only *real* problem here is you, borrowing trouble?"

"I mean—"

"If we survive this, if a meteor carrying an alien army somehow *doesn't* crash land on top of us in the next few hours, you need to find a mirror, give yourself one of those patent-pending, ridiculously named mediator smiles, and get your shit together, little bird. I don't understand what you see in that woman, but it's clear as day that you both love each other. Focus on that and everything else will figure itself out."

For a minute or two, the only sounds in the clearing were the continued and disturbing noises of sprite royalty dipping themselves into honey.

Juliette was right: I was just borrowing trouble. Anastasia was incredible and she showed me how much she loved me on a daily basis. If I didn't feel worthy of her love, that was on me, not her. Rather than obsessing about any perceived imbalances, maybe I should just focus on making myself the kind of man who *did* feel worthy.

And maybe I should also talk about all of this with the woman herself. Wasn't that what adults did?

I eyed Juliette. Having said her piece, she was lying on her back, propped up on her elbows, and looking at the canopy of leaves above us, presumably to *avoid* looking at the bacchanalian honey bath going on in front of her.

"What?" she asked. "I can feel you staring at me, you know."

"I was just thinking; it's hard to imagine you giving me a speech like that even three years ago."

"Three years ago, you *were* a juice box on legs. Now…"

"You're a good friend, Duchess."

"I don't understand your relationship," she admitted, "but it seems to work, and you getting sex regularly makes all of our lives a little bit less obnoxious. If I have to slap some sense into you from time to time… well, it'll hurt you more than it hurts me, that's for sure."

We had a moment, there in the clearing, irrespective of what was happening a deer-length away from us both.

"I love you too, Juliette."

"And just like that, you had to go and ruin it." But she smiled as she said it.

"So, now that we've dealt with Anastasia…"

"Yeah?"

"Did you want to talk about Angel?"

"Nah."

"Wait, what?"

She shrugged. "What's there to say? She and I are at different places in our lives. We want different things."

"But you care for her."

"Sure. But sex and affection alone aren't a recipe for a lasting relationship, even if I was looking for one."

"Have you talked to her about this?"

"Oh, dozens of times."

"Seriously?"

"Some of us are evolved beings, little bird."

"Covered in macaron crumbs and sitting next to an empty beer stein."

"Even so." She shrugged. "We want different things. Talking hasn't changed that. Maybe if I'd been a hundred years older or a different person entirely…"

"You seem a lot more comfortable with the idea of breaking up than you did in Payson."

"That was two days ago, and I just drank twenty-six ounces of beer."

"That's like two and a half bottles, you lightweight."

"I didn't say I was drunk. Just… mellow. Angel would kill to have a relationship like yours. I can't give her that. I don't want to give her that. Better to cut her loose to find what she's looking for."

I didn't ask what that would mean for our business, or Angel's employment, or a half-dozen other dominos that would be toppled as a result of their breakup. Those were just details. We'd figure them out as they came.

"That's a pretty mature way of looking at things, Juliette."

"Right? It's honestly horrifying what getting back to nature can do to a woman." She gave me a look. "I'm going to blow out the Corolla's speakers on our return trip to San Diego. None of this new age pop-punk stuff. We're going hard from dawn to dusk."

"Just as long as we get there in one piece."

"No promises."

CHAPTER 25
IN WHICH THE MERITS OF DOGS
ARE DEBATED

It was ten minutes past five when the sprites started to return, according to my wonderphone and its steadily dwindling battery. They didn't come in a single rush this time, but in smaller waves, and most seemed content just to fill the clearing with their hum. The emperor had finished his bath at some point, and the jar of… used… honey had been secreted away for future occasions that I didn't even want to consider. For all I knew, they'd tip that jar over once we were gone and the whole symposium of nature spirits would follow their ruler's example.

It was twenty after five when a small cloud of sprites flitted out of the trees and made a beeline for the emperor. More buzzing ensued; the spokesprite even woke up and joined in on the conversation. Eventually, it turned and floated over to us.

"The vehicle you seek has been located."

"A motorcycle?" I was taking nothing on faith.

"Yes. Red and white and shiny, as described. Scout cluster Bzzark located it near the edge of the forest, far from any black roads."

"Down by the town?"

"No. Approaching the mountain's crown."

I wasn't sure what mountain they were talking about, but the fact that it matched the description *and* was off the beaten path was a good sign.

"Did you see any giant stains nearby?"

"You promised shinies for finding the motorcycle."

"I did, and I'll give them to you. I'm just asking if your scouts saw anything more."

After more unintelligible dialogue, it turned back to me. "There were no giant stains or blood-drenched anywhere in the area. But we found the motorcycle and can take you to it. We have earned the shinies."

"Yeah, you have." Even if it ended up being the wrong motorcycle, twenty bucks wasn't worth pissing off an entire army of sprites over. "But the sun will be going down soon and I don't know what we'll be able to accomplish after dark. If I give you the shinies now, can you have someone ready to guide us to the motorcycle tomorrow morning?"

The spokesprite turned to the emperor and then back to us. "Their Exalted Eminence has agreed to your terms. Place the shinies before you, and you will be guided back down the mountain. Tomorrow morning, a sprite will wait for you by the anthill."

Again with the anthill.

"Tell them to look for a giant stain and a blood-drenched," I suggested. "If they don't see both, then it's not us."

This whole not being able to distinguish between individual members of a species thing was annoying. Not that I had much ground to stand on… every damn one of the sprites looked the same to me.

Another buzz, which I took for agreement or at least acknowledgement. I nodded to Juliette, who gathered up the two hundred dimes and carefully poured them into a small pile half a deer-length between us and the sprites.

"Their Exalted Eminence, Emperor Emeril Ellington, Esquire, will consider this matter closed with the fulfillment of tomorrow's duties. They bid you farewell, giant stain and blood-drenched. May your futures be ever-shiny."

That whole honey sex bath thing notwithstanding, Emeril seemed like a decent enough creature. I was pretty sure I liked sprites more than goblins, pixies, and the Illutu, if nothing else.

We stood, ignoring the sprites that swarmed Juliette's stack of dimes, and a glowing ball separated itself from the rest of the symposium to approach us. I couldn't tell if it was the same sprite that had led us up from Ghost Falls, but its behavior was almost identical, darting past us, and then waiting for us to turn and catch up.

"More hiking through the woods," groused Juliette.

"At least we'll be going downhill this time. We might even make it back before it gets dark."

ooo

In a shocking turn of fate, my optimistic prediction actually came true. It was half past six when Ghost Falls came into view, and the sun was, if not high in the sky, at least not busy hiding itself behind the horizon.

I tried passing Juliette her shoes, but she waved them off.

"I'm not putting them back on until my feet are clean again."

"So, Pearl's?"

"Gods, yes. I claim dibs on the first shower."

That was fine with me. While I was just as filthy after a day in the woods, I was also pretty hungry. "I might grab something to eat from the vending machine."

"You don't need to do that."

"I don't?"

"No. I'll clear things up with Mama Nita and Henry when we head over there. As funny as it was to watch them turn on you, it's not worth you not eating there anymore."

"Why wouldn't I be eating there?"

Her yellow eyes narrowed. "You just said you'd be getting something from the vending machine."

"Yeah, to tide me over while you showered! I figured we'd head over once we were both clean."

"The fact that they clearly think you're up to no good doesn't bother you?"

"I mean… not really? I can see it from their perspective, after all. I'm not that far from thirty and you don't at all look your age. Besides, I'm sure they'll come around eventually. I tend to grow on people."

"Yeah, like mold."

"Some of my best friends are mold, Juliette."

It was only five blocks to Pearl's, and even with Juliette barefooting it, we made it there in record time. I was way too dirty to sit on the bed while Juliette showered, so I stood by the slider that led to the balcony we weren't allowed to stand on. I unwrapped my Almond Joy and chewed through it slowly, watching darkness fall across the town, combatted here and there by interior and exterior lights coming to life.

Ghost Falls was a hell of a place, but I was ready to be home. Ready to tackle the goblin mediation and Mike's infidelity. Ready even to maybe share some of my insecurities with Anastasia, who I knew would have a thoughtful take on the whole thing.

But first, we needed to find Dulcinea and Pedro. And the fact that the sprites hadn't seen either of them near the motorcycle had me concerned. It had been a week since their disappearance, and while people could conceivably survive for years in the wilderness, the fact that they'd left their bike *and* hadn't come back down the mountain suggested they were injured.

Or worse.

Juliette emerged from the bath in a towel that a single person might have noticed left an awful lot of leg uncovered, running one hand through hair that, without any product, lay mostly flat instead of in its usual spikes. I squeezed past her, trying not to dirty her towel, and entered the steam-filled bathroom.

Twenty-five minutes and two impatient complaints by Juliette later, I toweled off again, pink and clean. I'd only brought two pairs of jeans with me, and one was stained with blood while the other was stained with sap, grass, and dirt, so I changed into a pair of shorts and pulled on my third-to-last T-shirt.

"We have to do something about your wardrobe," said Juliette. The femmepire was wearing a little black dress—sexy without looking like her usual club fare—and a pair of strappy blue heels. She even had a shawl that matched those heels draped over her shoulders and framing what was, especially for Juliette, remarkably restrained and tasteful cleavage.

"*My* wardrobe? *You're* going to be the best dressed person in Ghost Falls, by like a factor of ten thousand," I told her.

"You should try it sometime."

Given how well dressing up for brunch had gone over with Ana, I couldn't find it in myself to disagree. "I do have *some* nice things at home. Maybe I should try dressing up more often."

"They grow up so fast," murmured Juliette in mock delight, clutching her imaginary pearls as she looked at me adoringly. "Any day now, you'll figure out who you want to be when you grow up."

"And maybe *you'll* learn to pack sneakers or hiking boots when we go to the ass-end of nowhere. Three suitcases and not a single pair of shoes other than heels?"

"Nobody likes a know-it-all, little bird."

We went downstairs, waved to Pearl, and exited onto the street… where a patrol car was waiting for us, Sheriff Abbas standing beside it. He tipped his hat and walked over.

"I came by earlier to check on you two, but Pearl said you were out?"

"Yeah. We interviewed the rest of Dulcinea and Pedro's friends and families this morning and spent the afternoon familiarizing ourselves with the terrain outside town."

"Any luck?"

I hesitated, just long enough to know I'd be screwed if I outright lied. "Yes and no. We didn't learn anything new from our interviews, other than that Dulcinea is the town's worst baker—"

"Sadly, that much is common knowledge. Poor girl was actually banned from participating in bake sales in high school." His eyes sharpened, almost lost under the brim of his hat. "But you did find something?"

"Unconfirmed reports of a motorcycle matching the description of Pedro's, somewhere way up one of the eastern mountains," I said.

"Reports from whom?"

Damn it, he even knew when to use who vs. whom. There was no way I was talking my way out of this one.

"A source I can't disclose at this moment, Sheriff—"

Abbas stepped forward, eyes suddenly hard. I was taller than he was, but I was pretty sure he'd have the edge if it came to a fight, even without the taser or the 9mm in his belt holsters.

"I'm going to need more information than that, son."

"Or you could just take it on faith that we're doing the right thing," said Juliette, eyes glowing golden. "After all, we're on the same team here, right?"

"You're not wrong," said the sheriff, still looking determined and professional even as he unwittingly flipped positions entirely. "Do y'all have coordinates for the motorcycle?"

"We'll get them for you tomorrow," I said. "The bigger problem is that they didn't see any… they didn't see Dulcinea or Pedro anywhere near the bike."

"If we finally have a starting point, I might be able to get a loaner from the K-9 unit down in Santa Fe. Their focus tends to be on drugs and explosives, but they'd still be better suited for tracking than any of the dogs in town."

"How soon do you think they could have someone up here?"

He took off his hat and ran a hand through hair that was surprisingly thick for an early-forties man. "Forty-eight hours at the earliest, if I'm being honest. When I reached out to them previously, they blew me off."

"I think I might have a better alternative," I said, "but I'll let you know if that's not the case. You can at least get the wheels in motion."

I was pretty sure the sheriff would have never just accepted something like that, but with Juliette standing next to me, he didn't have much of a choice. He nodded and tugged his hat back on.

"Keep me informed," he said. "When your source gets you the bike coordinates, I'll be accompanying y'all. I'd suggest we bring at least a dozen others so we can put together a search pattern. More, if the path there's not too treacherous."

"Sounds good," I lied. More people wouldn't hurt—*too* much— but Juliette having to compel a dozen people at a time just to hide the existence of sprites sounded like a recipe for disaster. "We'll talk tomorrow."

He tipped his hat to first Juliette and then me. "Tomorrow it is."

As he flipped an illegal U-turn and headed back to his office, we started down the road to Mama Nita's.

"So?" asked Juliette.

"So what?"

"You said you have a better alternative to the K-9 unit? I'm waiting to hear what it is."

"What's the biggest problem with dogs, Duchess?"

"They drool on everything."

"True, but not the answer our judges panel was looking for."

"John, I'm tired, I'm hungry, and I'm probably going to have to find some new sucker to drink from tonight after spending energy keeping my feet healed. Just tell me."

"The biggest problem with dogs is they can't talk."

"Even if they could, they'd just say 'squirrel' all the time."

We shared grins. We'd had a Pixar movie marathon about a month earlier.

"True. So, what we really need is a dog with the brain of a human, or a human with a dog's senses."

She stopped dead in her tracks. "You've got be kidding me."

I smiled serenely as I crossed a narrow street and continued down the block. Eventually, she caught up with me.

"Werewolves? Again?"

"You're the one who originally suggested it. I'm pretty sure Audrey feels like she owes me, and their pack *is* still in Payson."

"And still wants us dead, last I heard."

"Not all of them. Or all of us, for that matter." I held up my hands to forestall the next wave of objections. "I'll ask for one wolf. If they leave shortly, they'll be here early tomorrow."

"I'd prefer the K-9 unit."

"It's already been a week, Duchess. Two more days might be one too many. Besides, if we run into something dangerous up there, would you rather have a German Shepherd with us or a wolf the size of a pony?"

"Is there a third option?"

I sighed. Genius was never truly appreciated in its time.

ooo

By the end of dinner, Henry was all smiles again. I didn't think I'd be invited to his granddaughter's Sweet Sixteen or anything, but I also didn't worry about running into him in a dark alley. As for Mama Nita, I still hadn't met her, although Juliette had disappeared into the kitchen twice, and the laughter that could be heard suggested she was making herself right at home.

After finishing Nita's unique take on meatloaf, I once again pulled out my wonderphone. I hadn't thought to charge it while waiting for Juliette to shower, so I was hovering around twenty-two percent battery life, but that would hopefully be enough.

Audrey was surprisingly amenable to sending a wolf up to help us. Maybe it was because I'd listened to her earlier cues and texted her instead of calling like some kind of boomer? She said our contact would meet with us at Pearl's in the morning, but that they'd have to be back in Payson by Sunday. That was a restriction I could live with… if we didn't find Dulcinea by then, we'd have bigger problems.

As usual, the young werewolf just sort of dropped off the text conversation without any pleasantries or goodbyes, but I was starting to think that was a generational thing. And that hanging around with centenarians was aging me way too fast.

I had another sip of my IPA, checked my battery life—eighteen percent—and then called Ana. It was early enough that they *probably* weren't out hunting yet, and I really wanted to talk to her.

It rang twice, and then she was there.

"Mr. Smith." I could hear the smile in her voice, undiminished by the miles between us. "We will be leaving to hunt shortly; I was hoping you might call before we did so."

"And I was hoping to catch you, so I guess we're even. How are you doing?"

"I am well. The house feels quiet without your presence. I think Gustavo and Teresa miss you."

"Just them?"

"I *think* they miss you. I *know* that I do."

That single sentence warmed me more than the entire beer.

"The feeling's mutual. I spent the entire day in the woods and I don't have a lot of battery life, but I just wanted to hear your voice."

"The woods? How goes the search for Simon's descendant?"

"We've had some bumps along the way, but I think we could be closing in." I shook my head, even though she couldn't see me. "I'm a little bit worried about what we'll find though."

"You can only do your best, John."

"Yeah. Hopefully, my best means Dulcinea and her boyfriend make it back home safely. What about you? How is the literal witch hunt going?"

"I too believe we are closing in and find myself rather relieved that you are away. What we have already found has been… disquieting."

"How so?" *Please don't be bodies*, I prayed to myself.

"We think Zorana is living on the streets amongst San Diego's homeless population. What we have been able to piece together of her recent actions suggests that her mental state may have deteriorated precipitously."

"She was never all that sane to begin with."

"No, she was not. Yet now…" I could hear her sigh. "I too fear what we might find."

"Don't take any chances. Please. I know that you're a necessary part of bringing her in, but—"

"On that subject, I have—"

"You have?" I frowned. "Hello?"

I looked down at my wonderphone and found a black, empty screen staring back up at me.

"Oh, come on! That was like a three-minute phone call! How the hell did *that* eat up eighteen percent battery?"

Neither my dead wonderphone nor the otherwise empty restaurant had a reply.

By the time Juliette was done talking to Mama Nita, it was too late. I gave Ana a call from Juliette's phone, but it went straight to voicemail. Still, I left a voicemail explaining what had happened so that my lovely girlfriend wouldn't worry.

Hopefully, we'd both have good news to share with each other the next time I called.

Juliette paid our bill this time—using the corporate card, of course—and we were soon back out in the cool night air.

"I'll see you back at Pearl's?" I asked.

"Unless you're offering free drinks in our suite."

"I'd say we could always raid the minibar, but I don't think there is one."

"That's not the kind of drink I was talking about."

"Yep, I know."

She sighed. "Time to go scout out the livestock again."

"Be careful; if they moo, they might *actually* be cows."

"You were a lot funnier when you weren't getting so much sex," she decided, completely contradicting what she'd said out in the woods.

"I think we'll have to agree to disagree on that one."

CHAPTER 26

IN WHICH A GIANT STAIN, A BLOOD-DRENCHED,
AND A FLOWER GIRL CLIMB A MOUNTAIN

Morning came far too swiftly, courtesy of a rapping on our suite's hallway door. I blinked away the last remnants of my dream—something about a ski chalet where the snow was ice cream and the instructors were cartoon cows—and glared toward the door I couldn't quite see.

"Can you get that, Juliette?"

"I will pay you ten million dollars if you get it instead."

I was pretty sure Juliette didn't have one million dollars, let alone ten, but *pretty sure* was a long way from completely convinced. I flopped my legs over the side of the bed until they found the floor and pushed myself up to a standing position. I pulled on a fresh tee and made my way to the door.

Whoever was there had stopped knocking as soon as I spoke, which meant that either Pearl had way better hearing than I'd have expected, or our werewolf escort had arrived. I opened the door, unsurprised to find it was the latter.

"Hey," I said. "You're frighteningly early. Come on in."

"Frightening, I understand, but early? It's almost seven."

"In the morning? Sweet Jesus, no wonder I'm exhausted." I took a step back and waved Hyacinth into our suite. "Come on in. We still need to get dressed."

She paused on the threshold. "I thought y'all were just business partners?"

"Oh goodie," came Juliette's voice, still foggy with sleep beneath the sharp edges irritation had given it. "It's flower girl. What fresh hell is this?"

Hyacinth had on a new variant of her riding uniform; black leggings, calf-high boots, a red tank top that wouldn't have looked out of place in Angel's closet, and a motorcycle jacket in black and gray. Her shaved head practically glowed red from the light bouncing off the sheer quantity of mahogany surrounding us.

"Fanger," she said, putting some swing in her hips as she rounded the corner into the bedroom. "I hear you missed me."

"Don't worry," said Juliette. "I've got a few rounds left in the magazine."

"Glad to hear not everyone's firing blanks." Hyacinth shot me a look over one shoulder.

"Please, leave me out of whatever this conversation is." I rolled my eyes and disappeared into the bathroom. Between the beer I'd had the night before and the water I'd followed it with in an attempt to stay hydrated, my bladder was ready to burst.

After more than a year living with Juliette, the knowledge that both women would be able to hear me tinkle didn't even faze me. Expectations of privacy disappeared fast when living around the supernatural. Hell, Valentina had walked—or floated—in on me in far more precarious situations than that.

By the time I was done, I felt awake again, but still a long way from human. Thankfully, a shower and a shave took care of that. I emerged from my steam-filled cocoon to find that neither Juliette nor

Hyacinth had moved; the former sitting on her bed in a nest of blankets, the latter leaning against the room's primary dresser, both arms folded across her chest.

Yet somehow, both had mugs of coffee in their hands.

"Where did that come from, and which of my children do I have to sell to get a mug of my own?"

'You have kids?" Hyacinth looked torn between horror and surprise.

"Of course not," said Juliette. "Before he started dating an executioner, he had the game of a choir boy. And now that he *is* dating her…"

The werewolf nodded, getting the point. Children were not in my future.

"Ana and I could be planning to adopt," I pointed out.

"Just so you can sell the poor kid for coffee? Have a heart, little bird." She waved to my bedside table, where a third mug was waiting, steam rising into the air like clear evidence of angelic intervention.

I was reaching for that mug when she spoke again.

"That'll be ten million dollars."

"Easy come, easy go, I guess." I picked up the mug and drank half its contents in one easy motion. "Get me a creampuff and I'll be good to go."

"You *are* a creampuff."

"Are the two of you always like this?" asked Hyacinth, clearly amused.

"Only when we're not collared by sociopaths."

"I think Shea's closer to being a psychopath, to be honest." The werewolf winced. "Can we put that whole thing behind us?"

"Yeah, Duchess," I chimed in. "Why do you have to go around dredging up ancient history?"

"It was two days ago!"

"Vampires," I said, rolling my eyes. "Always living in the past."

"Seriously though." Hyacinth ignored me and crossed the room to stand near Juliette's bed. Zippers jangled as she extended an open hand. "Could we maybe start over?"

My partner joined the epidemic of eye rolling sweeping the nation. "You and me and maybe Sparkles? Yeah. Ezekiel and Shae? If I never see them again it will be too soon."

"Audrey thinks that'd be best for everyone." Hyacinth wagged her outstretched hand. "Don't leave me hanging here."

Juliette climbed out of bed, wearing far less than what she'd had on when I went to sleep. She looked at the other woman's hand, and then sighed and shook it. "At least you ride bikes," she grumbled. "Even if yours doesn't have a chance in hell of keeping up with my Ducati."

"I've got an SV1000S back home that should do just fine."

"Not on a track."

"The world isn't a track, fanger."

"Not with that attitude it's not."

"90-degree V-twin. Horsepower *and* torque."

"And yet all *I* hear is *not-Ducati.*"

"Juliette, for the love of God and either of us having a future when we get back to San Diego, could you please put on some clothes?"

The femmepire spared me a glance and then looked back to Hyacinth. "He gets pretty temperamental from time to time."

"Kind of like a Ducati, you mean?"

"Oh, we are going to have ourselves a talk." Juliette slipped past the other woman. I had my eyes focused on the ceiling because there were limits and we were definitely pushing them, but something told me that she put just as much swing in her hips as the wolf had done.

I waited for the bathroom door to shut and the shower to start up and then reclaimed my mug, peering over it at the other woman.

"Juliette has a girlfriend, you know. A human girlfriend."

"Is she pretty?"

I blinked. "I'm probably not the best judge of that."

"Why? You only go for fangers?" She didn't wait for a reply, claiming a seat on Juliette's bed even as she planted her elbows on her knees and leaned forward toward me. "I've heard their kind tend towards kinky, but nothing I ever read about the Stone Lady said she liked to share."

"Ana and I are monogamous. And like I already told you, Juliette and I are *business* partners. That's why we have two beds."

"So, that show was for me?"

"I refuse to answer that on the grounds that it would require acknowledging that the show even happened."

"You do talk like a mediator. Or a lawyer, maybe. After the whole thing with Kevin, I didn't really have any doubts, but I guess this proves it. So, wanna tell me what the hell I'm doing in this little town?"

"Audrey didn't say?"

"She just said y'all needed help. It was either me or Ezra, and he wanted to spend time with his pup."

"Ezra has a kid?"

"With lifespans like ours, we have to get started early if we want to keep the gene pool viable, don't you know?"

"What about you?"

"Some people get special dispensation. Not all of us are the maternal type."

"Yeah, I can see that."

Her eyes glittered dangerously. "Can you?"

"I mean…"

"I'm kidding. Children have never been part of the plan."

I gave her a doubting look.

"You think I'm lying?"

"I'm trying to picture you having a plan at all."

Unseen chains jangled as she made herself more comfortable on Juliette's bed. "You're a lot more spunky than you were the other day."

"I've finally slept and eaten."

"That makes one of us." She growled, the sound a low rumble in the suite. "Now, are you going to tell me why I'm here, or am I going to have to get irritated?"

I yawned to show that I wasn't scared—and because I *was* still tired and waking up—but decided to answer her before she got truly testy.

"We're here about a girl…"

It took a while to cover the basics, and by the end of it, Hyacinth looked and sounded annoyed.

"We're meeting with sprites? Really?"

"Right?!" Juliette chimed in from the bathroom. She'd finished her shower during my not at all overly verbose recap of why we were all in Ghost Falls.

"Technically, we'll only be meeting with one sprite," I said, hoping that was true. "They'll guide us to the motorcycle they found, and you'll take over from there."

"To sniff out the humans."

"Y'all *are* hunters, after all."

She made a face like she'd just tasted sour milk. "Please, never say y'all again."

It was like having a second Juliette in my life. Which sucked because the first one was still hanging around and liable to join in the festivities at any moment.

"Anyway," I said, raising my voice as though Juliette couldn't have heard me whisper, "if my *business* partner ever finishes up in there, we can head up the mountain and get this done."

"Stay frosty, little bird," came Juliette's inevitable reply.

"Are you that eager to go hiking?" asked Hyacinth.

I shook my head, smile falling away. "They've been missing over a week now. If they're still alive—"

"Then every minute counts. Okay, I get that." Just like that, the werewolf was all business. "I'm ready when y'all are."

I gave her a look.

"Hey, it's charming when *I* say it."

When Juliette emerged from the bathroom, she was fully dressed, her tank top just a little bit tighter than Hyacinth's. She dug through the array of shoes in the closet and frowned, before pulling out a pair of sandals with only a three-inch heel.

"I'm not sure those are hiking material, fanger."

"Unless you've got an extra pair of boots in your saddlebags, they're going to have to do."

"What size are you?"

'Nine. Why?"

"I've got moccasins that might fit."

Juliette tossed her sandals back into the closet and gave the werewolf a considering look. "You're actually starting to grow on me, flower girl."

○○○

We didn't hike up the whole mountain; that would have been ridiculous. Not to mention ridiculously tiring, especially for those of us without supernatural powers to call upon.

Instead, we took the Corolla as far as we could, stopping to pick up the sprite that was waiting for us just outside town. I still didn't spot the now-mythical anthill, but the glowing ball was hovering by the wood's edge, its light barely visible thanks to the morning sun.

Getting it into the car was an adventure all on its own, but eventually, there were four of us in the Corolla's cozy confines, motoring our way up the surprisingly non-windy road.

Juliette had called shotgun, so Hyacinth had claimed the entire back seat, sprawled out on faux leather like some sort of noblewoman at rest, just waiting to be painted. The sprite, on the other hand, insisted on hovering roughly four inches away from my right eye.

I guess it wanted to make sure I could see it when it waved for us to stop.

We had driven for almost twenty-five minutes before that signal finally came, and I understood why Sheriff Abbas hadn't turned up a thing. Twenty-plus miles had to be far outside the suspected search area, especially given the town's limited population.

There wasn't a convenient rest stop or overlook, so I just pulled off to the shoulder. I hadn't noticed much in the way of traffic going through Ghost Falls in either direction, and at this time of the morning, we seemed to be the only people out on the mountain road. Hopefully, the Corolla would be fine until we made it back.

The sprite bounced off the driver-side window a few times before I got the door open, and then flitted across to the other side of the road. We joined it soon after and followed it into the woods. It was almost five minutes before Hyacinth pointed out what was almost definitely a tire tread, although the lightness of the track meant it was either old or it had barely been carrying any load. Given the lack of any real pathway, I was betting they'd been pushing the bike instead of riding it.

Why they'd decided to enter the forest here, of all places, remained an open question.

We walked for another ten minutes before coming across some sort of a trail, too narrow to be anything the townsfolk regularly used. Hyacinth was up front, just behind the sprite, and I tapped her shoulder. "Deer?"

She shrugged. "Could be a lot of things, really."

Behind me, Juliette snickered. "Real helpful."

"Lot of herbivores leave game trails, fanger. This one's big enough that I'm guessing it was from deer or elk, but it could be mountain goats or something too. Or maybe even a bear."

"Well, isn't that a happy thought?" I grumbled. The only thing I knew about bears was that some would kill you if you didn't lie down and play dead, and some would kill you if you did.

"Don't worry, mediator. You've got two big, strong women to protect you."

"Speak for yourself," said Juliette. "If I see a bear, it's every vampire for themselves."

"Won't Angel be proud."

"Angel is your girl?" Hyacinth asked Juliette.

"And our receptionist," I said.

The werewolf looked from the femmepire to me and shook her bald head. "Y'all really do like to mix business and pleasure, don't you?"

"That's a whole different story." Up ahead, the sprite bobbed in the air. I wasn't sure if it understood us at all, but it seemed impatient. No doubt there was some sort of honey orgy scheduled for later in the day. "Let's just keep going."

"You're the boss, boss."

It wasn't true, *especially* when it came to Hyacinth, but I didn't hate hearing it said.

After about an hour, the trail we followed intersected another one, this one leading uphill. My quads, already sore from yesterday's hike, ached just looking at it. Hyacinth had left her jacket with the Corolla, and her strong, tanned arms glistened with sweat, but she climbed the hill like she was half-goat herself. Behind me, Juliette was only slightly worse off, her borrowed moccasins finding careful purchase on an incline that had me slipping and sliding more than once.

Meanwhile, I staggered on like a seventy-five-year-old chain smoker, too tired to even feel grateful for the fact that I was wearing shorts instead of jeans.

If nothing else, I was pretty sure I was going to lose a few pounds in water weight by the time the day was done. It would be cold comfort to legs no longer capable of moving, but maybe I could get Juliette to drag the mirror over to my bed at Pearl's so I could at least meet and greet the newer, slimmer me.

As we ascended the mountain, the terrain grew rougher, the forest giving way to scattered trees and craggy rock. The actual peak was still way above us—lost in a cloud layer that had moved in sometime during our long hike—but the change in our elevation was clear. I turned to look below us for Ghost Falls, but it was lost somewhere behind those same clouds and the ocean of trees below us.

Our sprite guide darted to the left where a shredded tire jutted out from under an outcrop of rock.

By the time I made it over, Juliette and Hyacinth had dragged the whole thing out into the open; shredded tire attached to mangled wheel attached to the chrome forks that led all the way up to handlebars, a clutch lever, and a throttle.

"Please tell me this is the right dirt bike," said Juliette.

I compared it to the description in our notes.

"It's red and white, under the dirt," I finally said. "I'm not sure how long it's been here, but I think this might be it."

"Might be?"

"Pedro didn't have plates for it," I reminded her. "All we have to go off of are visuals. But it's a bike matching the description and it's out in the middle of damn near nowhere. I think our odds seem pretty good."

My partner scowled. "I guess that means you're up, flower girl."

"Let's check in with our guide firs—" I let my voice trail off as I realized the sprite was gone. "Did anyone see where they went?"

Neither woman had, which made me feel a little bit better about things. Sure, *I* was the trained observer, but *they* had supernatural senses.

"I guess the job's over and it's time for the honey orgy," I said.

"The what?!"

"Don't ask," Juliette told Hyacinth. "Seriously."

"Do either of you know how to get back to Ghost Falls from here?" I asked. "I wasn't really paying attention to the route."

"Just head down and keep walking until we hit either town or ocean," said Juliette.

As valuable as that advice was, I turned to Hyacinth, the only of us who truly seemed at home in the woods.

"The fanger's not entirely wrong. We follow the trail downhill until it reaches the other trail and then take that one south to the road."

"If you ever want to give up on the biker gang thing and enter the glamorous world of private investigation, give me a call," I told her. "I'm not sure my current junior partner is up to snuff."

"Says the man who's currently ninety-seven percent perspiration and one percent brain," said Juliette.

I frowned. "That only adds up to ninety-eight."

"Exactly."

I looked to Hyacinth for an explanation, but the werewolf was shaking her head.

"Y'all really need an off switch. Who's gonna carry my clothes?"

I patted the backpack I had slung over both shoulders. Without the jar of honey or the rolls of dimes, the only thing in it were the water bottles we'd been draining along the way.

"Fair enough." She took one long step away from the rest of us and shifted, her clothes falling away and through the cloud of smoke that replaced her human form. By the time those clothes had touched the rocky earth, a wolf stood before us, its head as high as my shoulders, its fur a gray so dark as to be almost black. The wolf twisted to look at its clothes, and then turned bone white eyes on me.

"Yeah, I'll get them as soon as you're out of the way." I waited for her to move and then turned word into action, kneeling to scoop the pile of clothing into my backpack. Somehow, her boots weighed even more than the water bottles had when they were full.

Hyacinth padded over to the dirt bike and snuffled around it, looking for all the world like a house pet sniffing out its treat. It was far too adorable a sight for something of her size, and I caught Juliette hiding a grin.

"Can you pick up their scents?" I asked. "Or *some* scents, at least?"

I'd never seen a wolf nod before, but she seemed to manage it just fine, turning to prowl in the direction that the still-rising sun told me was west.

"New guide, who dis?" muttered Juliette.

I rolled my eyes. We were not going to talk in memes. We just weren't. "How do you feel about carrying me the rest of the way?"

"I'm already carrying the agency, little bird. Maybe you should just move your feet."

I eyed the broad back of the werewolf in front of us. Would Hyacinth eat me if I asked to ride her?

CHAPTER 27

I ended up not asking Hyacinth for a ride, and deeply regretted that fact for the roughly seven additional minutes we traipsed around the mountain. The only good news was that the werewolf didn't lead us further uphill. Instead, we stayed in that strange no-man's land between forest and rocky crown. The low clouds above us had fragmented and the sun peeked through, casting the mountain into ever-shifting patches of darkness and light.

It would have made for one hell of a postcard. If Maria Elena or Sabina had been with us, I was pretty sure they'd have stopped every three feet for selfies. I just focused on putting one foot in front of the other, trying not to slip as we skirted the incline.

Growing up in San Diego, I'd never been much of a mountain person. The city had its share, from Mount Woodson to Cuyamaca Peak, but it had always seemed foolhardy to expend effort climbing a rock when you could instead have a burger, fries, and a beer while overlooking the Pacific. The only thing I really knew about mountains was that they were high, the air was sometimes thinner at the top, and people raced up them for the privilege of then having to race back down.

When Hyacinth finally came to a stop, I realized something new: some mountains had caves.

It shouldn't have been a surprise, really. New Mexico was famous for its caves, and even if the Carlsbad Caverns were well to our south, it made sense that other peaks might have caves of their own. And sure enough, a tunnel descended into the mountain we'd been hiking on.

"Look at that," said Hyacinth, pointing to either side of its mouth and then down the hill. I'd passed her clothes back over as soon as she shifted, but she had yet to pull anything on. A tattoo of a cluster of purple, flowering plants covered most of her back, their stems sweeping down over the curve of one butt cheek.

I didn't know a hyacinth from a haiku, but I was pretty sure this was the former.

I was also pretty sure the show was meant more for my junior partner than me. I coughed, cleared my throat, wiped the sweat from my brow, and did everything else I could to make it clear I was focused on more important things as I stepped up to her side to see what she was pointing at.

There were rocks on either side of the opening, some the size of my fist, others large enough that I wasn't sure even Hyacinth could lift them. More rubble spread downhill from the cave, forming a short-lived trail that disappeared into the tree line. The jagged, untidy edges of the cave mouth itself, rough rather than having been worn smooth by wind, water, or time, made it clear what Hyacinth was suggesting.

Even so, Juliette beat me to the punch. "You think this only opened up recently?"

"Looks like it to me. Something brought it all crashing down. Some sort of seismic activity, maybe." She frowned as she ducked her head into the tunnel, still putting the butt in butt naked. "Huh. That's weird."

"A full moon in broad daylight?"

Juliette's elbow caught me in the ribs.

"No." The werewolf turned back to us, and I fixed my gaze on her face. "I think the tunnel's older than the rubble that was blocking it. In fact, I'm pretty sure this was blocked deliberately at some point. Nature's not a huge fan of straight lines or ninety-degree angles, unlike whoever built this wall."

I didn't love the sound of that. "So, you're saying that at some point in the past—"

"Distant past, I'd say."

"Your distant past, mine, or Juliette's?" That phrase meant different things for a species whose average lifespan was four decades than it did for humans, let alone vampires.

"I'm not an archaeologist, but I'm guessing this was at least a few hundred years old. Maybe more, even." She eyed Juliette and squared her shoulders. "What do you think, fanger? Is that old?"

"Age is a mindset," said Juliette.

"Tell that to the boss." Hyacinth shook her head and finally started tugging on the clothes I'd given her. "Anyway, the trail heads inside."

That revelation didn't fill me with warm fuzzies. An old cave system that had been blocked off sometime in past centuries only to be reopened by nature's capriciousness and then discovered by two unsuspecting small-town lovers?

"Am I only the only one getting creepy horror movie vibes from this?"

"He complains a lot, doesn't he?"

"It's endless, really." Juliette turned to me. "If this was a horror movie, *we'd* be the monsters, little bird."

"Oh. Honestly, that hadn't even occurred to me."

"And then he says something like that, and you can't help but forgive him."

I wasn't sure what the femmepire was talking about, so I shrugged, hoisting the backpack back up onto my increasingly tired shoulders. "We're sure this tunnel *isn't* the mouth of a slumbering rock elemental or something, right? I'd prefer to not march right down into its belly otherwise."

"There aren't many nature spirits left in this country," said Hyacinth. "Sprites and the occasional dryad are about as close as you get."

So, if this *was* an elemental, it was likely long dead. I wasn't sure if that made it any better, but at least it didn't make it worse. If Dulcinea and Pedro had gone into the tunnel, then we would too, no matter how dark and possibly dank it might be.

I pulled my wonderphone from its pocket. Somehow, it had lost thirty percent of its battery during our climb. It might already be time for another upgrade. I toggled on the flashlight app and waved the bright light across the tunnel's walls.

I didn't see any teenagers.

I didn't see much of anything but stone.

"In we go, I guess."

○○○

Spelunking, I was swiftly learning, ranked up there with bungee jumping and skydiving on the list of things I shouldn't ever do. The tunnel we'd been following twisted and turned, narrowing and widening as it progressed deeper into the mountain. I could practically feel the weight of all that stone above us and the air, while still plentiful, had gone sour and stale.

Another tremor, like the one that had opened the tunnel, and we'd no doubt end up buried forever.

Until the superhuman killing machines at your side dig their way out, a voice in my head reminded me. Juliette might not be able to bench press a car, but between her and Hyacinth, there was little they couldn't shift or move.

We'd passed several side tunnels as we traveled, but each time, the werewolf kept us moving in the right direction. Most recently, she hadn't even had to shift, instead pointing out a scrap of cloth that had torn free as someone squeezed between sharp edges of stone.

It was the first visible sign since the motorcycle that we were on the right path, but I couldn't find it in myself to be relieved. There were very few scenarios that even my admittedly expansive imagination could come up with where two teenagers ended up stuck down in a tunnel for a week and emerged from the experience alive, let alone unscathed.

As soon as the sprites had found Pedro's bike in the mountains, I had known there'd be a good chance we'd be retrieving two bodies instead of saving two people, but still…

Just once, I wanted to offer more than closure.

I was deep into my own thoughts, flashlight pointed at the ground just in front of me in a futile attempt to reduce my stumbles, when first Hyacinth and then Juliette stiffened and stopped.

"What is it?" In the confines of the tunnel, even my whisper seemed too loud.

Juliette was behind me, but I felt her press up against my back, bringing her lips closer to my ears.

"Breathing," she said. "And I think heartbeats."

"As in plural?"

Ahead of us, Hyacinth stepped back into the small circle of light my wonderphone offered. I could hear the wolf in her voice. "Sounds like two of them," she agreed, "but the heartrates are slow."

"So are the breaths," said Juliette.

"Sleeping, you think?"

"Or unconscious."

Two heartbeats. For the first time in far too long, I allowed myself to hope.

We didn't hurry, but instead took the next twenty or thirty steps with even greater caution, Hyacinth a wall of superpowered muscle between me and whoever we were approaching, Juliette on alert for anything that might come at us from behind. It took almost a minute to reach the source of those heartbeats, but when we did, my flashlight app found two teenagers sprawled across the tunnel floor next to one another.

Pedro was darker skinned than I'd expected from his photos. He had one arm around Dulcinea, who was lying face up in the tunnel, hair spread beneath her head like a pillow. Both were dressed in tattered pants and long-sleeved T-shirts… relatively sensible hiking gear that hadn't held up to the rigors of the cave. And while their lips were cracked and dry, both of them were, as already predicted by my two companions, visibly breathing.

"Dehydrated," said Hyacinth, already at their sides. "It's a miracle they lasted this long, although—"

"Although?"

"Sometimes… sleep or… reduced activity can…" Her words slurred, like Juliette after a five Mai Tai pre-gaming session, and then there was a thud.

I turned the wonderphone in the werewolf's direction, but she was gone.

"What the hell?"

"Point it down, little bird."

I angled the wonderphone and found Hyacinth puddled on the floor next to the unconscious teenagers. Like them, she was unconscious, her eyes—celery green without the wolf's influence—vacant behind dark lashes.

"Trap?"

"Have you seen a trap that can tag a werewolf?"

"Magic trap?" I tried again.

"Huh. Maybe?"

"Why her and not us? And what do we do now?"

She didn't bother answering the first question. "I'll try to wake the wolf. You go deal with our sleeping lovebirds over there."

"If it's proximity-based…"

"Right. Okay, *you* go try to wake up the wolf. I'll stay right here."

"Why me?"

"If you pass out too, I can probably drag you all out of here. If I pass out…"

"Right." My frequent complaints aside, Ana and Kayla's fitness regimes *did* mean I was getting stronger… but I doubted I was up to transporting four bodies through tunnels I couldn't even see in without my light. "Wish me luck, I guess."

"Wait. Do you have a belt?"

"I'm wearing shorts, Duchess. Soccer shorts."

"Then maybe crawl towards flower girl instead. If you trigger whatever the trap is, I need to be able to pull you out. Having your feet stretched out behind you would help."

I nodded, although I didn't think even vampiric night vision was good enough for her to see it. I couldn't speak for the comatose teenagers, but *my* heartbeat was loud enough to challenge a marching band. I lowered myself to my hands and knees, and then further, to my belly, and started scooting forward, phone in hand, in the sort of army crawl I'd seen in movies.

There was a second benefit to approaching Hyacinth like this. While there was no barbed wire here for me to creep under—as far as I knew, anyway—it was possible the trap's trigger was set at a certain height. Maybe I could crawl right under it?

"Are you still awake?"

"Yeah."

"Then why did you stop moving?"

"I was just thinking."

"Well, stop it. I want to get out of these tunnels as soon as we can. *Someone* or *something* had to have set this trap."

Which raised the likelihood of that creature coming to investigate what its trap had caught. Yeah, that was enough to get me moving again.

I reached Hyacinth without issue, and poked the wolf in her leg, soft at first, and then harder when my touch failed to rouse her.

"She's not responding," I called back to Juliette. I reached out to my other side and tapped Dulcinea's leg. "None of them are."

"But you're okay?"

"Yeah."

"Okay… back away and try to bring Hyacinth with you."

Forgetting myself, I shot a look back behind me at the dark tunnel. Crawling was hard enough on its own. Crawling backwards while dragging a woman who was probably a hundred and fifty pounds of muscle?

"You're joking, right?"

"Just do it, little bird. Once you're closer, I'll pitch in."

"Fine. But you hold the light. Let me pass it over."

"Keep it. I've got my phone with me." A moment later, another light sprang to life, this one behind and above me.

I didn't ask where she'd kept it, given that her jeans were almost as tight as Hyacinth's leggings; more than a year living with two women had taught me some mysteries would never be solved. Instead, I turned off my own flashlight app, tucked my wonderphone away into a pocket, wrapped both of my hands around the supine werewolf's ankle, and pulled.

The angle sucked, and either I was weaker than I thought, or Hyacinth was heavier, but eventually, I had her moving, scraping across the stone in a way that would have had me wincing if she wasn't a werewolf with quite literally inhuman powers of regeneration. I pulled her in until my arms were at a ninety-degree angle, and then crawled backwards again, letting my arms extend back above me.

I didn't know if it was the most efficient way of moving her, but it kept me flat against the ground, and it was working, and that was good enough for me.

It took four full cycles of my inchworm maneuver before I felt hands on my own ankles. Juliette had no problems dragging me backwards—and apparently no concerns about any scrapes I might accrue along the way—and within moments, both Hyacinth and I were back to safety.

The werewolf still didn't move.

"Go get the next one," said Juliette.

"It would be faster if you did it."

"Obviously."

"But?"

"But we already *know* you can do it without getting knocked unconscious. It's still a question when it comes to me."

I hated it when Juliette used logic. Our assumption that this was some sort of trap, and that the magical tripwire or all-seeing-eye that triggered it was set somewhere above crawl-height, was just that: an assumption. Better to stick with what we knew worked than to risk our only remaining heavy hitter proving that assumption.

My wearing shorts instead of jeans had been a bonus in the outdoors heat, but the rough stone I was now crawling over had me wishing for pants instead. I only prayed that my latent werewolf virus would be able to keep up with the sheer number of scrapes and scratches I was accumulating.

I don't know how long it took to get both Dulcinea and Pedro back to Juliette and our presumed safe zone. My muscles told me it had been hours, my head said mere minutes, and the still comatose werewolf suggested it had only been seconds.

That or removing her from the spell wasn't enough to break it.

I patted my sore, abraded belly as I leaned back and dripped sweat all over the tunnel wall.

"This isn't working," said Juliette, rubbing her hand after delivering the sort of slap that would have had Hyacinth wolfing out if she was conscious. "What now?"

"I don't know."

"We could carry them down to Ghost Falls, I guess, and hope the spell wears off along the way."

"What if it doesn't?"

"Is that our problem? You were hired to find them, not cure them."

"I'm not sure Simon will be satisfied with us returning a pair of vegetables... and I *know* Audrey won't be happy if we don't help Hyacinth."

"Then how do you want to wake our sleeping beauties?"

"Sleeping beauties... Could it be that easy?"

"Nobody breaks curses with kisses, little bird."

"Tell that to Walt." I coughed. "Rock, paper, scissors to determine who has to do it?"

"It's a smooch, not a prison sentence." I couldn't see Juliette's face, but I could almost *feel* her roll her eyes. "I'll do it."

To absolutely nobody's surprise, she picked Hyacinth as the recipient, leaning over the werewolf for an almost-chaste brushing of lips.

Nothing changed.

"Well, shit."

CHAPTER 28
IN WHICH THE CHEESE STANDS ALONE

"Any other bright ideas? And no, I'm not slipping her tongue."

"I wasn't going to suggest it. She's not awake to give consent… although something tells me she would if she were."

"Wolves aren't particularly subtle, are they?" I could hear the smile in her voice.

"Neither are you, Duchess."

"That's fair. Anyway, even if the whole situation with Angel wasn't in the middle of falling apart, Hyacinth and me would never work out."

"Too similar?"

"Worse. My kind can't digest Infected blood, remember? What's the point of dating if you can't drink—" Her voice trailed off. "Shit. I'm sorry, John."

"It's okay."

"I'm in my first century, while Ana's approaching her fifth. It's not the same thing at all. I promise."

"Juliette, really… it's okay. I get it."

"You do?"

"Yeah. You're not responsible for my insecurities. And if it's something that's truly bothering me, I should talk to Ana. She's a hell of a lot smarter than me. If she knows there's a problem, she'll help figure out a solution." I coughed and changed the subject. "But first, you and I need to figure out what to do about this spell."

"I still stand by my *carry them to town* plan."

"Let's leave that as a last resort. I don't want to have to carry them back *up* here if it doesn't work."

"I'm waiting for any suggestions from your side of things then. Ones that don't involve kissing."

"I hear you. Let me think a second."

Our hypothesis that this had been some sort of magical trap remained solid. In fact, it seemed even more so given that they were still asleep now. Each of the victims had somehow triggered the trap, been hit by the spell, and gotten knocked unconscious as a result.

While I considered myself at least somewhat educated on the many supernatural species of San Diego, I still didn't know a lot about magic itself. Zorana used blood as both a power source and a tool, the spells themselves cast either through spoken word or sheer will, while Nepenthe and her now-deceased coven had used raw energy to fuel spells that were then channeled through runic circles.

In both cases, there was a power source and something that gave shape to that power. And that meant if I could find whatever was powering this spell, I might be able to end it.

Of course, disrupting a power source, assuming I could even identify it, might blow up the mountain too. I had no idea what kind of magic was at work here, and even less of an idea what breaking it might do.

Still, I didn't see much other choice.

Juliette was less enthused.

"You want to what?!"

"Crawl back over and look for whatever is powering the trap."

"That's what I thought you said. Why the hell would we do that?"

"If we cut off the power, we would break the spell. And then everyone could walk out of here on their own two feet, and Audrey wouldn't send the rest of the pack to hunt us down."

"That's…"

"Yeah?"

"I hate it when you use logic."

It was possible we'd been working together too long.

"What if we can't find it?" she finally asked.

"We? I thought you didn't want to risk triggering the trap?"

"If you can limbo under the trigger, so can I. The difference is I'll actually make it look good."

"Juliette—"

"However this trap was constructed, and whatever magic was used, chances are you're going to need someone stronger, faster, and with better senses to deal with it."

"Maybe we should just send you then?"

"Four hands are better than two, little bird." For the first time in far too long, Juliette snickered. "You can trust me on that much."

"Trust you to make everything sexual, you mean."

"I said what I said."

I sighed. The truth was, Juliette was right. About the trap, anyway. "Okay but follow right behind me. And if you start feeling sleepy, reverse course as quickly as you can."

"If I start feeling sleepy, I suspect it'll be too late."

I did my best to ignore that inconvenient truth.

"The same goes for you," she continued. "Keep up a stream of inane babble—you're good at that—so I can tell if the trap has started to affect you. I'll know to reverse, and I'll at least be able to drag you back out with me."

Leaving her to transport four bodies back down the mountain. I didn't envy her that task—super strength only partially mitigated issues like size and leverage—but at least I wouldn't be awake to worry about it.

I renewed my acquaintance with the floor, muscles groaning. Behind me, Juliette somehow made half the noise I did as she crawled in my wake.

"You're supposed to be talking, little bird."

"Right. I guess I don't have a lot to talk about." Or breath to say it with, not that I was going to admit it. "I'm glad we found Dulcinea, and I'm *really* glad that this whole trip might be over soon."

"Not the romantic getaway you were hoping for?"

"I'm starting to realize romance is something you have to squeeze in whenever you can, because there's always another calamity lying in wait."

"I think that rule might only apply to you."

"Possibly. Mediation has been a bumpy ride so far. But even for other people, things are always changing. I mean… look at you!"

"That doesn't count. I got sucked up into the vortex of stupid chaos that is the John Smith experience."

The John Smith Experience would make for a hell of a title for my eventual autobiography. Or my EDM show if I ever quit mediating and decided to become a DJ.

"And I guess you're giving Ana and Lucia the same excuse?"

"Obviously. One is bonded to you by a nightmarish connection that neither of you seem capable of breaking. The other took you as her thrall."

"Funny." It was hard to tell, but I was pretty sure we'd passed where Hyacinth and the others had originally fallen. I scanned my flashlight ahead of me but found only more tunnel ahead. Apparently, we'd just keep crawling. "Anyway, my point is that we have to make time to enjoy the good experiences when they come through."

"So, you're buying the beer at Mama Nita's tonight?"

"Technically, I've bought it every night."

"I know. It's awesome. But what were you trying to say then?"

I had lost my train of thought and it took me far too long to find it again. "I think I'm going to take Ana to Hawaii."

"Why Hawaii?"

"Sun, beaches, and a lack of things trying to kill us."

"That you know of."

I ignored that all-too-accurate point. "If she feeds before we leave, we should be able to spend a week or two there, just the two of us. And my earnings from the goblin mediation should cover the cost."

"You remember she's rich, right?"

"She can always pay for the next trip."

"Huh." She chewed on that, never more than a few feet behind in our two-person crawl-a-thon. "It's possible that you're not a complete waste of space as a boyfriend."

"I love you too, Duchess."

Fifteen feet past where we'd recovered our budget-brand sleeping beauties, I finally found something other than stone; my flashlight glimmered off markings set in the tunnel floor. Even better, I recognized what I was seeing: runes.

The sigils that Nepenthe's coven had used back in Vista had been chiseled into the warehouse foundation and then infused with power until they glowed. Whoever had created these had gone one step further... runic characters carved into the tunnel rock had then been inlaid with silver and moonstones. They ran from one side of the passageway to the next, making a gleaming, glittering, jeweled line.

"If this isn't what's powering the trap, it's at least a key component of the spell," I said. "Any ideas on how to break it? Without smearing blood all over it, I mean?"

Juliette's silence spoke volumes.

"Right. Maybe I can dig out the silver or something?" I leaned my wonderphone against the tunnel wall so that it illuminated the row of runes and reached into my pocket. I didn't have a knife—after the whole Nepenthe experience, I was more skittish around blades than firearms—but I did have keys. I wasn't going to use the keys to my Corolla, Juliette's apartment, or Ana's house because they might get broken, but the key to the swimming pool gate in Juliette's complex? In almost two years, I'd *never* used the pool or the attached gym, and if a broken key kept that streak going, I was pretty okay with it.

I held the key in my fist, jagged part poking downward, and hammer fisted the sleep spell out of existence.

That was the plan anyway. Unfortunately, my hand and improvised weapon were still inches away when the air solidified above the runes, forming a wall that deflected my blow.

I looked at the runes again and swore. Not a line, but a *boundary*.

Thankfully, this wasn't my first time playing with runes. I set my keys aside and ran one hand down my other arm. My knees and legs were a mess from crawling across the stone, but my elbows weren't much better, scraped, torn, and—most importantly, for my purposes—bloody. I ran my index finger directly through the largest and most painful of my accumulated injuries. When I held it out in front of me, it glistened wetly in the light of my phone.

"I'm really getting tired of blood playing such a central role in my life," I told Juliette. "It's time for ice cream to take its rightful place."

I reached down to draw a bloody X across the closest rune.

For the second time in as many minutes, a brilliant plan failed through no fault of my own. My blood-streaked finger met the exact same resistance as the keys had. Try as I might, I couldn't reach the runes.

Damn it. That was supposed to have worked. Now, I felt like an idiot for putting my no-doubt dirty finger into a clearly open and bleeding wound.

"If I get an infection, you might have to end up carrying me after all." I sighed. "Any ideas on what to do next? Maybe it's time for some of that strength you were talking about?"

Nothing. I grabbed my phone and pointed it back down the tunnel to find my junior partner flat on her face roughly five feet behind me.

"Very funny," I said. "You definitely got me. But I could use some help now. Seriously."

Still nothing.

I didn't *think* Juliette would take a practical joke this far, but I'd said the same thing about hot fudge and brand new Jordans, and we all knew how that had turned out. With a sigh, I left my wonderphone and keys behind, and crawled back over to her.

Juliette was a lot of things, but patient wasn't one of them. When she didn't spring her surprise on my arrival, I started to worry. When she didn't even react to no less than three pokes and one totally insincere offer to let her drink from me, I knew something was very wrong.

She'd made it further than Hyacinth or the two teens, but my femmepire friend had fallen to the same spell as the others.

"I can't even carry one of you, let alone four," I complained. "What the hell am I—"

Behind me, the battery on my wonderphone died, taking the clear, cold light of its flashlight app with it.

And just like that, the cheese stood alone.

Or... lay flat on his belly alone, anyway.

ooo

I didn't have a good history with dark places, even before the supernatural species of the world had made my life their dumping grounds, and the darkness that filled that tunnel was thick and all encompassing. I could feel my breath coming fast and short. I had to fight the urge to spring to my feet and run back up the tunnel for the exit I wasn't even sure I'd be able to find.

In a desperate panic that said as much about the things that might live in the dark as the darkness itself, I searched for Juliette's phone and found nothing. Either she'd dropped it as she was passing out, or it was tucked away inside a secret dimensional pocket I couldn't find.

Either way, I was screwed.

We were screwed. If I couldn't see, how would I find—

Wait a second.

I blinked and looked to my side where Juliette lay. For the first time since my wonderphone had died, I could actually see a vague shape in the surrounding darkness. As I watched, that shape solidified into the form of my friend and partner.

Somehow, my eyes were starting to adjust to the lack of light, giving me a limited view of my surroundings. Maybe that latent werewolf virus *was* more than just an ongoing joke that only I ever found funny? I was pretty sure my night vision had never been good enough to pierce total darkness before. Then again, I hadn't spent much time in lightless caves either. It was entirely possible this was just a hidden talent I was finally discovering.

Whatever the reason, being able to see, even a little bit, helped with the panic. My breath evened out and my heart rate dropped to safer levels. Finally able to think again, I tried to focus on what I knew.

It was pitch-black, but I could still see. I was somewhere deep in a tunnel, with the way forward blocked off by runes. I'd arrived with werewolf muscle and vampire snark, and both had been ensnared by some sort of sleep trap just as easily as the teens we'd come to find.

What did that mean?

First, it meant the spell almost had to use mental magic to knock out its targets. There was no other rational explanation for why Juliette would have succumbed while I remained upright. Well, not *upright*, but at least awake. It also explained why Hyacinth had passed out when and where she did; unless she was actively calling on the wolf, she was as susceptible to that kind of magic as your average human. Hell, Kevin had demonstrated as much with his spores back in Phoenix.

So, we were dealing with some kind of runic trap or spell field that used mental magic to put people to sleep.

Second, the barrier I'd found was either part of the spell trap or a secondary spell intended to keep anyone from making it to the first spell's power source. Either way, breaking through that barrier was more important than ever.

Third, given that the trap had caught Juliette, it clearly extended all the way down to the floor. And that meant there was no reason for me to be crawling about on bloodied hands and knees.

I rose to my feet, hands extended out to either side, partially for balance and partially in case my new and surprisingly impressive night vision had misjudged the location of the nearest wall. Five strides took me back to the runes, where I tried to step over them. As expected, a barrier stopped me, mid-step. I felt along that invisible wall, verifying that it stretched from one side of the tunnel to the other, and as high as I could reach.

With a lot of time, tools, and other resources, I could probably chip away at the tunnel rock to either side, maybe not enough to squeeze my body through but at least to reach around and see if I could disrupt the runes from the other side. Unfortunately, I didn't have any tools, time was running out for the two dehydrated teenagers, and the closest thing I had to *resources* was thousands of miles away, probably wearing an all-white ensemble and secretly putting the *age* in cleavage.

It was scary how quickly I'd come to rely on Lucia's powers, and how weak and incapable I felt without them. I shook my head, reminding myself that I'd gotten along just fine without vampiric abilities for most of my life. Hell, I'd survived without any supernatural assistance at all for almost as long. I just needed to put my thinking cap on and get some good old-fashioned human ingenuity going.

Chapter 29

IN WHICH HUMAN INGENUITY DOES ITS THING,
SORT OF

For all its supposed virtues, it turned out that human ingenuity was spectacularly useless against magic. I spent the first ten minutes of my imposed solitude trying to think of something—anything—to do and then the next twenty minutes verifying that all my ideas sucked.

If the runes reacted to any form of music or speech, they were looking for words I didn't know or notes I couldn't hit. My breath wasn't stopped by the barrier, but it had no effect on the jeweled sigils. Meanwhile, both my blood and my spit stopped dead, whether they were attached to me or not. I didn't know if that was a *me* thing, where both fluids were recognizably part of my DNA and a puff of carbon dioxide was not, or if the barrier simply understood basic high school chemistry better than I did.

If Juliette had been conscious, she'd have no doubt suggested physically breaking the barrier down—it was her idea of lockpicking, after all—so I tried that next. The barrier gave way under each punch, but then rebounded just as quickly. I tried putting pressure on it instead, a steady weight that would hopefully stretch its resilience to the breaking point. It deformed slightly but then, about two inches into the invisible layer of force, hardened to stop me cold.

I even tried screaming at both the barrier and the runes that powered it, but either the demigod of pointless histrionics was on vacation or they didn't judge my efforts worthy of an appearance. That made me think of other demigods, of course, so I tried calling out to Bill next. After all, being stuck with four bodies and a magical spell in the mostly dark somewhere under a mountain had to be *someone's* idea of a nightmare, right?

Maybe so, but the giant green asparagus didn't appear.

I tried summoning Kala too, even though the demigod never left his bar, and was unsurprised to find my call go unanswered. By that point, I'd mostly run through my mental phonebook of powerful allies who had some vague chance of hearing me without a cell signal.

Mostly.

There *was* one person I always had a connection with, and even if we *were* six thousand miles apart, that connection had to be at least as effective as an anonymous prayer. And so, for the first time since I'd left Rome, I found myself *actively* reaching out to Lucia Borghesi, Winter Queen, Ana's ex-boss, and the current and forever holder of my bond.

What had originally started as a tight knot of thoughts and feelings in the very back of my brain had long since been torn wide open, creating a space that felt as much Lucia as it did me, but the distance between us had kept that space quiescent since I left Rome. I never got much more than a vague direction, and maybe the tiniest hint of a mood.

Which was why I was surprised to have Lucia flooding into my brain… her presence, if not her active thoughts. In fact, I was pretty sure she was sleeping, dreaming dreams I had no interest in experiencing myself.

Even odder, she was somewhere above me.

I didn't know what to make of any of that, but wherever she was, and whatever was going on, our bond was alive and active; we felt fully connected for the first time in months. I took a breath and called upon the Talent that had given her the title of Winter Queen.

The temperature in the tunnel plummeted, my next exhalation a plume of frozen water vapor I could sense if not see. I gathered the cold of Lucia's power around me like a shroud and focused it on the runes at my feet, frost becoming ice that sheathed the floor.

Lucia had once flash frozen an entire wing of her house along with the vampires skulking through its halls to kill her. I was never going to be that powerful *or* that skilled, but with a few minutes and no hard limits on the amount of power I was allowed to waste, I could do a pretty good Jack Frost impression of my own.

Silver didn't get brittle under cold temperatures, any more than gold or platinum did. I knew that much from high school, even if I couldn't remember exactly why. But I was pretty sure gemstones were a whole different matter. If I could shatter or even just crack the moonstones in the runic barrier, it would almost *have* to affect the spell itself, wouldn't it?

I was about to find out.

I didn't hear the moonstones break, buried under the ice as they were, but the barrier they were generating went soft, then brittle, then collapsed entirely. I waved a hand in front of me and found nothing but natural, un-spelled air.

More importantly, I could hear noises start up behind me, the sound of people stirring from a deep and involuntary sleep.

Maybe human ingenuity wasn't all it was cracked up to be, but if you could combine it with a little bit of vampiric power?

Well, it didn't suck.

I let Lucia's power go, and the summoned ice almost immediately started to melt, forming a layer of slush over the now deactivated spell.

A part of me was curious about what might be waiting deeper in the tunnel. I mean… a barrier *and* a sleep trap wouldn't just be erected for no reason, right? Between this magic and the stone wall blocking the tunnel's entrance, someone had gone to extraordinary lengths to keep people out.

And I'd seen enough movies to know what that meant:

Treasure.

On the other hand, Dulcinea and Pedro had been trapped here for more than a week, and while their comatose state may have kept them from dying of dehydration, they were going to be thirsty as hell when they woke up, not to mention in need of better medical care than any of us could offer. We could start the rehydration with the leftover water in my backpack but would still need to get the pair down to Ghost Falls as quickly as possible.

People first, glittering possible dragon's hoard second. It had never been one of the immutable laws of my existence, but I decided to add it to the list.

Juliette was the first to recover, springing to her feet with an agility that reminded me she was an actual vampire. I had stayed carefully out of arm's—or fang's—reach, but when her flurry of motion stopped, I moved in.

"Welcome back, sleepyhead."

"What? How did—What?"

I shook my head. "All this time working together, and you've still only managed to remember two of the fundamental five questions."

"If you bring up that stupid class—"

"In Journalism 101, we learned better."

"I hate you, little bird." She looked about. "We're still underground?"

"Yeah. You made it about ten feet further than the others, then passed out. It's okay though; I saved the day. Again."

"How?"

"I found the runes for the spell trap and broke them."

"Just like that?"

"There's a reason I'm the senior partner, Juliette."

"And here I thought it was because I look eighteen and you're pushing thirty really, really hard."

"Well, that's just hurtful."

A low groan came from Hyacinth, and Juliette was at the wolf's side in an instant. "They're all waking up?"

"Yeah. I'm going to give Dulcinea and Pedro the rest of our water once they're conscious."

I made my way over to my backpack and dug through its contents. We'd started with seven full water bottles, and were already down to three, but I figured that'd be enough to at least take the edge off their thirst.

"You're moving pretty well for someone who was basically blind before I went to sleep."

"Yeah. Funny story, that: my phone battery died, and shortly after, my eyes adjusted to the dark well enough that I could mostly see."

"Uh huh." There was a rush of air and then Juliette was pinning me to the tunnel wall. "A likely story."

"What?"

"It's so dark in here that *I* can barely see. So, you tell me, what's more likely... you suddenly develop better than human senses, or whatever thing crawled inside your head is helping you see?"

"I don't think Lucia would appreciate being called a thing."

"I'm not talking about Lucia, you idiot!"

"Then I'm totally lost."

"Think for once in your life, little bird. Magic spell traps. A walled-off tunnel—"

"The runes made a barrier too."

"Runic barriers," she added, the edge in her voice making me rethink future interruptions. "What does that all say to you?"

I'd already done this equation. "Treasure."

"Exact—" She stopped. "What? No! It says cage or prison."

I didn't agree with that take *at all*, but Juliette did have almost seventy years of experience on me. "And you think that whatever was imprisoned crawled inside my head?"

"How else do you explain suddenly being able to see in the dark? And if you say anything about a werewolf virus, you're walking home."

I snapped my mouth shut so fast I almost chipped a tooth. "I don't know," I admitted, "but there's one problem with your theory."

"And what's that?"

"If something—some spirit or haunt—is possessing me and that's what improved my night vision, then why was I able to see in the dark *before* I broke the barrier?"

"That's—huh." I could almost hear the gears turning in Juliette's head. "Assuming that said haunt isn't forcing you to say that, then I guess you might have a point."

"We can have Valentina scope me out when we get back to San Diego," I said. "I'm pretty sure she'd be able to tell if I was possessed or not, and I doubt she'd stand for it."

"No kidding. That woman is all kinds of protective."

"It's mutual."

"Well, if there is no wraith… then, maybe we should take a peek at what was being protected?"

I opened my mouth to explain my newest rule to live by to Juliette, helpfully offering her the benefit of my painstakingly accrued wisdom, when Hyacinth ruined the moment by waking up.

Much like the vampire before her, she was on her feet in a move I could see but not quite parse, but where Juliette had taken a moment to shake off her confusion, Hyacinth did something neither of us expected.

She took off in a dead sprint, heading down the tunnel toward the barrier I'd dispelled.

"Juliette, stop her!"

If our one-time captor had been calling on her wolf, it might have been more of a contest, but for whatever reason, Hyacinth was staying one hundred percent human, and Juliette caught her like she was standing still. Caught her, and physically lifted her into the air. At this distance, even my suddenly supernatural vision was insufficient, but I was pretty sure I could see the other woman's legs still churning, even though her feet weren't touching the ground.

"What the hell, flower girl? You flirt like a pro all morning and then take off running because of one little kiss?"

My sigh carried all the way down the tunnel. *Of course* Juliette assumed it was all about her.

"I don't think she's running from you, Duchess. It seems more like she's running *to* something."

"Maybe you're right." Juliette pinned the woman against the wall with one arm. "She's not responding either. Are you sure you broke the spell?"

"Maybe she's only half awake?"

"I'm *not* kissing her again."

"Then what do you—"

A sharp crack filled the tunnel, and Hyacinth's head snapped back like she'd been shot. Her legs went still and a low growl started somewhere in her chest.

"I will rip your gods-damned head off," the werewolf snarled, "and piss on whatever remains."

"Just like a wolf to mark her territory," said Juliette. Her words were light, but I could see the tension in her arms as she now had to fight to keep Hyacinth restrained. Juliette was at least a century from being able to match strength with an Infected calling on their beast.

"Fanger?" Hyacinth went still, but before she could say anything, another crack sounded. "What the hell? Could you stop hitting me?"

"Hold on to your wolf, flower girl," said Juliette. "You've already been unconscious once, and something else in these caves seems to be affecting your mind."

I blinked, forgetting the freshly opened water bottle in my hands and the two teenagers still stirring from their own sleep.

Sometimes, Juliette was way smarter than I gave her credit for. The biggest weakness werewolves faced, beyond their own lifespans, was that they spent most of their lives being every bit as vulnerable to glamor and magic as any mundane human. They only had some level of protection when shifted or when the wolf was close to the surface.

It was why Davis Hawthorne, Carolyn's uncle, had kidnapped me and tried to turn me. He'd hoped that my odd genetic quirk might breed true and strengthen the pack.

But if *Hyacinth* had fallen prey to some siren call from deeper in the tunnels, wouldn't—

Dulcinea's fist shot up and caught me in the face like a miniature cannon, spinning me about and sending me sprawling to the floor. By the time I could see straight, she and Pedro were both up and moving, sprinting toward the dispelled barrier just like Hyacinth had done.

Despite the darkness and their merely human eyes, they charted a course right down the middle of the tunnel.

Thankfully, my two companions were quick on the uptake, and a hell of a lot stronger than humans. Juliette dropped Hyacinth, and both women tackled the incoming pair.

I winced at the impact. It was bad enough that both townies were dehydrated and apparently ensorcelled… they didn't need broken bones on top of all that.

"Now what?" Hyacinth's voice remained a low growl.

"That's… a great question."

"I could slap them too," suggested Juliette.

"That only worked because you roused Hyacinth's wolf."

"Save the dirty talk for the bedroom, little bird."

I sighed. After her sexts with Angel, the femmepire had no room to mention dirty talk. "Not my point. Dulcinea and Pedro are entirely human, right?" I was pretty sure they'd have already mentioned it if that wasn't the case.

"Right," both women answered.

"So, they don't have wolves or other inner beasts to awaken. Slapping them won't do anything to help them fight off whatever's going on. Instead, it'll just give them bruises we'll have to explain to the sheriff."

"So, what do you want to do then? I mean, my *carry everyone down the hill* plan is still on the table."

"I think it's better if I try to figure out what's deeper in the tunnels. If it's another spell or something, I'll break it."

"We'll all go together," said Juliette.

"What if the spell or the siren call or whatever this is grows stronger the closer you get?" I shook my head. "That sleep trap took you out just like it did Hyacinth, and I don't have a chance in hell of restraining you if you go nuts on me."

"Wait, *you're* the one who saved us all?" The werewolf gave me a look I couldn't parse, paying no attention to the human male struggling ineffectually in her grasp. "Who the hell are you?"

I met her eyes across the tunnel. "No one to be trifled with."

There was a moment of deeply impressed silence and then Juliette broke down, laughing so hard that Dulcinea almost wriggled free. "Gods, little bird. Did you workshop that or something?"

"I mean—" Not *all* my free time was spent in front of a mirror, practicing smiles.

"Who the hell says *trifle* anymore?"

"Lots of people, I'm sure."

"Yeah, keep telling yourself that."

I looked toward Hyacinth to see if she, at least, had been impressed, but her grin was obvious even in the pseudo-darkness.

"That job offer stands," I told the werewolf. "I'm not sure my junior partner is going to be around much longer."

Juliette had finally straightened back up and her snicker told me how seriously she took my little threat.

Which… was fair, really. She was practically family at this point.

"Anyway, for whatever reason, I'm best suited for stuff like this," I said. "And you all are better suited to restraining our missing teenagers without hurting them. So, I'll go in, look around, and report back to you both. Sound good?"

"No, but I don't see any better options." Juliette paused, lowering her voice as if somebody else might be listening. "This is going on the list of things you can't tell Anastasia about."

"I think that ship has already sailed."

"Because I made fun of your superhero one-liner? Come on, John, have a heart so I can keep mine."

That wasn't what I'd meant, but I decided to roll with it. "It's okay; I doubt she'll be *too* pissed. Hopefully. Then again, you *did* say she was both possessive *and* overprotective." I pretended to give it some thought, then shrugged. "I guess we'll find out what that means."

With a smile of my own, I moved past the two supernatural women with their mundane, still struggling burdens, and on down the tunnel. I grabbed my dead wonderphone on the way, managed to avoid slipping on the melting ice patch over what remained of the runic barrier, and descended into a darkness far less all-consuming than it should have been.

I didn't have to go far. About twenty feet after the runes, the tunnel twisted to the left, and ten or feet after that, it opened into a small cavern. Not even my new and improved night vision allowed me to see to the far side, but what I did see dispelled any lingering dreams of a dragon's hoard.

There were no Scrooge McDuck style piles of gold. There were no endless shelves of precious artifacts like in the Indiana Jones movies. There wasn't even a broken-down wagon with three or four treasure chests stashed within. Mostly, there was just a lot of empty space.

The sole exception was a pile of detritus in the room's center.

If my enhanced vision *was* a result of Lucia's relative nearness as I was starting to suspect, then it might fade as she continued traveling west. And since she almost had to be on a plane—likely part of Borghesi International's private fleet—that moment could happen at any time. Even so, I circled the small cave and verified that there was nothing else hidden within... no runes on the walls, no dusty pentagrams on the ceiling or floor, and no hidden pools of surprisingly fresh blood.

The cave was every bit as empty as it seemed, except for whatever waited at the center. I approached that object carefully, letting both Lucia's physical strength and her wintry power fill me. The vampire would find herself tapped out whenever she landed and woke up—my draw on her abilities was anything but efficient—but hopefully she'd have gotten over that by the time we saw each other again.

Nothing leaped out to attack me as I neared, which had been my main concern. I used a shoe to stir what appeared to be a pile of wood, only to have that pile crumble on contact. My HGTV-watching experience and a handful of construction-related conversations with Mike told me I was dealing with rot, even though I doubted there had been water intrusion or termites this far into the cave.

"I think this was some sort of box, originally."

"What did you say, little bird?"

I raised my voice, no longer concerned that something would hear us. "I think I found a box!"

"Whatever you do, don't open it!"

"We're well past that point, I'm afraid!"

I couldn't quite hear what Hyacinth said to Juliette, but the words *we* and *die* were unmistakable.

More wood disintegrated as I stirred the pile with my foot. Soon I was left with a mound of rot dust and… something else lying almost buried beneath it. I nudged it into the open and found…

"Huh."

"What?!"

"It's a statue! Clay not gold!" I didn't even try to hide my disappointment about that last part. With the statue being the only thing in this cave, it was almost definitely the source of the magic affecting Dulcinea and Pedro… but still, it kind of took the shine off *buried treasure* when it barely even qualified *as* treasure. "I don't suppose our teenage rescues have calmed down?"

"Not in the slightest!"

"Okay. I'm going to touch it then. If you don't hear from me in one minute…"

"Yeah?"

"Call the president!"

Boom. Hero status unlocked.

I didn't listen for any answering replies, confident that Juliette and Hyacinth were appropriately awestruck. Instead, I picked up the statue, ready to drop it just as quickly.

Nothing happened. The thing was about the length of my forearm and a lot heavier than it looked. It crudely depicted a standing figure with hands held before him, palms facing forward. Diagonal lines in his chest suggested either armor or ribs, and his slightly oversized head was bare. Either the hair he'd been given had been made from a less enduring material, or the figure had been bald from the start.

Old, somewhat creepy statue? Check. But what I *didn't* find were runes or anything else even vaguely recognizable as magical.

"John?"

"I'm still here!"

"And you're not possessed by any sort of evil djinn or anything, right?"

"Not that I know of! Should I try making a wish?"

"No! Just figure out how to end the spell and get back here!"

That was easier said than done, given that I wasn't a secret sorcerer in disguise. Assuming sorcerers were even a thing… so far, I'd only met different kinds of witches. I set the statue back down on its feet and called on Lucia's powers to cover the statue in a thin layer of frost.

"Any changes with the kids?" I shouted.

"Are you even trying?"

That sounded like a no. But how did I break a spell that didn't appear to be operating along any of the scant forms of magic I was familiar with?

Hmm. Maybe *break* was the operative word here?

In a move that would no doubt have had junior archaeologists across the world shrieking in horror, I picked up the statue, this time by its feet, and swung it at the hard cavern floor.

The statue didn't shatter into a thousand pieces like I'd expected, but it did break, and the manner of that breaking was almost *more* disturbing: the head toppled off to bounce—once—on the floor.

"That's some durable clay." As a kid, I'd knocked over my mom's ceramic vase while roughhousing with Mike, and it had broken into so many pieces that even Humpty Dumpty's men would have thrown their hands up in despair.

As I waved the statue around, its left arm dropped off to join the head. Still, three fragments was a lot fewer than a million.

"That did it!" Juliette sounded as surprised as me.

I eyed the statue pieces. My job was done, but leaving what had been some sort of spell-worked artifact behind didn't sit well with me, especially when some other Ghost Falls resident might stumble onto the place. I scooped up the head and arm in my free hand, gave an apologetic shrug to the empty cave, and headed up the tunnel to where the others were waiting.

I was halfway there when I heard the howl.

CHAPTER 30

IN WHICH BLOOD TAKES ITS TOLL

By the time I made it back, that first howl had been followed by at least two more, accompanied by what I was pretty sure was Dulcinea and Pedro screaming. I rounded the corner and found two oversized figures going at each other in a flurry of blood and fur.

Werewolves in their hybrid forms. One of them had to be Hyacinth, but then who was the other? And where was Juliette?

Even as I tried to make sense of what I'd come back to, one of the wolves slashed through empty air as the other, larger wolf dropped to a knee, their own claws tearing through the unprotected belly of the first. More blood splashed against the tunnel wall, and the injured wolf dropped to the ground, all the fire and fight gone out of them. The second wolf lashed out again, lifting the downed wolf into the air with the force of their kick, a move I distinctly remembered from the Comfort Inn parking lot. I didn't need the snarling voice that issued from the bipedal nightmare to know who it was.

"Not so high and mighty now, are ya?" growled Shae through a maw not meant for speech. "Poor Audrey's gonna weep her little four-eyed head off when you go mysteriously missing." She tilted her head upwards, scenting the air, and then landed another bone-breaking kick. "Smells like the man of the hour's arrived. Stay down like a good pup and I'll come back to you in a second."

Shae's hybrid form was at least seven feet tall, her wingspan so large that clawed fingers brushed both sides of the tunnel. She stalked toward me.

"Hello, mediator."

"Does Ezekiel know you're here? Does Audrey?" Behind Shae, Hyacinth's large form lay still, blocking my view, but I could hear whimpers from Dulcinea. At least she was still alive. I wasn't sure the same could be said for Juliette or Pedro.

"What they don't know won't hurt them. Can't say the same for you though, can we?"

She moved as she spoke, zigzagging down the tunnel toward me as if to keep me guessing as to where she was. If my eyesight had been purely human, it might have been terrifying. As it was, what I could see of her visage was horrific enough.

In human form, werewolves ran the full gamut of attractiveness, just like the rest of us. In wolf form, they were scary but also kind of majestic in a *holy crap, how is anything that big?* sort of way. But every single hybrid form I'd ever seen had one thing in common: they were all total nightmare fuel.

I swallowed and tried to control my breathing, knowing she'd be able to hear my heart pounding even from twenty-five feet away. "What's the play here, Shae? Are you still trying to use me as bait?"

She paused. "That was Plan A. You just had to go and screw that one up, didn't you? Plan B is simple."

"Simple how?" I took a few steps back, for all the good it would do me. Even if I ran, even if I was fast enough to not be caught in a matter of steps, there was nothing but a dead-end cave behind me.

"Everyone dies."

I mean… to be fair, that *was* pretty simple.

"Hyacinth and the fanger get left here for the scavengers," she continued, now twenty feet away, now fifteen. "But you, you I'll eat."

"Excuse me?"

"Eat you up, shit you out, put it in a box I'll send to San Diego. Maybe then your other fanger will learn what it's like to lose someone."

"She's been around for centuries. I'm pretty sure she learned that a long time ago." I tried not to gag as I bladed my body to make it a smaller target for the unstoppable death machine. "Also, that's the nastiest thing I've heard in my life. Seriously, what is *wrong* with you? Did you kiss your sister with that mouth?"

If I survived the next few minutes, maybe I'd feel bad about going for the throat with the sister comment, considering Laika was dead and my Ana was the one who'd killed her. In the meantime, it had the desired effect.

With a howl, Shae abandoned her slow prowl and charged.

Lucia's power was the only thing that even let me see her coming. Even then, my body was still human, my reflexes and capabilities all restrained by a purely mundane form. It was like watching a car coming at you, far too fast to even think of getting out of its way.

Thankfully, the tunnel was straight, and Shae ended up having to charge a whole lot further than she would have if I hadn't pissed her off.

Also? I'd played Little League Baseball growing up.

The head of the possibly magical, unquestionably ancient statue caught Shae right in the face. I heard something crack, and it was anyone's guess whether it was the fired clay or one of her cheekbones. Either way, the werewolf spun to one side, bounced off the wall, and dropped.

Which left me all the time I needed to give Jack Frost a sequel.

I'd once skewered a demon with an icicle the size of a car, but this time, I went for something smaller and faster, a spear to impale the wolf before she could regain her footing. Lucia's power swirled around me, the temperature in the tunnel plummeted for the second time, and then…

Nothing.

Lucia's power was gone like it had never existed. I reached out again and found the femmepire now tracking somewhere far to the west and south of me. Close enough to sense, yeah, but too distant for anything else. Even my night vision started to deteriorate, plunging the area around me back into shadow.

I'd long suspected an airplane might be involved in my death, but somehow, I'd never predicted that it would be the plane *leaving me behind* that did it.

Shae was back on her feet already, whatever minimal damage I'd done to her no doubt healed. I threw the rest of the statue, and this time, she batted it out of the air.

"Kill you," she snarled. "Eat you. Shi—"

Her words cut off as something hit her from behind, kicking the back of her right knee to collapse that leg in a mirror of the move I'd attempted at the Comfort Inn. Then, a shape I only barely recognized as Juliette was there, pinning that leg to the ground with her foot even as she pulled the werewolf's arms back behind her.

Juliette was strong, but she was a hell of a long way from *werewolf* strong. I could hear my partner's strangled grunts as she fought to keep the other woman immobilized, but the outcome was a foregone conclusion. Shae slowly started to pull her arms forward, like a gym rat doing chest flies, and the vampire on her back couldn't do a thing to stop her.

So instead, Juliette leaned forward, tilted her head to the side, and drove her fangs into the other woman's neck.

Shae's howl filled the tunnel, shockingly loud, but I knew even that respite was short-lived. If Juliette had been a werewolf herself, she might have been able to do the kind of damage even another wolf couldn't easily heal, but vampire fangs were meant for feeding, not crushing vertebrae or tearing out throats.

I hated that I knew that, hated that there was this inescapably bloody side to the life that had otherwise given me so much, hated that I'd either be dead in the next few minutes or have new nightmares to add to my highlight reel.

But mostly, I just hated this woman who had collared my friend and was now doing her level best to kill us both.

I stepped forward, closing the space between the struggling Shae and me, and lashed out. Not with a fist… I was pretty sure I'd break every bone in my hand trying to punch Shae's monstrous face. Instead, I struck with my elbow, dropping my weight, and rotating through the hips like Ana had taught me.

It probably hurt me more than the werewolf, but her head snapped back anyway, and for just a second, she was too stunned to struggle against Juliette. So, I did it again, and again, and again, switching to my other elbow even as adrenaline muffled the pain of the bruises I was racking up like frequent flyer miles.

At best, I was a distraction or an annoyance, that mosquito flitting around that makes it impossible to focus. But all the while, Juliette was there, keeping the werewolf immobilized, draining her blood, and digging ever deeper into her throat.

I don't know how long it took. I just know that at some point, Shae stopped struggling and started writhing in pleasure instead. I stepped back and Juliette rode the werewolf's body to the floor. She ripped her bloody fangs out, grabbed the back of the woman's head, and smashed Shae's face repeatedly into the tunnel floor, her movements so fast I couldn't distinguish them.

Juliette wasn't werewolf strong, but she *was* a vampire, and bones—even supernatural ones—have a breaking point. By the time my partner finally stopped, hyperventilating like she'd just run an ultra-marathon, there was nothing but gore left above Shae's tattooed shoulders.

"Holy shit, fanger," came a strained whisper from up the tunnel. "Remind me to never piss you off."

My junior partner shakily rose to her feet, eyes glowing a gold that did little to illuminate the increasingly dark tunnel, and then turned to one side to puke her guts out.

It was all I could do to keep from joining in, but I hadn't liked whatever it was I was hearing in Hyacinth's reed-thin voice. I fumbled about to find the closest wall, and then followed it up the tunnel towards the werewolf. The adrenaline had drained out of my body sometime in the middle of Juliette's blunt force decapitation, and my legs were rubbery beneath me. Even the sound of my shoes squelching through fluids I didn't want to think about was faint and indistinct.

Without my borrowed night vision, I ended up almost walking right into Hyacinth. Her clawed hand first stopped me, then helped hold me up as I staggered backwards.

"Y'all might not want to go stepping around here," she wheezed. "Some of my insides are taking a field trip, and I'd like them back undamaged."

And that *was* enough for my stomach. I took two steps back, turned away, and tossed up what little remained of the breakfast I'd had at Pearl's.

Up the tunnel, either Dulcinea or Pedro made a sound that told me they had joined in on the sympathetic vomit parade. They were going to have to fumigate this whole tunnel before anyone tried spelunking again.

"What can I do to help?" I finally managed, when there was nothing left to puke up.

"Things will heal, but until then, I'm kinda stuck. If you could help push some of the organs back into place… and maybe without adding your own upchuck to the mix?"

Down the tunnel, Juliette hacked and coughed up another cup or two of undigestible werewolf blood.

Worst. Trip. Ever.

ooo

It wasn't fun helping Hyacinth make sure her organs went back where they belonged—more or less—but that effort still paled in comparison to the task of calming down Dulcinea and Pedro. The two teenagers had, as far as they knew, been out hiking, only to wake up a week later, exhausted and feeble, in pitch-black darkness, with what sounded like monsters fighting and dying mere feet away.

It took me half a conversation to realize my mediation skills weren't going to be up to the challenge.

"Juliette, if you're uh… done… back there, can I get some help settling these two down?" I turned back to the kids, although neither they nor I could see each other. "My colleague is a bit of an amateur therapist. She'll get you both on your feet, so we can get you home."

The *on your feet* part was a bit of an exaggeration; neither Dulcinea nor Pedro were in any shape to walk on their own without a supernatural statue's siren call, and Hyacinth and Juliette would almost definitely be carrying them down to town. But we needed the teenagers calm and we needed them to *not* spread stories of monsters on the mountain, and a vampire's compulsion was the quickest route to both of those things.

There was just one problem with that.

"I'm tapped out," said Juliette, her voice a whisper in my ears. She'd pulled me away, back down the tunnel, although Hyacinth seemed focused on her own healing and the young couple didn't seem to be listening to anything but their own whimpers.

"Tapped out?"

"Blood, little bird."

"You just fed last night!"

"And wrestled a werewolf today, *after* healing from the damage I took in her initial ambush." She sounded even more tired than I felt. "I can compel them, but I need to drink first. Which of them is in better shape for me to feed from?"

"Which of who?"

She didn't say anything, just waited for me to get it.

Dulcinea or Pedro?

The problem was… the answer almost had to be *neither*. I wasn't a doctor, but I knew being stuck in a cave for a week was the sort of thing that took its toll on the body. They were already in a state that required medical attention, and I was pretty sure drinking their blood would push them that much closer to the edge.

So, I did the only thing that I could think of, something that would no doubt send Lucia into fits of rage, and possibly stir even the slightest bit of displeasure from Anastasia herself.

I extended my arm in front of where I assumed Juliette was standing.

"What are you doing?" The voice came from three feet further to the left, showing me just how blind I had become again.

"You need blood. I'm the only one here who can afford to give it."

I was prepared to detail the reasons that was the case, to override Juliette's objections, and to slowly wear her down with the full weight of my unassailable logic.

What I *wasn't* prepared for was her taking me at my word and biting down instantly.

I'd been bitten way too many times by vampires, and the two bites from Lucia notwithstanding, it had hurt every single damn time. At three bites, Juliette lagged only behind Zorana on that particular scorecard, but I don't think she cared as she lapped up the blood gushing from my wrist.

I'd been told my blood smelled good and tasted better so often that it had long since ceased to be a compliment and instead felt more like a threat. With that threat once again realized, it was all I could do to grit my teeth and take it, giving my partner the nourishment she required.

And to think, I could've been an accountant, like my dad, if it hadn't been for a pesky but persistent hatred of math and an incurable allergy to ties.

I was fully prepared to pry Juliette off of me, but the femmepire stopped on her own. My arm still held in her two hands, she delicately licked the puncture holes in its wrist. Anticoagulants would ensure I didn't bleed out on the way down, and my curiously quick healing would likely have me right as rain by morning.

It didn't make the pain I'd suffered any better, but hearing Juliette move easily for the first time since our battle at least gave that pain purpose and meaning.

"If Ana got to drink this every day," Juliette murmured, her words slightly slurred, "I might really have to hate her."

"I'll let her know."

With a shudder, she seemed to shake herself fully awake, her next words the usual blend of sharp-edged snark.

"Uh, think we can add that comment—and this whole feeding— to the list of things you're *not* telling her?"

I reached to pat her shoulder with my good arm, and missed entirely, once again misjudging her position. "Duchess, I'm going to tell her everything."

"What? Are you serious?"

"Of course I am."

"Why?"

"Why am I serious or why—"

"You know what I'm asking, little bird."

"Because secrets are dumb."

She waited, but I was done.

"That's it? Secrets are dumb?"

"Yeah."

"I'm going to die."

"Ana's not going to kill you just because I freely offered my blood to help you recover. Lucia, on the other hand…"

"Good thing that walking breast show is in Rome."

"About that. I'm pretty sure she just flew to San Diego." Maybe it was the blood loss, but I couldn't even find it in myself to be irritated by that fact. Before we'd gotten cut off, Ana had started to tell me something… and having sensed Lucia literally passing overhead on her way to the coast, I was guessing I knew what that was.

Anastasia and a bunch of House vampires against Zorana was dangerous enough to put me on edge, but if you added Lucia to the side of truth, justice, and non-insane, millennium-old Blood Witches? I was a lot less concerned for the woman I loved.

"If you help me gather up the pieces of the statue I broke, I won't tell Lucia," I finally promised.

"Really? I thought secrets were dumb?"

"I guess it depends on the people involved."

"She'll probably just pluck it out of your mind, you know."

"Probably."

"Vegas is looking better and better."

I smiled but didn't respond.

"Anyway, I'm running at about seventy percent now. Shall we get these two sweetlings home to their parents? I could do with one of Mama Nita's mole enchilada plates."

I frowned, standing in the darkness. "I don't remember seeing those on the menu."

"They're on the secret menu. Friends and family only."

I was right. Secrets *were* dumb.

CHAPTER 31

IN WHICH SOME STORIES DON'T HOLD UP
AND OTHER STORIES DO

By the time Juliette had finished giving the teens their vampire-powered pep talk, Hyacinth was back on her feet. We headed back through the tunnels in a group, the werewolf carrying Dulcinea, the vampire carrying Pedro, and me carrying my own tired and slightly woozy ass. I had Juliette's phone with me this time, the flashlight app doing what it could to light my way.

It was strange stepping out into sunlight. It felt like we'd been underground for ten or more hours, but the sun, while well past its high point, was still a long way from the western horizon. What had started out as a hot, kind of muggy day had only doubled down on those two facets, and if we hadn't given all of our remaining water over to help rehydrate the young couple we'd rescued, I'd have drained a full bottle then and there.

As it was, there was nothing to do but keep going. I blinked away the brightness and looked to my companions. Juliette seemed almost perky despite the dried blood on her face and tank top, while Hyacinth…

"Are you okay?" I asked the wolf.

"I'll live. Why?"

"You just look…"

"Like I haven't had a meal in over a month?"

"Exactly." Before we'd entered the cave, the werewolf had been a specimen, the red tank top showing off her toned and muscular physique to its best advantage. Now, that same tank top hung loosely on her frame. The muscles were still there, but her face was gaunt, her eyes slightly hollow, and it looked like she'd dropped every possible percentage of body fat… and then a few percentages more.

"Healing takes energy," she said, nodding to wounds across her stomach that were well on their way to becoming scars, "and we can't all top up our tanks at the full-service blood station."

"More like self-service," said Juliette, cheerfully joining the conversation.

"Oh?" Despite her horrible appearance, Hyacinth's humor remained intact. "So, he didn't hold his arm out for you to drink from, like a mama bird feeding its babies?"

I laughed. After years of Juliette calling me little bird for no reason whatsoever, it was nice to see her end up in a bird-related metaphor.

"No, he did," said Juliette, not troubled at all by the reversal, "But I'd expect snacks and complementary window washing at a full-service stop. What kind of low-rent, fly-by-night operation are you running here anyway, little bird?"

"The kind that's free, on the spot, and might not end with you a Juliette-sized popsicle."

"Might not?"

"I guess it depends on what I'm going to get to eat tonight."

Hyacinth looked back and forth between us. "Should I ask?"

"I wouldn't recommend it," said Juliette. "Not now anyway, when we have sweetlings still to finish saving. We can all discuss it tonight over mole enchiladas." She eyed the other woman, looking her up and down in a way that would get most men an ass whooping. "You might want to get a couple orders."

"I'm getting four or five and y'all are paying."

I just nodded, still flush with the realization that I'd negotiated myself access to Mama Nita's secret menu.

During that whole conversation, Dulcinea and Pedro had been happily passed out in their respective carrier's arms, and that didn't change as we hiked down the mountain. Whatever Juliette had told them had completely erased their fear, but the lack of food meant they were still listless and exhausted. Pedro had stayed awake longer than his girlfriend, stubbornly doing his best to keep watch over her, but I'd heard his snores even before we exited the cave.

Over the course of the next hour, I found myself envying the two sleeping teenagers. I was hot, I was covered in blood, and my arms and legs were competing to see which could scream the loudest, but there was nobody left to carry me. I picked up one foot at a time, trudging after Juliette, who in turn followed Hyacinth, as the only one of us who knew where the hell we were going.

When we saw the road again, I honestly thought it was a mirage, a flicker of black that didn't really exist but served to keep us hiking further through the endless hills. It was only when my gore-covered sneakers hit asphalt that I realized it was real.

Even better, my Corolla was waiting there, still parked on the shoulder.

"Hurray," said Juliette dryly. "A Toyota. We're saved."

For a terrible second, I thought I'd left my keys back in the caves, but a second check found them in my left pocket rather than the usual right. Instead of unlocking the doors, I popped the trunk.

Both werewolf and vampire turned to look at me.

"You want us to put them in the trunk?" asked Hyacinth.

"What? No. I have some towels back there. And water, though it's probably a week or two old at this point. I wouldn't suggest drinking it, but maybe the three of us could…"

"Could what?" asked Juliette, dried blood flaking away from her chin as she spoke.

"I think he wants us to clean up."

"Exactly. Dulcinea and Pedro are fine as they are, but if the rest of us show up in town looking like this, someone's going to have a stroke. And the sheriff will toss us all in jail."

"Like I'd let that happen," muttered Juliette. "It's going to take a shower to get all this crap out of my hair and clothes, but I suppose it wouldn't hurt to remove the more offensive bits."

I dug through my trunk and emerged with the towels and a two-liter, previously opened, and very old bottle of water. I passed two of the towels over to Hyacinth and Juliette, took a third for myself, and spread the remaining few over the Corolla's seats. Her Royal Snootiness had given the Corolla an all-white interior, and I didn't want that interior to get stained. Especially not with the foul cocktail of guts, blood, and vomit that most of us were currently sporting.

○○○

Even though we'd only been gone for a matter of hours, part of me was convinced the Corolla wouldn't start, its battery dead and its engine a nest for a squirrel family of twelve. Maybe Juliette's relentless comments about me being a walking catastrophe were starting to wear on my otherwise ever-shiny optimism?

In this particular instance, optimism would have been justified. The Corolla came to life with a purr, its many vents dispensing a short blast of hot air that quickly turned ice cold, just the way I liked it. I adjusted my mirrors, even though I'd been the most recent driver, made sure that everyone was buckled in, waited to make sure there were no cars coming from either direction, and flipped a careful U on the mountain road.

An *illegal* U-turn, admittedly, but I had no interest in driving up and over the mountain in search of a place to turn around. And it wasn't like anyone was around to see it anyway.

I'd driven all of three hundred feet when a patrol car passed us, going in the opposite direction up the hill. Less than a minute later—far too swiftly to have found a legal turning spot of their own, that patrol car was behind us again, its cherry lights flashing in my rearview. I pulled over onto the shoulder and stepped out of the car to go speak with Sheriff Abbas.

"Mr. Smith," he said, voice casual in a way I didn't trust, "I heard you and your partner headed out early today with a stranger. I'm guessing he or she's the owner of the Harley parked outside the B&B?"

"Pearl's a bit of a gossip, isn't she?"

His smile came and went, dry as a rattlesnake's freshly shed skin. "When we spoke last night, I thought you were going to get me the coordinates to Pedro's motorcycle?"

"We did one better."

He frowned, eyes hidden under the brim of his sheriff's hat, and then looked toward the Corolla, mouth dropping open. "You found Dulcinea?"

"And Pedro, yeah. Both are alive and uninjured, but they're really dehydrated. We were bringing them down to Ghost Falls; maybe you could take them to the hospital for us?"

"We don't have a full hospital in Ghost Falls, but we do have a doctor and a vet both. We can get IVs in them now and then medevac them south if there's more to be done. How did you find them?"

"It's a long story," I said, which was kind of a lie and kind of not. "That stranger Pearl mentioned is a tracker. She came up to help us out.

Once we found the motorcycle, we followed their trail. Found them in a cave up on the mountain… I think they got lost."

I think they got lost was a pretty flimsy excuse, given that both kids had grown up in the region and even *Juliette* knew enough to just walk down the hill until you hit the town. Still, it was a better explanation than *they either were summoned to a cave or wandered in on their own where they came across a spell trap that put them to sleep for an entire week.*

Sometimes, 'simple and rational' was better than 'factually correct and impossible to believe.'

The sheriff gave me a hard look, as if to let me know there were holes in my story large enough to drive his patrol car through, but just nodded. "I'll want to get the full story from all of you later today."

"Not a problem. We're going to get cleaned up and then head over to Mama Nita's for a late lunch and early dinner. Feel free to stop on by, Sheriff."

"I'll do that. In the meantime, why don't we move Dulcinea and Pedro over to my car so I can get out of your hair."

It was the work of a few minutes, but neither Dulcinea nor Pedro even woke up during the handoff. Abbas closed the rear door on his car and shook his head. When he spoke, his voice was soft.

"I'd honestly given up hope," he said, words almost reverent. "We're going to have words about what actually happened on the mountain, and why you and your partners look like you wrestled a bear, but for now… thank you."

"What matters is that they're safe."

"That's the main thing, yeah," he said, making it clear that *other* things mattered too.

Clearly, Juliette was going to have to use her mojo again.

A few minutes later, I watched the patrol car pull back onto the road, headed down the mountain to what passed for medical facilities in

Ghost Falls. I ran my hand through my hair, found some bit of *something* I'd missed in our hurried roadside baths, and joined Juliette and Hyacinth back in the Corolla.

"All's well that ends well?" said Juliette.

"I know you both could hear that conversation as well as I could."

"If we'd been listening, yeah."

I was too tired to even sigh. "He's not dumb. He knows there's something more going on. I told him we'd be at Mama Nita's tonight, and he's going to stop by." I craned my head in Juliette's general direction. "Will you have enough juice to compel him?"

"Does the pope wear women's underpants?"

"I don't think so? Not that it would matter if he did."

"Maybe we're thinking of different people then." She smirked. "Yeah, our good sheriff will leave with a fresh brownie and an unshakeable belief that everything we saw and did was completely aboveboard." I could feel her giving me the once-over. "What about you? Are *you* going to have enough juice to make it down the hill, or do I need to put you in the back with flower girl?"

"If he sits in the back, I'm calling shotgun," said Hyacinth.

"I'm fine. Just tired and disgusting and hung—"

"Hung?" asked Hyacinth.

"Believe me, it's *not* what you think," said Juliette.

"Hung*ry*," I clarified, shaking my head as I turned my focus to something Juliette had said earlier. "I'll be okay to drive. What I want to know is where Abbas is going to get a brownie from?"

"There's a bakery on Main St. I grabbed some sweets there last night after I fed."

"I wondered why I smelled chocolate on your breath this morning," said Hyacinth. "You didn't want to share?"

"There was nothing left *to* share." Juliette felt my hard-eyed glare and turned to me. "What?"

"New agency rule," I told her. "When you use the company card to buy sweets, bring enough back for everyone."

"I didn't even know flower girl was coming!"

"I'm not talking about Hyacinth, Juliette. I'm talking about *me*."

"Oh." She thought that one over and shrugged. "My bad."

○○○

An hour later, we were all freshly showered, and dressed in whatever clean clothes we had left. Pearl had volunteered to run a load of laundry for us, and Juliette had gently encouraged her *not* to notice any strange or suspicious stains on those clothes. With the sun headed down, Hyacinth shrugged back into her motorcycle jacket, while Juliette grabbed her own coat and swapped her borrowed moccasins for a pair of heels that made my ankles ache just from seeing them.

Having been born and raised in San Diego, I hadn't thought to bring a jacket, but I'd been hot all day; I didn't mind being cold instead for a change.

Mama Nita's was bustling when we arrived, busier than I'd ever seen it. Thankfully, there was still one table free, right in the middle. Henry took our orders—giving me the smallest hint of a genuine smile—but soon after, the reason for the crowd became clear.

One by one, a representative from each of the surrounding tables made his or her way over to thank us for finding Dulcinea— and occasionally Pedro. I recognized a few of the faces and names from our interviews, but most were strangers, townsfolk who had heard the teenagers were safe and decided to come break bread with those responsible.

I'd never lived in a small town, and I'd never really wanted to, either. You always heard the horror stories of everyone being up in everyone else's business, of the tiniest communities hiding the biggest and darkest secrets, and of the way those towns diminished with each new generation. Ghost Falls had some of that, I knew, but I was also getting to see the positives. A community that knew each other rallied around each other when something went wrong. There was genuine care and compassion in a way I wasn't used to in bigger cities, not even a city like San Diego which was so often said to have a small-town feel.

I still didn't want to live there, but it was kind of nice.

Both Jeremiah and Pedro's brother, Edu, made separate appearances, although neither stayed to eat. Instead, they simply thanked us—Jeremiah with tears in his eyes, Edu with a hug that threatened to rearrange my vertebrae—and then left again, heading back to the doctor's office where their relatives were being treated.

I shared a look with Juliette. "This is one of those times the job doesn't suck."

"Yeah." I thought she was going to say something more, maybe pointing out that we'd nearly died multiple times and hadn't even gotten paid, but instead, she just grinned, looking for all the world like a delighted teenager as she dug back into her food.

With the parade of well-wishers, our meal took longer than usual. By her fourth plate of enchiladas, Hyacinth was back to looking like herself, and by the time we polished off our sopapillas, we were all roughly twenty minutes away from food comas. Most of the restaurant had cleared out around us, with only a handful of tables—younger groups without children—still going strong.

That was when Sheriff Abbas made an appearance. He took off his hat and tucked it under one arm, nodding to Henry as he made his way over to our table. "Can I have a word with you, John?"

"Pull up a seat. Mama Nita is brewing some sort of dessert chocolate for us apparently."

"It's hard to say no to that, but I'm afraid I'm still on the job." He waved to the front door of the restaurant. "Shall we? This will only take a few minutes."

I nodded slowly, pushing my chair back so I could stand up. "Not a problem, Sheriff. Juliette, do you want to tag along?"

"And miss out on dessert chocolate?" She shook her head and yawned. "I'm sure you've got this."

I gave her a look that said, in no uncertain terms, that I needed her to use her vampire mojo on the sheriff… and she gave me one back that said, in slightly less certain terms, that she had no idea what I was trying to say but that she was looking forward to her second dessert.

I swallowed a sigh. If I got arrested, I had no doubt that she'd come take care of it. In the meantime, it seemed I was on my own.

It had already gotten cold enough outside that I regretted my lack of a jacket. I looked for the sheriff and found him waiting just to the right of the entrance. The good news is that his patrol car was nowhere in sight. The bad news was that we were only three blocks from the station, and he could walk me there in handcuffs easily enough.

I tried not to let any of those thoughts show and took up a spot along the wall next to him. "What can I do for you, Sheriff?"

"You could do me the courtesy of not blowing smoke up my ass."

"I'm sorry?"

"Your story today was leakier than a hundred-year-old pipe. I want to know what you aren't telling me."

"What did the kids say?"

He gave me a look, as if surprised that *I* would call anyone a kid, then shrugged. "Pedro's still out, but Dulcinea gave pretty much the same tale you did. Word for word, in fact. They went out to go off-roading, crashed, got lost in the woods, and then y'all found them and brought them home."

"So, what's the problem?"

"There isn't a person in Ghost Falls that can't find their way back to town. If they had been injured, then maybe things would make sense, but the doctor confirmed it… all they're suffering from is dehydration and a lack of food. And for them to even have lived this long means they either found water while up there or they were just lying around, not using up any energy the whole time."

He was a lot closer with that guess than I'd expected.

"And then there's you, your partner, and the woman who rode into town today. A tracker, you said?"

"Yeah."

"Interesting, because I ran her plates, and the computer told me the owner of the bike belongs to one of the largest biker gangs in the state."

"I mean… she's *also* a tracker."

"Maybe so, but when a member of a notorious biker gang joins two other strangers in my town, a man can't help but pay attention. And when those three people all show up roadside with blood on their clothes, that man finds himself wondering a few things. Like what the real story is, who got killed in the middle of it, and why Dulcinea's telling me tales to protect you all."

I winced. Still no sign of Juliette. "Would you believe me if I told you we ran into a bear, like you thought?"

"Not with all of you still in one piece, no."

I sighed. I genuinely didn't know what to say. The sheriff wasn't going to buy any lies I gave him and there was no way I could tell him the truth.

Abbas fished a pack of Marlboros out of his pocket, tapped a cigarette into his hand, and lit it, all in the motion of a man who'd done the same thing literally thousands of times before. "I don't think y'all are the bad people in this story you're not telling me," he said, sucking in until the end of his smoke glowed red. "But I'm gonna need more than a made-up fairy tale before I see my way to letting any of you leave town."

"Funny you mention fairy tales."

"I'm sorry?"

I waved away the question. "Nothing. Just talking to myself. I wish I could help you, Sheriff, but that's the only story I've got."

"Then maybe I'll tell you one of my own."

I had a feeling this story ended up with me in jail, banging a metal mug against the bars as I waited to be shipped off to prison.

This once, I was wrong.

"I didn't grow up here, if you hadn't already gathered as much," he said, waving his cigarette in front of him and letting its light wash across his features. "I was born and raised in Turkey, in a mountain town I doubt you've ever heard of. Came to the United States of America for college and then liked it well enough I decided to settle down. A lot of people probably don't think much of small towns like this, but it reminded me of home."

"I get it. Really, I do. And I'm not trying to—"

"That's not my point, son. I haven't gotten to my point."

I waved a hand. "Go ahead."

"The old country's different in a lot of ways. More settled. Thousands of years of history. Generations upon generations of people all living and dying in the same towns, passing on knowledge, passing on life experiences. Here, people like to pretend that we know everything there is to know, that science has an explanation for it all. Someone disappears, they've run away, or been kidnapped by human traffickers, or hitchhiked with the wrong individual. Back home, they acknowledge all those possibilities but also wonder if something in the woods, or the seas, or the mountains came and took them.

"That's not how policework here goes," he continued, "and I'm alright with that. Even if I wasn't born in this country, I do my best to live by its rules. But when someone comes in from out of town, accompanied by a woman who looks eighteen but has eyes as cold and old as my nana's, I pay attention. When I realize I've somehow opted to let crucial questions slide, like how and where y'all found Pedro's dirt bike, I start to worry. And when a woman biker who seemed to have one foot in the grave when I met her this afternoon is looking like one of them CrossFit world champions just an hour later, I can't help but think that something is going on. Something that science can't fully explain. Something that would fit right in with the stories my nana used to tell." He turned to me, eyes dark and glittering behind the red light of his cigarette. "So, you tell me, Mr. Smith. How close am I?"

The smart thing would have been to keep lying until Juliette finally—finally!—showed up, but if Sheriff Abbas was *already* suspicious, there was no guarantee he hadn't already shared those concerns with someone else, or even left himself some sort of note to try to guard against inexplicably changing his mind again. I'd seen *Memento*, after all.

"You're not far off," I told him. "We didn't come here expecting anything but a regular missing persons case, but what we found was a little bit more than that." I didn't understand what the statue was, or why it had been stashed in a trapped tunnel with its entrance sealed off, but with that statue now in multiple fragments, it didn't really matter all that much. I'd give it to Lucia, let her experts in Rome analyze it, and hopefully never see it again. "I can't tell you everything, but—"

"Is the *bear* still out there?"

"No. We uh… we took care of it." I wasn't too worried about anyone finding the cave or Shae's body, not with the statue's siren call silenced and Juliette having wiped the location from Dulcinea and Pedro's brains. "It won't be coming back."

"Good to know, I guess."

"That's it? You're not going to arrest me? Or us?"

"Y'all came to town, all on your own, and helped us find our missing kids. Jeremiah's gonna sleep well tonight for the first time in a week. Edu's going to stop showing up at my office at odd hours, demanding to know why I'm sitting on my Arab ass instead of doing something. And let's be honest…" He sighed, took a long drag on his cigarette, and then flicked the butt off to the side. "How long would any of you bother to stay in my little jail? You seem human, at least, but the other two? Sometimes, the old stories speak true, Mr. Smith, and those stories tell me to thank y'all and get the hell out of your way. And maybe I can get your card, in case something else strange happens around these parts?"

I didn't have any business cards on me, so I rattled off my phone number instead. And then, once he'd finished adding me as a contact, I gave him a considering look of my own.

"What did your nana's stories say about coexistence with these other things?"

"Depended on the creature. A lot of their kind were around before we were. They had as much right to the land as anyone, maybe more. We got a fair amount of native folk here in this state, and their philosophy tends to be live and let live. Hard to argue with that, unless we get another bear. All I really care about is keeping my town safe, you know?"

I did know, and I could empathize. Maybe that's why I said what I said next.

"Do you know the anthill east of town?" I couldn't even find it in myself to be amazed or irritated when he nodded yes. "Okay. Well, if you want to meet the people who helped us find Pedro's bike, you're going to need to bring a jar of honey…"

Chapter 32

In Which Nothing Good Ever Happens at Two in the Morning

There's nothing quite like a barbershop quartet, especially when that quartet is comprised of cartoon wildlife. The hippo, surprisingly enough, was a soprano, and every time he hit the high notes, the crystal blue sky behind him would explode in golden light. The meerkat, almost as surprisingly, was a baritone, singing a harmony that sometimes matched and sometimes wove between the three-headed dog's countermelody. And last but not least was the pink giraffe, standing tall on still-wobbly legs, her head and lengthy neck lowered almost to the grass. With the music building around her, she had yet to sing, but as she lifted that odd head high into the air, I knew her part in the song had finally come. Eyes fit only for a cartoon widened and she breathed out her first triumphant note.

Bzzzzzzzzzt.

The three-headed dog's countermelody sputtered to a stop. Even the hippo lost his tune as he turned to look at the giraffe who, instead of singing at all, was now vibrating in place, a metered buzzing emitting from her every time she opened her mouth.

Bzzzzzzzzzzt.

I looked to the meerkat, but she just threw up her hands and gave up on the harmony. A cigar appeared in one paw, and she folded herself into the chair that sprouted behind her, looking at me with a tilted head, as if to say: *What are* you *going to do about this?*

So, I did the only thing I could:

I woke up.

The buzzing was coming from my left. My wonderphone sat on my nightstand, where I'd plugged it in after dinner, and now its screen was bright, lighting up the room. It vibrated like a pay-by-the-minute massaging bed as notifications flooded in: texts and emails and even multiple calls I'd missed while the battery was dead.

I checked the display for the time: 2:05 a.m.

Yeah… no.

I was ready to dismiss the notifications, turn on Do Not Disturb, and go back to bed when the phone buzzed again. This time, it wasn't a notification, but yet another incoming call.

Worse, it was a number my phone recognized, plastering the caller ID *White She-Devil* across the screen.

Well, shit.

I yanked out the charging cord and took the phone with me into the bathroom in the vague hopes of keeping Juliette from waking up. That cost me another two rings; and I was only one away from once again consigning my caller to voicemail when I finally answered.

"It's two in the morning, Lucia. What the hell?"

"Where have you been?" If I'd ever thought the vampire queen had mellowed, her tone dismissed that fantasy immediately, so filled with ice that it might have drawn blood if we were face to face.

"Doing my job."

"I have called you thrice."

Somehow, at 2 a.m., it was that much more obnoxious to have her say *thrice* instead of *three times* like a regular person. She was clearly spending too much time with the ancients back in Rome.

"I was out of cell range all day and my phone was dead until about a minute ago. If this is about me pulling on your power, we can talk about it later."

"We *will* talk about it later, but that is neither here nor there. A plane is departing the Santa Fe airport in three hours. You will be on it."

"What?"

"You are needed here in San Diego, Mr. Smith. Posthaste."

Maybe it was the fact that she called me Mr. Smith instead of thrall. Or maybe it was the utter lack of humor in the femmepire's voice. Either way, my blood went cold. We were too far to feel each other's emotions, let alone thoughts, but somehow, I knew exactly what had prompted the call.

"Anastasia? Did Zorana—?"

"The Blood Witch has been neutralized. My *Secundus*—" On that last word, her voice did something I had never heard before: it broke, like fine crystal shattering into a thousand shards.

In the middle of the night, in the bathroom of a bed and breakfast in Ghost Falls, New Mexico, I broke out into a sweat.

By the time Lucia spoke again, her voice was firm, but I could hear the cracks in it, hear that she was holding it together through nothing but will. "Lady Dumenyova is not well. Get to Santa Fe. Board the plane. You have already been sent the details."

And then she was gone, leaving me to look at my phone in still groggy disbelief.

I didn't know what had happened, what Zorana must have done to Anastasia before they were able to, in Lucia's own words, neutralize the thousand-year-old pre-teen. Nor did I know what I could to do to help, assuming I could do anything at all. All I knew was that I needed to be there, and that meant getting to the plane Lucia had mentioned. Literally everything else was secondary.

I splashed water on my face, slapped myself twice when the water didn't seem to be working to wake me up, and darted into the suite's bedroom. I didn't need anything but my keys, phone, and wallet.

"John?"

"Juliette, did you hear?"

"Most of it." The femmepire was already getting dressed.

"If Hyacinth can give you a ride tomorrow, do you mind picking up my Corolla at the Santa Fe airport and driving it back to San Diego? I have to go."

"I have a better idea," said Hyacinth, from the hallway outside our suite's main door. "I'll give you a ride tonight, so the fanger can pack up and drive your car to San Diego tomorrow."

Sometimes, supernatural hearing actually worked in my favor, even if it did mean Lucia's call had apparently woken up the werewolf in the neighboring suite.

"Are you sure, flower girl?" asked Juliette.

"Yeah. Someone told Shae I was coming up north, and I need to find out who that someone is. Sooner I'm back to Audrey, the better, and Santa Fe's not that far out of my way."

"That works for me. And thank you." I pulled the key fob off my keyring and tossed it to Juliette, who, despite the late hour and lack of light, snagged it out of the air like a professional shortstop. "You'll be back by Monday?"

"Definitely," she said. "With all due respect to Arizona, I'm planning to drive straight through."

"Great." I tugged on some clothes and my soiled shoes, then scanned the room one more time, checking to see if there was anything I needed, or anything that couldn't be replaced when I was back home.

There wasn't, and I was burning time. I could hear Hyacinth still tossing clothes and toiletries into her saddlebags but headed for the hall anyway.

Juliette caught me by the arm. "Little bird… John… she's going to be okay. Anastasia's like the Terminator; nothing's going to keep her down for long."

It would have been more reassuring if I hadn't seen all five Terminator movies. Even if only the first two *really* counted, the cyborgs died in all of them.

Still, I didn't have time to debate the finer points of post-apocalyptic time travel cinema. I just nodded.

ooo

Five minutes later, Ghost Falls was a handful of lights in Hyacinth's mirrors. I wrapped my arms around the biker werewolf, wishing yet again that I'd thought to bring a jacket. The weather up here in the mountains was considerably chillier than what I'd experienced down in Phoenix and being on a bike in the early hours of the morning was deeply unpleasant.

It was still more comfortable than Juliette's Ducati though.

Most of that drive passed in a blur of darkness, interspersed with the occasional tail- or headlights. There weren't a ton of vehicles on the road at that hour, and most of those were long-haul truckers no doubt skirting the sleep regulations to get a few more miles in. We wove our way through them, like ghosts passing in the night.

Two hours later, we'd arrived. At least… I thought we had.

I'd never been to the Santa Fe airport. I hadn't even known there *was* a Santa Fe airport, with the flights I'd looked at and then discarded all landing in Albuquerque. Even as we followed the signs and reached a small, squat building, I *still* wasn't sure there was an airport.

"Is this it?" It made Lindbergh Field back home look positively palatial.

"That's what the signs say."

I checked my phone for the email Lucia had sent me. Or someone had sent to me on her behalf… I couldn't see the vampire queen sitting down and typing out instructions, especially when her oldest friend and servant was—

I shook my head. No point in dwelling on the unknown, especially when I'd already been doing that for the entire ride down.

"Looks like I go inside and look for someone who can direct me to the FBO." I frowned. "What's an FBO?"

"Fixed-base operator." Hyacinth had dismounted from her motorcycle and pulled off her helmet. "They're the people who take care of airplane storage, maintenance, and sometimes even private jet charters. You didn't think commercial flights left on demand, did you?"

"I've done my best not to think at all about airplanes," I admitted.

"Well, chances are you're about to see how the other half lives. Either that or they're putting you in a crop duster with no chance in hell of making it to the coast."

"One or the other." I checked my pockets and made sure I still had what little I'd brought with me. "I guess it's time to find out. Thank you for the ride. And for helping us find Dulcinea. Tell Audrey we're even."

"Given that Shae followed me all the way north and nearly killed us, I'm not sure Audrey will agree… but I'll tell her." She ran a hand over her shaved head. "I uh… hope things work out for you."

With Anastasia being persona non grata with the pack, even for those who *hadn't* lost a relative or loved one, I appreciated the effort. "Stay safe. Good luck with Ezekiel."

And that was that. As I turned away, the rumble of her Harley filled the air. By the time I'd made it off the curb, she was gone. I entered the sleepy terminal, took maybe three steps, and was swiftly intercepted by a sleepy-eyed, smiling Latina in a blue blouse and black skirt.

"Mr. Smith?"

"That's me." She had curly black hair and a small nose too perfectly cute to be natural. I had never seen her before in my life.

"My name is Alicia, Mr. Smith. I'm with JetSet. It's our pleasure to serve you and Borghesi International for today's flight. If I could just check your license for verification, we'll head over."

"To the plane?" I fished out my ID and handed it over.

"To our private pilot and passenger lounge." Her smile was warm, if professional, as she handed my license back. "Your plane is scheduled to board in just over forty minutes. We'll get you settled in as soon as we can. In the meantime, there are refreshments and pastries available."

Between the impending flight and the uncertainty of Anastasia's condition, the last thing I wanted was to eat or drink, but my stomach gurgled anyway, eager to express its own opinion.

Instead of leading me deeper into the terminal, Alicia took me right back outside, to a golf cart I'd ignored on the way in. A minute later, we arrived at a second building, this one larger than the airport's main terminal. It bordered the tarmac, where numerous planes were parked next to one another, looking like North County mall on a busy weekend. One plane, sleek and white, had left the 'lot' and was parked near the building, uniformed personnel swarming around it like ants on a candy bar.

"There's your plane now," said Alicia. "As you can see, it'll be ready to go on time, as expected."

I spared the airplane another look as we turned and entered the facilities. I didn't know much about private charters, but that plane was *small*. It was hard to imagine it being able to stay in the air if there was any wind at all, let alone make it all the way across three states.

But maybe that was my recently discovered aerophobia talking. One of these days, I was going to see Bill in my dreams, and I was pretty sure he'd be wearing a pilot's uniform.

The passenger lounge was small, but it was also empty and a lot nicer than anything I'd see at a normal gate. I hit the restroom like I hadn't had time to do before leaving Ghost Falls, got a glass of orange juice, and took a comfortable seat near the exit, swiftly reaching a fugue state of tiredness and anxiety.

Thirty minutes after that, we were in the air.

Flying private was, obviously, an entirely new experience for me. It was also a mixed bag. On the one hand, I felt like a rock star or celebrity: the plane was well appointed and absurdly spacious, if not quite as luxurious as the ones you saw in hip hop videos, the flight crew was professional, nice, *and* attentive, and I hadn't had to stand in a single line or even get patted down by TSA to board.

On the other hand, it was still an airplane, and because it was significantly smaller than the plane I'd flown in to London and then Rome, it was also noisier and far more prone to turbulence. So far, I'd kept down last night's dinner, but there'd already been a few close moments.

And on the third hand, I didn't have to sit next to anyone, especially a demon disguised as a hyperactive toddler.

To distract myself, I ordered a coke and a sandwich, the latter freshly made to my exact specifications… meaning a triple serving of ham on honey parmesan, with each layer of meat separated by a slice of cheese. There was alcohol on offer, including bottles I rarely even saw in my day-to-day life, let alone got to taste, but I passed on the opportunity. There was no way in hell I was showing up in San Diego buzzed, especially since I *still* didn't know what had happened to Anastasia.

I sent my fifth set of texts to Lucia, demanding answers, and for the fifth time, she ignored those texts as only a jilted ex or someone of royal blood possibly could.

I tried sending a mental message instead, because I knew from experience that there was nothing quite as annoying and unavoidable as having a voice in your brain that just won't shut up, but even with our bond wide open, we were well out of range for that sort of communication.

I napped as much as I could. It wasn't much, given both my own jitters and the mix of emotions from Lucia that appeared about ten minutes out of San Diego. Anxiety, fear, rage, grief… we weren't even in the same city yet and I was already struggling to separate her feelings from mine. I fell back on my tried-and-true approach of building a mental wall around the bond in my head, but it had been a lot easier before Rome. The best I could manage was a crude dam, where emotions leaked through in drips instead of a flood.

By that point, we were already preparing for landing. The whole flight had been much faster than I expected; I'd be back in San Diego before I would have even woken up in Ghost Falls. Which said something, since I'd been sharing a suite with Juliette and the vampire had a bad habit of throwing open the curtains to our nonfunctional balcony at ungodly times like eight in the morning.

"We'll be landing at Carlsbad airport soon, Mr. Smith," said the bright-eyed, blonde flight attendant who had greeted me when I boarded the plane and then personally delivered the masterpiece that was my ham sandwich. "I'm told your car is already waiting, so once we come to a complete stop and lower the gangway, you'll be able to depart at your leisure."

"Thank you, Stephanie. You've all been fantastic."

"It's been our pleasure to serve." Her grin turned mischievous. "And I went to school at UCSD, so I always jump on the opportunity to accompany a VIP here and visit some of my friends."

"Hopefully, you can all have a great dinner out on my dime." I'd looked up tipping etiquette on the flight, and ended up more confused than when I'd started, but I pulled out my wallet anyway. I didn't have much in the way of cash, but if they accepted plastic…

She waved away the offer and flashed a set of award-winning dimples. "Your company has already provided a more than generous tip to the pilot and flight crew on your behalf, sir, but thank you."

That didn't sound like Lucia *at all*, but I just nodded. I'd have been billing Lucia for my tip anyway, so it all worked out.

I had no idea if the landing was bumpier than normal for a plane that size or if the pilot was instead a secret maestro of the skies whose skills I'd likely never experience again. Either way, I didn't die, and that was what really mattered. We taxied a short distance and then came to a halt. Shortly afterward, the gangway was opened, and I was saying goodbye to the people who had kept me safe and fed as I took my first step back into the city I loved.

May Gray and June Gloom were far behind us, but this close to the coast, there was still fog and low cloud-cover in the direction of the ocean. Nevertheless, I paused when I hit asphalt, and just took a moment to breathe in that San Diego air.

It… smelled a lot like jet fuel and exhaust, to be honest.

I'd never been to the tiny Carlsbad airport before, but as Stephanie had mentioned, there was a car waiting. A limo, in fact, and a white one, which was a good sign that it had been sent by Lucia. The driver was a human I'd never met, dressed to the nines in the sort of three-piece suit you only saw on the supernatural or Europeans. He tipped his chauffeur's cap to me and came around to open the rear passenger door.

I could really get used to the luxury of private charters, if it wasn't for the whole flight part of the experience.

I waved to my sainted flight crew, nodded to the chauffeur, and had just slipped into the white limo, like Cinderella entering her pumpkin coach, when the theme music that had been slowly building in my brain—something stately, but energetic… classy but sensual—came to a screeching halt.

Someone was waiting for me in the limo, and it *wasn't* a curvaceous, easily enraged platinum blonde vampire.

Instead, it was her accountant.

"I see you somehow continue to survive, monkey," said Marcus.

He sounded disappointed.

CHAPTER 33
IN WHICH YOU CAN'T GO HOME AGAIN

"Marcus." As I took my seat in the limo, I gave the vampire a once-over. As usual, he was small, dark, and handsome, dressed like he was headed to Wall Street or a movie premiere. "I thought you were living on your private island somewhere?"

His sneer lacked some of its usual edge. "My exile from Rome was lifted along with that of the queen's. Why would I choose to continue wasting away in solitude?"

"Sun? Sand? Fruity drinks with little umbrellas in them?" I shook my head. Maybe vampires had a different concept of paradise. I should ask Ana where she wanted to go instead of just buying tickets to Hawaii. Assuming we… "How is Ana? Lucia wouldn't tell me anything."

As the limo pulled out of the airport, he straightened up but wouldn't meet my eyes. "Lady Dumenyova is… not well."

"That's not helpful, dude."

"I am not your dude. I am your elder and superior in every way that matters. I am—"

"An accountant with unparalleled abilities to screw me over financially. I know. I get it. Can we stay focused on Ana please?"

When he turned back to me, his look was almost considering. "You have changed, human."

"That's how life works, Marcus."

"Is it?" He looked away again and shrugged. "I know little more than you do. I was not with them when they bearded the Blood Witch in her lair."

"So, Zorana *did* do something to her?"

"That is the assumption, yes."

"And she's not healing from it?" I'd never thought of myself as a violent person, let alone a bad one, but after what had happened with Shae, I was no longer so sure. And if Zorana had hurt or somehow crippled Anastasia…

"I can say no more. The queen wishes you to see Lady Dumenyova's condition with your own eyes. I believe she hopes that your unique perspective might provide answers we have missed."

I watched out the window as we waited to merge onto the 5. It was the nicest thing he had ever said to or about me, and I couldn't even enjoy it. I wanted to press for more, but this once, I was going to trust that Lucia had thought things through. If going in blind could help Ana somehow, I'd do it.

We rode in silence for a bit, before something else occurred to me.

"If you didn't come to help with Zorana, why are you here?"

"The queen's former House remains entangled with certain assets that are hers by birthright. I am here to see them divested of those assets."

"Like what?"

"The building itself and many of the possessions contained within."

"I didn't know you worked in real estate too."

"You could have simply stopped after *I didn't know.*"

Marcus had clearly *not* changed.

"Where are they going to live?"

"Who?"

'Shouldn't it be whom?"

His lip curled and I could practically see him flipping through his mental database of insults. Finally, he let it go. "If you are asking about the traitors who stood by as the queen was ousted from her own home—"

"See? I knew you could figure it out all on your own."

"—then my question to you is why do you care?"

"I have friends at the House. Still. Sort of."

"Then perhaps you should raise your standards, monkey." Dark eyes flicked down to the shoes on my feet, and he made a face. "And learn about dry cleaning."

I wasn't sure even dry cleaning would save them, honestly.

Ana's house in Cardiff was just a short drive away from Carlsbad, even with early-morning traffic in San Diego. The cloud cover was thicker on the coast, a cool breeze sweeping in from the ocean, but I didn't take my customary few seconds to appreciate the view. As soon as the limo came to a stop, I was out and headed for the front door, leaving Marcus behind.

I kicked off my shoes as soon as I was inside, not wanting to make more of a mess for Teresa or Gustavo. Strangely, there was no sign of either one as I made my way to the stairs. Lucia's presence rang like a beacon in my mind, above me and down the hall. It put her in one of the spare bedrooms, not the master I sometimes shared with Anastasia, and I headed there first. It was time someone told me what the hell was going on.

I passed by Ana's bedroom—empty—and kept going. Two rooms down, a door was open, and I could feel Lucia inside, a roiling cauldron of emotions, as turbulent as the rage that had so often bubbled beneath her icy exterior. It hit me like a sledgehammer to the breadbasket and I reached out to the wall to keep from falling.

Lucia and I didn't see eye to eye on many things, but she had proven to me that she valued Ana enough to free the other woman rather than lose her entirely. The sorrow leaking across our bond into my mind made the depth of her emotion that much more apparent.

I rebuilt my mental dam as best I could. The construct was even less effective now that the queen and I were a single room away. Maybe I could—

You're stalling. For a second, I wasn't sure if it was Lucia's voice in my head or mine. The lack of insults proved to be the deciding factor. *You're stalling because you're terrified of what you might see.*

I was and I was. But running and hiding wouldn't help. Not when everything I wanted was in the room in front of me.

Lucia notwithstanding, of course.

I took a breath, in through my nose, out through my mouth, and pushed inside.

Lucia stood by the window like in a painting, but the early morning cloud cover ruined the image, robbing her of the sunlight that might otherwise have highlighted her platinum blonde locks. She was dressed all in white, as usual, in skyscraper heels that brought her up to an almost average height, and her hands were clasped behind her, clasped so tightly that her fingers were pale and bloodless.

Behind her, in a bed usually reserved for guests, lay Anastasia.

She had the sheets wrapped around her, auburn hair fanned out over the pillow beneath her head, and she looked… wrong.

Either I made a noise or Lucia finally paid enough attention to the bond to realize I was there. Either way, the femmepire queen turned. Her usually flawless makeup was nowhere to be found, face streaked by dirt and what I was pretty sure was soot, but her voice was hard enough to drive railway spikes through solid concrete.

"Mr. Smith—"

"What's wrong with her?" I crossed to Anastasia and cupped her cheek in one hand. She was cold to the touch, her skin sallow, and she didn't even stir at my touch.

"She is starving, and I do not understand why."

"What?" Food was one thing that *wasn't* a problem. Not with two blood donors in the house. "Gustavo—"

"He and the other one both donated all that they can, and now sleep in their own room downstairs."

"All that they can?"

"If I thought it would help, I would have Asya drain them of every drop, and damn what she thought of me when she woke." For a moment, Lucia's crystal blue eyes blazed… but only for a moment. "She has drunk enough for any three fledglings, and yet her condition remains unchanged."

"Zorana."

"Perhaps. I did not see a spell… She did not appear to have time to cast one before we struck her down, but… perhaps. You and I will meet with the Blood Witch shortly and find out."

"She's here?"

"She is being transported here." Lush lips thinned. "I came to reclaim her, like a shepherd recovering a lost lamb, yet if she is truly responsible for this, I will make her fate a lesson for all who think to oppose me."

"If? She's a witch who specializes in blood magic. Ana's a vampire who can't seem to get enough blood. Why is there even a question?" I held out my arm—*not* the one Juliette had fed from only hours earlier— over Anastasia's mouth.

"What are you doing, my thrall?"

"What does it look like? If she needs more blood, I can give it."

"What would your blood do that her donors' wouldn't?"

"I don't know. But I'm here. We might as well try."

"He speaks wisdom for once," said Marcus, standing at the door despite the fact I'd never heard him come in. "And what do we lose should he fail or fall?"

I… didn't love the way he phrased that last bit, but I couldn't disagree with the sentiment. I pushed my bared wrist to Ana's mouth.

She didn't move.

"You will have to make the incision yourself, Mr. Smith." Lucia's voice was low but somehow filled the bedroom anyway. "She will swallow any blood that enters her mouth but has yet to willingly bite."

"I don't have any—" My words cut off as the queen grabbed my outstretched hand in hers, and ran a fingernail across the inside of my wrist. Skin separated almost effortlessly, and blood immediately started to flow. "Ow."

"If you wish to feed Lady Dumenyova, then do so, my thrall. Neither she nor I have time for your usual complaints."

I shuddered and brought my wrist to Ana's lips. There was a whole bundle of rules and social mores tied up in where a vampire drank from, with the wrist being the sole one that suggested the drinker was subservient to the drinkee, but clearly we were past caring about any of that. I rotated my arm and watched the blood drip down into Anastasia's open mouth.

To hear Juliette talk, my blood was the next best thing to the second coming of the Clash, but whatever properties made it tastier than most didn't help with Ana. She swallowed the blood that I fed her, but barely even stirred in the process.

Even so, I looked up to find both Lucia and Marcus staring at me.

"What?"

"That is the most reaction we have seen from Lady Dumenyova since her return," said Marcus.

"Keep going," urged Lucia.

Unfortunately, a few minutes later, I was so lightheaded I could barely stand, and Ana's condition hadn't changed at all.

The femmepire queen pulled my hand from Ana's mouth, absentmindedly licking the incision she'd made in the wrist. I tried not to shiver, focusing instead on the fact that the cut had already started to heal and clot even before Lucia's actions. I healed far too quickly, even on normal days, but with Lucia literally feet away from me, the effect was that much more pronounced.

"Now what?" I was pretty sure I'd slurred the words, but it was difficult to care.

"Now, you refuel," said the queen. "Marcus, fetch Mr. Smith something to eat."

"My Queen?"

"I want him upright and clear minded when we interrogate the Blood Witch. For that, my thrall requires food."

"Yes, but…"

"Were. My. Words. Unclear?"

"No, Your Majesty."

"Then make it so."

I didn't have the energy to needle Marcus, or even the desire. Because honestly, something to eat sounded really good, and if that made us temporary allies, then I'd bear that burden. In fact, I would—

I blinked and found myself sitting in an armchair, Ana and the bed a good six feet away.

"What happened?"

"That is my question as well." Lucia was standing next to me, looming in a way she'd only ever be able to do while I was seated, her overexuberant chest level with my head. "You did not give so much blood that you should be feeling this faint."

I yawned, leaning back into the chair's pillowy cushion. "I guess I haven't fully recovered yet."

"Recovered from what?"

"From feeding Julie—" My eyes, which had begun to sag comfortably shut, snapped open as rage suffused our bond, white hot, and sharp as any rose's thorns. "We were *attacked*, Lucia, and barely survived. It was the only way. It was necessary."

"And now you lack sufficient blood to heal the woman you have professed to love."

"Really? You want to go there?" I found enough energy to straighten up in my chair, allowing me to look past Lucia's chest to her deceptively angelic face. "*You* were the one with her when she faced down Zorana. When whatever this is was done to her!"

"Casting blame in the event of catastrophe is a fool's game, Mr. Smith," she said, conveniently ignoring the fact that she'd been the one to start that game. "What matters is Asya."

"On that, and maybe only that, we agree. But I just fed her more than she drank in Rome after having been stuck in the Tower for literal weeks!"

"Yes. You are right."

"And I'm sorry if I crossed some sort of boundary, yet again, by saving my friend's life, but—Wait. What?"

"I said that you are right, Mr. Smith. I will not repeat it a third time."

"I thought doing things thrice was sort of your deal."

"I am starting to believe that Rome is not sufficiently distant, that this planet as a whole is rapidly becoming too small for the two of us."

"You could always go back to Venus."

"What? Why would you think I have ever been—"

"I just figured that was where you were from."

Lucia's phone, out and on the nightstand next to my chair, buzzed. "This is neither the time nor the place for your usual stupidity, my thrall. You proved an able investigator in Rome, surprising us all. I will be relying upon you as an observer when I speak to Zorana."

"What am I supposed to be observing?"

"The Blood Witch herself, of course. Zorana teeters on the edge of sanity at the best of times. Like any wayward child, she requires stability and a firm hand to remain true to herself."

"She's not a child though."

"A part of her will always be a child, Mr. Smith. Physiology is more than just skin deep."

I didn't know what that meant, and I didn't care. "I still don't understand what you want from me."

"I want you there, beside me, watching for any clues the Blood Witch might let slip."

"I thought she just needed a firm hand?"

"Only a *part* of her is a child. The rest is a conniving schemer that has outlasted three kings. I will see that she is brought back under control, or I will permanently deprive the world of its last remaining Blood Witch, but that is a concern for the future. Today, it should be expected that every word that passes her diminutive mouth is a lie. You will assist me in disentangling those lies so that we might find the truth of Asya's condition."

I swallowed. I didn't want to be in a room with Zorana ever again, but that fear paled in comparison to the thought of watching Ana waste away. "I'll do my best."

"You will do better than that. I did not travel seven thousand miles only to watch Lady Dumenyova die."

It was an odd thing, feeling our emotions echo our words across the bond. The one thing I knew was that, for the second time in a too-long year, Lucia and I were fully aligned.

ooo

If Marcus ever retired from his role of royal bootlicker and financial assassin, he might have a career as a sandwich maker. I had some suggestions for future attempts but couldn't deny that what he had put together mostly hit the mark in terms of size, quality, and variety. Some chips, sprinkled in above the top layer of roast beef, would have added crunch and texture, but given the circumstances, I wasn't going to complain.

Zorana was delivered about three bites into that sandwich, and I had to scarf the rest of it down before joining Lucia in what she called *the salon*, and what was, to me, the upper den that got a lot of light in the afternoons. Both queen and witch were already present, and as I slipped in through the open door, pulling it closed behind me, I found two sets of eyes doing their best to pin me to the wall.

"Mr. Smith," said Lucia. "You finally grace us with your presence."

"Don't hate the player, hate the sandwich," I told her absently, unable to tear my eyes away from the other, smaller woman, barely propped up on the opposing couch.

Zorana looked eleven… would always look eleven, because that was the age she'd been forcibly turned. It had given her features that were forever stuck in the awkward phase between childhood and adulthood… large ears and a too-wide mouth paired with a button nose and eyes that were cloudy gray when not filled with blood.

That much was as I remembered. But her curly dark hair had been hacked off just below the ears, the remainder matted and thick with dirt and fluids I didn't want to think about. Her face was similarly stained, like she was auditioning for a role as a fifteenth century runaway, and despite clear efforts to at least hose her off at some point in the recent past, she still stunk like the dumpsters behind Juliette's condo building.

Below that dirt-stained chin, a truly impressive number of chains had been wrapped about her, pinning her arms to her side, and hiding her small legs from view. If someone dropped her into the Pacific, she'd sink so quickly that she'd probably leave an impact crater on the ocean floor. Even on dry land, those chains seemed sufficient to keep her contained, and the manacles on her wrists and ankles, attached together by a bar of steel as thick as my forearm, only sealed the deal.

Someone had taken the traditional hog-tie to a whole new level.

If Zorana was at all inconvenienced by her bonds, she didn't show it, gray eyes widening with delight at my appearance. Her wild smile presented both sets of fangs, fully extended.

"Hello, pet."

Chapter 34

IN WHICH THE WITCH IS NO SNITCH

I was half a second from stepping right back out into the hallway when the vampire shuddered and dropped her eyes, twitching as she did her best to crane her head around to scan the room. Chains clanked against one another as she seemed to test her bonds, less attempting to escape than just verifying they were really there. For the first time since I'd met her, I heard Zorana's breath: short, sharp gasps.

"Zorana." Lucia's voice was mild, but there was iron in that single word, the unmistakable strength of authority.

The Blood Witch stilled, eyes pulled almost magnetically to the woman sitting across from her. She breathed out, one long exhalation that was almost a sigh, and then giggled.

"Lucia. When did you get here?"

I frowned. I was used to Zorana's voice twisting my guts into a knot, but there was none of that going on right now. And her tone and even inflection was changing with each sentence.

"A day ago," answered Lucia. On the surface, she seemed cold and indifferent, but our bond told a different story. "We met last night, the three of us."

Gray eyes darted my way, but before the pre-teen could speak, Lucia shook her head. "I speak of you, me, and Lady Dumenyova."

"Stone in the heart, stone in the soul, stone at the head of each grave waiting to be filled." She rocked back and forth, chains clanking with every movement.

"Does she have meds she's supposed to be taking or something?"

"Mr. Smith, you are here to watch, not speak." Behind the sharp words, an equally sharp whipcrack of emotion came across the bond. It couldn't hurt me, but I almost flinched anyway. I scowled and sent my own message back across that bond, repeating the question I'd just asked.

There are no medicines in the world that can help, came the silent reply.

Are you sure? Anti-psychotics have gotten pretty good, I'm told.

"It is impolite to hold a conversation that excludes one of the people you are seated with," said Zorana, now sounding as prim as a governess hired to wrangle unruly children. "Surely, I must not speak to you of manners, young Lucia?"

"I am not that child anymore," replied the queen. "I am at the height of my power, the Winter Queen in truth as well as name. And I have come, Zorana, to take you home."

"Home burned to feed the Mad King's hunger." From her voice, it had happened yesterday.

"I speak of Italy, not France."

Zorana stirred. "Rome?"

"The wrongs of the past have been righted. My star is ascendant once more. And you—"

"I tunnel into the darkness, so that she cannot see me."

This time, Lucia's emotion across the bond was every bit as bewildered as mine. I felt her desire to ask who or what Zorana was talking about, and then, just as quickly, felt her crush that urge like a ladybug beneath her stiletto heel.

"Be that as it may," managed Lucia, "I am here, and you remain sworn to my service."

"The servant turned. The service is over."

"It is over when I say it is over, and that time has not yet come."

Zorana shook her head, more to herself than in a denial of Lucia's words. "Rome?" she asked again, this time in the voice of a child even younger than she appeared to be.

"The city stands. House Borghesi stands. And you will stand with us."

"Hand in hand, we stride through waters thick and red."

"Yes. And in return, I will give you the structure you require."

A small smile crept across the other vampire's face, terrible for all its sweetness. "Boundaries must be tested."

"They will not be found wanting." Lucia spoke simply, but every word was burnished steel.

Zorana shivered and shook herself like a dog that had gotten wet. A small pink tongue darted out across her lips, and her gray eyes locked onto Lucia like a lifeline. When she spoke, her voice was strong. "It is agreed, and it is good."

"Not quite yet," said the queen, stealing the words right out of my mouth. "My *Secundus*—"

"Will watch from the shadows through eyes of stone that have forgotten how to weep. I know, I know."

This time, Lucia and I *did* exchange glances, equally confused.

"Lady Dumenyova has been unwell since our encounter last night," said Lucia finally, choosing her words with obvious care. "I cannot see a way toward resumption of your service until that malaise has been lifted."

"Then we wait?" Zorana nodded to herself and tried to kick her feet up and onto the coffee table between them, rattling her chains and accomplishing little else. "I can wait. A spot of tea and a crumpet or three as we toast the future."

Juliette had once called Zorana as nutty as a fruitcake, but I was starting to think that was an insult to fruitcakes. Maybe there was something to what Lucia said about the vampire needing structure, because she was significantly less collected than the last time I'd seen her.

"Are you saying that you have nothing to do with her plight?"

Zorana paused, mid-headshake. "We met, last night."

"As I said, yes."

"She was first, smooth but not slow. A distraction?" With every word, the Blood Witch's voice crept closer to the cadence and tone I was used to. My intestines clenched in fearful anticipation of the pain to come.

"Yes," Lucia admitted. "I entered, moments later, to restrain you."

"With the ice and cold of winter's grasp." Zorana frowned. "It has been centuries since I was taken so easily. Your powers have grown."

"They have." Lucia waited for more, and then prompted. "And Lady Dumenyova? What did you do to her?"

"Nothing."

"Nothing?"

"We fought, in the space between heartbeats. If I had remembered who and what I was, the outcome may have differed. As it was, our clash should have done little but tax her reserves."

Reserves? I asked Lucia.

Blood, she replied. *Now, be silent.*

Even in my brain, Lucia was the worst. *Especially* in my brain.

"Then how do you explain her current condition?"

Gray eyes darted back and forth between Lucia and me. "Neither you nor your pet monkey have told me what her condition is."

"She appears to be blood starved," said Lucia. "She will not drink on her own, but even when she is fed, that blood appears to have no effect, like a drop of water vanishing into a bottomless well."

Zorana nodded, as much as she could with chains wrapped about her. "How many humans have you fed her?"

"Both of her blood donors, as well as my thrall."

I self-consciously held my bitten arm behind me. *Both* bitten arms. When had I become a chew toy for the supernatural?

"And the result was the same each time?"

Lucia paused. "No… when Mr. Smith fed her, she stirred, if but for a moment."

The eyes that haunted too many of my nightmares turned again on me. "Then I must see what makes his blood different. With your permission, Lucia?"

"*My Queen* or *Your Majesty.*"

Zorana turned back to Lucia. "What?"

"When you speak to me, you will utilize my title. Names must be earned once more."

The smile that spread across Zorana's face was that of an old woman finding comfort in the unexpected.

"My Queen," she purred. "May I taste your thrall's blood?"

I stiffened, my mental objections flooding the bond so strongly that Lucia actually turned and gave me a glare.

This is for Asya, she told me.

I… I can't. If she touches me again…

Do you trust me, my thrall?

Every time you call me that, it reminds me why I can't.

Mr. Smith, then. John, as Asya deigns to call you. One drop, and she will not touch you. I give my word.

Maybe it was the bond, or maybe it was three years of quasi-relationship with Lucia, but I knew it ultimately didn't matter what I decided. Anastasia meant a hell of a lot more to the queen than I did, and if she had to forcibly take my blood… well, she'd done worse in the past. This so-called *choice* was purely ceremonial. And yet…

Was it ceremonial to me? Or would I remember that I'd had the option of willingly giving yet more of my blood to help Ana and had chosen otherwise? That I'd let my fears of the woman who had imprisoned and tortured me win out over the love I had for my auburn-haired vampire?

Maybe. Maybe not. This wasn't the sort of situation I had a ton of experience in, but in the end, it didn't matter. Lucia and I had one thing in common, and only one thing.

We would both do whatever we had to for Anastasia.

One drop, I said.

Zorana had watched us both during the exchange, clearly aware that some sort of dialogue was happening, even if she couldn't listen to our words. As Lucia turned back to her and I took a careful, cautious step forward, she smiled again.

"You will not make contact with Mr. Smith," said Lucia, pulling me closer. "Tilt your head back and open your mouth."

"Am I then a baby bird, Your Majesty?"

"For this moment, you shall be."

"Very well." She started to lean back, paused, and smiled again. "I have always liked birds."

Maybe she shouldn't talk either?

Lucia didn't bother to respond. She brought me over to stand above the practically mummified Blood Witch. "Your arm, Mr. Smith. The one you fed Lady Dumenyova from."

I wasn't sure why or how the specific arm would make a difference, but nobody seemed interested in giving me a primer on blood and its many intricacies. I just stuck out my left arm and waited.

Once again, Lucia opted not to bite me. Maybe it was the connotations of drinking from my wrist, or maybe she just didn't want me to collapse into a pile of pre-orgasmic jelly. Instead she cut another hole in my skin, a fraction of the size of the previous one, and shallow enough that blood oozed rather than pooled. She turned my arm over, wrist down, and waited as the drop slowly gathered and then fell.

It hit Zorana in the eye, and the Blood Witch hissed like a cat, startling a laugh out of me that was far too close to hysteria. Before I could collect myself, Lucia had shifted my arm slightly, and the next drop fell right into the so-called baby bird's open mouth.

Another touch of Lucia's tongue to a wrist already clotting on its own, and then she was tugging me back away until a coffee table stood between me and the chained vampire on the couch.

Zorana, for her part, was rolling her head around on her shoulders in strange, looping patterns. I tensed for the near-inevitable betrayal and subsequent attack, but instead, she simply opened her eyes. Both were filled with blood this time, and I was pretty sure none of that blood was mine.

"What in the ninety-seven hells have the two of you done to your bond?" At a hard look from Lucia, she added on. "No disrespect intended, of course, my Queen."

"We did what was necessary. What have you found?"

"His blood has echoes of House Borghesi in it."

Lucia went still, physically and metaphysically. "What?"

"I have never tasted the like, even during your pet's prolonged stay in the House dungeons last year. One of the People, but not. A monkey, but also not. Fascinating, and it explains much."

"So far, I haven't heard a damn thing about how we're going to help Anastasia," I said, speaking out loud for only the second time since entering the salon.

"Lady Dumenyova is not suffering under a curse," said Zorana, her eyes reverting to gray even as her smile turned wicked. "She is not injured or crippled. Yet, she will die unless she gets what her body needs." She looked to Lucia. "If you would give it a moment's thought, Your Majesty, you would recognize the symptoms. You have witnessed them in others of our kind, even as you consciously chose to avoid them yourself."

"Just spit it out—" began the queen, only to trail off as something, something I couldn't quite parse, came to her. There was a moment of shock across the bond, as white and bright as the noon sun on a field of freshly fallen snow, and then that moment crumbled, consumed by a rising tide of red-hot rage. *How?*

"What?" I asked, adding onto the pile.

Lucia spun on me, eyes blazing. The anger on her face was a shallow representation of the sheer weight of the emotion flooding our bond and giving me the mother of all headaches.

"Leave us," she snarled. "Return to Lady Dumenyova."

"Excuse me?"

"Go," she said, "or I will not be responsible for what I do next."

I… didn't know what was happening, but I had a wealth of experience dealing with angry women, not to mention three years of an angry Lucia, and the queen was far past the state where she'd tried to kill me last spring. I couldn't help Anastasia if I was dead. I bit back a half-dozen ill-considered replies and one sweet comeback that would have *absolutely* gotten me killed, and left the room, head held high.

Lucia's rage followed me all the way down the hall like a thundercloud.

∘∘∘

I sat with Anastasia for a good thirty minutes, doing my best *not* to pay any attention to the part of my brain that was Lucia. I could feel her rage slowly fading but focused my attentions on the woman I loved.

Ana looked peaceful, open in a way I had rarely seen her. Even when she slept, there was a part of her that was usually primed, listening for threats and ready to respond in the manner she'd been trained. I'd been privileged enough to see some of that soften over the past few months of occasional bedsharing, but I knew what she had gone through in her training, and also knew some of those lessons would never leave her.

Whatever was wrong with her, whatever Zorana and Lucia knew and weren't sharing, was different. She looked ill, yes, and hungry and malnourished, and a thousand other things that all added up to something that had gone horribly awry, but she also looked… younger, somehow. She had fed at twenty-five, so I was already technically older than her purely physical appearance, but the way she carried herself, her poise and emotional reserve, had always lent her an air of maturity and elegance that most twenty-somethings lacked.

Despite the unknown illness that had struck her down, she looked young and innocent, soft, and oddly vulnerable. It was a side of her I saw only in private, and even then, all too rarely.

"I'm going to help you," I told her. "Whatever this is, I'm going to fix it. And then we'll go to Hawaii or Lake Tahoe. Anywhere you want. Even Rome again, if Lucia will cover the flight."

I waited for the inevitable correction to *Queen-Regent Lucia*, but of course, it never came.

"Did you know there's an intelligent fungus living under Phoenix?" I asked, carrying on the one-sided conversation. "What am I saying? Of course, you do… it was in your briefing. Well, apparently his name is Kevin, and he's big into philosophy…"

I was thirty minutes into my not-at-all-exaggerated-for-comedic-effect retelling of the trip to New Mexico when the door finally opened. Instead of Lucia, however, it was Marcus. He gave me the barest of nods and held the door wide as Gustavo and Teresa entered, each carrying a tray of food.

Ana's blood donors looked terrible—pale, listless, and slow to move, every step a struggle against gravity.

"What the hell, Marcus? They should be in bed."

"It was they who insisted," he said simply, all the usual snooty awfulness missing from his voice.

Teresa took her tray across the room to place it atop the dresser there, while Gustavo brought his over to me. He laid that tray—piled high with red meat and dark leafy greens—down onto the end table next to my chair and grabbed my hand. Warm brown eyes met mine before he looked to the femmepire sleeping in the room's only bed.

"I know," I told him. "We're going to fix it. Somehow. I promise. Nothing else matters until she's better."

He squeezed my fingers with the one hand and patted my shoulder with the other, eyes still trained on Anastasia, the woman he and Teresa had served for so many decades. Finally, he turned to Marcus, and rattled off something in Italian. I could hear the question in it even if I couldn't understand the words.

The manpire replied in kind, and both Gustavo and Teresa nodded reluctantly. With a soft sigh, the older man went to help his wife, and the two of them made their way back out into the hall.

"What did he ask?"

"If they could offer more blood."

I winced. Between the two of them, I doubted they had a fluid ounce left to spare.

"I told them it would not help," continued Marcus, "and that Her Majesty has the situation under control."

"Does she?"

"Eat, human. All will be made clear shortly."

Apparently, I was the only person who still didn't know what was going on. Still, the full tray of iron-rich foods made one thing clear.

"I'm donating blood again? Who's the second tray for?"

"Eat and be silent. I was not put on this planet to cure your ignorance."

"No, you were put here to do taxes and count beans." I rolled my eyes and grabbed a forkful of spinach off the plate. I wasn't a big spinach fan, but Teresa had added some sort of vinaigrette glaze that balanced it perfectly.

"Is not your father an accountant?" asked Marcus.

"Maybe?" Honestly, I didn't love that he knew even that much.

"Then why is it that you persist in your belief that any mention of my profession will function as an effective insult?"

"Uh…" It was an oddly good question, and the answer I eventually arrived at didn't spawn warm fuzzies in my soul. "You're good-looking, you're rich, you're successful… I guess your job seemed like the closest thing to a vulnerability."

"A wealth of experience dealing with literal wealth is anything *but* a vulnerability. Take it from the soon-to-be Royal Treasurer."

"I don't think I've met him or her yet."

I could hear his teeth grind from across the room.

"Oh! Congratulations then… I guess?"

"Your praise is as meaningless as your criticism," he said, not at all preening like a peacock in his three-piece suit. "As ever, I am simply honored to serve."

Of course he was.

CHAPTER 35

IN WHICH THE ANSWER IS SOMEHOW ALWAYS MORE BLOOD

I was done with my platter of food, and feeling comfortably full again, when Lucia finally saw fit to rejoin us. The vampire queen swept into the bedroom, riding a cold wind that was as much literal as it was figurative, but whatever conversation she'd had with Zorana had clearly helped temper her killing rage.

"Are you going to finally tell me what's going on?" I asked her. "Tweedledum over there has been no help at all."

Marcus didn't even have the grace to look ashamed of the fact.

"We must first prove out the hypothesis," she said.

"What hypothesis?"

She answered my question with one of her own. "You do truly love Lady Dumenyova, yes?"

"Of course."

"And you would do whatever is necessary to save her?"

"I've already fed both her *and* Zorana, so I think you know the answer is yes." I waved to the now-empty tray. "What I don't get is why you think a second go will have any more effect than the first."

"You will not be feeding her your blood alone."

I blinked, and it was only my years of experience as a mediator that allowed me to properly respond.

"What?"

Lucia held one arm out, and Marcus was at her side in a second, unbuttoning the cuff of the sleeve on that arm, and rolling it up to expose her forearm and wrist. When he was done, the accountant retreated, leaving the queen with her bare arm outstretched.

"You will feed from me, and then Lady Dumenyova will feed from you."

"What?" I asked again.

"Which part of this very simple arrangement is unclear, human?"

"The part where I'm drinking blood? I'm not a vampire!"

"Nevertheless, it must be done."

"Why?"

"You will be told if the attempt is successful." She met my eyes, and I could see her anger even as it bubbled up over our bond. "If it is not, then we were wrong, and we will move on to a new hypothesis."

"Still, I don't get—"

"Your purpose here is not to *get it*, Mr. Smith," she said, unknowingly paraphrasing a line from one of the greatest movies ever. "It is to do whatever is necessary to see Lady Dumenyova healed."

"Fine. But if I throw up all over you, you're paying for the dry cleaning, not me."

"Come now; this is not the first time you have tasted my blood."

Lucia was right, but the last time, I'd been too blissed out to care.

Still, if it could help Ana *and* get me answers…

I nodded and something in her cold, hard gaze softened, just a bit. She ran her index finger across her own wrist—the same finger she'd used to cut me open twice, I couldn't help but notice, although I guessed we were past the point of worrying about blood contamination—and motioned to me.

Our height difference, even with her heels, was even more apparent up close. I had to bend over to latch onto her wrist, squeezing my eyes shut as the foreign liquid entered my mouth. Much like the last time, it was very different from human or even werewolf blood: spicy instead of salty, sweet instead of bitter, and thick in a way that reminded me almost of molasses.

None of that made it any easier for me to drink it. I choked it down, swallowing the slow trickle that came from what, on a human, would have been a gushing wound. Lucia placed her other hand on my head, keeping me close, her fingers strangely hot against my scalp.

"Apply suction or the wound will close on its own."

How had *this* become my life?

I followed her instructions. What other choice did I have? This time, my strange feeding went on a lot longer than our purely ceremonial exchange of blood back when I was declared an ally to the House. I swallowed down mouthful after mouthful, waiting for my notoriously untrustworthy stomach to express its dissatisfaction.

That dissatisfaction never came. I didn't want to know what that said about me, and I wasn't much interested in thinking about it either.

Finally, Lucia's hand tightened in my hair, and she tugged my bloody mouth away from her golden wrist. Without my active suction, the wound closed at a speed that made my own regeneration seem almost ordinary. There was a ring of gold around the vampire queen's pupils, but she otherwise showed no signs of strain.

"What now?" I asked her.

"Now, we wait."

"For what?"

"For my blood to integrate with yours to the greatest extent possible."

I sighed and stalked over to the armchair that was starting to show an impression of my butt. Keeping me in the dark was doing nothing but pissing me off.

"Is that second tray of food for me too?"

"Don't be obscene, my thrall."

"What?"

"Gluttony is a cardinal sin and one you have clearly already overindulged in."

"Does that mean no?"

"It does." As she spoke, the hallway door opened again. A black-clad stranger, too handsome to be anything but a vampire, escorted in a blond, blue-eyed, and shirtless Adonis who had clearly never had a cheat meal in his life. The latter guy crossed to Lucia and dropped to both knees, tilting his head to one side.

"Normally," the queen said to me, "I would feed upon you, as is my right. However, doing so would defeat the entire purpose of this act. Thankfully, there was no shortage of individuals wandering the beach who were happy to be of service."

Even kneeling, the walking CrossFit advertisement was almost as tall as Lucia. She didn't have to bend down to bite into his neck.

I looked away. I knew from experience how good that bite could feel, but I didn't need to be a witness to it. What I needed was eye bleach and earplugs.

Lucia drank from the other human for a far shorter time than I had from her, but when she was done, the man was a quivering mess, held up only by the femmepire's iron grasp. She nodded to the manpire in black, and he dragged the blissed-out donor over to the far chair and the platter of food that awaited him.

I highly doubted Lucia—or the black-clad manpire who was almost definitely a member of the Crown Watch—had asked my fellow human if he'd wanted to have his blood sucked... but I also highly doubted he would find it in himself to care, even if they dismissed him without first compelling him.

Which, of course, they wouldn't. Too many humans already knew enough to be afraid of the dark.

Eventually, the other man roused himself enough to see the tray laid out next to him, and he fell upon it like a starving hyena, utterly demolishing the piles of food without any regard for basic manners, let alone utensils.

He was halfway through when Lucia had had enough. She glanced to the black-clad manpire. "Take him to the kitchen for the remainder of the meal. It is bad enough that his blood is thin and underdeveloped; I should not have to listen to him feed like an animal too."

"It will be done, Your Majesty," came the reply, and just like that, both human and guard were gone again.

"You brought the Crown Watch with you?"

"Some of them, yes. I am, after all, the ruling queen."

"Until Sabina is ready to take the throne."

She waved a golden hand, though not the one I'd fed from. "Trifles, Mr. Smith. Mere trifles."

Juliette was right. Nobody said trifle anymore.

"Sufficient time has passed. It is once again your turn."

"You want me to feed from you again?"

"Don't be absurd." She crossed the room and took my wrist. "It is time for you to feed Lady Dumenyova."

That much I was happy to do. And since Ana wasn't well enough to bite, the only pain I'd deal with was the wound Lucia was opening, for the third damn time in the same damn arm.

Anastasia hadn't moved at all during the whole blood gravy train. Mindful of the Zorana mishap, I pulled the sheets down below her shoulders to make sure I didn't get blood on them, and placed my wrist against Anastasia's open mouth.

At first, it went just like it had before, Ana stirring an infinitesimal amount before settling back down. Then, I heard murmurs from the peanut gallery of Lucia and Marcus, responding to something I couldn't see or sense.

It was the only warning I got before Anastasia's eyes snapped wide open, gold having almost entirely displaced the jade. Hands that could shatter concrete pinned my arm more tightly against her mouth, and two sets of teeth bit deep into the waiting flesh.

I had just eaten a whole cow and probably eight heads of spinach, but either the rumors of their iron-rich content had been greatly exaggerated, or my body hadn't yet had time to finish processing it and replenishing its own stores.

Whatever the reason, for the second time in as many days, and the third time in the past week, I passed out.

ooo

When I came to, I was in bed. The size of it told me it belonged to one of Ana's guest rooms, and the lack of a beautiful femmepire lying next to me said it was most likely *not* the same one that she had been convalescing in.

The good news was that my head only kind of hurt. The better news was that, for once, I had all of my clothes on, although someone had taken off my socks before they tucked me in.

Lucia, Marcus, or the guy from the Crown Watch? It was hard to imagine any of them even bothering to carry me, let alone tucking me into bed, but Gustavo and Teresa could never have managed it, even if they weren't currently suffering from exhaustion and blood loss themselves. *Anastasia then?*

I shook away the moment of hope. Even if she was better, and I had no guarantee that she was, Ana was the sort of person who would keep a vigil by the bedside, doing everything to ensure she was present when I woke.

As mysteries went, it wasn't one of the more engaging ones I'd dealt with. Nor was it difficult to solve, with the answer no doubt waiting for me elsewhere in the House. I felt for Lucia and found her two rooms down, presumably still in the same bedroom where Ana was convalescing. Her emotions were a muddle, which at least made for a difference from the usual white-hot anger.

My wonderphone had been left on the nightstand next to me, and miraculously, someone had even thought to plug it in. I checked the time, blinked, and checked again.

It hadn't even been eleven in the morning on Sunday when I fed Ana for the second time… so how was it already noon on *Monday?*

"Jesus, Juliette's probably back in San Diego already."

I had literally dozens of notifications, but they would keep for another time. I swung my legs out of bed and stood, grateful to find them stable beneath me, then made my way out and down the hall. My senses told me that Lucia was still in the bedroom where we'd fed Ana.

The femmepire queen met me at the door, one golden finger silencing my protests as she pulled me away.

"She is sleeping," she told me, her voice strange and thick with an emotion that seemed half relief, half concern, and half soul-weary frustration. "Truly sleeping, this time."

I sagged in relief. "She's better? She's cured?"

She paused, visibly considering her words. "The treatment worked," she finally said, "but it will have to be repeated in the future."

"For how long?"

"Until it is no longer necessary."

Which told me absolutely nothing at all. Again.

"Is this… how it starts? Do all of the People go through this as they near the end of their lives?"

"What? Curb your useless tongue, human! Asya is no older than I am, and my uncle has three centuries on us both. We will all be walking this earth long after you are but a faded memory, an itch that no longer needs to be scratched."

Well, Lucia was back in fine form.

"Then what's going on? You promised you'd tell me if the hypothesis or whatever proved correct."

"What I said was that you would be told, and you will be. It is, however, not my place to tell you. Nor is it my decision to make."

"Whose decision is it, then?" I read the answer in her eyes. "Anastasia?"

"Once she herself has been made aware, yes."

I didn't know what to make of that, which kind of summed up my life experiences with vampires, in general. Still, if there was one person I trusted above all others in the world, it was Anastasia. She would tell me when she could, and if Lucia was right about her recovery, she would be able to do so soon enough.

I turned back to the bedroom Lucia had kept me from entering. "I'll keep watch over her. You deal with queen stuff."

"Queen stuff?"

"*Queen-regent* stuff then. I'm sure your subjects need to be reminded of your existence before they try to stage another coup."

"The Italian Court is well in hand, Mr. Smith. *I* will be watching over Lady Dumenyova, ensuring that none disrupt her recovery."

"I'll watch with you then."

"Do you truly have nothing else to do?"

"Nothing important, no."

She tilted her head to the side, the diamond pins in her hair sparkling. "And yet, I had been told you had a mediation underway."

"I do, but those meetings aren't until—"

Tomorrow, I'd been going to say. But *tomorrow* was now Tuesday, while two of those initial interviews had been set for…

"Ah, crap." I fished my wonderphone out of its pocket and scanned the notifications. Twenty-seven spam emails, two spam calls, a text thread from Juliette saying she was home, and yes, two missed calls and a text from the half-goblin, half-troll I'd named Junior… who I was supposed to have met roughly an hour earlier.

Worse than that? There was a recent text from Wubby-Lubby Rivers Tomlinson, saying he had arrived and was waiting.

But the biggest problem was that I'd set both meetings up at the same taco shop, reasoning that it would save me from having to change locations between interviews. Only… I'd failed to show. If Junior hadn't already left in disgust, that taco shop was now potentially ground zero for the next phase of the goblin war.

"I've got to go, if we don't want San Diego overrun by angry green men," I said. "Like immediately. Can your driver drop me off, or should I take one of Ana's cars?"

CHAPTER 36

IN WHICH ABSENCE MAKES THE HEARTS
GROW FONDER

Lucia sent me out in her rented limo… which was probably the safer choice. If I'd come back with even a scratch on the paint job of one of Ana's Jaguars, I wasn't sure even true love would have been enough to save me from the fallout.

I texted Junior my apologies, texted Wubby Lubby that I was on my way, and put my wonderphone away. The taco shop we were meeting at was in Del Mar, near Torrey Pines. In fact, it was the same place where I'd met with Jason, back when he was one of my mediation clients. I hadn't been back since—not after the missing guacamole disaster, the werewolf attack, and my subsequent kidnapping—but it was convenient, and open-air dining when meeting with goblins was pretty much a must.

"Thanks for accompanying me," I told the black-clad manpire who, at a word from Lucia, had followed me into the limo. "I'm John."

"I am Castor," he told me. His English was heavily accented, but he was still doing a hell of a lot better than I would have in speaking whatever his native tongue was.

"Like the oil?"

"Like the mythological figure."

I nodded, even though I wasn't familiar with Castor, and wasn't sure what his connection was to cooking products.

"Good to meet you," I said instead. "And again, thanks for coming."

"It is my honor."

That threw me for a loop. "Really?"

"Of course. Not only are you the bondsworn of the queen-regent, you brought King Tomasso's murderers to justice. While I was fortunate enough to witness some of your performance in the trial against Lady Dumenyova, I deeply regretted never having the opportunity to meet you while you were in Rome."

"Oh. Well, that's…" I trailed off and shrugged self-consciously. "I'm nobody special, but that's really nice of you. Do you know Niccolo? Or Yovanna?" I asked, citing the name of two other members of the Crown Watch.

"I know them both. Yovanna is a treasure. Niccolo…"

"Right?! I still don't get what Maria Elena sees in him." I shook my head. "Anyway, I hope you won't be needed on this little excursion, but I'm glad you're coming along, just in case."

"Who are we meeting?"

"A goblin. And potentially a half-troll, assuming he stuck around too. Which I hope he didn't, as that would just make it that much more likely your services would be required. I'm mediating between two goblin tribes," I explained.

"And the half-troll?"

"Is the son of one of the tribe's chief."

"Impressive. Not many survive sex with a troll matron."

"TMI, Castor. Way too much."

He grinned, teeth brilliantly white in his bronzed face, and I knew for a fact that we were going to get along just fine.

A short time later, we were parked up the street from the taco shop, our limo drawing more than a few eyes. It wasn't every day someone traveled in style just for tacos… which seemed a shame, really. Maybe someone would grab a picture and post it to social media and Castor and I would find ourselves the unwitting originators of the latest trend or challenge.

It kind of made me wish I'd dressed up, but I hadn't moved any of my nicer clothes to Anastasia's place yet. Clean shorts, a T-shirt, and my badly stained sneakers would have to do.

And who knew? Maybe the contrast between the quality of our ride and the slovenliness of my appearance would factor into that social media challenge somehow?

"I'm going to get a burrito," I told Castor, as we walked back down the block toward the restaurant. "And maybe a beer. What can I get you?"

"I am here to protect you," he reminded me, "not to eat or drink."

"I'll get you some enchiladas and a Coke then."

"Do they have raspberry lemonade?"

"You know what? I have no idea, but for you, I'm going to find out."

Despite the banter, I was tense as we neared the shop. I hadn't seen any signs of a brawl or bloodbath as we drove past, but I wasn't always the most observant of people. It was a potentially fatal flaw for someone pursuing either of my two careers.

Before going inside to order, I peeked around the corner at the outdoor seating. Wubby Lubby was there, sure enough, wearing a Philip Rivers jersey in celebration of the contract extension the quarterback had just signed, but he wasn't alone. And given the sheer size of the person seated with him, Junior had opted to stick around.

That was not good.

And yet, as I continued to peep, my worries of a knock-down, drag-out battle royale slowly faded. The two young men didn't seem to be staring each other down, sizing each other up, or any other sort of directionally oriented phrase that might lead to bloodshed. Mostly, they were just… eating. And talking.

Junior threw his head back, his cackle so loud that it caught the other outdoor diners' attention, even through the glamour he was no doubt employing. As I watched, he pounded the table, barely keeping his food down as he continued to laugh. A moment later, he smacked Wubby Lubby on the shoulder, the blow hard enough to almost lift the smaller goblin out of the chair, but when I changed angles, I saw Tikky-Wokka's son was laughing too.

"Huh."

"They do not act like tribes at war," said Cantor, proving he had the requisite observation skills to join my agency.

"They really don't. Let's get some food and see what's going on."

∘∘∘

It took a while to get my burrito, in part because I stared down the cook putting it together until I was certain he wouldn't skimp on my guacamole. If asking for extra guacamole really *was* gay code, nobody here seemed to know it; mostly, the staff just seemed weirded out by my intensity. Clearly, none of them had ever been cheated out of their proper measure of condiment before.

I could only pray that they would continue to live such blessed and carefree lives.

Castor's enchiladas were cauliflower because the dude was apparently a vegetarian. And Greek, not Italian, despite my earlier assumptions. He seemed more focused on the lemonade anyway, which was strawberry instead of raspberry, but, judging by his expression, every bit as tasty as he'd hoped.

When my food finally came, I checked the guac levels and tipped the cashier accordingly before carrying the tray back outside. Castor took a nearby table while I approached the goblins. Wubby Lubby and Junior were still chatting, so deep in their conversation that they didn't notice me until I had set my tray down and pulled up a chair.

"Sorry about the delay," I told them both before turning to Junior. "Especially for you. We had a bit of an emergency last night."

"Is everything okay?" asked the half-troll, his squeaky voice still an odd match for that massive frame.

"I think so. I hope so." I took a bite of my burrito—which, in another stunning sign of caloric restraint, I had opted *not* to make ranchero style—and waggled my fork between them. "Did you two know each other before all of this?"

"No," said Wubby Lubby. "Charles was up in Seattle with his mom."

I felt like mentally slapping myself. *Charles* was a *much* better nickname than Junior. It was also a syllable shorter, which would have saved me a ton of mental headspace.

"Well, you seem to be hitting it off pretty well."

"Wubby plays League," said Junior. "He's a Maokai player, but you can't win them all, I guess."

"Exactly what someone who rolls with Alistar would say."

I… didn't know what either of them were talking about, but they were trading grins, so I guessed it wasn't serious.

"Well, I didn't mean to stack your appointments one after the other, and then miss the first one entirely," I admitted, "but with you both here, and getting along, how do you feel about doing this as a group instead?"

The two kids traded glances.

"I don't think my dad would—" began Junior.

"Mom won't like it if—" said Wubby Lubby at the same time.

"Don't think about them," I said. "They wouldn't have brought you to the initial meeting if your opinions didn't matter. You're both future leaders of your respective tribes. Maybe this is the right time to assert yourselves?"

The two goblins traded looks, their nonverbal communication already on a whole different level than what I'd managed with Juliette after three freaking years.

"Is it true you know Lord Beel-Kasan?" asked Junior.

"He helped me out with Wubby Lubby back in the day."

Wubby just nodded, although he'd gone a little pale under the green.

"Is he… scary?" squeaked Junior.

"He can be, yeah."

"How do you talk to him then?"

I frowned, giving it some thought. Something told me this *wasn't* about Bill, but the key to mediation was communication, and I was happy to go wherever this tangent took us. "Mainly, I try not to focus on that aspect of him. He's a person. A strange person, and a powerful one, but still, a person. I try to treat him like one, instead of a source of fear and horror, and I think he appreciates that."

"My dad is scary," said Junior, his voice almost too low to hear.

"Mine was too," admitted Wubby Lubby. "He didn't like me spending all my time on YouTube and Twitch. Mom doesn't really care about what I do. Or about me at all, really."

"Parents are hard," I told them, speaking from a place of complete ignorance, given that my own mother and father were saints just waiting to be canonized. My mom would be the patron saint of patience, and my dad the patron saint of never growing up. "Just by virtue of being born in different times, they don't always see things the way we do or understand why we act a certain way."

"We?" Wubby Lubby cocked an overly hairy eyebrow. "Weren't *you* born all the way back in the 80s or something?"

Junior snickered.

"Accurate, if hurtful," I said. "I'm not saying I understand people your age any better than your moms or dads do, especially since I'm probably closer to their ages than yours. But I bet when they were younger, they went through the same thing with *their* parents."

"I can't imagine my dad being younger," said Junior.

"What about your mom?"

He shrugged massive shoulders. "She spends a lot of her time as a statue."

That… wasn't really an answer, but I just went with it.

"I get it. But I can tell you that this is something every generation goes through. People your age try out new things and people my age— or older—just shake our heads and don't get it."

"Do you have children?" asked Wubby Lubby. "Are they scared of you?"

"I don't," I said, hiding my wince. "Children aren't really in the cards for me, but even if they were, could you imagine anyone being scared of me?"

"My mom is," said the full-blooded goblin. "I heard her talking to the Elders last week. She was reminding them what happened to the witches."

"And the vampires," said Junior. "And the crabs."

"Werewolves too," added Wubby Lubby. "Although I think some of them are still alive at least."

Lord Kala, owner of the Bitter End, had once told me he found me fascinating because death followed me everywhere. I hadn't realized that rep had spread as far as the goblin tribes.

"I'm not a violent person," I said, trying not to remember how I'd kept Shae stunned until Juliette could finish draining her just two days earlier, "but I'll admit our world sometimes doesn't care who or what we are. But if I did ever have kids, I can promise you I would love them and protect them. And," I added, trying to pivot back to the point of our lunch meeting, "I would listen to them whenever they had something important to say."

"I don't want to go to war," said the massive, damn-near unstoppable tank of muscle and bone that I'd nicknamed Junior.

"War's dumb," agreed Wubby Lubby, "and you're the coolest guy I've met in ages."

For a brief, shining moment, I thought he was talking about me, but his eyes were clearly locked on Junior instead.

"Then what we need to do," I said, finally remembering to take another bite of delightfully rich and creamy burrito, "is convince your parents of that."

"How?"

"A mediation is essentially a dialogue through which both parties can arrive at a compromise," I said, citing a passage from one of my books with the casual aplomb of someone who had thought it up on the spot.

"Huh?" Junior screwed up his broad features, while Wubby Lubby just sent me a look like he could physically smell the bullshit I was peddling.

"We figure out what your mom and *Charles'* dad want and then work backwards until we find a place where they're both partially satisfied. And that means the two of you," I continued, nodding at both goblins, "have some homework to do."

By the matching expressions that greeted me, one thing our generations *did* have in common was a distaste for homework, but I let their disapproval roll right off of me. I wasn't here to do the heavy lifting after all; I was just here to facilitate.

ooo

"That was educational," said Castor, accompanying me back to the limo.

"The enchilada?"

"The mediation. I've never seen a mediator at work before."

"There aren't any mediators in Rome?" Come to think of it, I hadn't run across any *brothers or sisters of the compromise* while I'd been there.

"The council moderates any disputes that reach the level of possible disruption."

"That makes sense. Sort of." But there was no way in hell I was including Vigo or Dog in my imaginary global fraternity.

"Do you think they will be able to convince their respective parents to pursue peace?"

"My one-on-ones with Madonna Adele Beyoncé Swift and Charles the Elder aren't until tomorrow, but I'm hopeful. For all the blood that was already spilled during the coup and initial retaliatory attacks, everyone now seems more focused on potential concessions than the lives that were lost."

"Goblins are ever greedy."

"*People* are ever greedy," I countered. "Goblins might just be a little less subtle about it than the rest of us."

Castor gave that some thought, nodding as we reached the limo and he opened the door for me. "So, if the children can identify what those concessions are *and* defuse talk of more violence…"

"They'll do my job for me, yeah."

"Niccolo and Yovanna both had stories to tell about you," said the manpire, sliding into the limo across from me, and tapping the privacy glass between us and our driver. "Yet neither one mentioned your subtlety and guile."

"It's not just the small who are sneaky."

"I… beg your pardon?"

I coughed. "Never mind. Definitely one of those things where you had to be there."

"They *did* mention your strangeness." He softened the words with a smile that would have brought most straight women and at least as many gay men to their knees.

"Yeah, somehow *that* always seems to be remembered."

Chapter 37

In Which a Hero Plays Hooky and Gets Hit with a Bomb

I probably should have stopped by the office while I had transportation, but I was pretty sure Angel and Juliette would have things covered. And showing up in Logan Heights in a limo might be the sort of faux pas that ended the recent armistice between me and the local gangs, and my Corolla would end up paying the price.

But the real reason I told our driver to head north to Cardiff was to get back to Ana, both to make sure for myself that she was okay again, and to find out what had happened in the first place. If Zorana truly hadn't done anything, did that mean Anastasia was sick? Was that even possible? The only time I'd ever seen a sick vampire was when Lucia's energy was being drained out of her through our bond.

I didn't push Castor for information. It would have put him in a tough spot, and there was every chance he didn't know anyway. After all, if Lucia had been the sort of person to be kind or even transparent with the *help*, she probably wouldn't have had her House stolen right from under her.

Instead, I decided to be productive on the drive back to Cardiff. I texted Juliette to let her know I was still alive, I checked to see if Mike *or* Susan had called, emailed, or texted me, and finally, I called Simon on the number he'd given me.

"What?" Either zombies could get colds like the rest of us or he'd lost another piece of himself; his voice was scratchier than I could remember it being, even over the shaky quality of the call.

"Hey Simon, it's John."

"I know. I've got caller ID like every other person with a cellphone in the damn world. What do you want? I'm watching *Better Call Saul.*"

"Didn't that come out back in the spring?"

"I'm not watching anything until I can binge it, kid. Bad enough that I'll have to wait until next year for season two."

"Right. Well, I just wanted to let you know that Dulcinea's safe."

"Yeah, I heard."

"You did?"

"Jeremiah gave me a call. I think he's sweet on that partner of yours."

"I hope Pearl never finds out."

"Who's Pearl?"

"It's not important." I waited for a thank you, but there was only silence. "So, we're good?"

"Yeah yeah. Consider the favor repaid. Next time my great-great-granddaughter gets stuck in a cave, I guess I'll offer cash for you to get her out."

"That's not exactl—"

"Kid. John. Captain Smith."

"Yeah?" That last title got my attention. I'd never been a captain before, and honestly, I didn't hate it.

"What part of *I'm watching Better Call Saul* did you not get?"

"Fine. I get it. I'm just glad she was safe."

"Me too," he admitted after a long pause. "Anyway, bye."

I looked at my phone to see the call had already ended.

Goblins might be greedy, but I think I preferred that to the undead being ungrateful. On the other hand, the scales were balanced. No more favors hanging over my head. No butcher's bill waiting to be paid. No…

Crap. I couldn't think of any other suitable sayings. Maybe all this guacamole was weighing down my thoughts. *Also*, I realized, *I still need to help Kevin, as promised.*

Obligations remained.

We turned off the 5 onto Birmingham and headed down the hill toward the ocean. There was no trace left of early morning fog, just deep blue waters extending from the town's skyline all the way out to the horizon.

Juliette was right. It was stupid to keep my own place now that Ana had given me the key to her house. Cardiff was a beautiful, sleepy little seaside town, and it was hard to imagine better people than Gustavo, Teresa, and Anastasia herself to share it with.

The limo parked in the driveway, the driver apparently paid to keep hanging out in the car while Castor and I went inside. I headed straight for the downstairs kitchen, *not* because I was hungry, but because it really was the heart of the home. If Ana was awake, she'd no doubt be there with Lucia and her donors.

Instead, I found only Teresa, still looking like she should be in bed. The elderly woman was making hot chocolate in a saucepan, which seemed complicated but also tasted a lot better than the instant stuff I was used to. She handed us both mugs and shooed us out of her kitchen.

"I'm going to look for Lady Dumenyova," I told Castor.

"I will report in with my lieutenant." He headed off in the opposite direction.

"If he gives you any grief, let me know," I said. "I'm pretty sure I outrank him."

"Her," he clarified, "and how do you figure?"

"You heard Simon on the phone." It wasn't a question. He'd been in the limo with me so of course he had. "Captain beats lieutenant every time."

"I will be sure to let Claudia know."

He grinned as he said it, only solidifying the fact that Castor was a good dude.

"Castor and Claudia," I said to myself after he was gone. "Is it just coincidence, or did Lucia really pick only members of the Crown Watch whose names start with the letter C?"

I was laying heavy odds on the latter. It seemed like the sort of thing she would do, probably as repayment for some imagined slight three hundred years earlier from someone unfortunate enough to share the same starting initial.

Well, I hope Cory or Cornelius or Caline or whoever it was, knows just how badly they ruined things for everyone else for the rest of forever.

Although… Castor *had* gotten a strawberry lemonade out of the deal, so there were clearly some upsides to being forced to guard Lucia.

I didn't see Gustavo as I carried my hot chocolate upstairs. Hopefully, *he* was resting, even if Teresa had chosen to do otherwise. I skipped the salon entirely, under the assumption that Zorana was still there, looking like a heavy metal mummy in all her chains, but instead turned left and went down the hall where I could sense Lucia still camping out in the same bedroom where I'd fed Anastasia—twice.

This time, the queen didn't head me off at the entrance. I eased the door open and slipped inside, using my best ninja-adjacent skills to be as stealthy as possible.

Clearly, I shouldn't have bothered. By the time I had the door open, the conversation within had ended, and two vampires were looking my way.

Lucia had pulled one of the armchairs over to the bed—not the one I'd camped out in, I couldn't help but notice—and stood next to it, long white skirts almost hiding the equally white heels beneath. In lieu of hot chocolate, she had a glass on the table next to her, the rose color telling me it was wine, not blood. She had a bone-handled comb in one hand, and was gently running it through the tangles of the woman who sat in front of her, propped up on enough pillows to fill a small swimming pool.

"Ana." For the first time since I'd left Ghost Falls, I felt something in me unclench, a tight knot of fear and tension finally coming undone.

"John." The vampire still looked sick, unhealthy rather than just pale, with circles under her eyes, but she was sitting up on her own and her eyes were open.

I'd never seen anything more beautiful.

I sent her a smile that couldn't hope to convey even half of what I was feeling, hoping for that slow half-smile I loved in response. Instead, she looked almost… pensive behind the poker face I'd been learning to interpret.

"My Queen," she said to the woman who hadn't stopped brushing her hair upon my arrival, "may I speak to Mr. Smith? Alone?"

I was pretty sure she didn't need to ask for permission since Lucia had freed her from her service, but apparently old habits died hard.

"I will be nearby," said Lucia, patting the other vampire on the shoulder and handing the comb over. She gave me a hard look that I hadn't earned at all, and then brushed past me as a strong sense of admonition, still mixed in with a heavy dose of anger, poured in over our bond.

I didn't know what the hell was going on with Lucia, but if I spent my life worrying about her moods, I wouldn't have time to do literally anything else. I sent back the mental equivalent of a shrug and crossed over to the woman I'd come to see.

"Here," I said, plucking the comb out of Ana's hands. "I can take care of that."

"How are you doing?" she asked, her usually rich voice oddly strained.

"Isn't that my line?"

"When Queen Lucia first arrived, she said you had pulled upon her abilities while she was asleep and in flight."

"Oh, that." I ran the comb through her long auburn hair, pausing to tease out a knot. "We ran into a spell trap, some sort of magical relic, and an enforcer from the New Mexico Pack, in that order. No big deal."

"You… what?"

Apparently, the rumors of coma patients hearing what people spoke to them were *not* true when it came to vampires, as I'd already recounted most of the trip for her on Sunday.

"It's okay. The kids are safe, the werewolf's dead, the relic is broken, and nobody was permanently hurt. Other than the werewolf, I mean."

"How did you even encounter an Infected?"

"Well, that's a whole different story. It all started—" I stopped. "You know what? It can wait. I'm here and I'm fine. You're the one who had us all worried. How are *you* feeling?"

"That is a difficult question to answer, if I am being honest."

I paused, mid-stroke. "Really?"

"Truly."

"Okay. Well, I don't want to push or anything, but—"

"John," she said, "we need to talk."

I shook my head even though she couldn't see it. "No."

"No?"

"I'm not going to let you break up with me. Not this time."

"John—"

"I'm not losing you. Hell, I almost just did. *Again.* Whatever is going on, we're going to deal with it, and we're going to deal with it together."

Finally, she turned toward me, her moves almost painfully slow as she placed a cool finger against my lips. For just a moment, the smile I'd been looking for peeked through her mask.

"I am not leaving you, Mr. Smith. You are mine, and you will remain mine until you request otherwise. However, there are matters that we must discuss."

"Oh, thank God. I mean… I… uh… kind of have a history with those particular words, in that particular order."

"What words?"

"We need to talk."

"I see."

I tapped her shoulder with the comb. "Turn back around. Lucia didn't finish your hair, and I'm not done yet either. We can talk as I work. Is this about you falling sick?"

"Yes, although it is not a sickness, per se. It…" She trailed off, sounding uncharacteristically tentative.

"Take your time," I said. "And if you need something to drink, in either meaning of the word, just let me know."

"I will. Need to drink, that is. Not now, but tonight, and every day for at least the next few weeks."

"I'm not sure Gustavo and Teresa will be up for donations anytime soon, but I'm here and available."

"Their blood would not suffice, regardless."

"Can you tell me why?" I didn't want to press, not when she'd very nearly wasted away and still clearly wasn't alright, but it was impossible to offer solutions when I didn't know what was going on. "Is this something Zorana did to you?"

"No. If anyone is to blame, it is you and me."

"What? When? How?"

She sighed. "I am making a mess of this, but it was not a conversation I ever expected to have. Not in my fourth century, and especially not with you."

"Maybe just come out and say it," I suggested, focusing on another, particularly difficult tangle. "I love you, and nothing will change that, but I also have literally no idea what you're talking about."

"Very well." She was already facing away while I worked on her hair, but she seemed to turn inwards even further, as if to remove any possibility of meeting my gaze. "I am neither sick nor cursed, nor suffering from any form of spell or magic. Instead, it appears that I am feeding for two."

"Well, at least it's not—Wait. What?"

"I am pregnant, John."

I dropped the comb.

○○○

"Is…" There was no polite way to ask if the baby was mine, and thankfully, I stopped myself from even trying. "I thought that wasn't possible? Our two species…"

"Breeding? You are correct. It should not be possible, even if we discount the fact that I am past the usual age of fertility among the People. Yet here we are."

"How?"

"Lucia and Zorana believe that it may be a result of what has happened with your bond."

"I don't get it." My thoughts had taken wing, flying in a thousand different directions. I tried to grab the comb, still hanging in Anastasia's hair, but my hands didn't want to listen.

"The People are neither human nor animal, Mr. Smith. We are a blend of the physical and the metaphysical, and it is in the latter realm where our two species prove incompatible."

"Except apparently not, given that I'm human."

"Are you? Even if the Lady Manassa's suspicions about you being more than human are incorrect, your bond with my queen gives you access to at least some of her power."

"So, what… I *tricked* your body into believing I was a vampire?"

"Lucia said Zorana tasted House Borghesi in your blood. If you had been pulling on Lucia's power when we were mid-coitus… then, perhaps?"

"That's…" Well, it wasn't *totally* impossible. The pulling on the power part anyway. But it would have to have been during our first night, back when I was trying to make up for a disastrous first attempt, and before Lucia was thousands of miles away. "Wait, does that mean *Lucia* is the father, technically?"

"*You* are the father," said Anastasia, the firmness of her response leaving no room for misinterpretation. "Yet she played her role as well."

This was all manners of messed up, and that was saying a lot, given that I'd recently both debated philosophy with a fungus and stood reluctant witness to the love between a sprite and a jar of honey.

"Okay. So, you're pregnant." There was a *lot* to say and unpack about that, but I tried to focus on the bigger issue. "What does that have to do with your condition? You said you're feeding for two? I thought vampires didn't drink blood until the Thirst hit?"

"When a child is still in the womb, they are nourished by the blood of their parents. Both parents. The gap between requisite feedings widens as the pregnancy continues, but such feedings remain a necessity until the child is born."

"So, fighting Zorana thinned out your reserves, and…"

"Triggered our child's need for blood, yes. It is a little bit early, if conception occurred that night in Rome, but it is not *too* early. However—"

"It needs my blood along with yours." I frowned, putting the pieces together at a pace that would make a preschooler feel superior. "And Lucia's?"

"While your blood *tastes* of House Borghesi, it remains predominantly human, and is thus insufficient to fill the metaphysical need. Whereas Lucia's blood, while pure, lacks the markers that identify her as the biological father."

"Which is why she had me feed from her before you fed from me. Because my blood infused with hers is what the baby requires."

"Indeed."

"Huh. I… uh… Huh." Thank God I'd already done my mediation meetings for the day, because my current level of eloquence wasn't going to impress anyone. "I didn't see that coming."

"Nor I."

I sat there for far too long, trying to put my thoughts in order. This was nuts. My life was a single-camera sitcom on the best of days, but this was something straight out of a telenovela.

I didn't realize how long the silence had gone until Anastasia straightened, doing her best to sit up against the pillows. "You have my apologies, Mr. Smith. If I had known this was a possibility, I would have informed you of such and we could have taken action to prevent it. I understand that this is not something you had sought—"

I blinked and started to reply, but she spoke right over me.

"—and in truth, I never sought to be a mother either. Nevertheless, I will not let this child pay the price for my mistake. If you wish to go, all I ask is that we work out some manner of arrangement, wherein you return for feedings."

"What are you talking about, Ana?" I ignored impropriety and climbed right into the bed with her. "Why would I leave?"

She refused to meet my eyes. "You are not even thirty yet. A child, particularly one that will likely bring with it unforeseen challenges as a member of both our species, is—"

"Nothing short of a miracle," I told her. "And I will love them every bit as much as I do their mother."

She went still. "Truly?"

"Truly. I never bothered to dream of having a family with you, because everyone kept saying it was impossible. And yeah, maybe I'm not strictly ready to be a dad, on an emotional *or* intellectual level, but I think that's something I share with *every* first-time parent. None of that means I'm not thrilled beyond belief."

For the first time, she met my eyes. "Are you certain?"

"I am." I tried to beam that message straight into her brain, using our eyes as a delivery mechanism, but it was made more difficult by one oddity. "Why are your eyes stone, Ana?"

"Because stone does not cry." She shook her head and released her Talent, dark granite melting back into jade green pools.

"You really thought I was going to take off?"

"I am perhaps not at my best right now," she admitted, "but our baby is, as you yourself said, an impossibility. Human and vampire both. This pregnancy is already uncharted territory, to say nothing of what they will be like once they are born. Will they feel the Thirst after puberty as my kind do? Will they age like you, or like me, or some combination of the two? I would not blame any man for running from such uncertainty."

"Anastasia Dumenyova," I said, forcing steel into my voice. "You've known me for three years now, and you still haven't figured out how much I hate running in general? Seriously, it's the absolute *worst*, even before you throw in the nipple chafing."

"Clearly, I should have said *walking away from it*, then," she said. For the first time all day, her eyes sparkled.

"I don't care if it's walking, running, or paragliding… I'm not going anywhere. And when it comes to the whole *great unknown* thing, I've got a leg up on you."

"How so?"

"I almost *never* know what's going on or what to expect. You call it uncharted territory? I call it my life… and honestly? It's not that bad. You'll see. Come to the dark side with me, Ana. We've got cookies and hot cocoa."

"Speaking of cocoa, I believe yours might be getting cold."

"No," I said again.

"No?"

"I'm not drinking my hot chocolate until you kiss me and accept that everything's going to be okay."

Her lips curved into a wicked smile. "This is blackmail, Mr. Smith, pure and simple. You well know how greatly it pains me to see Teresa's hot chocolate wasted."

"Like a certain femmepire keeps teaching me, I use whatever weapons are at my disposal, Lady Dumenyova."

"Oh, for the love of gods, would the two of you just get it over with already?"

I shared a look with Anastasia. "Has Lucia seriously been standing outside the door this entire time?"

"Should not *you* have been able to tell as readily as me?"

"I was focused on more important things."

"That, my heart, is a very good answer." She leaned forward and brushed my lips with hers, a feather-soft gesture that just left me hungry for more. "But for now, I believe we should let my liege and oldest friend back in before she batters down the door. After all, you have hot chocolate to drink, she left her wine here on the table, and I—"

"Still have a comb stuck in your hair."

"Precisely."

"Okay." I gave her another kiss, just because I could. Then, I grabbed my hot chocolate and climbed right back into bed where I wrapped an arm around her shoulders and cuddled her to me. Hell if I was going to stop snuggling just because Lucia was around.

Especially since she'd be around a lot in the short term, until the baby's need for blood started to dwindle.

The baby. *Our* baby.

Holy shit.

CHAPTER 38

That night, we repeated the whole feeding process: Lucia to me to Anastasia. It didn't get easier with repetition, not the part where I drank blood from a blonde bombshell, nor the part where I then fed the mix of my blood and hers to the woman I loved to keep our baby from draining her dry.

Really, there was nothing easy *or* normal about the situation, but by the end of it, Anastasia had color in her cheeks and ample energy to walk over to the upstairs dining room, and that made it all worth it.

Gustavo, up and about for the first time all day, brought me some ibuprofen while the previously unseen Claudia took Lucia's latest snack back to whatever terrible singles bar they'd found him in. And that left the three of us—Ana, Lucia, and me—sitting in the upstairs dining room, a charcuterie board, two glasses of water, and one glass of wine on the table between us.

The wine was for Lucia. Ana wasn't drinking, obviously, and I'd decided to join her, partly in a show of solidarity, and partly because I was already plenty lightheaded from the blood I'd given.

According to Anastasia, we would eventually be able to scale back to weekly feedings, and then phase those feedings out entirely somewhere around the last trimester, but first, I had to make it through at least two weeks of daily feedings.

By the end of those two weeks, I suspected I'd be really tired.

Of Lucia, if nothing else.

Once we switched to weekly feedings, Lucia would hopefully return to Rome, but for now, she seemed committed to staying glued to Ana's side, lending blood every night while spending the rest of the day being… well… Lucia.

Those hundred years of freedom she'd given us had sure gone by fast.

The most annoying thing about it was that I couldn't even complain. Ana needed us both, and Lucia voluntarily putting her queendom on pause to care for her friend was objectively admirable.

Still, I gave it less than a week before she tried to kill me again.

"Where is Zorana?" I asked, after Lucia had finally finished regaling Anastasia with all the amazing things that had happened in Rome in the five days that they had been apart.

The queen favored me with an imperious look. "She and some of the Crown Watch are at my former House."

My blood went cold. Whatever was left of it anyway. "What?"

Lucia waved the hand that held her wine. "Be calm, my—" She paused, and reconsidered. "Mr. Smith, that is. Those traitorous fools have nothing to fear from me. A queen may afford to be magnanimous."

"Since when?"

"Since I chose to make it so."

Anastasia headed off the inevitable trading of insults by nestling deeper into my embrace. Her hair, glossy and free of tangles, tickled my chin and the side of my face, and I breathed in the scent of her. By the time I breathed back out again, the words that had been on the tip of my tongue were gone, along with the irritation that virtually any conversation with Lucia provoked.

"I informed my queen that I would not have Zorana stay under this roof. Under *our* roof," Ana told me. "Not with you present, along with Gustavo and Teresa. Her assistance with my condition was appreciated, but the slate is far from clean."

"Precisely. And she will need to pack up her things anyway if she is to return to Rome." Lucia drained her glass, and glanced over the charcuterie board, ruby lips curving as she took the piece of prosciutto I had clearly been eyeing for the last few minutes. She popped it into her mouth, chewing it with exaggerated relish.

I swallowed my annoyance and took another sniff of Anastasia's hair. If I could bottle that scent and sell it on a commercial scale, I was willing to bet divorce rates would drop across the world.

"You're sending her back by herself?"

"The Kingmaker will meet her in Rome. Zorana needs structure, and as we all know, my beloved uncle is as stiff and unbending as the city's aqueducts, if not quite as old. His presence will suffice until I return."

"Are you certain you can afford the time away, my Queen?"

"Asya, we have spoken on this already. As you well know, the court measures its intrigues in decades, not days. Two, even three months here will hardly cause a stir."

"Did you say *months?*"

Icy blue eyes met mine across the table. "I will not spend two days of travel time every week to commute back and forth between Rome and San Diego, Mr. Smith."

So, she would be around until the start of the third trimester. Fabulous.

"I bet your room at the House is still available," I said, not even trying to be subtle.

She sniffed. "As if I would spend a minute there after it was befouled by the former Duke Barros."

"I have invited the queen to stay with us, John," said Anastasia.

"Right." It was Ana's house, not mine, whether I had a key to it or not, but… "Any thoughts on how we stop the dreams then?"

"I believe our time together in Rome taught me how to keep you out of my dreams," said Lucia, "and perhaps even how to settle yours."

"That was before we blew our bond open," I reminded her. "Frankly, I'm shocked we didn't share dreams last night."

"I did not sleep yesterday," admitted Lucia.

"Seriously?" At my age, an all-nighter left me looking like an extra from *The Walking Dead*. She had four hundred years on me and looked like she'd just stepped out of a magazine cover.

The Rich, the Gorgeous, and the Criminally Obnoxious.

I hated to admit it, but I'd totally pony up for a subscription, if only to count how many new objects were gold-plated in each issue.

"I am always serious. As you have aptly demonstrated, comedy is the refuge of those with nothing interesting to say."

"My Queen—"

"Now, *that* was a joke," Lucia said, seemingly delighted with herself. "Surely you can see the difference?"

"How did I know you would be into insult comedy?"

"Our bond, as you said, is wide open. I can only assume your intellect is growing marginally as you benefit from my presence."

"Another joke, Your Majesty?" asked Ana.

"For your sake and that of your unborn child, I dearly hope not, Lady Dumenyova."

Not even the ambrosia that was Anastasia's nearness could keep me from grinding my teeth.

○○○

A few hours later, we stood on the balcony and watched the sun set over the Pacific, hues of orange, red, and purple spreading out across the ocean's dark waters. The wind off the beach was cold, the vanguard of autumn's arrival, but even so, there was something peaceful about the moment: Anastasia standing in front of me, my hands resting on a stomach that was as flat and rock solid as ever, the slow and steady murmur of the waves washing against the shoreline.

To nobody's surprise, it was a moment that couldn't last.

To my amazement, it wasn't Lucia who broke the peace.

"Sorry," I said, as my phone buzzed persistently in my pocket, "I probably need to get that."

I frowned at the name showing on the call and put on my metaphorical PI hat—a fedora, obviously—before answering.

"Hey Susan, what can I do for you?"

"How about the job I hired you for?"

"Trust me, there's no agency in the city working harder on your behalf," I said, hoping she wouldn't realize that was because we were the only agency she'd hired.

"So, you have someone tailing Michael? Because he left the house. At night. Again."

I frowned. "What was his excuse this time?"

"He said he got word that someone broke into a job site, so he's heading over to secure it. I offered to come, but of course he refused."

I was about ninety-five percent sure Angel wouldn't be following Mike, not with Juliette having just come back from New Mexico, and the pair no doubt getting reacquainted with one another. If I wanted to get to the bottom of this case, if I wanted to prove Angel wrong, or give Mike a piece of my mind if he really was cheating, this was the perfect opportunity.

"We're on top of it," I told Susan. "Don't worry."

I ended the call before she could demand information I didn't have.

"I assume you have to go?" asked Ana.

"Sorry, but yeah. The sooner I get this off my plate, the happier I'll be. Whether I end up a friend down or not."

"I hope there is an alternate explanation."

"For my sake?"

"Yes. And because their wedding was lovely, and I would not have the memory of you in a tuxedo tarnished by your friend's actions."

On the other side of the balcony, Lucia guzzled her fifth glass of wine. I'd have said something, but at least it was keeping her mouth full.

"I'll be back as soon as I can," I promised. "Don't wait up though. You need your sleep."

"I believe you are correct." Anastasia yawned. "I continue to feel fatigued and out of sorts."

"Hopefully, that'll go away as soon as we get your blood equalized again." And hopefully, it *wouldn't* be replaced with morning sickness.

"I will be accompanying you," announced Lucia.

I rolled my eyes. "No offense, Lucia, but I don't think Ana needs you to sleep in our bedroom. There are plenty of other rooms available."

The queen scowled. "I will be accompanying *you*, Mr. Smith, on your nighttime rendezvous."

"Oh." I already knew I wouldn't have a choice in the matter, but… "Why?"

"Two reasons, human. First, your life is, for a brief and painful moment, secondary in importance only to mine and Lady Dumenyova's. Without you, both child and mother could be lost, and while I believe we could avoid that issue simply by draining you entirely of your blood and storing it properly, to be mixed with my blood before each feeding, my suggestions to do so have been largely ignored. As a result, you must be kept safe."

I didn't even know what to say to that. Part of me was surprised Lucia had managed to think up an alternate solution, and part of me wasn't surprised in the slightest she'd actually proposed it to Anastasia. "And second?"

"I wish to have words with you."

I sighed. "I already got your blessing, Lucia."

"Yes, you did." I could feel just what the femmepire queen thought about that, but she at least opted not to give those thoughts voice. "Nevertheless."

"Fine. It's your limo anyway."

"Yes, it is."

We escorted Ana to her room, where I kissed her goodbye. Again. It felt odd to leave her behind, when she was the only truly competent one of the three of us, but the brief burst of energy she'd had after feeding was clearly starting to fade.

"John," she said to me, as we parted after one final hug, "friend or not, remember that this is a job, and you have a client. Whatever you discover, choose to follow your brain and not your heart."

"Juliette gave me the exact same speech in New Mexico."

"Did she?" Anastasia cocked her head. "I am glad to hear it. Perhaps I will factor that single piece of solid advice into the conversation she and I will be having in the foreseeable future."

"Conversation?"

"About werewolves, kidnappings, unsanctioned feedings from the man I love, and, of course, leaving you alone to deal with Kcythxcklmnrtvsphlskz."

I wasn't even vaguely surprised she knew how to pronounce Kevin's real name. "She's my friend," I said simply.

"That too will factor into the conversation."

I reminded myself to send Juliette a warning. Anastasia was the least bloodthirsty vampire I knew, but she *did* seem to make exceptions when it came to me.

With a nod to Anastasia, Lucia led the way downstairs, looking like an overexposed photo in her white, hip-length coat, blouse, skirt, heels, and purse. We traded nods with Claudia and a member of the Crown Watch I didn't recognize and followed them out into the crisp night air.

The limo was waiting right where Castor and I had left it.

"Where are we going, Mr. Smith?" asked Lucia, once the four of us were seated within.

That was a great question. I'd texted Angel to ask for an address, but our receptionist/junior investigator hadn't answered. Thankfully, I was pretty sure I'd recognized the location where Mike had been photographed making out with not-Susan.

"Pacific Beach," I said, raising my voice so our purely human driver could hear. "Crystal Pier."

"How do you know the target will be there?" asked Claudia, taking notes on her gleaming black phone.

"He's not a target… he's my friend. And it's where he met the woman last time."

"So, this Susan person was correct to be suspicious?" Lucia nodded, as if to herself. "She seems intelligent for a human. Pity she did not bend her mate to her will before he could choose to stray."

"You're *never* getting married." I made it a statement instead of a question.

"Of course not. Even were it common practice amongst our kind—and it is not—I have little interest in allowing someone to make demands upon my time or emotions."

"That's what I figured." Also, anyone who *did* marry her would set a speed record for requesting a divorce the very moment they sobered up.

I could practically feel her pick that thought off the top of my brain, our physical closeness such that it didn't even require effort to send words across the bond. I sent a smile right after, deciding that she could figure out on her own whether I, too, was a budding insult comic.

"It'll be at least thirty minutes to get there," I said aloud, as we started up the steep hill to the 5. "What is it you wanted to talk about?"

Lucia gave Claudia and the other guy a sharp look. "I will be conversing with my thrall across our bond. Focus on preparing for the tasks I have assigned you."

"Yes, Your Majesty." Their reply came in chorus. I still needed to ask what the dude's name was. Caden? Cristo? Coriander? I was pretty sure that last one was a kind of spice, but I'd already met a vampire named after a vegetable, for God's sake.

What did you want to talk about? I asked again, this time in my mind, using a connection that would have been the coolest thing ever if it weren't for the woman at the other end.

I am no happier with our arrangement than you are, Mr. Smith, said Lucia, responding to the thought I *hadn't* meant to send. *As for my intentions, I wish to discuss Lady Dumenyova's pregnancy.*

I think Juliette has dibs on being the godmother.

What?

I'm just saying… She lives here. You don't. Maybe you can be a friendly but inevitably distant aunt or something instead.

I have words of my own for Juliette Middleton, promised Lucia, in a mental tone that had me moving *warn Juliette* way up on the priority list, *yet neither she nor this godparent nonsense are subjects I care to discuss today.*

Okay? Then what do you want to know?

I already know what I must. I hardly need one such as you to provide answers.

I sighed. Telepathic dialogue with Lucia was somehow even *more* tiring than the real thing.

I'm all ears, I finally said. *Figuratively speaking.*

Your child, she said, in words so clear I could almost hear them, *is an abomination.*

Wait just a second—

They are an offense against nature and a crime against the heavens. There is no telling what they will be or become, let alone what damage they might cause along the way.

That sounds like every *baby to me.*

This is not a joke, Mr. Smith.

No, you talking shit about our unborn child is the joke. A baby that you also kind of had a part in.

And yet, the truth remains.

I don't care. Ten hours ago, I didn't expect to ever be a dad, and honestly, I'm pretty sure I'm going to suck at it. But boy or girl or bat-winged, scorpion-tailed hippo hybrid, this baby will be mine and Ana's. And if you really are her friend—

I paused.

Wait, if you feel so strongly about our baby, why are you even helping? Isn't there some sort of Plan B pill you should be trying to force on Ana instead?

I am helping because Lady Dumenyova has earned as much. She desires this child, whatever its nature, and I will see to it that it is born.

But—

Which does not change the truth of its nature nor how the world will respond to it. Half my council would demand the infant be slain out of hand. Much of the other half would take it away so that it could be studied, as something that might be the twisted solution to my species' own fertility concerns.

And you?

I will stand by Asya, as she has stood by me, even should the world stand against us.

That was not where I'd seen this going.

Then... what was all this about?

I am informing you of the reality of the situation. Build your crib, plan your baby shower, reveal the gender through pyrotechnics that imperil your own home and its surrounding environment, but know that this child—your child—will have the world set against it even before it draws its first breath.

I can live with that.

Yes. Her wintry blue eyes met mine. *But can you die for it?*

For once, I didn't flinch. *I think I answered that in Rome.*

Lucia was the first to blink, turning to look out the window as San Diego slid by. *I suppose you did. I will do all I can to keep this pregnancy a secret, but should word leak out...* She shook her head. *Whether on the run or under someone's thumb, your child will not have a normal life. You will not have a normal life.*

I'm a PI turned supernatural mediator. My best friend might be having an affair four months after his wedding. My other best friend is a vampire who works for a living and has an unnatural obsession with punk music. I eat ice cream with a demigod, talk philosophy with a fungus, drink tea with nagas, and accidentally usher in new systems of government for werewolves. What part of any of that sounds normal to you?

There wasn't much Lucia could say in response. I let my satisfaction at finally winning an argument seep across the bond, confident—this once—that she wouldn't try to kill me for it.

After a long moment of blessed mental silence, she spoke again.

Why would your baby have bat wings or a scorpion tail?

They wouldn't. I was making a point. I frowned. *Why ask about those aspects and not it being a hippo hybrid?*

I have seen both you and hippopotamuses feed and found myself largely unable to distinguish between the two. That part is at least within reason, but scorpion tails? She shook her head. *I think not.*

Funny.

I am thrilled you finally have the wit to appreciate true humor. Perhaps these next few months will not be as tedious as I feared. But Mr. Smith?

Yeah?

Her eyes blazed like stars, and the temperature in the car dropped to 'I bet my tongue would stick to this flagpole' levels of freezing.

Hear this, and hear it well, she said, each word thrust down the bond like a spear. *Whatever you say, whatever you believe, there is no power in this world that can stop me should I decide to become the child's godparent. Accept that reality or perish.*

In a very Lucia-like way, it was almost sweet.

Chapter 39
IN WHICH PIER PRESSURE IS NO BASIS
FOR A RELATIONSHIP

We were ten minutes out when Claudia cleared her throat from across the limo. "Your Majesty?" she asked. The black-clad femmepire had cheekbones that could give Juliette a run for their money and a level stare that reminded me uncomfortably of my third-grade teacher, Mrs. Jefferson.

"You may speak."

She gave the queen a short bow, a neat trick since we were all still sitting down, and turned to me. "What is the situation on the ground? Exactly what are we walking into?"

"There's not much to say. Or to worry about, from a security perspective, I guess. As you probably already gathered, the target—" I winced. I didn't even like it when *I* said it. "Rather, *Mike* is suspected of cheating on his wife. I was hired to prove this was the case."

I didn't mention the photos that *already* proved it.

"And what is this… Mike? Besides your friend?"

"A lying asshole, apparently."

"I'm sorry?"

"He is but a mundane human," interjected Lucia.

Oh. Right. "Yeah, he was my best friend growing up."

"I will be with Mr. Smith throughout the encounter," said Lucia.

Claudia nodded. "So, our role will be to secure the perimeter and ensure that there are no attacks from the rear?"

"That sounds good to me." I wasn't entirely sure why we were treating this like a military operation in enemy territory, but I wasn't going to complain about it. Not this time, anyway. Safety was a good thing.

On a Monday night, Pacific Beach was only mildly less chaotic than on the weekends. Our limo got some looks—albeit not as many as an out-of-towner might expect—while making its way through the ever-present traffic before it finally stopped at the lot closest to the pier. Claudia and Coriander exited the limo first, like Secret Service agents scoping out the environment. I was next, followed by Lucia, the queen's white-on-white-on-white ensemble ensuring that we had no chance in hell of sneaking up on anyone, even in the dark.

"That's Mike's car over there," I said, nodding to the candy apple red '66 Mustang in the lot. I couldn't see the fuzzy dice hanging from its rearview mirror, but I knew they were there. "I guess he's not even bothering to vary their meeting spots. That means he should be out on the pier itself."

"Let us finish this task then and be on our way," said Lucia.

"Right. Maybe you should hang back and let me talk with him first? This could be awful. And awkward."

"I have become accustomed to such things since making your acquaintance, my thrall, and I will not have Lady Dumenyova perish because you chose privacy over security. We go together or not at all."

"Fine. They're going to see you coming from a mile away though." Against my better judgment and all basic laws of humanity, I found myself offering her my arm. "We might blend better as a couple."

"I do believe my ancestors just turned in their graves."

"Please; I've *seen* your memories. This barely even rates on your personal scale of romantic cringe. Starting with, but by no means limited to, the Horny God himself."

"What Asya sees in you remains one of life's great mysteries." She sniffed, but took my arm anyway, her skin, as always, uncomfortably warm. I would have pitied anyone, man or woman, forced to cuddle her in the heights of summer… if it wasn't impossible to imagine Lucia ever cuddling.

Behind us, the two Crown Watch members spread out, silent and ever watchful. And if they had any thoughts on our repartee, let alone my odd relationship with the queen and her *Secundus*, they were smart enough to keep those thoughts private.

Crystal Pier was almost a hundred years old, wide enough to have a row of cottages on each side of its initial length, while still leaving sufficient room for a marching band to parade right down the center. With the sun having long since set, the usual crowds were absent, but there were still quite a few people wandering up and down its wooden length, enjoying the night air and gazing out over the waters. There were a fair number of couples too, some wrapped around each other simply for warmth, others sucking face like nobody was watching. Lucia and I fit right in, more or less. Any looks we got were mostly for the queen, followed by the kind of puzzled glances my way that I'd become all too accustomed to in dating Anastasia.

This time, those looks didn't bother me. After all, I wasn't dating *Lucia;* I felt no need to justify what I, as a man of at-best average appeal, was doing with the kind of woman whose mere existence could stop traffic.

I don't think anyone noticed Claudia or Coriander traveling in our wake, even though both were vampires too, and thus, preternaturally attractive in their own right. Lucia was undoubtedly the star of the show, just the way she liked it.

"That's him," I said, as we left the cottages behind. Mike stood at the very end of the pier, where the walkway widened into a large square. He was alone, gazing out over the waves, dressed in the pink button-up he'd always called his #1 date-shirt, work boots poking out from under his nicest pair of jeans.

"Are you certain he's not part troll?"

I shrugged. "He's a big dude, yeah, but there isn't a violent bone in his body. And he's headed off more than one barfight just by buying everyone involved a beer."

"Perhaps *he* should be the mediator then?"

"That would only work until one of the involved parties compelled him."

"Ah yes. Sometimes, I forget that you are unique in that regard."

"Was that… a compliment?"

"It was not." She frowned. "Where is his supposed paramour?"

"I'm guessing he's waiting for her still?" I guided Lucia to the side of the pier, where we could keep an eye on Mike from a distance. "We should hang out until she shows."

"I am well familiar with the concept of *proof*, my thrall, and that a man standing by himself does not constitute such." She released my arm and leaned back against the pier's wooden railings, looking for all the world like an influencer posing for her seventeenth photoshoot of the day. "What shall we do while we wait?"

"My vote is for silent meditation."

"Maybe you and Asya *do* make a good pair." She shook her head, platinum blonde hair shimmering like silk.

"There's no maybe about it." Although to be honest, I wasn't really into meditation. It just seemed more appealing than *another* conversation with Lucia. Still, as long as we were stuck out here waiting… "How is Princess Sabina doing?"

"Are you not in contact with both her and her flirt of a friend?"

"More Maria Elena than Sabina, to be honest. And even then, I mostly just get grainy pics from whatever bar or nightclub they end up going to."

"My niece does enjoy the social aspects of her position." Lucia, against all odds, actually sounded mildly approving. "Thankfully, she has begun to apply herself to mastering the political side as well. She has decades before she will be ready to take the throne, but her time on the council serves her well."

"And gives you an extra vote in your pocket, I'm guessing."

For the first time since we'd left the car, Lucia's eyes locked onto mine, and she tilted her head in a gesture I was pretty sure she had stolen from Anastasia. "That is far more insightful than I would have expected from someone of your limited means and background."

I let the backhanded compliment slide past me, like wind from the ocean. "I saw how the council worked when I was there. It's not a huge leap of logic to realize that stacking the deck in your favor would be a good thing. Especially with people like Dog and Vigo still presiding."

"In truth, Duke Marte," she said, referring to Vigo by title, "has performed quite the turnaround since my innocence was thoroughly proven. His desperation to return to my good graces has been gratifyingly pathetic."

"And Divya? The Lady Manassa, I mean?"

"She was naturally always in my good graces as both a steadfast ally and loyal supporter," said Lucia, conveniently forgetting that she'd been utterly convinced the naga was involved in her brother's murder. "However, I suspect she and her daughters will be leaving Rome soon to return to India. Tomasso has been mourned, avenged, and buried, yet the palace holds far too many memories for one such as she."

"I can understand that—" I stopped, forgetting that I was supposed to be incognito as I turned to face the end of the pier. A figure, dripping wet, had just finished climbing the outside of the pier. As I watched, she flipped over the railings to land in a low crouch, slowly rising back up on wobbly feet as she looked about.

Somehow, I wasn't shocked at all to see her march toward Mike.

"You're seeing this too, right?" Nobody else on the pier had reacted, which told me either this was a common occurrence, or the newcomer was more than just an odd woman who liked to swim in the ocean and scale wooden piers like a mountain climber.

"I am." An iron grip on my shoulder held me in place, even as Lucia signaled to the two guards with us. "Wait until you have your proof, my thrall. In the meantime, the Crown Watch will cut off any escape routes."

Given that the target—and I had no issue whatsoever calling this strange woman that—had come out of the ocean and was now standing on a pier surrounded by that same ocean, I wasn't sure how Claudia and Coriander would be able to accomplish that... but I also wasn't a trained professional in these matters.

"What is she?" I'd seen the Mer, and this woman was no Mer, though the pier's lights shimmered off something that might be scales.

"A siren, I suspect. Flighty as a pixie and with half the brain for all their size. This one appears old enough to leave the water, yet too young to trawl the depths for her prey."

"*Prey?* I'm not going to stand here while she eats him—"

"Sirens are like succubi, Mr. Smith, if far less formidable. They take their nourishment in a hundred small meals."

"Do you think she compelled him? Or is he here on his own, fooled by her glamour into thinking she's human?"

"I think the line between willingness and compulsion when dealing with what your mind tells you is a beautiful woman is razor-thin and sharp enough to shave off that thing you call a beard, my thrall."

"I don't agree. At all."

"And yet, I have seen you led around by your nose by more than one such woman." She sniffed again, her disdain practically a physical presence. "If she *has* ensnared your friend, we will need to force her to release him. Move before the stage is properly set, and all could be lost."

"You sound almost like Anastasia sometimes."

"And wouldn't my instructors be proud to hear that, were they not all dead and buried, as deeply dull now as they were every day of their dry, pointless lives?"

Nobody had asked me, but I was really starting to question Lucia's suitability as a role model and regent for Princess Sabina.

I hadn't seen our two guards slip past us, but they were somehow already at the far end of the pier, each taking up positions that flanked Mike and his supernatural potential seductress. Claudia looked back and nodded in our direction, and Lucia took up my arm again.

"Slowly, my thrall. We are but another ill-fated romantic pairing, out for one last walk together before I shatter your sense of self-worth forever by ending the relationship. You should have ample experience to act out this scenario."

"And *now* you sound like Juliette."

"Bite your tongue, lest I have Constantin do it for you."

Constantin, not Coriander? At least it fit the naming convention.

We closed the distance between us and the siren. Neither she nor Mike saw us coming, both lost in their own world as they locked lips like teenagers trying to squeeze in every second of smooching before curfew. The siren was only marginally taller than Lucia, which meant Mike topped her by well over a foot; even with her clawed and webbed feet wrapped around the railing's lowest rung she still had to tilt her head upwards so he could bend down to kiss her.

My PI instincts kicked in as we approached, and I took a handful of pictures that put Angel's earlier efforts to shame. The siren was mostly human-looking, with long dark hair and skin that, while slightly blue, could pass for simply being pale under the moonlight. The scales and eyes that were entirely black were a little bit harder to camouflage, however. Clearly, she had some sort of glamour in effect.

Idly, I checked my phone and saw she was human in every picture. And gorgeous to boot. Huh.

Mike never picked up on our approach at all, but we were ten feet away when the siren stiffened in his arms. Before she could move, Lucia was just *there*, leaving me behind like I was standing still, a golden hand wrapped around the other woman's neck.

"And where were you thinking of going, little one?"

"What do you want, vampire?" The siren didn't *look* like a Mer, but she kind of sounded like they did, all clicks and gurgles instead of the melodious tones that were supposed to lure sailors to their doom. "This meal is mine!"

Mike just stood there, saying nothing, eyes blank and distant. To my experienced eye, he might as well have been wearing a sign saying *I've been compelled through no fault of my own to become fish food*, and I spent the next few seconds silently apologizing for every bad thought I'd had about him since New Mexico.

"—already claimed by another," Lucia was saying, when I finally turned my attention back to her and the siren.

"Another what?" demanded the siren. For someone caught in the grip of a far stronger opponent, she showed a serious lack of self-preservation.

"A human," I said, cutting in. "His wife."

She ignored me, still turned toward Lucia. "When have such as we ever let other humans stand in the way of destiny? Or are you saying that you, yourself, have never poached from another?"

"This is neither a discussion nor a negotiation," said Lucia, hand tightening on the other woman's neck, even as frost started to gather about us. "Release him or perish."

"Should I die, he will never be free."

"Yet you will still be dead."

I recognized a Mexican standoff when I saw one, and not just because Mike was a second-generation immigrant.

"There's no need for anyone to die here," I said, switching hats from private investigator to mediator in the sort of fluid shift that would have made even Hyacinth jealous. "Let him go, be more judicious in your future meals, and you can walk away. Or… swim away. Whichever it is that you do."

"Why do you let this human speak to me, vampire?"

"I'm John Smith," I said, cutting in before Lucia could reply. Judging by the emotions swelling across the bond, the queen had already reached the limits of her patience. That was fast, even for Lucia, but I was pretty sure I still held the all-time speed record for pissing her off. "San Diego's mediator."

The siren formed a silent *O* with her mouth, the parallels to a fish unfortunate and undeniable. "You are working with the Mer."

"At the moment, yeah."

"Then you surely know of my kind as well. Would you have me starve, mediator?"

I mean… if the alternative was her killing people up and down the coastline, the answer was *kind of* yes, but saying so seemed counterproductive.

"No," I said instead, "but your choice of prey is problematic. He has a wife and a family. If he dies, they will dig into why, and who knows what they might find?"

"Dies?" Her alien features weren't great at conveying emotion, but she seemed offended. "Why would he die?"

"Aren't you eating him?"

"A bit at a time! I would never take so much that he perished. What sort of a monster do you take me for?"

One with scales, teeth like a shark, and a penchant for married men, I very carefully did not say.

"No children, not ever," she continued, "and no kills either, save those lost at sea and already presumed gone. Those are the laws of our people, and I have not broken them."

"I'm glad to hear that," I admitted. And I truly was, because otherwise, my conscience would have struggled with the idea of letting her go. "However, I'm still going to have to ask you to let this one go."

"But I love him!"

"What?"

I felt Lucia's eyeroll across the bond, an utterly disturbing sensation given the telepathic setting. *All sirens are like this, my thrall. Serial monogamists, and each new target eclipses all targets before it.*

"Have you ever *spoken* to him?" I asked the siren.

"Well…"

"What's his name?"

She screwed up her face, and for the first time, I saw the gills in her neck flapping. She'd already been out of the water longer than Glub had been on Bill's boat but showed no signs of fatigue or strain.

"Is it Fabio?" she finally asked.

"God, no." Although part of me wished Mike was conscious enough to hear her call him that.

"Rufus?"

I just sighed. "What is your name?"

"Lillithilan."

I blinked and took a desperation shot in the dark. "Is it okay if I call you Lily?"

"That's *not* my name."

"Okay… well, if you don't know *his* name, and you've never even spoken to him, I don't think you can say you're actually in love."

"Our bodies speak for us."

"*His* body is—" I stopped. "Actually, I have no interest in talking about my best friend's body, now or ever. The problem is… you've compelled him."

"And?"

"And nothing says *I love you* less than forcing that person to be with you."

She screwed up her face again, but this time, it looked like she was about to cry. Seconds later, my premonition proved correct as fat tears, far too large for human tear ducts, slid down her face. "Are you saying it's over?!"

I held back my sigh. "Sure. Let's go with that. It's time to let him go."

More tears. "I really… I really thought he was the one."

"I'm sure your true love is still out there waiting." And if he was smart, he'd avoid the ocean like the plague.

"You really think so?" Just like that, the tears were gone, absorbed right back into her pale blue flesh. "Really truly really?"

"Of course. After all, there's plenty of fish in the—I mean, a lot of humans wandering the earth."

"*Too* many, by most rational people's standards."

I didn't reward Lucia with a response.

"Will he be a prince?" asked Lily.

"Maybe? It feels like you can't take a step without tripping over royalty these days." I shot the femmepire queen a look. "That said, if I can make one suggestion…?"

"Of course!" Lily had seemingly forgotten Mike's existence entirely, black eyes fixed on my face, mouth hanging wide open to show off her needle-sharp teeth. "Anything!"

"Maybe talk to your next meal first. Make sure he's single?"

"Why?"

"So he can love you with all his heart."

"Oh." The smile that spread across her face was truly horrifying, but I tried to keep my reaction hidden. "Yes! I like that!"

"Great." Part of me still struggled with the idea of letting a predator go so she could keep hunting, but… was Lily any different from vampires in that way? Hell, *Lucia* had plucked two random strangers off the beach in the past two days. As long as nobody was dying, could I begrudge another sentient species their sustenance?

It's not the sort of dilemma you'll solve right now, I told myself. *Better to hold off until there's plenty of time and even more beer.*

What? came Lucia's voice in my head.

Nothing. I wasn't thinking that to you.

I focused back on the siren in front of me. "So, we're in agreement then?"

"We are! I will tell my sisters that the stories told of you are not true, Mediator Smith!" She tried to turn back to the railing but was stymied by Lucia's heavy-handed grip. "Excuse me? Vampire? Hello?"

"You need to release Mike first," I reminded her.

"Who's Mike?"

"Rufus."

"Oh. Oh! You're right." She patted Mike's face with a webbed hand. "I'm sorry, Rufus. It's not me, it's you. My true love is out there and this was never going to last." She trilled a series of notes that sounded, to me anyway, kind of like baby's first attempt at music, and I watched the light slowly turn back on in my friend's eyes.

"I knew it!" screeched a voice I unfortunately recognized, so loud that even the nearby teenagers stopped their kissing to see what was going on. "You lying asshole!"

Mike was shaking his head, clearing cobwebs that had gathered through no fault of his own. He hadn't even noticed me yet, but his eyes widened as he looked to the source of that noise.

"Susie?"

CHAPTER 40
IN WHICH HARD DECISIONS ARE MADE
BY SOMEONE ELSE

I don't know what Claudia and Constantin had been doing, but Mike's wife, red-faced and furious, had made it almost all the way to us before they reacted. It was almost like they had simply discounted her as a threat due to her being human, a decision that spoke poorly of the Crown Watch's judgment outside of the statue-strewn halls of Villa d'Borghesi.

Susan ignored both Lucia and me, stepping past us to stick a finger in Mike's face. "This is the *work* you've been doing, Michael? Some dark-haired floozy?"

"It's not... I don't... What?" Mike finally stopped shaking his head long enough to take notice of Lily, still close enough to touch. "Who are you? What's going on?"

"And now you've got amnesia? Real believable!"

"It's okay," said Lily, smiling that grotesque smile neither my friend nor his wife could apparently see. "Rufus isn't my true love after all! You can have—"

I'm not going to say Susan's slap came in at vampire speed or anything, but I was pretty sure *I* wouldn't have been able to avoid it.

Lily, who seemed to be anticipating a thank you, didn't have a chance. Her scaled head snapped back, and her strange black eyes widened. She hissed, like a feral alley cat, and held her webbed hands in front of her, and began to sing.

"Nope." I stepped between the two women, my still-confused best friend towering over all of us. "We're not doing that, ladies. Not now, and not ever."

I sensed more than saw Lily swipe at me from behind and heard an impact and pained cry as her blow was stopped cold by a black-clad vampire. Claudia may have discounted Susan as a threat, but she was on the ball when it came to the supernatural.

"This is not what it looks like, Susan," I told my friend's angry wife. "Seriously."

"Isn't that supposed to be *his* line? How long did you know? How long have you been stringing me along, John?"

"If you would just take a breath and calm down, I can explain."

In the history of the world, the times that telling an angry someone to calm down has worked can be counted on a single hand. And not a human hand, but a goblin one, meaning four fingers at most, and even then only if said goblin somehow made it to adulthood with all of their fingers intact.

Shockingly, I didn't add to that number.

"Michael can tell me himself. He doesn't need you to protect him. Not you and not your partner—" She scowled, finally taking in Lucia's appearance for the first time. A note of incredulity entered her voice. "Really? Another one? And you wanted me to believe they *weren't* prostitutes?"

"Constantin," said Lucia, voice cold as ice. "Bring me that one's tongue."

Coriander, if he had ever been anything but a figment of my imagination, would never have followed that order. Constantin, on the other hand, had apparently grown up to be a Grade-A bootlicker. He moved toward Susan.

I pulled on Lucia's speed and interposed myself between the guard and his target.

"Nobody's taking anyone's tongue," I said, with a glare that encompassed both Constantin and Lucia. "Nobody's calling people names either."

"Don't forget about me! I was slapped!" Lily seemed torn between delight and dismay.

"What the hell is going on?" asked Mike. The sleepy confusion was starting to leave his voice, replaced by a growing anger.

"You know *exactly* what's going on, Michael!"

"Everyone needs to chill for like thirty seconds." I didn't raise my voice, but I *did* pull on Lucia's power sufficiently to coat the pier around us in more frost. "Be quiet, and I will explain. But first…" I turned to Lily. "Is it done? Is… uh… Rufus free?"

"Is anyone truly free when fate is in play?" She dropped her head at whatever expression she saw in my face. "His will is his own. He was not the one."

"I think you should probably take off then. Maybe head up the coast a bit? There are a lot of pretty people in L.A."

"There is no love in the City of Angels," she told me. "Just faded dreams and base instincts."

Apparently, we had similar views on the city. "Maybe try Del Mar then? Or Oceanside? Anywhere but here?"

"I will go where my heart takes me," she said brightly, patting her bony, scaled chest. "Eyes open and with a song in my soul." She turned to Mike and Susan. "Goodbye, Rufus. Goodbye, strange shouty thing. May you know for even an instant the blessing and favor of love, and may it inspire you each to dance below the waves."

I owed Glub an apology, maybe over a lager. After meeting my first siren, the Mer seemed downright normal. And far, far less annoying.

With a chirp and another trilling note that seemed more goodbye than songspell, Lily hopped over the railing, a splash announcing her return to the Pacific.

Moments later, Susan blinked. "Wait… what? Where did the floozy go?"

"What floozy?" I asked innocently.

"The one who was—" Her voice trailed off, as she looked about us. "No, I don't know where she went, but she was right here. I'm not crazy."

"I think that might make one of us, Suze," said Mike, running a hand over his face. "Where are we? Is this Crystal Pier? How did I get here? And why am I wearing my #1 date shirt?"

With Lily gone, I could focus on the crisis that was my best friend and his marriage. The problem was, I didn't know what to do. Part of me wanted to just spill the beans, like I had with Sheriff Abbas back in Ghost Falls. Mike—and by extension, Susan—knowing the truth about the world wasn't the worst thing ever, was it? It would take some convincing, sure, but it would also make it clear that nothing that had happened was his fault… that a siren stealing some smooches from a man stuck under her spell was a very long way from that same man actively and willingly cheating.

Even better, it would mean I could take my best friend to the Bitter End.

On the other hand, it would potentially expose both him and Susan to the same sort of supernatural dangers that I dealt with on a near-daily basis… and they had neither my immunity to compulsion nor my ever-growing cadre of vastly more powerful friends to protect them.

With three vampires present, I could take the easy way out instead, and just have them compelled, all memory of Lily and Mike's supposed betrayal wiped from their minds. But despite every assurance to the contrary, I still wasn't certain that specific usage of glamour was entirely safe. I'd nearly blown a gasket when my mother was compelled by Duke Barros' lackey, Thales, and Mike was practically family too. Strangers were one thing, but did I really want to take a risk like that with my best friend?

The answer to that was a definite no. I opened my mouth to tell them everything, prepared to weather Susan's scorn and disbelief, when Lucia took the decision out of my hands, her eyes glowing golden.

"You followed your… husband…?" She nodded, as if to herself. "Yes, husband, Michael here to this pier, worried that he had been up to no good. Instead, you discovered that he had been planning a romantic dinner out as an apology for his recent late nights on the job."

"I had?" asked Mike, voice slow and once again confused.

"Really?" squeaked Susan. "That's so sweet!"

"It's because I love you, Suze," said Mike, the new reality settling into his brain. "I've been working hard to try take care of you, of us, and our little family, but I realized it's not just about money. It's about seeing to your emotional needs too. Only, the pier isn't as nice as I remember. I was thinking maybe a picnic at Balboa instead?"

I sent Lucia my own mental eyeroll. *Seriously? Isn't that laying things on a little bit thick?*

The fact that you think so tells me Asya has yet to train you properly. Rest assured, I will see to it that this changes before I return to Rome.

"A picnic would be lovely, and I'm sorry for doubting you," said Susan, in the surest sign yet that she was operating under Lucia's compulsion. "You know how I worry sometimes."

My friend folded her into his arms. "You never have to worry when it comes to me, babe."

We should have waited to send Lily away. She'd have eaten this Hallmark moment up.

You'd be surprised. For sirens, there's no such thing as making up. If there's an argument, it means they were never the one in the first place.

That was kind of sad. Not that I *wanted* to get into a fight with Anastasia, verbal or otherwise, but in my admittedly limited experience, making up was often a big part of growing up.

"Wait… why are *you* here, wey?" Mike asked me.

"As the best man at your wedding, Mr. Smith felt honor bound to ensure that this misunderstanding was resolved," said Lucia, in the sort of explanation that would not have flown *at all* without supernatural help.

"And you are?"

"Most decidedly *not* a prostitute."

"This is my girlfriend's former boss," I said.

Former and *future*, corrected Lucia.

"She's in town for God knows how long," I continued out loud. "I was showing her and some of her other employees the sights when we saw the two of you."

"Weren't… weren't you here when I got here?" asked Susan.

"That wouldn't make any sense at all, would it?"

She frowned. "No, I guess it wouldn't. I swear, this whole thing has me turned around."

"We should get you home, babe," said Mike. Either being compelled twice in a row made the whole story easier for him to swallow, or he was just naturally extra-susceptible to mental magic. "It's too cold for you to be running around without a jacket. We can order in tonight. Sandwiches?"

"Maybe noodles instead?"

"I can roll with that." He spared me a glance as they wandered off. "Catch you later, hombre."

"Sounds good. I still owe you that birthday dinner." I took a long breath and decided to be the better man. "And Susan, we'd love to have you join us. There will be cake."

"I don't eat cake anymore. Or processed sugar. But I'll consider it," she added, snuggling into her much bigger husband. "And maybe send you a list of acceptable restaurant options."

I waited until they were gone.

"You couldn't have fixed her personality while you were in there tinkering?"

"If you recall, *I* wanted to remove her tongue."

There was nothing I could say to that.

"Now then, do you wish to get your histrionics out of the way immediately, my thrall, or would you prefer to save them for the car ride north?"

"My what?"

"I know that you are overprotective and touchy when it comes to the people in your life."

"But you decided to compel them anyway?"

"It was a matter of expedience."

Annoyingly, I once again didn't have an argument, despite my misgivings. If she'd given me enough time to think, I might have asked her to compel them both anyway. Instead, she'd taken the choice out of my hands and unwittingly absolved me of any guilt in the matter.

"Why go with *that* story though? Couldn't you have convinced them both that none of this ever happened?"

"Of course. However, if the woman encountered other evidence of her past mistrust, whether through records she made or discussions she had had with individuals other than you, the cognitive dissonance would have created a strain on her mind. It is preferable to make the new reality as close as possible to the old. *Half a truth is often a great lie*, as one of your less idiotic founders once said."

"Abraham Lincoln?"

"Was *he* one of your country's founders?"

"George Washington then?"

"I should have Zorana check Lady Dumenyova for enchantments," decided Lucia, as she turned and marched back down the pier. "It would explain everything about your relationship."

ooo

An hour later, Anastasia and I were in bed, the queen thankfully bunked down two rooms away from us and the primary suite. I still wasn't convinced that distance would be enough to prevent any shared dreams, but we weren't spoiled for choice. For all its size, Ana's house held most of the bedrooms on the same floor and off the same hallway. The lone exception was the downstairs bedroom shared by Teresa and Gustavo, and there was no way in hell I was kicking them out just to increase my chances at a decent night of sleep.

"Are you well, Mr. Smith?"

'I think that's supposed to be my line," I reminded her.

"I am already returning to my full strength," she assured me. "You, on the other hand, appear more distracted than usual."

"It's been a really long week. It's hard to believe Kayla and Darlene got married just eight days ago. So much has happened since they took off for Australia."

"Then, you will have much to share with them when they return." I could hear the smile in her voice, even if my view was blocked by a headful of sweet-smelling hair. "You have a right to be exhausted, you know. Much of your life—much of *our* life together—is quiet and peaceful, but other times—"

"Yeah. Everything happens at once."

"Are you sure there is nothing else troubling you?"

I sighed. "No, I'm not."

Instead of pressing for more, Anastasia just waited, a comforting weight against my side.

The problem was, I didn't know what I wanted to say. I hadn't really formulated my thoughts yet, hadn't even known I needed to, really. That answer had just sort of slipped out of me, unprompted, and now I realized there was something bothering me.

As we lay there, and the silence grew, Anastasia shifted, rising up onto one elbow to look down on me. I didn't know if her glow was from the pregnancy, our most recent successful feeding, or simply a trick my mind was playing on my eyes, but she was especially lovely just then.

"I love you, John Smith. And whenever you wish to talk, I promise that I will listen. For now, I would suggest we both get some sleep."

"I'm scared," I said, forcing the words out.

Her only reaction was a slow nod. "Fear is often a healthy response. What are you scared of?"

"A lot of things. The future. Not being enough for you. Failure and the possible consequences when there's more at stake than just a goblin war. The fact that I can even say things like *just* a goblin war." I shook my head. "Lucia mindwiped Mike and Susan all on her own and I was glad about it, because it meant I could pretend that she overstepped and that I wouldn't have asked her to do it anyway."

"It was—"

"Yeah, I know. And I couldn't think of a better way to handle it, anyway. Still, this is my best friend. Not only did I let the creature that had been screwing with his mind go to no doubt snack on her next victim, I then stood by while someone else mucked with his brain even more. And on the way home, you know what I kept thinking about?"

"I do not."

"Shae, of all people."

"The werewolf Lady Middleton slew?"

"That's the one. The woman I elbowed in the face until she died."

"Even with as much death as you have seen, my heart, it is understandable that such things bother you. Admirable, even."

"That's the problem… I'm not sure it does. Bother me, that is. Tonight was the first time I even thought of Shae after we left the cave. I know she had it coming. I know it was her or us, and I don't regret her death, but even so, shouldn't I feel *something?*"

"So, your fear is that that you have grown callous?"

"It's not who I was raised to be." I swallowed. "I think I'm afraid of what I might be becoming."

"Change is inevitable," said Ana. "It is one lesson even the ancients learn. The only true stasis is death."

"I think Simon might have something to say on that front."

"True death," she clarified. "As for your fears…"

"I know," I said, forcing life back into my voice. "I'm being ridiculous. Let's just forget about it. A good night of sleep and I won't be such a mess, I promise."

"I killed my first man when I was eleven," said Anastasia, in a voice empty of emotion. "I am told he was a convict, given a knife and sent for me as a test of my training, but he could have been anyone, really. A peasant, taken from the fields. A father, snatched off the city streets. By the time I was your chronological age, two years after finally quenching the Thirst, I had enough bodies to my name to fill a small cemetery. That was more than a century before your country came into being, and the years where I did not add to that total have been few and far between."

"And here I am, complaining—"

"Killing takes a toll, Mr. Smith, whether it is your hand on the bloody weapon or another's. It took me multiple human lifetimes to realize that, to recognize that I could and should be more than just a knife in the darkness. It's a lesson I continue to learn, a lesson I continue to teach myself each day. Some deaths are unavoidable. Some deaths are justified. The world is better without some beings in it. But violence leaves its mark on all of us. It is to your credit that you already feel that mark and fear its deepening stain."

"What should I do about it?"

"Talk. If not to me, then to another. Inside, none of us is stone. The wounds we bury beneath the surface will continue to bleed unless they are treated. I do not have answers, let alone solutions, but I can promise that I will listen, I will love, and I will not judge."

I nodded, almost to myself, lost in her eyes. "That goes both ways, you know."

"Much like so many of the People."

I frowned for a moment, puzzled, before the meaning hit me. "Wait. Was that... a joke? Was that *my* joke?"

"I fear your humor might be contagious," she admitted. "Gods help us all."

"You've never been hotter than right now." I held my grin just long enough that she would know I meant it. "But I'm serious. I've been in this life for three years and most of my job is focused on *avoiding* conflict."

Not that I was doing a bang-up job of that, but still, it was the thought that counted, right?

"Meanwhile, you were a *Secundus* for centuries. I'm not so shallow or self-absorbed that I don't realize you've had it far worse than me. Any time you want to talk about any of it, whether to vent, to mourn, or just to remember, I am here."

"I know you are. Just as I know you are a good man."

"I'd say more like mediocre—"

"Good enough to be troubled by a momentary lack of compassion for enemies who would kill you and those you love. Good enough to willingly shoulder the burdens of those you encounter. Good enough for Queen Lucia to give us to one another."

I'd been kind of with her until that last bit. Lucia's whole life was a litany of bad decisions and worse judgment. The fact that one of those decisions had worked out in Ana and my favor didn't say a thing about my quality as a human being.

Anastasia turned my head back to her, her hand gentle even as the force she exerted was impossible to resist. She scooted up the bed to place a smooch on my forehead.

"Since the moment of our first meeting, you have been a breath of fresh air, John, a reminder that there is more to life than politics, death, and loneliness. If one such as I can ever be saved, then you are that salvation. Trust that I will do everything in my power to be yours."

"I do. I can. I will."

"Then trust also that you are enough for me."

I coughed. "I wasn't sure if you'd heard that part."

"Fear is natural," she reminded me. "But in this case, it is unwarranted."

"But I can't give blood—"

"These past two days have proven otherwise. Yes," she acknowledged, silencing my protests with a kiss. "I know that is not what you meant. And I know that when Teresa and Gustavo pass, it will introduce new challenges for us. I feed from you now because I must, but when this pregnancy is done, our time sharing blood will be too."

"I could—"

"There is neither satisfaction nor pleasure in causing you pain, John. I will need a donor. But we will meet that challenge, and every challenge after, together, as a family. And if you suggest for even a moment that you are insufficient or that I deserve better..."

"Yeah?"

"Then I will steal the blankets from you in the dead of the night, to leave you shivering in the air-conditioned cold you Americans prefer."

"You… kind of already do that."

"Yes. And only now have you learned why."

I… didn't *think* that was true, but to be honest, it was within the realm of possibilities. The femmepire was scarily perceptive sometimes.

"I just hope our daughter is half as smart as you," I sighed. "And that she shares *my* taste in hamburgers."

"Our daughter?" Ana arched an eyebrow. "What makes you think the child will be a girl?"

"I just get that feeling." I placed my palm against her stomach. "She's going to be a badass like her mom."

"I will make sure to tell our son about this prediction," promised Ana, "as a lesson that even the best of men is not infallible. And I hope *he* has your heart and my taste in entertainment."

"I don't think any child born in the twenty-first century is going to like opera, Ana, no matter what gender they end up being."

"We will see, Mr. Smith. We will see." She lowered herself back down to my chest, a cool hand snaking under the T-shirt to find bare skin. "For now, you should sleep. We will talk on the morrow, and every day after that."

"That's a lot of talking," I teased.

"We are worth it."

Normally, I fell asleep long before Ana, but for once, she was out mere seconds later, even as sleep continued to elude me. I hit the light switch and lay awake in the darkness. All my fear was still there, all my insecurities and doubts, but they seemed just a tiny bit more distant, somehow.

It wasn't much, but it was a start.

I held Ana close for a long while and listened to her breaths. Only when sleep finally started to close in on me, did I reach out to the part of me that was now all Lucia, all the time.

Goodnight, Lucia, I said. *And thank you for helping with Mike.*

Her response came immediately, the subdued tone to her thoughts ample evidence that two rooms' distance had not been enough to prevent eavesdropping.

Keep her safe, Mr. Smith. Keep her happy.

CHAPTER 41
IN WHICH THE PAST COMES CALLING

For the second time in three nights, my phone started buzzing just after 2 a.m., although this time, I couldn't remember the dream it interrupted. Which was either a sign that I'd been dreaming one of Lucia's memories and my brain had thankfully decided to scrub it away with bleach, or that the queen's promises to settle my own dreams still held true.

Either way, I fumbled for my wonderphone. At some point in the past several hours, Anastasia and I had moved to separate sides of the bed, but I knew she had likely awoken with the very first vibration. Still, I did my level best not to make *too* much noise as I rolled about like a beached whale.

"Yeah?" I croaked into my phone. I hadn't had a drop to drink the previous night—unless you counted blood, not alcohol—but it felt like something had crawled into my mouth and died.

"Is this your work, Smith?"

"What? Simon?"

"Yeah, it's Simon. How many other zombie princes do you even know?"

"Just you." I army crawled my way up the bed until I found my pillow again, then used that to prop myself up. "What are you talking about? What's going on?"

"Big energy pulse. Kind of reminds me of when those witches you killed last year were trapping ghosts. You sure you're not doing anything?"

"I was sleeping."

"At two?! I thought you were in your twenties."

"Goodnight, Simon."

"Whatever, kid. All I'm saying is, if it's not me and it's not you, you might want to stay away from whoever it is doing whatever they're doing in the cemetery."

"Cemetery?"

"Mount Hope, where we first met. I was planning on crashing there later this week, but hell if I'm putting myself anywhere near whatever that is, you know?"

"Good to know." I mumbled my goodbyes and moved my phone back to the nightstand. I was a mediator, not a problem-fixer, and weird stuff happened in San Diego all the time. Whoever had decided to throw a supernatural kegger in the cemetery, I was sure one of Anastasia's contacts would find more about it in the morning.

I had just rolled over and closed my eyes when my phone buzzed again. For the first time in my short life, I was starting to hate technology.

"Simon, I'm not—"

"Little bird? Hey! It's me!"

"Juliette?"

"Yeah! Have you seen Angel?" She was slurring her words, just enough to tell me she'd been drinking, but not enough to disguise her worry.

"No? I assumed you two were busy celebrating."

"Earlier, yeah, but then I went over to Brenna's to talk her down off the ledge again."

I assumed she was speaking figuratively, but with Brenna, it was always hard to know. Juliette's friend was an uber-fit femmepire that had been part of the San Diego flock before the House came into existence. Her taste in men was odd, to say the least—like, purple skin and multiple heads odd—and she hadn't had a relationship that lasted more than a month since I'd known her.

"Did Angel go out too?"

"No… she was sleeping." Juliette's snicker told me she was still a long way from sober, despite Angel's disappearance. "I wrung her out like a dishrag before I left."

That was the sort of mental image I didn't need.

"Anyway, when I was at Brenna's, one thing led to another, and we had a few drinks. Maybe a bunch of drinks. When I came back, Angel was gone. She left her phone behind and the apartment door unlocked."

"Do you think someone took her?"

"Nah. I don't smell anyone else in the house. Just her, me, and a little bit of you. That's why I thought you might have come by."

"You've got my luggage from the New Mexico trip," I pointed out. "That's probably why you're smelling me."

"Huh." I could hear her walking through the condo. "Yeah, that's what it was—"

Her voice trailed off.

"Juliette?"

'Are you *sure* you haven't been home since I came back?"

"Very. I've been helping Anastasia."

"Oh, right. Is she—"

"She's fine. We've got some news to share, but it can wait. What were you going to say?"

"If you haven't been here, then why is your suitcase open?"

"What?"

"Oh. Oh crap."

Something in her tone cut through my sleep-addled brain, and I was upright before I even knew I was moving. "What's wrong?"

"Remember that statue you broke into pieces?"

"The one we found in the cave? Of course I remember it."

"It's gone."

Well, shit.

Lights flickered on in our bedroom, and I squinted through the brightness to see that Anastasia was out of bed and pulling on a robe. Normally, it was the sort of sight that would have left me tongue-tied and without a functional brain cell, but tonight—

"Hello? Are you still there, John?"

Okay; tonight, it had the same effect as always. I coughed and tried to focus back on the call: my business partner, her missing girlfriend, and the equally missing, presumably cursed relic.

"So, Angel is gone and so is the statue? Do you think she took it? And if so, why? It was clay, not gold, and I'm not sure how much historical value it has after I broke it and then threw the pieces at Shae."

"This is the statue that was attracting the two Ghost Falls humans?" asked Anastasia, looking comfortable—and still somehow breathtakingly beautiful—in her fluffy robe.

"Yeah. Once I decapitated it though, that stopped."

"And you brought it back to San Diego, Lady Middleton?"

"Hi, Anastasia." Juliette didn't bother raising her voice, since everyone could hear each other just fine. "Yeah, John had mentioned something about giving it to Queen Frosty herself so her people could analyze it. And I figured it would be hard for a centuries-old relic to get pissy with me if I gave her something almost as old as she was."

I winced. Juliette was shaking off the effects of the alcohol as the conversation went on and her fear and anxiety spiked, but she was clearly a long way from sober still.

"Some relics," said Anastasia, as the only one of us with any real experience with enchanted things, "have been known to reconstitute themselves."

"Re-what?"

"You're saying the clay statue repaired itself?"

"I am only saying it is a possibility, if the enchantment was strong enough. It is rare that physical strength alone proves sufficient to permanently damage such items."

"And if it reformed," reasoned Juliette, "it might have activated again. But Angel's not in the spare bedroom with the statue. Instead, she and it are both gone."

I didn't love how easily *my bedroom* had turned back into *the spare bedroom*, especially since I hadn't even told Juliette yet that I'd be spending my nights in Cardiff for the foreseeable future.

Not that any of that was important right now. I was just having trouble keeping my brain on track.

"We don't know *why* the statue was trying to lure people to it."

"Perhaps, the statue's goal was to attract someone capable of carrying it away."

I nodded at Anastasia. "Right. And to prevent that, someone else buried it in the caves, put up some sort of runic barrier *and* sleep trap to keep people out, and then walled off the tunnel entrance."

"All of which you broke," added Juliette.

"I mean… not the tunnel entrance. Clearly, that happened before we made it to Ghost Falls. But if the statue did *want* to be taken somewhere, the question becomes where? And why."

"And just like that, we're back in Journalism 101."

"Did Angel take her car?"

"I don't know. I saw she wasn't here, tried calling her, and then called you to fix it."

That was almost flattering.

"Does her junk heap have GPS? Maybe your contacts at the local precinct could track it for us."

"That's—Okay, that's not a terrible idea. I'm going to put you on hold. Don't go anywhere."

I looked to Anastasia. "I swear I don't normally get phone calls in the middle of the night."

"You do not need to fear, Mr. Smith. I am not going to force you to sleep in another room." Her half-smile warmed me better than any hot chocolate ever could. "However, I think it might be best to discuss this statue in greater detail. What did it look like? How did it feel to the touch? From your tale, you were clearly immune to its call, but did you sense anything else about it that might aid in identification?"

"Identification?"

"A totem's purpose can often be divined through the figure— deity, spirit, or demon—that it was crafted to represent."

"Oh. Uhm. Working backwards through your questions, I didn't sense anything at all, it felt just like clay, if a lot sturdier than I'd expected it to be, and it looked like a creepy bald dude. Oversized head and big ears." I racked my brains for more detail. It had been a very long few days since we'd recovered the statue. "It had its hands held up in front of it, although I couldn't tell if it was defending itself or about to attack. Oh, and either its ribcage was on the outside of its chest or it was wearing some sort of rib-like chest armor. Does any of that help?"

Anastasia had her phone out and was tapping through screens. She finally held up the screen to me. "Did it look like this?"

I blinked. "Almost exactly like that, but small enough to be carried. What is it and how did you find it so fast?"

"You were in New Mexico, and by your and Lady Middleton's reckoning, the statue and its cave system were easily multiple centuries old."

It was actually Hyacinth who had guessed that, but I just nodded.

"Given the crude design you described, I leaned toward the upper end of that estimate, which would make the statue itself older than the country. That left native iconography to search; the rest was elementary. The true question is what a statue of the Aztec god Mictlantecuhtli was doing in New Mexico."

I didn't know a ton about ancient North American history, but I was pretty sure the Aztecs had restricted themselves to Mexico. Old Mexico, in this case. Only to then be wiped out by the Spanish.

"Maybe it was carried north by someone?"

"Perhaps."

I added it to the long list of mysteries we'd probably never solve.

"So, what was Mict—"

"Mictlantechutli."

Mickey, I decided. "Yeah, what was he god of?"

She scrolled down, and then her eyes met mine. "He was the Aztec god of the dead."

Because *of course* he was.

"And something's going on over at Mount Hope Cemetery? There's no way those two things aren't connected."

"You're never going to believe this, little bird," said Juliette, as she switched back over to us. "They pinged her car and she's at—"

"Mount Hope Cemetery," I finished for her.

"I hate when you do that."

"That statue we found is a representation of Mickey—"

"The mouse?"

"The Aztec god of the dead. I don't know why it wanted Angel to take it to a cemetery, but Simon just sensed an energy pulse at Mount Hope a matter of minutes ago."

"More witches?"

"I think the statue itself might be doing something. Maybe Mickey's trying to make a comeback? A graveyard seems like the place for a god of the dead."

"I'm headed there now." I could hear the door slam as Juliette exited the apartment at full speed.

"We will join you shortly," said Anastasia, surprising me.

"Don't do anything dumb or heroic before we get there, Duchess. Just scout things out and report back. If this is another coven, we might be able to talk things out. And if it's something worse… well, we might need reinforcements."

"Right. I'll let you know what I find."

I set my phone aside. "It's times like this that I wish Kala could leave his home dimension."

"He is a demigod, Mr. Smith. If this totem has even a portion of the power of its deity invested in it, Lord Kala might find himself outmatched."

Which didn't say great things about our chances on our own, assuming the statue *was* up to no good and not just in search of a brief, festive powwow with the long dead.

"Are you sure you feel up to going?"

"I am with child, not dying. I will not be coddled and confined while you put yourself again into danger."

"Neither of you should be going anywhere," said Lucia, entering our bedroom like she owned it. The queen was fully dressed, clad in the white leather she wore when she wanted to cosplay as a warrior queen. "The risk is too great, and the loss of Mr. Smith means the loss of you both. *I* will take the Crown Watch and deal with the matter."

"You are as much a part of our continued survival as we are, my Queen." Anastasia didn't back down, tossing off her robe—yay!—and pulling on her matte-black workout garb—also yay. "If you fall, so do John *and* my child."

Jade eyes clashed with crystal blue. As much as I wanted to see who won that war of wills, time was wasting.

"Nobody says we have to throw ourselves into harm's way," I said, sneaking the Encourager™ into the fray. "Juliette will let us know what she finds, and we can decide then what to do. I've got some moves now, sure, but I'm totally cool with staying back and coordinating our response."

Lucia nodded. "For once, you speak sensibly, Mr. Smith."

I ignored the barbed compliment, my smile undiminished. "It's what I do. Are you cool with that, Ana?"

"I am. Will Lady Zhukova be accompanying us?"

As if summoned by her name, Valentina manifested in the room, dark hair hiding her equally dark eyes. She clutched the sides of her old-fashioned, bloody nightgown in two small fists, offering me a black-gummed smile, Anastasia a curtsey, and Lucia a scowl.

I'd almost forgotten the two didn't get along.

"I'm not sure it's a good idea," I told the ghost. "I don't want you tangling with another god. Especially not a god of the dead like Mickey."

"Mictlantechutli," murmured Anastasia.

"Right. Mickey." Despite the potential seriousness of the situation, I sent my lover a grin.

Valentina floated over until she was directly in front of me, so close I could have tasted her breath if she had any. She motioned to the nightstand where the necklace and the wedding ring that was her tether still sat.

"Are you sure?"

The ghost nodded resolutely, more solidly present than I'd seen her since coming back from Rome. Whatever the other White Ladies were doing to help her appeared to be working.

But still…

"Okay," I said, "but stay immaterial and safe unless you have no other option. I mean it! I don't know if this god is still around, or if the statue is just a cursed relic that was made in his image, but I don't want you attracting that sort of attention again."

She blew the hair out of her face—a neat trick, since neither she nor that hair was corporeal—and nodded, sketching a near-perfect military salute as she mimed kicking her heels together.

I slipped the necklace over my head, letting the small ring rest against my chest. "Alright then. Let's go save the world."

Anastasia coughed. "Are you sure you wish to go out like this, Mr. Smith?"

Given that *she* had been the one who'd told Juliette we'd meet her, I didn't understand her sudden concern. Thankfully, Lucia cleared up that confusion right quick.

"Pants, at a minimum, are a requirement to ride in my limo."

Oh. Right.

CHAPTER 42
IN WHICH THE MEDIATOR HAS A PLAN

In the end, I didn't ride in Lucia's limo, even after pulling on pants. Instead, the queen rode with the members of the Crown Watch who *weren't* watching Zorana at the San Diego House, which meant the rest of us took one of Ana's Jaguars. The F-Type was just a two-seater, so we went with the XJR instead, Valentina bobbing about in the backseat like a child on a joyride.

We were rocketing down the 5, Lucia's limo somewhere behind us, when Juliette finally called.

"You're going to need those reinforcements, little bird."

"What do you mean? What's going on?"

"Apparently, Mickey wants an army. Packs of the walking dead—zombies, skeletons, *and* ghouls—are roaming the cemetery and more keep crawling their way out of the ground to join them. Give it an hour or two and the whole graveyard will have risen."

I hadn't had zombie uprising anywhere on my to-do list for the week. Clearly, that was a mistake.

"Any sign of Angel?"

"I found her car. She must be somewhere in the cemetery itself, but I don't... I'm not..."

"It's okay, Juliette. You won't do her any good if you end up dead yourself. Especially since Mickey would probably just raise you too."

"I'm at the main entrance on Imperial," she said. "Hurry. Please."

I turned to Anastasia, who was coolly weaving between the surprising number of cars on the road. "Thoughts? You're better at this stuff than I am."

"I believe you are selling yourself short, as usual, my heart. Still, there are two, possibly three, avenues of concern. First, this army that is being raised will need to be contained. Should they spill out into the surrounding city…"

"Yeah." The cemetery was squarely in the center of a wide swath of urban sprawl, from Mountain View to Stockton to Lincoln Park. Hell, my office in Logan Heights was just a few minutes away, by car. The number of casualties that could happen even in a short window of time was staggering. "Concern number two is Mickey himself, I take it?"

"Or at least his totem, yes. Breaking it again should disrupt whatever magic is being done."

"But we already know that it will just repair itself."

"Indeed, which is why we must find someone with knowledge in matters like these to break the enchantment for good."

"Zorana?"

She shook her head, cutting across three lanes of traffic and back again so smoothly that the drivers she danced around didn't even think to honk. "Hers is the magic of blood. We need someone who deals specifically in divine curses or, barring that, all base energy."

"Like a witch. A normal one, I mean, not a Blood Witch."

"Yes." She didn't say anything more. Together, we had wiped out the Temecula coven, and they had, as far as I knew, been the only witches in the area.

"Well, we can always just keep breaking the idol until we find someone," I muttered. "What's the third concern?"

"Your species, in general."

"I'm sorry?" Ana had always been one of the few vampires who *wasn't* anti-human, so I knew I was missing something.

"The cemetery is closed for the night, but all it takes is one human with a cellphone passing by for this entire event to be uploaded to the internet. The dangers of a zombie uprising pale in comparison to humanity realizing that at least some of their legends and horror stories are true."

I nodded. We'd talked about it in the past, and Anastasia and a few others believed the time their species could remain in the shadows was coming to an end, but even so… there was a difference between a carefully planned emergence of the many things that went bump in the night, and the world finding out through YouTube videos of the undead Armageddon.

"So, keep the zombies pinned in the cemetery, keep the news of the outbreak from making it to the internet, and find someone to break the curse? And hopefully find and save Angel along the way?"

"I believe those should be our main objectives, yes."

I tapped my wonderphone's screen and started scrolling through my contacts. "Good thing we got almost three hours of sleep. I'd hate having to do this tired."

In the back seat, Valentina giggled.

ooo

At the end of the day, whatever the Lady Manassa thought, whatever Ana's own biology had decided, I was just a human. I didn't have any real power of my own outside of what I borrowed from Lucia. No super strength nor magical abilities. Hell, I didn't even have a properly heroic jawline.

What I did have, at least most of the time, was a phone. A phone and an address book full of people more powerful than me.

I started with Lucia first, because she would be the hardest sell. The queen's limo driver hadn't been able to keep up with us, and that left her and the Crown Watch far behind, well out of range of any mental speech.

"Yes, my thrall?"

"We heard from Juliette. The whole cemetery is coming back to life. Or unlife. Whatever."

"How large is this cemetery?"

"I don't know… seventy, maybe eighty acres?"

"I was asking for the number of corpses interred within."

Then maybe you should have said so. I buried the thought, on the off chance that it might leak through our bond and checked my phone. "Holy crap. It says something on the order of 76,000 people."

"Of those, many will be beyond raising, but even so… the seven of us, eight if you include your pet ghost, will be insufficient."

She said it as if it had required real consideration, and not the simple recognition that we would be literally outnumbered 10,000 to one.

"Yeah, it might have been different if you'd brought the Lord of Bones with you to San Diego. Anyway, I'm going to round up some allies," I said, "people who can keep things contained while a smaller squad tries to cut the head off the snake."

"Wise. I sense Lady Dumenyova's hand at work."

"Well, obviously." Ana didn't say anything, content to leave the conversation to me and her queen. "Anyway, while I do that, I was hoping you could reach out to your former House."

"Zorana will be of limited use against those who lack blood entirely, Mr. Smith. Although," she admitted, "her strength alone is something to reckon with."

"Bring her if you want—and if you don't mind the near inevitable mid-battle betrayal—but that's not what I was going to suggest. We need to keep word of what's happening from getting out. Didn't the House have contacts in the press? Tech-savvy computer people? Disinformation specialists? Even an in with the mayor? It might be time to leverage all of that and get a media blackout in place before zombie videos start showing up online."

"Such was never my area of interest nor expertise, but I will speak with the House's current sham of a council and instruct them to redeem their traitorous souls by dealing with the matter."

I winced. "Maybe don't use those exact words?"

"I will say what must be said."

That didn't fill me with a ton of confidence.

"Well, good luck, I guess. We're going to assemble at the main entrance. If your driver doesn't step on it, you might miss the whole thing."

"We will be there, Mr. Smith."

I shook my head, but there wasn't time to bitch about Lucia, no matter how much I wanted to. Instead, I tapped another number, and waited for a reply.

"Smith? What is it now?"

"We found the source of the energy you felt, Simon."

"More witches?"

"No, it's a relic of—" I turned to Anastasia for help.

"Mictlantechutli," she said, raising her voice enough for it to carry over the phone to Simon's largely mundane ears.

"Right. Him. Aztec god of the dead. Anyway, the whole cemetery's getting raised, and I thought to myself, *John, who do you know that's good with the dead* and *a snappy dresser besides?*"

"I sure hope the answer's not what I think it is, kid."

"You're a zombie prince. We've got zombies out the ass. It's time to leverage the power of your throne, dude."

"Yeah… no."

"What?"

"I'm not going anywhere near the influence of a god of the dead, whether you're talking Aztec, Greek, or that bag of bones in the Bitter End."

"But why?"

"Think about it for half a second."

Even on three hours of sleep, half a second was all it took. "Oh. You're dead too."

"Give that man a prize! I don't got much left, kid, but my free will is one of those things. I go near your god of the dead, and I can kiss that goodbye. Sorry, but that's not an ending I'm up for. Wish I could help more. Best of luck to you, the dame, and anyone else with you."

"Wait!" I said, before he could kill the connection.

Simon sighed. "Look, I know you think you're hot shit at this whole persuasion thing, but if you think you can talk me into giving up my long life just to help you—"

"No, I don't. Honestly, I get it."

"Then what do you want?"

"You've been in San Diego longer than anyone, right?"

"Your demigod pal's got me beat, as well as a few others, but yeah, why?"

"We're looking for someone who knows magic."

"Rabbit out of a hat type magic?"

"Not unless it's a real rabbit and the person doing it is creating them out of pure matter. We need someone who specializes in curses. Or general energy, if the first isn't available."

"You killed the crap out of the experts last year."

"Someone *other* than the Temecula coven."

"Huh." I could hear him chewing on something over the phone, and hoped it wasn't his lip. "Don't know any other witches in these parts, but you could always go see the wizard."

"San Diego has a *wizard?* Seriously?"

"Sure does, but before you get your hopes up… let's just say that, last time I saw him, my body was doing a whole lot better than his brain."

Given the number of pieces Simon had lost over the years, that was deeply concerning. Still, beggars couldn't be choosers.

"He's the only wizard in the city?"

"Yeah. There were a couple others, but they all split town when someone went and wiped out the largest coven in the region."

That was always going to haunt me, wasn't it? Now, I knew how Lucia felt about her whole fateful decision to enthrall me.

"I guess he'll have to do then. Any idea where we can find him?"

"Not really. He lives on the streets but isn't really a part of the community, you know? Doesn't care for shelters or even the tent towns in the canyons. Sorry. Guy's a bit of a nutter, like I said."

And that was coming from a zombie who spent his afterlife watching streaming television.

"Does he have a name at least?"

"He's had a lot of names, kid. Last I saw him, he went by Dale. If you find him, don't tell him I sent you… and for the love of all that's alive or undead, don't get him started on the perils of communism."

I stared at my phone long after Simon had hung up.

"Is not Dale the name of the man who sits outside your office building?" asked Anastasia.

Somehow, we had just passed the 52, even though that was normally a twenty-five-minute drive from Cardiff. I leaned over and peeked at the speedometer and blinked.

I'd never gone ninety-seven before. No wonder we were passing everyone in sight.

"Mr. Smith?"

'What? Yeah. Sorry. It is. And he's hyper-obsessed with communists too. Do you think they could be the same guy?"

"I have learned not to question chance, when it comes to you."

Which was, I was pretty sure, the *nice* version of Juliette telling me I was a walking disaster magnet.

"Can we spare the time to swing by? The office *is* pretty close to the cemetery."

"If Mr. Dale is, in fact, a wizard, his help could be invaluable. I will take us there first."

"And I'll get back to my phone calls."

ooo

By the time we reached my office, I was done rallying the troops, and Lucia had called to assure me that the House was doing whatever they could to keep word from leaking about the necromantic stylings of one Mickey the Death God. As Anastasia came to a stop, I scanned the curb outside the building and came up empty.

"Damn it, where is he?"

"Is there anywhere else that we can check?"

"I'll check the alley if you check across the street?" At almost three in the morning, Logan Heights was quiet and still, but not the sort of quiet stillness you'd find in a suburb or fancy gated community. Instead, it felt like a predator waiting to pounce.

It was a strange way to describe a neighborhood, but it fit.

I left the Jag behind, confident that Valentina would keep anyone from even thinking of touching its paint job, and rounded the corner to the alley that threaded its way between my office building and its neighbor. When first starting out, I'd parked my previous Corolla in that alley, doing my best to keep it safely out of sight. It had worked wonders until my first mediation, when, after multiple weeks of it being parked there, the local gangs had decided I was gifting them a mobile canvas on which to demonstrate their inspirational street art.

Meaning dicks and curse words, obviously.

These days, I parked out front, but the alley was just the way I remembered it: dark and smelly. I made my way down it, stepped past the dumpsters, and found a large heap on the asphalt. Was it trash that someone hadn't bothered to take to the dumpster? A body that didn't merit careful disposal? Or the man of the hour, the wizard I'd unwittingly fed sushi just a few days earlier?

A careful tap with my foot answered that: it was definitely trash.

I made my way through the rest of the alley and then back again, finding nothing. Ana was already waiting, and I didn't need to see her face to know that she'd come up empty too.

"Back to the *assign someone to keep breaking the statue until we find our wizard* plan," I said. "And if it turns out that Dale's taken off for good, we could always try to hire someone up in Los Angeles. Hell, we could just leave it *in* L.A. I'm pretty sure there's enough bad vibes up there to drown out something as petty as a death god's curse."

I was kidding. Sort of. And maybe a little bit salty that the freaking Dodgers were good again while the Padres continued to suck.

Even with our detour, we reached the cemetery before Lucia, let alone any of the other allies I'd called. Juliette was waiting, crouched by the closed gate.

"Any updates?" I asked her in a hushed whisper.

"There're still more crawling out of the earth," she whispered back, now perfectly sober. "But the rest seem to be organizing themselves into ranks."

"From most dead to least dead?"

"More like an army getting ready to march."

"I wonder where Mickey learned that from. I don't think the Aztecs marched in file."

"Pantheons and mythology are human creations, little bird. Mickey could just be another name for Hades or Hel or a dozen other death gods."

"I'm pretty sure Hades is dead." I'd seen the ruins of Olympus myself, presided over by Minerva and patrolled by the chained form of the Fenris wolf.

"Still, you get my point. What's the plan?"

I eyeballed the walking dead. The only good news was that they seemed to be accumulating here, with more arriving from other parts of the cemetery all the time. If we'd had to guard the entire perimeter of the cemetery, we would have lost even before we started.

I glanced over to Anastasia, who had taken up position on the opposite side of the entrance, and tried not to let my worry for her show. She was better, yeah, but even I could tell the femmepire was a long way from full strength, whatever she claimed. Still, Ana at half-strength was better than Juliette and I could do together.

Valentina was hidden away now, dematerialized or whatever it was she did to enter the ghost plane, and I hoped to God we wouldn't have to call on her at all. Because if *Simon* was worried that he might lose his free will to Mickey, then we had to believe Valentina was at risk too… and I was pretty sure she'd be able to kill most of us without even straining.

"We wait for our backup," I finally answered. "Most of them will be on containment duty. The rest of us will go in and find Angel."

Lucia wasn't going to be happy with Ana and me being part of that second group, but I didn't see much choice in the matter. I didn't have enough allies in the world to hold thousands of undead at bay for long, and that meant someone had to go in and break the statue. Anastasia was easily the most competent one of all of us, and baby or no baby, she had made it clear that she would not be sitting the mission out. And if she was going, I was too. Hopefully, rather than writing us both off as imbeciles, Lucia would choose to come with us. As much as I disliked the queen, she had the kind of power that lent itself to moments like these.

I reminded myself not to draw on that same power too deeply. I remained a thoroughly inefficient vessel… if Lucia's Talent were a glass of water, I would spill most of it onto the floor every time I took a sip. And the last thing we needed was for her well to run dry while battling our way through the undead.

"When is that backup getting here?" demanded Juliette, eyes still fixed on the gathering undead. "I don't even know how long Angel's been in there, but—"

"We'll find her," I said, once again breaking the first rule of private investigation. "We'll find her and save her. I promise."

She glanced at me, fear sitting oddly in place of the usual smirk. "They need to hurry then, damn it!"

"WHO is it that NEEDS to hurry, LADY PAC-MAN?" boomed a voice literally inches from our ears, baritone with a southern twang.

CHAPTER 43
IN WHICH NOBODY LIKES NUMBERS

It was only the lack of hydration that kept me from peeing myself. Even so, I'm pretty sure something close to a shriek made it out before I could stop it. I turned to find Bill, all seven feet of him, crouched down, leafy green stalk extended above us as his magic marker mouth wiggled to and fro.

Whatever Juliette saw when she looked at Bill, familiarity hadn't lessened its impact. She blanched and looked away, shuddering as she brought herself back under control.

"The others, Bill," I answered for her. "Some of the pack is on its way, along with goblins and pixies. Also…"

"THE QUEEN OF REFUSE AND THIEF OF MOONBEAMS," shouted Bill, turning his coal eyes around his stalk as Lucia's limo finally arrived.

"She's on our side this time, Bill."

"That is NOT a VERY JOHNNY-ONE-NOTE thing to SAY."

"No kidding. Still, she's here to help. And she's not all bad. She let Tiny Flower come over to play back when Summer was still in San Diego."

"She DID?" Bill shook himself, which was an odd thing to see a seven-foot-asparagus spear do. "She DID! Now I REMEMBER!"

I breathed a sigh of relief. We couldn't afford to have any of our allies crucified on twenty-foot candelabras today.

Behind Lucia, another line of cars pulled up, and vampires from the House spilled out with Zorana. They were followed by the rest of the Crown Watch who had accompanied Lucia to California: Castor, Claudia, Constantin, and at least three other vampires whose names almost definitely started with C. I nodded to them and the others I recognized: Steve and Brenna, as well as Tasha and Kale, the vampires who'd caught the bouquet and collar at Kayla's wedding.

More vehicles arrived, including one sweet motorcycle whose rider I recognized immediately. Emilio's mustache was as awe-inspiring as ever, though the man himself looked a decade older than when I'd last seen him.

"You called and we came, son," said Jason, stepping out of the first car in that second caravan. He was trailed by almost a dozen other wolves, all but three of them younger men. To a man (and woman), they each spotted Bill, froze, and then did their best to never look his way again.

"Jason… thanks for showing up. I really appreciate it."

"Yeah well, Cara says if you get anyone killed, she's going to eat your heart."

I blinked.

"Hormones," Jason stage whispered. "Pregnancy is a beautiful but also terrifying thing, bro."

"You don't say."

"No, I really do. Anyway, what's the sitch?" He looked through the gate and then backed away slowly. "That's a *lot* of dead people."

"Yeah." And like an idiot, I'd left my gun in the safe at Anastasia's house. I doubted it would have done much against the undead, but it might have at least made me feel better. "You, the goblins, Lucia's former House, and Bill are going to try to run containment."

"Containment? There's barely enough of us to even hold this gate. What's to stop them from just climbing the fence, or following the railway tracks out?" That was Brenna, who had apparently recovered from her latest relationship disaster sufficiently to remember she didn't like me.

"Nothing," I admitted. "But they seem to be gathering here on the south side of the cemetery so far. I've asked Kristin and her congregation of pixies to watch the rest of the perimeter. They won't be able to stop the dead, but they'll at least be able to spot them for us."

"I don't even want to guess what *that* cost you," murmured one of the unknown vampires.

"You really don't." I wasn't sure what value *my* endorsement could have when it came to a product, but Kristen had seemed thrilled with the exchange. Although she was still trying to sell me on her pyramid scheme too. "Anyway, we may have to do some cleanup afterward, but if you all can stop the main force here…"

"And if they completely overrun us instead? What then?" asked another wolf, one that I recognized.

"Hey Matt," I said, scanning the crowd, and feeling my heart sink when I also spotted the werewolf I'd once called Longhair. Was it a bad sign that all three werewolves I'd almost gotten killed against Nepenthe's coven had shown up, or was it just proof of my growing mastery of the mediator's bag of tricks? "The hope is that you won't be overrun."

"Hope in one hand and—"

"I'm sure John has a better plan than *stand here and die*," said Steve, joining the conversation.

"There are NO SNAKES in the vicinity," bugled Bill. "There will be VICTORY and ICE CREAM!"

"Not if you persist in announcing our presence to the world, demigod." Lucia's voice was literally icy, water crystals forming in the air and shattering as she spoke.

"The plan," I said, trying to take back control before everything fell apart, "is simple. You all stay behind and do your best to keep anything from getting out. The rest of us go in and find the relic behind all of this. In all likelihood, some or most of that army over there will focus on the strike team once we make our presence known. You and the goblins, whenever they show up, are here to take care of whatever stragglers make for the gates."

"When is a GATE NOT A GATE?" asked Bill.

"When it's a jar?"

"No." He frowned. "Why is there a jar? What does IT HAVE in it? Is it MILKSHAKE? Is it STRAWBERRY?"

"Exactly *who* is going into *that* mess?" asked Lucia, interrupting our meeting of the minds.

"My Queen—" began Anastasia.

After four hundred years together, Lucia knew immediately what was coming. She went cold and still. "This was not what we discussed, Lady Dumenyova."

"The world is what it is, Your Majesty. We do what we must."

Juliette shot me a look. "Should I ask?"

I shook my head. "Not until after this is done."

"You're buying the beer then."

"I can live with that."

"I hope we all can. And do."

An array of vehicles that looked suspiciously like souped-up vanagons headed for the other gate. I spotted little green men inside. From the looks of it, the entire Padres tribe had decided to come to the party. With Petco Park just a few miles away, Anastasia had said this was ostensibly that tribe's territory, and their chieftain had been surprisingly eager to defend it. Granted, he'd been extremely drunk when I called him, but even so… Junior and Wubby Lubby aside, it had been the nicest conversation I'd ever had with a goblin.

There was a reason baseball was my favorite sport.

"If you insist upon entering, then I will be accompanying you, Lady Dumenyova," said Lucia. "The Crown Watch can help man the gates with my former House."

"Your Majesty—" began Claudia.

"I have made my decision, Lieutenant."

"The three of us, then, and Juliette," I said.

"I will GO too!"

"We need you to hold the gate, Bill."

Those pieces of coal rotated around the stalk to face me, and the magic marker mouth flattened into a straight line.

"I will BE there for the MOUTH-WIGGLING that is to come and the beer that comes after! And TINY FLOWER WILL KNOW that her MR. BILL did his part as one does when parts are to be done."

"But what about the gate?"

"There is a place for those who sin, John."

I didn't know what any of that meant, but I literally couldn't keep Bill from doing whatever he wanted. So, I shrugged and held out my hand, waiting as Bill grew an arm of his own and shook it.

"Alright. The five of us, then."

"FIVE is a GOOD NUMBER, Jack and the Beanstalk!"

Honestly? I'd have been happier with five thousand.

ooo

Before we could move out, Lucia and Anastasia exchanged glances, and the vampire I loved crossed over to me. There was only cold static over the bond and that, along with Ana's sudden poker face, put me on alert.

"John—"

"No." I was saying that a lot more than I'd expected when dreaming of finally having a relationship with Anastasia. "If you're going in, I am too."

"I need you to be safe," she said.

"The safest place in the world is next to you."

She struggled against my unassailable logic. Unfortunately, she'd brought reinforcements.

"Listen to my *Secundus*, Mr. Smith," said Lucia. "Your presence in battle is a distraction. I need sole access to my gifts, and Lady Dumenyova needs her focus, and we will not have either with you nearby, vulnerable and requiring protection. You will make us all weaker by going."

"Lucia." Ana's voice was stone, that tone almost as surprising as her dropping the other woman's title.

"I am saying what must be said, Asya. Our chances of success diminish if he accompanies us."

Anastasia turned back to me. "I'm sorry, John, but…"

"She's right, isn't she?"

"Yes."

It was one thing to know I was almost always the weakest person in any room I walked into. It was another to have that truth laid bare when it mattered. So far, I'd found ways to contribute, but when it came to a straight up war, I was so outclassed by even Juliette that it wasn't funny.

"You're right," I said, trying not to show how much that admission hurt. "I'll stay back and coordinate or something. Bring Zorana with you instead."

"I think it might be too late for that," said Steve.

I followed his gaze and swallowed.

Every undead I could see was in motion… and they were all coming straight for us.

ooo

Mount Hope Cemetery was supposed to contain almost eighty thousand bodies, but either a lot of them were too far gone to raise, or Mickey didn't have as much juice as we'd feared; I doubted there were more than five thousand undead swarming the cemetery.

It was still enough to almost completely overrun us in the very first minute. Zombies didn't heal, as Simon had so aptly demonstrated, but they were insanely strong and didn't feel pain. Nor, we soon discovered, did they stop due to minor injuries like decapitation. That first wave went down easily enough, torn apart by werewolves and vampires, but when the second wave hit, our line of defenders found themselves also beset by the limbs, disembodied heads, and other body parts left over from the prior assault.

Things had already dissolved into chaos when a thick square of skeletons charged the gate, led by a handful of the gray-skinned, feral creatures I assumed were ghouls.

Bill trumpeted, and something unseen but massive swept out of the darkness and through the onrushing skeletons. Bone shattered and at least a hundred enemies were casually wiped from existence. Only the ghouls avoided that initial strike, too fast and agile for whatever was hunting them. Even so, a hundred skeletons were barely more than a percentage of the force we faced. Undead swarmed past the hidden attacker, and while not a single group made it through intact, there were more than enough to flood the gate, putting our already shaky defenders on their heels.

The ground just inside that gate shuddered and split, a crack widening where no fault line should have been. From my vantage point, I couldn't see down into that crack, couldn't see the fields of candelabras that dotted Gehenna's horizon, but more undead fell, this time tumbling into the dimension where Bill held dominion. The hunter I couldn't see came from behind, a multi-tentacled creature of darkness that crushed more of the undead, devoured others, and drove still others into the rift.

Still, it wasn't enough. Either the undead had functioning brains of their own or Mickey was actively directing them, because more and more started to peel away from the main group, headed for the flimsy chain-link fence surrounding the cemetery instead of the gate itself.

"Spread out!" I yelled. "Don't let them past you."

One of the Crown Watch I *didn't* know shot me a look that said exactly what he thought of my plan, only to be taken to the ground almost immediately after by a swarming mass of severed limbs. He wasn't the only one down either. At least two werewolves had fallen, and I rushed over to help drag them away. Both vampires and werewolves would heal with sufficient time and rest, but... I wasn't sure we would get that time.

At the front of the line, Lucia dropped to one knee, driving a golden hand into the cracked asphalt. Walls of ice formed out of nothing, closing off one half of the gate completely, and spreading in each direction along the fence, creating a barrier the undead couldn't easily climb. A moment later, she was back in the fight, but I could feel what those walls had cost her, the deep well of her power already half depleted. Worse, even in September, this was still San Diego ... I knew the ice would already be starting to melt.

Anastasia fought next to Lucia, often venturing out past the increasingly tight circle of Crown Watch trying to defend their queen to dispatch attacker after attacker. Only her arms and legs were stone, and it took me a moment to realize why: she had no idea how her Talent would affect our unborn daughter and wasn't taking the risk of transforming entirely.

Unfortunately, that left her just as vulnerable as the other combatants.

Zorana was cackling as she fought, relying on her great strength instead of her magic as she tore through anything in her path, but even the Blood Witch was just one woman, and a small one at that. A space grew around her, but that just meant more undead falling upon the other defenders.

And if Anastasia, Bill, Lucia, and Zorana were so far proving unassailable, the rest of our line wasn't nearly as fortunate. Claudia had grown chitinous armor that reminded me unsettlingly of the Illutu in Rome, while Steve was moving like the ninja I'd always accused him of being, everywhere and nowhere at once, but their allies and Jason's wolves lacked that same destructive power. Juliette had been wounded at least three different times and was staggering about like she'd spent a night at the Bitter End drinking nothing but Long Island Iced Teas.

The enemy's numbers were overwhelming.

Just as our line was about to break, something shifted in the attacking horde. A dozen zombies, then several dozen, turned, lashing out at the skeletons and ghouls around them. Though vastly outnumbered by the long dead, for a moment, they stalled the onslaught.

I smelled Simon before I saw him, the other man shuffling up to join me with a scowl.

"You came."

"I figured it was worth a shot," he grumbled. "And I'm too old to find someplace new. San Diego is *my* city."

"And you're still… you?"

He paused and considered it. "I guess I am. Either your death god's running on fumes, or that relic you mentioned just holds an echo of his power. For all the good it does us."

In the field, the zombies Simon had turned were torn apart. The remaining limbs continued to move under his direction, but any impediment to the oncoming horde was gone. Undead crashed into our reformed lines, and the battle was underway again.

"Too many skeletons and ghouls," said Simon, summing up the situation, "and nowhere near enough zombies. Sorry, kid."

"They don't quit, do they?"

"Goddamn communist bastards never quit."

'I doubt too many of them were—" I stopped, turned to my right, and blinked. "Dale?"

"They get in your head," said the homeless man who regularly camped out next to my office building and might be San Diego's only remaining wizard. "They get in your head and take your treasures."

With Simon on one side of me, and Dale on the other, it was a struggle just to breathe, let alone think. Thankfully, my mouth had never required my brain's permission to speak.

"How do you feel about stopping the red tide?" I asked him.

Something shifted behind rheumy, unfocused eyes, something cold and dark. His hungry grin exposed crooked and yellow teeth.

"Wizards are stronger than witches on an individual basis, kid," said Simon, chewing on his lip like it was a cigar, "but they ain't on the scale of the people you've already got in this fight."

"That's okay. I don't need him to be." I touched the ring hanging around my neck. "Valentina, are you here?"

She materialized before me, slim and unassuming in the nightgown that was once again turning bloody, in the endless replay of the wound that had killed her. She cocked her head at me in a silent question.

"Can *you* feel the death god's influence?"

She shook her head, dark curls swaying.

"Do you feel up to a little ghost walk? With two passengers?"

Her lips spread wide, revealing a black-gummed smile.

Anastasia was *so* going to kick my ass.

ooo

I'd ghost walked with Valentina twice before. The first time, she'd taken me to a hill that didn't exist in our world so I could be hired to find the missing leader of the White Ladies. Even though we were going to a physical place this time, the mechanics remained the same: Dale and I each took hold of a hand made just corporeal enough for us to touch, and then the world began to move around us. Both people and objects went slightly indistinct, visible but as if through cracked glass, and entirely intangible. The undead were, by contrast, brighter here, the core of their energy visible on this plane of existence in a way it wasn't in the real world.

Still, our trio phased right through living and dead alike, slowly picking up steam.

I didn't have directions to give Valentina. We didn't know where Angel was, if she and the statue were still together, or if she was even still alive at all, but the way the dead glowed gave me an idea.

"Look for the brightest light you can find, and head for it," I said, the words ripped from my lips to fall somewhere behind us, faint echoes of real noise. "I bet we'll find the statue there."

Valentina didn't reply, but the world shifted around us as she briefly spun in a tight circle. I squeezed my eyes shut, only now remembering how nauseous I'd been after our last lengthy ghost walk. When I opened my eyes again, the world had stopped spinning, but my stomach seemed unconvinced. There was a harsh light on the horizon, like a cold sun peeking through the trees.

The world dissolved into streaks of color as we flew forward, blurring straight through each and every obstacle in our path. And then we were there, in the shadow of a mausoleum not unlike the one where I'd first met Simon. The world came back into focus around us.

Angel was upright. That was the good news.

The bad news was that her mouth was open and her eyes were shut, the muscles in her arms tight like steel wires as she held Mickey's statue aloft in front of her. She was leaning backwards at an angle, but somehow, that small statue was acting as a counterweight that kept her from falling.

I rushed over and tried pulling the statue from her hands, but it wouldn't budge. I tried shaking her awake, tried breaking the statue even while it was in her grasp, but nothing seemed to work, and Angel didn't even stir.

She was breathing, but there was nobody home.

Don't borrow trouble, I told myself. If Dale could break the statue's enchantments, maybe it would free her too. And if not, we would do whatever was necessary to get her right again. But first, we had to stop Mickey from taking over the world.

"I think you're up, Dale."

No answer.

"Dale?"

The other man had been turning slowly in a circle, his expression almost as vacant as Angel's, but as I called his name a second time, he stopped.

"Where's my stuff?" he demanded.

"It's safe." I hoped so anyway. He was possessive of his pack, even if it was mostly knickknacks and garbage. "But we have to deal with this first."

I pointed to the statue. I could swear it was watching me, a creepy rictus smile on its clay face where none had been.

"It's a girl," said Dale.

"A woman, but yeah. She's trapped by the figure she's holding, the same figure that's raising the dead. Can you break whatever enchantments are on the statue?"

"Of course not."

My heart skipped a beat. "What?"

'She's not even real," he growled. "None of you are. Just another trick by the Russkies. Just another worm in the brain, wriggling about and firing off neurons." He spun about, looking at things I couldn't see. Things that presumably weren't there at all. "You think this is funny? Really? I'll show you funny!"

I was starting to question Simon's sources, starting to wonder if Dale was even a wizard at all, when he spread his hands wide, and blue flames flickered to life in his palms.

"I'll show all of you!" he shouted.

Well, shit.

ooo

The first handful of fire flared brilliantly as it lanced outwards from Dale's palm, burning through vegetation and dirt to leave behind a smoldering chasm in the earth, waist-deep and almost as wide. The second handful came my way, and I only barely threw myself aside in time to avoid it.

So much for wizards sucking at combat.

"I've been training my whole life for this, Mother!" yelled Dale, throwing fire indiscriminately around him. Each burst of light seared my eyes but they also exposed the creeping forms headed our way. More undead. Far too many for me to fight, even if I knew how.

Lucia, I said across the bond.

Mr. Smith? Where are you? She was worn down, I could tell, her initial delight in the savage simplicity of combat giving way to the dawning realization that nothing they were doing was enough.

You need to fall back, I told her. *I'm about to do something really dumb.*

I gave her five seconds, an eternity with all that was going on around us, then reached for her power and pulled.

Strength, quickness, and winter… what I got was barely a tithe of what Lucia lost on her end, but it would have to be enough. I mimicked Lucia's earlier gesture and spikes of ice thrust their way up from the earth around us to form a makeshift barricade. As the undead— some skeletons, but mostly ghouls—started smashing their way through, I ran for Dale, this time dodging an errant blast of fire with considerably less difficulty.

Valentina had appeared beside the man, her face twisted in rage, black hair streaming behind her in a wind that wasn't there. Her killing hand swept forward, but I was already there, tackling Dale to the ground, rolling away with him.

"We need him!" I shouted to her. "We need him to end this!"

Beneath me, Dale shook and kicked his legs, as if undecided whether to stand up or roll away. I didn't know a damn thing about mental illness, especially whatever he was suffering from, but I did know—I'd been taught—that the correct response was compassion, patience, and kindness.

Unfortunately, we didn't have time for any of that.

The power I'd taken from Lucia had almost all been funneled into the ice spike barricade the undead were swiftly dismantling. I used the remaining dregs to form an icicle in my hands, long, and sharp like a dagger. Blinking away images of Nepenthe, I plunged that icicle down toward Dale's chest.

A hand, wrinkled, twisted, and stained, reached up and stopped my thrust cold. Whatever I'd seen before was back in Dale's eyes, hard like uncut gemstones.

"That was foolish." The voice that emerged was barely recognizable, smooth and controlled, every syllable dripping with menace. "And now you die."

I don't know what he hit me with. It wasn't his fists, that much was clear, but it felt like I'd been kicked by a skyscraper-sized donkey. I was literally tossed up into the air and even before I landed again, something in my chest went numb.

Valentina had had enough. She stalked forward again, murder in her black eyes.

Dale rose to his feet and frowned, ignoring the ghost coming to kill him. "This isn't Prague."

"It's San Diego," I wheezed through ribs that were almost definitely broken. "We need your help."

'Stabbing a man's a funny way to show it." He scowled, still looking about. "Class two necromantic creations, and by the sound of it, a lot more where these few came from. But what's the source?" He turned on Valentina and something in his face brought the ghost to a halt.

"No," he decided, speaking to himself, "it's not the spirit."

"It's the statue," I said, squeezing each word out with effort.

Dale finally took notice of Angel and the figurine in her hands. "Ah. That's a nasty piece of work."

"Can you break it?"

"Breaking is easy. Breaking is *always* easy. Break break break and break some more," he muttered, his voice starting to lose its considered cadence before he visibly pulled himself back together. "Dispelling. Banishing. Curing. All so much harder. All so rarely done."

He lapsed into more mutters, pacing in a circle around the figurine. Below us, I heard the last vestiges of my spike barrier crumble, followed by the gibbering of ghouls as they loped up the hill toward us. I made a brief, if valiant, effort to get back up, and then sagged to the ground.

I spend way too many of these battles on my back, I realized. *Ana was right: I really need to learn how to fight.* After a moment's consideration, I couldn't help but add: *Maybe I should stop getting in the way of vastly more powerful beings too.*

When the ghouls arrived, Valentina was there to meet them, spectral winds whipping about her and tossing the undead about like bowling pins. But a ghost's greatest weapon, the chilling, killing cold of their touch, had no effect on creatures who were already dead. All she could do was delay them, and with every passing second, they drew closer.

"Dale?" It was a quiet little whimper, barely audible even to me. I dug down deep, did my best to ignore the pain, and somehow found it in me to shout. "Dale?!"

"What?!"

"We're out of time." Those words were just whispers, but he heard me just fine anyway.

"Plan B, then."

The world went white.

CHAPTER 44

IN WHICH THE DUST THAT SETTLES
MIGHT ALSO BE ASH

I woke to low murmurs and a hand caressing my face. My eyes didn't want to open, but I knew that scent, even when it was almost lost beneath far fouler odors.

"Ana."

A wealth of experience with passing out in the middle of the action had me taking a quick inventory of my surroundings. Grass under my hands meant I was still outside, the lack of warmth on my face meant it was probably still night, and the quiet conversation in the distance meant we weren't alone.

If I were a betting man, I'd have bet I was still in the cemetery.

Since I didn't have enough money to gamble, I instead opened my eyes, and found out I'd been right.

"Mr. Smith," said Anastasia, her hand still stroking my cheek, "I am very cross with you."

"Is our daughter okay?"

There was an exclamation from nearby, quickly muffled.

"Our *son* is just fine. More to the point, how are you?"

"I think I broke some ribs, but…" I experimentally shifted my upper body and winced. "Okay, that really hurts. Still, I'm guessing it'll heal with Lucia here."

"How fortunate that I am, at last, good for something," said Lucia, in a voice that made deserts seem waterlogged.

"Took the words right out of my mouth." I tried a smile, relieved to find that at least there was no pain involved in that. "Did we win?"

"Indeed. Whatever it was you did to the statue seems to have emptied it of power," said Ana. "The undead still on the field of battle collapsed at once, though I suspect the city will have a difficult time figuring out how to re-inter the remains."

"Tomorrow, the mayor will hold a press conference to announce a previously undiscovered sinkhole," said Lucia, "as well as an already-approved initiative to find new resting spots for the recovered bodies."

"Your former House came through," I said.

"I suppose they did. This once."

"And Angel?"

"See for yourself," said Anastasia, propping my head up so that I could see my surroundings.

As expected, we were still right next to the mausoleum… what was left of the mausoleum, anyway. Where Angel had once stood, holding the statue, there was now only a scorched patch of earth, the ground shiny like obsidian.

Jesus. There's nothing left for Juliette to even say goodbye to.

Lucia's voice echoed down our bond, full of the exhaustion she refused to show in public. *Look further, you cretin.*

I tore my eyes from the bare, black patch of glassy rock, and scanned further, to find Juliette, looking much the worse for wear, but still standing on her own two feet. Her yellow eyes gleamed in the near-darkness, full of words and emotions that I couldn't interpret. And in her arms, leaning more than standing, but otherwise whole, was Angel.

The former barista turned receptionist turned junior investigator didn't look my way, clinging to Juliette like the vampire was the only thing in the world. Even so, just seeing her alive and well had me breathing more easily.

Or was that my ribs healing?

Probably a bit of both, I decided.

Then, something Anastasia had said finally sank in.

"Wait, what do you mean what *I* did to the statue?"

"Was it Lady Zhukova instead?"

"No, it was…" I frowned. "Were we the only ones here when you arrived?"

"Yes." Ana stopped touching me just long enough to cast another look around the clearing. "You, Valentina, and Angel herself, along with a statue that crumbled as soon as we touched it."

"The ghost departed ahead of the coming dawn," added Lucia.

"Who else should we have found, Mr. Smith?"

I shook my head, fighting back a sorrow I hadn't expected. I guess I knew what Plan B was. "Just San Diego's last wizard."

○○○

As fast as my injuries were healing, I was still only able to stand with Anastasia's help. By the time I was upright, Juliette was there, practically carrying her girlfriend.

"We're headed back to the condo. Angel needs to sleep and recover." She nodded awkwardly to me, her eyes wide and solemn. "Thank you, John."

"I'm just glad she's okay. And that you are too."

"Castor and Crete will bring Zorana on the morrow," Lucia told Juliette. "She will check your donor's blood for lingering effects of the curse and nothing more. On this, you have my word."

The queen playing nice was a pleasant surprise, but it paled in comparison to further confirmation that every vampire she'd brought with her from Rome had a name starting with C. The story behind that oddity would either be utterly diabolical or deeply banal, with absolutely no chance of it falling somewhere in between.

"Fine," said Juliette, clearly too tired to be confrontational. "I guess we'll see her then. Goodnight, everyone. Lucia, Anastasia, little bird…"

"We'll get that beer another time, Duchess," I said back.

"Better believe it."

She walked away without any of her usual preternatural grace, but as soon as Lucia and Anastasia had turned back to me, she stopped, spun to meet my eyes, and held her free hand out in front of her stomach, like she was patting a round belly. She looked to Ana then back to me, and for the first time in our short but overstuffed history, I had no problem reading Juliette's nonverbal expression.

It helped that she actually mouthed the words:

What the f---?

Apparently, it would be beer *and* a confession.

I could live with that.

"Shall we?" I asked the two remaining women. Now that I was standing, I could see other members of the Crown Watch, scattered through the cemetery around us, but there was no sign of the werewolves, pixies, or goblins. Or Bill, for that matter. "Did everyone else already leave?"

Anastasia was busy supporting me, but Lucia nodded.

"To take care of their injured, yes."

That… didn't sound great. "How bad was it?"

"The Padres tribe faced far fewer enemies than we did, but lost twelve of their number, with almost five times as many injured."

I felt a weight settle on my soul. I didn't even like goblins, not really, but these ones had died because I'd called them to the fight. "And the others? The pack and the House vampires?"

"I don't think a single werewolf emerged unscathed," said Lucia, "but the Infected are hardy creatures, despite their paltry life spans. They should all recover. As for the People… half my detachment of Crown Watch is down, but with blood and time, they should all walk again. Our former House fared better by virtue of fighting in the second and third ranks."

"No other deaths?" It seemed too good to be true.

"Even a minute more, and the toll would have been much greater for all but your pet demigod," said Lucia. "As it was, I had barely retreated from the front lines when some smelly barbarian tried to drain my power from me like I was the monkey and he the vampire."

"My Queen…" murmured Anastasia.

"Yes, yes, I know. We are alive, this death god's artifact is nothing but dust, and the world is what it is. It is quite possibly my least favorite of all your sayings, Asya." She sniffed, turning away. "Shall we go? I desperately require a shower and these clothes will need to be burned."

○○○

Two weeks later, I was out on the balcony of Anastasia's house, a house that I hoped would one day be filled with the screaming laughter of our impossible daughter. A plate of corn dogs sat in front of me— bought from Costco and heated up by Teresa at my request—and I was working my way through the fifth of seven dogs. They probably didn't have anywhere near as much iron as the charcuterie board and veggies she'd previously prepared, but still… corn dogs felt a whole lot more *me*.

A few feet away, Valentina swayed back and forth, unconsciously moving in time with the ocean. She'd shown no ill effects from her efforts at the cemetery, and for the first time in a long while, I was starting to believe that the wounds Minerva had inflicted on her were finally healed. Or… whatever the correct term was for someone both dead and incorporeal.

She pointed to my wrist and raised an expressive eyebrow.

"Yeah. Another feeding. We're still a month or more away from the baby being able to grow on its own, apparently. Still, once a week is a lot better than when it was daily."

Valentina nodded and smiled her terrifying smile—a smile that warmed my soul almost as much as Ana's—and then mimed rocking a baby in her arms, dancing and twirling with the motion. The sadness I'd previously seen when she encountered children was still there, but only because I knew to look for it. Mostly, there was just open and honest joy for me and Anastasia.

"I keep telling Ana it's a girl," I said, "but it's way too soon to know for sure. Son or daughter though, that kid is going to know they're loved from the moment they take breath."

She nodded happily and kept dancing.

"And on that note, I wanted to ask you for something."

She paused, and cocked her head, floating closer on feet that only occasionally remembered to touch the balcony floor.

"According to Lucia *and* Zorana, there's never been a child born to a human and a vampire before. Our son or daughter will have enemies just for existing."

Valentina scowled.

"I know, right? That's… well, it's just *one* of the reasons, really, because we've been talking about it anyway, but…"

The ghost just waited.

"Would you like to be her godmother? Or his, if Ana is right?"

I don't think I'd ever seen Valentina surprised before. Her mouth dropped open, exposing her black gums, white teeth, and what was left of the tongue she'd lost even before dying. She shuffled a few steps back, and then, looking at me in confusion, pointed at her chest, right where the ever-recurring bloody wound began.

"Yes, you. You're dear to me—to us, rather—and it's hard to imagine any child having a better protector or friend."

I didn't even see her hug coming… it just happened, and then it was over, and Valentina was back on her side of the balcony. She nodded happily, and then paused.

"What is it?"

She opened her mouth again and made a face, pointing her index fingers down like they were incisors, followed by fingers sticking up from her head like spikes.

"What about Juliette?" I translated.

She nodded again.

"She's going to be a godmother too."

That won yet another nod before she pantomimed a second vampire. This one had its nose stuck in the air and a scowl on its face.

"Yeah, Lucia as well. We figured there's nothing traditional about this family—honestly, I don't even know which *god* we're referencing when we say godmother—and there was no reason we couldn't have three of you."

Even as Valentina nodded, Lucia's voice sounded in my mind.

By virtue of age, breeding, and power, I shall reign supreme among the three. This much I swear to you, my thrall.

ooo

The goblin war ended a week later, not with a bang or ritual bloodletting, but instead a shaking of hands. No doubt the stories of my awesomeness as a mediator would spread even further in the wake of another spectacular success, but this once, I'd had very little to do with the outcome. Instead, it had been the work of the two tribal heirs. Over the course of the mediation, Wubby Lubby and Junior had forged a bond of friendship that not even their overbearing parents dared threaten… especially when Junior casually put his fist through a steel door while demonstrating just what *I can bench six-fifty* meant when applied in other arenas.

As far as I knew, the two had been playing online games together since well before the mediation officially ended.

In truth, I hadn't had much to do with that happy ending. Except that it had been *my* tardiness that put Junior and Wubby Lubby in contact with one another in the first place. In a very real, if mildly exaggerated, way, I'd been the architect behind their whole friendship, and thus the mastermind behind another successful mediation.

Whoever deserved or even received the credit. I was taking it as a win. And somehow, it was just one of many such victories: a successful practice, a great circle of friends, and a baby on the way with the woman I loved. Almost as great, the time until Lucia returned to Italy could now be measured in weeks instead of months. Caleb Van Stahl's murder remained an open mystery, of course, as did more than a few of the loose threads we'd left behind in Rome, but otherwise?

Life didn't suck.

○○○

It was late October when I exited my office. The sun had long since gone down, and I nearly tripped over the man lying out front. He'd made a small fort out of blankets, and sat in the middle of that fort, tinfoil and assorted pieces of trash arrayed in front of him.

"Dale? Is that you? I thought you were gone!" I went in for a manly bro hug, but he leaned backwards, dodging the attempt.

"These are all mine," he told me, gesturing at his possessions.

"Yeah, they are." I didn't see any trace of the wizard lurking inside of him, and I didn't even care. "I'm just glad you're okay, dude."

"None of us is okay. Not while the commies have their orbiting alien death rays. You've heard about those, right?"

I tucked my car keys back into my pocket and took a seat on the curb, far enough away that he wouldn't worry about me taking anything from him, but close enough to have a conversation.

"I haven't," I said, "but I'd be happy to listen."

John Smith and his friends will return in *Godswar*

In the meantime, the action continues in a free Christmas story, *SANTA WILL BURN!*, available at my author site, christullbane.com.

Author's Note

Thank you for reading *A Dead Man's Favor!*

In many ways, this was a story about John's growth. Yes, he's still absurdly silly, still lazy, and still often unprepared for the realities of the world, but he's now coming to grips with his responsibilities and obligations to loved ones and allies. As much as he remains a mid-twenties fratman, the John of *A Dead Man's Favor* is very different than the John we first met in *Investigation, Mediation, Vindication.*

The thing I appreciate most about him is that, however much he changes, he still always tries to meet people where they are, to treat them with compassion, and to remain, at heart, a genuinely good person. Lucia's powers notwithstanding, John really does get by on the power of friendship. And when you have friends like Bill, Anastasia, and even Kevin, maybe that's all you need.

We'll find out soon enough.

In *Godswar*, we're going to see many of the threads I've put out there for the past five books finally come together. This will be a big one, I promise. And yes, John will still probably end up kidnapped and naked at some point… after all, it's kind of become his thing.

If you enjoyed *A Dead Man's Favor*, please tell a friend or seven and then leave a review! As an indie author, I depend heavily on word of mouth and the feedback and support of my much-loved readers.

Thank you, stay safe, and keep reading!

About the Author

Chris began life as a gleam in someone's eye, but birth and childhood were quick to follow. He's been fortunate enough to live in Spain, Germany, and all over the United States of America, and is busy planning a tour of the distilleries of Scotland.

A graduate of the Johns Hopkins University's Writing Seminars program, he put that degree to ill use for twenty years as a software engineer but has finally circled back around to the idea of writing for a living.

Chris currently lives in Nevada with his angelic wife and ever-expanding whisky collection and occasionally ventures outside to peer upwards, mutter to himself about 'day stars', and then scurry back into the house.

A Dead Man's Favor is his ninth novel and the fifth book in *The Many Travails of John Smith*. Chris regularly shares updates on his author website at https://christullbane.com.

www.ingramcontent.com/pod-product-compliance
Lightning Source LLC
Chambersburg PA
CBHW030836190726
48285CB00004B/1240